Ark of Ice

Canadian Futurefiction

---

edited by Lesley Choyce

Pottersfield Press
Lawrencetown Beach, Nova Scotia

Canadian Cataloguing in Publication Data

Main entry under title:
Ark of ice

ISBN 0-919001-73-4
1. Science fiction, Canadian (English) *
2. Canadian fiction (English) -- 20th century.*

I. Choyce, Lesley, 1951-

PS8323.S3A74 1992 C813'.0876208054 C92-098507-6
PR9197.35.S33A74 1992

Front cover painting by Robert Rutherford, West Petpeswick, Nova Scotia.

Published with the financial assistance of the Canada Council and the Nova Scotia Department of Tourism and Culture.

Pottersfield Press
Lawrencetown Beach
R.R.#2, Porters Lake
Nova Scotia B0J 2S0

Contents

Introduction by Lesley Choyce

Macroethics		11
Terence Green	Blue Limbo	13
Andrew Weiner	The Letter	36
Phyllis Gotlieb	The Newest Profession	49
G.M. Cunningham	Letters Home	68
Monica Hughes	The Price of Land	71
The Art of Escape		83
Jean-Louis Trudel	The Falafel is Better in Ottawa	85
Tom Marshall	Scenes From Successive Futures	95
H.A. Hargreaves	In His Moccasins	124
Katherine Govier	The Immaculate Conception Photography Gallery	134
Candas Jane Dorsey	Living in Cities	144
Eco/Logical		161
Douglas Fetherling	Memoirs of the Renaissance	163
Eileen Kernaghan	The Weighmaster of Flood	170
Timothy Findley	What Mrs. Felton Knew	181
Garfield Reeves-Stevens	Outport	197
Geoffrey Ursell	Greenhouse	209

Robert Sawyer — Where the Heart Is — 216

Political Alienation — 233

John Bell — Centrifugal Force — 235
Margaret Atwood — Shopping — 243
Sansoucy Walker — Invasion — 250
Spider Robinson — User Friendly — 253
Lesley Choyce — Patches — 263
W.P. Kinsella — These Changing Times — 274

Afterword by Judith Merril — 277

Contributors — 280

Acknowledgements — 286

Introduction
Some Notes Concerning Fact, Fiction, Ice Floes, Immigration, Solar Panels, Bay Street, Books and Best Intentions.

You and I have no choice but to proceed into the future. I can figure no way around it, death notwithstanding. But our skills at plotting a happy path in that direction are severely limited. Having barely recovered from our own past and not having had a fighting chance to come to grips with the here and now, we blunder ahead. It's the best we can do.

The confession is old news, but just for the record let me say it again: science fiction writers do not sit down to predict the future. We tamper with the present; we collect data; we sit in awe of the potential for disaster stored up in the techno-consciousness of our day and age; and we sometimes reminisce about a future that will never be, as if it has already happened.

And on top of that we dream a lot. We worry and dream with a little egojuxtaposing thrown in. Space—the white space of the clean unbroken, uncorrupted page—is still the final frontier. *Change the world for me, please,* the voice in my head pleads. Sure. Just let me begin again with another version, another future, this one more interesting, more terrifying, more challenging that the last.

My criteria for what stories would be included on this *Ark of Ice* was a simple matter of time-frame and political geography. I was looking for answers to my vague question: what might happen when tomorrow swallows up this country of Canada? Worries (and dreams) about Free Trade, constitutions and Quebec separation pale compared to the robust revolutions that the primary passage of years will bring.

I should also point out that this is an anthology of English Canadian writers. There is a thriving SF literature in Quebec that deserves to be regarded on its own terms and I felt I would be overstepping my abilities and knowledge as an editor to represent those writers here. This is not to say I've already accepted separation as a fact, just that I accept the distinction of Quebec society as a reality.

Fiction writers work from guesswork and hunches. We make the world up as we go along. Like big-time investors, we speculate about possibilities; we invest the capital of our imagination in life-as-it-is to produce a yield of life-as-it-could-be. It came as no big surprise to me that some of Canada's finest fiction writers dabbled in futures from time to time while other full-time SF writers mined the world of the day-after-tomorrow on a daily basis.

What exactly is it like in the Canada of the imagination, adrift in this Ark of Ice, on the cold-fusion fluid of tomorrow? Apparently there is still a problem with crime in Toronto, according to Terry Green. Tom Marshall's Kingston is just like it used to be...as long as you don't go too far from downtown.

Garfield Reeves-Stevens (writing from Beverly Hills) suggests that the fog is still thick in a Newfoundland outport, shrouding some surprises for would-be American rip-off artists of the worst kind. Western cities are only for the true connoisseurs of urban life, suggests Candas Jane Dorsey. There seems to be plenty of employment for Jean-Louis Trudel's globetrotting cyboghost bounty hunter and Phyllis Gotlieb's professional surrogate mom.

John Bell envisions my own Maritime neighbours turned militant and mad as hell at Upper Canada. Margaret Atwood depicts a worst-case scenario for North American women that has already seeped into our public consciousness through books and film. People, it would seem, are an endangered species for Monica Hughes, Rob Sawyer, and Timothy Findley, while the rest of us take a crack at damage control or wrestle with the problems of freedom in an unfree world.

Early Canadian literature suggests that this land was viewed as a harsh and unforgiving place. As an immigrant to this country 14 years ago, a refugee from Reagan, righteousness and urban rage, I felt that nothing could be farther from the truth. My newfound Canada was a haven of magnificent splendour and uncompromising kindness. It was, I believed then and still do now, an improved version of what the United States is supposed to be.

One of my first jobs in Canada was working under contract for the federal government in the area of renewable resources. I studied the high tech and the low tech and I communed with backyard wizards who tapped sun, wind and tide to produce heat and electricity. I lived with one foot solidly in the future and one foot still dancing a jig in celebration of my new country.

But when the government decided that the future wasn't all it was cracked up to be, they pulled the plug on bucks for new energy and decided that we'd worry about the end of oil when it was all gone. Sun, wind and tide would always be around. Oil wouldn't. We could work with Mother Nature later, only when it was absolutely necessary. Suddenly the future began to look a little more like the not-so-fabulous fifties and I still find myself waiting for that decade to go away.

Not long after the energy work dried up, John Bell and I put together one of the first anthologies of Canadian science fiction and fantasy titled *Visions from the Edge*. Our focus was pretty tight: we only included Atlantic writers but there was a storehouse of several generations' worth of fine speculative fiction there to work with. Upon publication, I discovered that we had achieved the impossible. Don't get me wrong. I'm not bragging. I just mean that we had created a book that in the mind of the public simply could not possibly exist. Maritimers and Newfoundlanders simply did not write science fiction. Or so the booksellers argued. Nobody knew what to make of the book and sales were pretty weak. But through some dark underground network of communication in the SF and F kingdom, foreigners kept finding out about the book. And for some bizarre reason, while orders were nearly nonexistent in Canada, a flurry of interest came in through the mail from buyers in Zurich, Moscow, San Diego and Madrid.

A decade or so has gone by and Canadian SF is diverse, literate and alive. But it has not come centre stage. Many of our most prolific SF writers are still published by American publishers. And our greatest strength in SF publishing is, I would argue, on either coast. The edges still have vision. Beach Holme Press (formerly Press Porcepic) in Victoria is probably the first Canadian publisher to make the big leap of faith into SF publishing. This volume pays homage to Judith Merril, Gerry Truscott and the rest for keeping the SF anthology tradition alive.

As suggested, one thing that all of these stories have in common is this: they all worry about the future. There are so many things that can go wrong! I think I was expecting to find more up-beat tales of future-perfect but I know now that those stories are all locked up in the muddle-minded but gleaming buildings of Epcot Centre at Disneyworld in Florida. The next holocaust, we have learned, is not necessarily nuclear. It could take on many forms and, quite possibly, it will come in a version that we have not even considered. So where will Canada sit in a world gone mad?

Probably, we stand a better chance than most. We still have land that is not bumper-to-bumper industry/high-rises/ roads. We still have a few trees and some drinking water. We are not completely driven by the sort of overzealous patriotism that destroys empires. We make plenty of bad moves but we have figured out some of the basics for survival: birth control, socialized medicine, a three-party political system and serious legislation concerning guns.

But as Marshall McLuhan (the first Canadian writer I ever read) astutely observed, "We look at the present through a rear-view mirror. We march backwards into the future."

In the spring of 1987 a spectacular field of ice washed out of the Gulf of St. Lawrence and came ashore here near my home at Lawrencetown Beach. No scene I had ever viewed in any science fiction movie could compare with the cold, alien beauty of this ice pack. It appeared one foggy morning seemingly out of nowhere. At first I studied it tentatively along the shore—the jagged white piles of cold blue-white crystal forms. Then, on a beautiful clear blue April day, I danced from one ice island to the next and studied the artwork of ice. The field stretched as far as the eye could see toward the horizon of the Atlantic. The ocean was gone; the world was transformed, perhaps never to return to its former self. I got carried away with my dance among ice islands and soon found myself very far from shore. One false step and I'd be up to my ears in a sloshing tonic of bone-chilling seawater. But the ice was kind; it gave me a circuitous path back to shore.

My foray along the ice islands gave me new admiration for the beauty of cold. I became a big fan of ice.

Canada sits near the top of the world with a better view of what goes on to the south. I'm not the first or the last to have found refuge on this ark. We float this crystalline entity above the tides of despair, ever mindful of the disasters that await, not always trusting the cold geometry of the economics and politics that keep us afloat. On this voyage there is no real destination expected, no Ararat of the future. Only the beauty of the vessel, the thrill of the sunlight at work on the frozen structure and the worries and dreams that fuel our voyage.

Lesley Choyce
Lawrencetown Beach, Nova Scotia
July 1, 1992

Macroethics

Blue Limbo

Terence M. Green

I

Huziak watched as Mitch Helwig left Karoulis's office. He was pretty sure what had transpired. Everyone in the police station could feel the vibrations. They had been expected for some time now—like aftershocks after the earthquake.

"Mitch."

Mitch turned to meet the face of the staff sergeant.

"You okay?"

Mitch nodded, smiled. "Thanks."

"What happened?"

Mitch was quiet for a moment. Then he said, "I'm going to be suspended." A pause. "What's new with you, champ?"

Huziak tried for a soft smile. He felt compassion, even if he wasn't very good at showing it. Everybody knew what Mitch had been through, what he had done. He shook his head, ran a hand through his thinning hair, and shrugged at the paperwork covering his desk. "All this stuff, I still got to wade through, and they take a good man like you out of service." He shrugged again. "Why don't they give you to me to use?" His hand passed over the clutter in front of him. "Help me clear up this stuff."

Not knowing what to say, Mitch smiled again. "What's the big item today?"

"Big item," he muttered. "Big fucking items." He shuffled through the papers. "First it's lasers, now it's zappers."

Mitch watched him, half listening, half lost in his own thoughts.

"Guy who manages three Burger Kings in the downtown core has just armed his entire staff with zappers." He held a sheet of paper at arm's length. "One of his waitresses complained — isn't sure it's legal." He looked up. "Or," he continued, "there's the betting pool we've uncovered, which tries to predict the date of Toronto's next police slaying. Vice searched a house in Parkdale, found about five hundred grams of marijuana and a pool chart with several names and eight columns numbered 1 to 31. What do you think of that one?"

"Christ."

"My sentiments exactly. Organized crime here and in the States reaps more than $200 billion profit, costs more than 700,000 jobs, is bigger than the paper, rubber and tire industries, and we've got zappers in our Burger Kings. Guys are betting when we'll get iced. And they come down on guys like you in their never-ending battle against the Bad Guys. Go figure."

They said nothing for a few seconds.

"If I can do anything, Mitch..."

Mitch nodded. "Thanks. I just might have to take you up on it."

"What do you do now? Go home for a while?"

Without answering, Mitch turned his gaze very slightly toward the wall behind Huziak. His eyes focused on something very far away, something not in the room or the building, something he had lost and did not know how to find.

II

"The Queen got her annual six percent raise." Paul Helwig, Mitch's eighty-four year old father, stared at his son as if the money had come out of his own pocket. He swiveled his head from the TV set which was his constant companion and held Mitch steadily with his weakening eyes. "Her annual salary's now $15.2 million. Not bad for an old broad with a crown."

Mitch noticed that his father's sweater was buttoned up incorrectly.

"The whole family of inbred imbeciles have now got $20 million a year to polish their crowns with. Wonder they can get 'em on their heads, the way they must be swellin' up." He shook his own head in disdain. "She's nearly as old as I am, for God's sake. Where did I go wrong? Eh? Where?" He continued to shake his head at the imponderable.

"Maybe next time you'll get it right." Mitch smiled at his father.

"Next time. Yeah. Right. Next time. I'll hold my breath."

Mitch sat down in the worn, green, cloth-covered chair in the corner of the apartment opposite to where his father was sitting. It was a chair that had been a fixture in the home in which he had grown up — the home that had been sold only last year. His father had lasted less than a year in the house after Mitch's mother had died. His parents had been married for fifty-two years. His father still didn't know where he was. It had all happened too fast.

Mitch knew how he felt.

"How're you doing?"

The older Helwig gazed at his son. "This is a strange place. I guess it'll take some gettin' used to." He paused. "I know I'm old. But everybody here's old. Makes me feel weird. Don't think it's natural."

"You wanted to come here. You said you'd researched it, that it was the best spot."

"I know. And it is. Still—"

Mitch nodded. He understood.

"A ninety-nine year old Japanese guy reached the top of Mount Fuji yesterday. A record. Forty-five hundred meters. Guy used a cane. The other climbers all shouted 'Banzai'." He gestured with his hand. "Nobody around here's doin' anything like that."

"Where do you get stuff like that?" Mitch asked.

"Where I get everything from. Goddamn TV."

Donahue blossomed to life on the screen as they sat there. It was ten A.M.

"Guy on 'Canada A.M.' this morning confirmed what I always knew. Bald guys are sexy." He smiled under his shiny dome. Mitch smiled too.

"Scientists have found the molecular missing link. It's all tied to overactive male hormones."

"That one's been kicking around for years."

"It's confirmed. Scientists said so."

"Scientists where? Who?" Mitch continued to smile as he felt himself getting drawn in further. The old man could do it to him every time.

"University of Miami. Oil glands in the scalps of guys with pattern baldness..."

"Pattern baldness?"

The old man stopped for a second, stared, then continued. "They got molecules, called receptors. with 50 to 100% greater capacity for binding the ingredients of testosterone. Receptors catch the hormones as they enter the scalp, convert 'em to testosterone, then pass 'em on to the gene structure in the cell's nucleus."

Mitch knew that he was getting exactly what his father had heard on TV. The old man's mind and short-term memory were as good as ever. As his eyes had faded, the world came to him, as it did to so many others, via the Tube.

"Guess the babes around here better look over their shoulders when you come strolling down to dinner."

"Be like shootin' fish in a barrel. Couldn't even give me a good chase anymore. It's ninety per cent women here, you know."

"I know. You've told me."

"Lot of 'em are Baptists, though. Don't know what to make of 'em yet."

"Just don't ask them to dance."

A corner of the old man's mouth finally smiled.

Fellowship Towers it was called. Senior citizens' apartments, right on Yonge Street, north of Bloor, right near the revamped Canadian Tire store. It *was* a good spot. There was a considerable waiting list—much longer for women than for men, as they tried in vain to balance their numbers. The facts were, simply, that women outlived men.

His old man, as usual, was the exception.

There was a dining room on the second floor, along with an elaborate, tasteful sitting and social area. His father had opted for the three-meal-a-day plan freeing him from most shopping and cooking. With his fading eyes and his fading strength, and his lack of familiarity in the kitchen in general, it was a good deal.

Mitch had listened for years about what a loner his father considered himself to be. When his mother died, the old man had lasted less than a year on his own. Sometimes, when Mitch would phone, his father would ruefully admit that he was the first person in three days that he had talked to. In bad weather, in winter, this was not unusual.

Donahue, resplendent beneath his full, white hair, was holding forth into his trademark microphone, his piercing blue eyes twinkling with life—the Dean of daytime TV.

The older Helwig jerked his head in Donahue's direction. "Guy's got too much hair." He smiled. "Poor bugger."

Mitch watched the thin profile that was his father, wondering what to tell him, wondering where to start.

Paul Helwig began again. His eyes riveted on the tube, he said, "News last night said they'd found a guy, a World War I soldier, found him in a glacier." He turned and looked at Mitch. "Guy spent eighty-five years in a glacier. Can you imagine? Glacier moved down the Italian Alps. They said his uniform was still in good condition. Found a note in his pocket that said: 'In the event of my death, notify my mother, 5th District, Vienna.' Poor bastard."

Mitch didn't know what to say.

"Eighty-five years in a fuckin' glacier."

"What're they doing with him?" Mitch asked.

"Guy had a tag around his neck. Born in 1874. Didn't release his identity." He swiveled back to Donahue. "They're gonna look for next of kin." He breathed out, heavily. "Good luck."

Then he mumbled it again. "Poor bastard," he said.

III

"Donahue's got one of them Revivalists on."

"Who?" asked Mitch.

"Revivalists. You know. With the Spiricom device."

They watched.

"—guest today is Dr. Victor Heywood, a physiologist at the Stanford Medical Center in California. He's going to tell us more about the Spiricom, what it is, what it can do. And maybe," he paused, "he can tell us what it all means. I know I could use a little enlightenment on it all," Donahue said, with the proper touch of humility.

It was big news lately. Mitch was more than a little curious too. He glanced at his father. The old man's concentration assured him that he was not alone in his interest.

He slouched back, listening.

"Doctor," Donahue said the word slowly, defining its proper parameters. "Can we really bring people back from the dead? That is the question, isn't it, in a nutshell?"

"I believe that is the question, Phil." The doctor was fortyish, personable; he had obviously done the circuit successfully to end up on Donahue's show. Information with panache: Sesame Street for adults, thought Mitch.

"The answer," said Heywood, "is Yes and No."

"Yes and No," repeated Donahue, smiling.

The audience chuckled, in response to his orchestration.

Heywood smiled too. "Sounds ambiguous, I know. But like most things in life—and death—it is ambiguous in many ways."

He paused. Donahue didn't interrupt him this time. Nobody said anything.

He continued. "When someone dies, if the body, especially the head, is still in good condition—not crushed, mangled, etc.—we can now normally Revive the person for a maximum of four weeks."

"How, Doctor? How can this be done?"

"The dozen major blood vessels carrying blood into and out of the head are attached to a heart-lung machine, which in turn pumps and oxygenates the blood."

Donahue was rapt.

Mitch Helwig was fascinated.

Paul Helwig, at eighty-four, had his own reasons for wanting to hear every word.

"Artificial kidneys are used to remove metabolic wastes. The liver is replaced by glass columns filled with absorbent chemicals to remove poisonous elements. Nutrients are also added to the blood, in addition to substances that balance the blood's acidity. Brain fluid is also maintained. An electrode, a tiny chip, is implanted inside the skull, where the bone resists electrical interference from muscles; this chip is outside the dura, a tough membrane that surrounds the brain. It can send signals from the cochlea to a computer for analysis, synthesis and translation, which can then, in turn, be received by someone operating the computer. In this way, communication is possible." He paused. "People can now communicate with the dead."

"But are they dead? Isn't that the question?" asked Donahue.

"That's certainly one of the questions. It would appear, now, that it's a matter of definition."

"You mean, how are we now to define 'death'?"

"Exactly. Do we now mean the first time one dies? Or the second, and so far the final, time one 'dies'?"

"Sounds like a combination of science fiction and voodoo mumbo-jumbo."

Heywood smiled. "In a way, it does. "But," he added, "electrical signals produced in the visual cortex of the brain and picked up underneath the skull have been used since the late 1980s to drive word processing software, or a speech processor. It was one of the methods used to treat amyotrophic lateral sclerosis—ALS—a degenerative disease which affects the nerve connections in the cortex. Used quite successfully too, I should add. And, little known to most of us, a patent was applied for and received by a St. Louis lawyer way back in 1988, describing a machine to keep a severed head alive. Most of the equipment necessary for all of this has existed for fifteen or twenty years. We've finally just put it all together."

"Scientific synthesis, piercing the ultimate barrier."

Heywood smiled. "If you like. Grandiosely phrased, but not essentially incorrect."

"Are there not," asked Donahue, leading his guest, "a couple of steps toward death, in medical terms?"

"In both medical terms and in legal terms, up till now there appeared to be two stages. A person could be brain-dead without being legally dead. The body had to die as well. But there's always been that grey area—the area of the brain-dead, the realm of the comatose. None of this has been clear. As long as the body could hold together without deterioration, hope always existed. We've tapped into that."

"By hope always existing, you mean—"

"I mean that there have always been cases of someone drowning—especially with children—where they may be submerged at the bottom of a pool or something for fifteen or twenty minutes, and for all intents and purposes are dead, but we have the occasional miraculous revival. In 1989, in a small town in Ontario, Canada, a seventy-nine year old man, who had been diagnosed as brain-dead ten weeks earlier, was taken off life-support systems and given the last rites of the Catholic church. His two year-old grandson shouted 'Grandpa!' and the man sat up in bed and stretched out his arms to the boy. A month later, he bought a new car and was driving around visiting family members. It's all documented at Ottawa Civic Hospital. The man's doctors have no medical explanation for his recovery. Brain scans showed no activity after he'd had heart surgery, leading to the conclusion that he'd suffered irreparable brain damage."

"And cryogenics?" asked Donahue.

"Cryogenics assumes the same basic sense of boundless optimism: that as long as the body can be kept in good shape, that perhaps someday the mind can be revived. We've been waiting for years for science to catch up to Death. Well, we're getting there."

Mitch watched his father. He had not moved.

The TV faded to a commercial.

"Tell all that," his father said finally, "to the guy in the glacier."

IV

"Why only four weeks?" Donahue asked.

Heywood shrugged. "Not sure about that yet. It's something like heart transplants used to be—a form of rejection sets in. We're working on it."

"And there've been how many done now?"

"Up to last week, over six hundred in the United States and Canada. Europe is beginning to equip its hospitals. Australia, China... It'll spread rapidly."

"Why though, Doctor..." Donahue leaned forward so that the camera could capture his earnestness, "*Why* would we really want to do this thing?" He spread his hands elaborately. "What's the point?"

Again, the man from Stanford, California shrugged. "There are as many reasons as there are people, Phil. The extra four weeks can be used to finalize personal relationships the way most of us would like them to be finalized. Business can be more effectively transferred. Both the military and the police forces have expressed considerable interest. The ability to Revive—even temporarily—a person who suffered a violent or criminal death, to have them explain how they were killed, who killed them, well, you can see for yourself where all this could lead."

"I'm not sure you're right, Doctor. I'm not sure we can see where it will all lead."

"It leads right into the next century, Phil. We're all headed there, whether we want it or not."

"Tell us about the subjective effect reported by the subjects themselves—the one the media have picked up on—the colour."

Heywood smiled. "Yes," he said. "That is interesting. All the senses seem to disappear. The mind works, and memory exists. The only sense that seems to operate even partially is something that tricks the sense of sight. Those Revived report, consistently to a person, that they see a world of Blue, nothing but Blue. They describe it as an endless void, an ethereal space." He shrugged again.

"Blue Limbo," said Donahue.

Blue Limbo, thought Mitch Helwig. It's the year 2000, and we've now got Blue Limbo. He looked at his father, thought about Elaine, Barbie, Mario, Karoulis, and everything that had happened, everything that would happen.

V

"Why aren't you at work?" The old man clicked the TV into silence with the remote.

Now it was Mitch's turn to pause. "I've been sent home. Things are changing. My status is up in the air."

His father waited for more. When it didn't come, he asked, "You still getting paid?"

"For now."

"You in trouble?"

Mitch shrugged. In spite of being almost forty years old, he was beginning to feel like a kid. "There are a lot of questions to answer downtown. The warehouse explosion. Last Fall."

His father nodded.

"I was involved. I spoiled a lot of parties."

His father continued staring at him for a while, then put his hand to his chin and stared back at the dormant TV set. "I heard," he said, "that every sort of filth was going on in that place, that its demise was a blessing to civilization." He glanced back at Mitch. "That true?"

"Yes."

"Fuck 'em then. They want to play their little political games, you step aside. There's more to life than a lunch pail and a job, if you can't hold your head up."

Mitch rose up out of the chair, put his hands in his pockets and walked to the window nine floors above Yonge Street. He stared down in silence.

Then the old man asked him, "Why don't you go home?"

Mitch turned and stared at him.

The answer was too long in coming. Even with his half-blind eyes, Paul Helwig could see the truth etched on his son's face, and for a moment he thought, that having survived everything as he had, the hurt that he saw there might by itself be enough to kill him if he would let it. His heart sank and he sagged visibly.

"Elaine and I aren't living together right now."

His father said nothing.

"I've moved out, at least for now."

He still got no response.

"It's been about a month now. I've got a small place— top floor of a house in the Queen and Pape area."

"Barbie?"

Mitch dropped his eyes. "She's with her mother, for now." He paused. "We'll work it out."

"Why didn't you tell me? Why didn't you come to me?"

Mitch shrugged, still unable to meet his father's eyes. "Couldn't."

His father nodded. At his age, nothing much surprised him anymore. But he was surprised at how badly he could hurt for his son, how badly he wanted to make the trouble, the pain disappear, just as he had when Mitch had come to him as a toddler with a scraped knee. "Do you need anything? Money?"

Mitch shook his head.

But Paul Helwig knew that it was not true. His son needed a lot.

And he felt helpless.

VI

Mitch felt a sense of relief as he drove south on Yonge Street after leaving his father. He had stayed for lunch at noon in the second floor dining room with him, fascinated by the array of senior citizens around them, the number of people with walkers and wheelchairs. Everyone who went by the table had stopped and spoken to them. In a way, his visit to his father was a visit to all of them as well, and they all enjoyed as much of it as they could.

His father was right. It was strange.

He had enjoyed the lunch. He was with survivors. These were people who had made a peace with life and what it had dealt them. They had come to terms with their own flaws. Life could make you crazy, Mitch knew. You had to hang on.

He was trying to hang on.

It was 1:30 P.M. Mitch took in the street scene of joggers in luminescent suits, wired to their walkmans; a swarm of Asian kids with safety helmets and their new striped roller blades were legging it out in the inside lane a few car lengths ahead of him; and when he crossed Bloor Street, he drove slowly past a group of black and white kids, between the ages of twelve and fourteen, their heads shaved up on side, the steel toes on their boots glinting in the afternoon sun, idling under the Uptown marquee, waiting for the theatre to open for the first showing of the latest splatterpunk film in town.

He could never figure why they weren't in school. How did their parents stand them? Could it happen to him? He thought of Barbie, and weakened at the image.

He had to see her again. Soon.

VII

Mitch eased his aging Chev to the curb on Queen East near Broadview. The 7-11 store had an automatic teller inside, and he needed some cash. His father had been good, he thought as he sat behind the wheel thumbing through his wallet, doing a quick inventory. The old man never passed judgement, Mitch realized. At least, he never had on Mitch. He certainly had opinions about everything else. Looking up and through the windshield at nothing, it hit him suddenly the power of the bond that had been forged silently between him and his father.

They were both alone. They were both disenfranchised from the mainstream.

There was nothing left except their children.

Every man became his own father, every woman her own mother, to varying degrees. He understood that.

It was the speed with which it had happened to Mitch Helwig that surprised him. That, and the clarity of his life that it produced, made him sit where he was for an extra minute.

A bit of commotion at the end of that extra minute caused him to refocus on the external world with equal clarity.

It was the middle of the afternoon. The woman getting into the cab some twenty meters ahead of him was Chinese and matronly. Her purse hung on a long leather strap over her left shoulder. Mitch watched without knowing what he was seeing until it was happening.

Two youths, a young Chinese male about seventeen and a blond Caucasian who seemed slightly younger, appeared from the 7-11 behind the woman. In a movement that was both precise and deft, betraying much practice, almost elegant in its quickness, the Chinese boy cut the shoulder strap of the woman's purse as she leaned forward into the cab and tossed it to the other boy. It had all transpired in a second. Then the two youths sped around the corner on foot, running south on Broadview.

The woman stood stunned.

Mitch felt the adrenalin begin to pump. They had probably watched the woman withdraw cash inside the store, knew exactly what they were doing, had done it many times before in many places.

The engine was still idling. But it was more than instinct or training that made Mitch pull out into the traffic and go around the cab and the shocked woman, make a right at the corner and sight the two miscreants running ahead of him. It stemmed from a quiet outrage against all that had happened to him, and all that was still going to happen. Instead of making his brain blur, it calmed it into a cold steel.

The woman getting into the cab would lose enough in life. She didn't need to lose this as well.

He felt under the seat beneath him to make sure it was there.

VIII

The sun painted on the side of the gaudy Caribbean restaurant smiled down on him through its sunglasses over his left shoulder as he watched the two snatchers run past the chain-link fence on his right and head west up the alley beside the five-storied red-brick factory. Mitch pulled up to the mouth of the alley, gazing down its length through the passenger window. There was another chain-link fence at the far west side, with the plastic pennants of a used-car lot fluttering aloft above it. They turned left, heading south, out of his line of vision, behind the factory.

Mitch cruised slowly down Broadview, along the front of the factory, to the lane which bordered the south side of the building. The lane ran around the factory in a squared-off U, surrounded by wire fence on all sides. Directly in front of him, along the south border, the entrance ramp for the Eastern Avenue expressway across the Don River isolated the spot even more.

The youths had not reappeared here. They were back of the building, or they were inside. There was no place else to run to.

Mitch looked at the signs on the structure. Gateway Auto Collision, Dubois Marine Insurance, M. Cutrara & Son, Wholesale Fresh Produce. And in spite of the blue, diamond-shaped sign that read *For Lease*, there was definitely business transpiring inside. It was certainly not abandoned.

They were at the back then.

IX

The Chev moved quietly down the north alley. Ahead of him the red and white plastic pennants, time-worn and weathered, fluttered at the edge of the wire fence, announcing rows of grey, assembly-line Toyotas, the dust from the nearby expressway covering them like urban delta silt.

Mitch made a left, along the building's rear.

They were there.

Turning, they watched him come, defiantly.

On an abandoned loading platform, the two youths had dumped the purse's contents, spreading it about: wallet, coins, credit cards, a few bills, comb, small make-up kit. Their arrangement of the contents was in itself an affront.

Mitch pulled up about ten meters away, staring at them through his opened driver's window. He let the car idle for fifteen seconds before shutting it off, while the two youthful felons studied him silently.

Approaching age forty, Mitch thought, gave a man many second thoughts. One of them was the uncertainty regarding just what one was and was not still capable of doing physically. As he eyed the two young and seemingly fit males, this thought did flit across his mind.

He reached under the seat and extracted the bag that he kept stored there. Clutching it in his hand, he opened the door and stepped out.

The two thieves straightened, unblinking.

Mitch reached into the bag and pulled out the Barking Dog. It had been a while since he had used it. In fact, he remembered having sworn to try to avoid using it. But then, he thought, these things happen.

Their eyes narrowed as they watched him attach it. They knew what it was: the ultimate in modern lie detection technology. Not even the police were supposed to have it, and they knew this too.

Who was this guy?

Mitch Helwig snapped the pocket-sized silver trinket to his belt where it could gaze unhindered at the faces before him. He then attached the sticky electrode to the bare flesh of his rib cage under his shirt.

The two young jackals watched him.

"What's that?" The blond Causcasian spoke first.

The Chinese lad turned a disdainful gaze on him for breaking the silence in any way.

Mitch smiled. The smile was cold. "Easter Bunny left it." He focused the eye. The dog's microcomputer would cross-reference voice pitch, body odours, face temperature, pupil and retina response; the microwave respiration monitor would measure stomach palpitations caused by rapid breathing under stress; and the video input would scan for the spontaneous, subcortical facial expressions that could register with the machine's coding system.

If either of these two told even the slightest lie, the Barking Dog would howl by sending a jolt of icy sensation to Mitch's side where the electrode clung to his flesh.

The Oriental picked up a knife from the loading platform behind them—the same knife, Mitch assumed, that had originally severed the purse's shoulder strap. The sun glinted from its surface hotly. Mitch also noted the look in their eyes: like distant thunder.

Then he noticed something else about the two. The hand that held the knife also flashed in the sun, its metal fingers twisting the light, glinting white fire. The blond lad sidled a meter or so to the left of his cohort, his silver foot creating the slightest trace of a limp as it sparkled lightning from the rubble about it.

Bionic limbs, Mitch realized.

These two were well on their young ways to whatever technological future awaited them. Piece by piece, they were ceding their humanity, tying motor and sensory nerve impulses to an electronic, computerized control system.

Mitch was struck by the irony of the confrontation. The human-machine interface was all about them. The Barking Dog. The limbs. Even the automatic teller that had complied with the Chinese woman's electronic commands. And it was just the beginning.

The Chinese boy had apparently been thinking. "If you're a cop," he said, "then you'd better read us our rights. If not," the silver hand clutching the knife remained poised aloft in the sunlight, "then you'd better fuck off."

Nobody moved.

Mitch could not tear his eyes from the hand, the foot. Individual nerve fibers, axons, regenerated through holes mere microns in diameter, like string beans growing through chicken wire, he thought. Commercial plasma-etching technology. Iridium microelectrodes, coated with silicon nitride to protect them from degradation caused by body fluids.

One day cops, he had once been told at a criminology seminar, might be able to plug their nerve impulses directly into their skimmer's control system.

Silicon nitride versus bodily fluids.

He thought of Elaine, Barbie, Karoulis, Mario, his father. He thought of Blue Limbo and the light-speed at which they were all approaching it.

The planet seemed to tilt, sliding the two steel-enhanced creatures dangerously near to him. He observed them with a brilliant clarity, suffused by the surrounding heat and cinders.

Mitch licked his lips. "You stole that purse." The Barking Dog waited, infinitely patient.

The Chinese youth stepped forward. He tried to assess Mitch Helwig, the Barking Dog. Mitch saw the knife more clearly now—a simple Arkansas toothpick, polished carbon steel, twenty-four centimeters overall. The other boy took a Ni baton from his belt, pressed the release bar and automatically extended it from its closed twenty centimeters to its fully extended fifty-two centimeters. Mitch knew all about them. The Taiwan Provincial Police still used them. Steel tubing, light. Capable of delivering stunningly painful blows.

"You made a mistake coming here," the blond one said.

Where did creatures like these come from? Mitch wondered. From under what rock? And we patch them up with new and better limbs, so they can continue. He remembered the story of the so-called Crocodile Man in the recent news, the name the health experts had given to a particularly brutal punk who had been apprehended while dismembering his latest victim. They said the "crocodile" brain condition was brought on by the assailant's having been born with the umbilical cord wrapped around his neck. The Crocodile Man, so went the contention, operated hyperactively, unhindered by functions of that portion of the brain governing emotions, morals, or the ability to judge reality.

Moral imbeciles. Egocentric instead of ecocentric. How many of them were out there? What else caused that portion of their brains to cease functioning?

"You stole that purse," Mitch repeated.

"We found it," said the blond boy. His silver foot ground into the cinders as he shifted his weight.

The cold of blatant fabrication froze Mitch's side. It began to freeze Mitch in other ways too. He could feel his anger rising and tried to control it.

Fuckers, he thought.

They began to move apart from one another, leaving the purse forgotten between them, never turning from the still figure of the man confronting them.

Mitch immobilized them again. "Are you two a pair of morons? You think I'd just waltz in here and submit to a pair of assholes like you?"

They stared without comprehension. The sun was at the stranger's back, making them squint, outlining him incandescently.

"I guess you figure you're a pair of real bad guys. Tough guys. Guys who'd kill for nickels and dimes." Mitch was taunting them, waiting to hear their voices.

"We never killed nobody," said the blond boy.

But it was a lie. The Barking Dog told Mitch Helwig so.

The Chinese boy glanced at his cohort. He was sharp enough to at least determine that the stranger now knew something more about them than that they were a couple of minor purse-snatchers. What he didn't know was what this man would do about it. The guy wasn't following any of the patterns that they'd seen before, and this new scenario wasn't computing smoothly in his jangled synapses. The Barking Dog wasn't any legal threat. Its data was inadmissible. The courts hadn't figured out how to deal with it yet.

So what was this all about?

It was about Mitch Helwig's anger, his frustration. He felt it bubbling to the surface, beginning to smoke silently.

They began to move toward him. As they did so, he reached once again into the bag from which he had taken the Barking Dog. He aimed the small laser that he pulled out in their general direction.

They stopped.

"The bag of goodies is surprising, isn't it?"

They said nothing. The lightweight plastic Sanyo could burn a hole in them as neat as a pin.

Mitch gestured casually toward them with the laser. "Put those things down and relax."

"Suppose we don't," said the older one.

Mitch shrugged. "You only look stupid is what I figured." He waited. "Maybe I was wrong. Maybe I'll have to kill you." He straightened his arm, targeting.

They lowered their weapons to the ground.

"You two little pigs stole that lady's money. I watched you. Then you run like little pigs back here to your pigpen to play with it. And now," he took a breath, "you tell me that you're killers."

"We never told you nothin'."

Mitch eyed them steadily. "You boys are all confused. You're all mixed up."

The staring contest continued.

"Consider me your new social worker."

The darker, older boy tried one last bit of bravado. "Don't mess with us. You don't know what you're messin' with."

Mitch smiled slowly, chillingly. "Lines from old, bad videos. It's your stock in trade, all you know." He stepped closer to them. He was no longer a cop. He was no longer even Mitch Helwig. He didn't know what he was or how this happened to him, but it happened more and more often of late. His job as cop was so limited, his desire to make a difference overwhelming. Maybe he was going crazy. In fact, he knew that it was partly true. It was as he had thought while driving from Fellowship Towers on Yonge Street: the world could make you crazy; it was making him crazy. There seemed to be no end to it all.

"As your new social worker," he said, "I think we'll start with basic Pavlovian conditioning. You do something mean to somebody else, you break the law, and you pay."

"What about if you break the law?" The question came from the Oriental boy and hung in the air like a storm warning.

A cloud of memories, of dark perceptions billowed up behind Mitch Helwig's eyes. "I pay," he said. The swirl of knowledge eddied away. "Everybody pays."

There was a sheen of sweat on the blond boy's brow now. The hot afternoon sun was a very small part of it.

"You pay me. I'm the reason you're going to try real hard to behave from now on."

They waited.

"First lesson," Mitch said. "Empty your pockets. Now."

Coins, billfolds pocket combs tumbled out. Each of them had one more weapon as well—the blond a Black Stallion knife, with solid brass liners and buffalo horn handle; the Chinese lad dropped a more conventional folding trench knife with built-in knuckle duster.

"Over there." Mitch gestured to the fence with a wave of the laser. They made their way across the cinders, the blond's silver foot an eerie, alternating glint. "Now," he added, "you, flashfoot, over there." He motioned to a spot some ten meters away.

The boy obeyed.

"Both of you," Mitch said, "lie face down."

"You could kill us," blurted the younger one.

"I could kill you now, as you stand there." Mitch held the laser steady. "A sweep of this across the area would cut you both in half." He paused. "Any doubts?"

They both knelt down, then spread themselves forward on their stomachs.

"Maybe this is what your victims always feel like," Mitch added.

Glancing over at their sprawled forms, an image of the walkers and wheelchairs that he had seen at lunch surfaced, superimposing itself on the reality of the bionic limbs in front of him. The stark injustice, the skewing of balance was not lost on him.

Leaving them there for the moment, Mitch went over to their pocket contents and picked up their billfolds. Briefly, he flipped each open to assure himself that there was some form of ID inside, then popped them into his own pocket.

It was in this moment of inattention that it happened. The Chinese lad must have had it inside his sleeve, and Mitch Helwig later chastised himself for his uncustomary lack of thoroughness, his distracted focus. It took a slice of skin a half centimetre thick from his left shoulder as it passed by, finally thumping numbingly into the wooden door atop the loading platform.

The pain, he knew, would follow in seconds. By all rights, he should be dead by now.

The hilt of the ballistic knife remained in the youth's hand. Good to a range of about ten meters, the weapon was capable of being fired silently and accurately; the penetration was more than five times that of a forceful manual stab. In close quarters, it was merely a knife. He'd seen them for sale on Yonge Street for fifty-nine dollars.

With the onset of pain, he felt the warm trickle of blood down both his back and chest.

Mitch moved quickly toward the prone figure, the sudden pain alerting his primal instincts. The youth lay frozen, fear in his eyes, with the knowledge a big-game hunter might have after a failed shot had turned a rhino in his direction. Mitch kicked him full in the face, swiveling in one fluid motion to face the blond, the Sanyo quivering in his tensed fist, his mind trying to regain total control. He bit down hard on the pain and anger, the laser trained like a cobra on the remaining youth.

"Don't," the boy said.

Mitch remained silent, his glare like ice.

"Don't kill me."

A wave of pain from his shoulder unsteadied him momentarily. The blood from the wound began to flow past the Barking Dog's electrode, gathering at his beltline. In his eyes, Mitch felt the sting of salt water, uncertain whether it was sweat or tears.

The Chinese youth was unconscious at his feet, his nose and mouth bleeding. Alternately glancing between his two prisoners, Mitch Helwig came to a decision. The bionic hand of the boy at this feet—the hand that had missed taking Mitch Helwig's life by inches—lay sprawled open like some metal spider creeping from its black sleeve.

He bent to pull the sleeve back, exposing the silver forearm.

The other boy watched with wide eyes.

Training the Sanyo at the middle of the forearm Mitch cut the hand off.

Even in the stupor of unconsciousness, the youth's feet jerked spasmodically. Bionic limbs, unlike simpler prosthetics, sensed heat and cold.

And pain.

Mitch kicked the hand away dramatically. Then he turned toward the blond boy, and gritting his teeth at his own pain, focused the laser on the boy's foot.

"Don't." The boy was terrified now, his eyes wild.

"You guys should think about this," Mitch said. "What it feels like." He continued to aim the Sanyo.

"Please."

Mitch was shaking now, a combination of rage, fear, and massive jolts of adrenalin. The blood loss was increasing too, making him light-headed, mistrusting his own anger. He tried to steady his hand.

"Please."

Mitch walked slowly toward the prone boy. "You shouldn't hurt people. You should leave people alone who don't bother you, who don't deserve to be treated the way you treat them."

The boy had a real, deep fear etched on his face. His voice quavered. "I'll try," he said.

Mitch halted as the Barking Dog registered the statement. There was a drop of cold attached to the phrase, but there was also the tremor, the shiver of uncertainty.

There was hope, even if it was born of fear.

Mitch lowered his laser. He stared at the boy's metallic foot. Then he met the young man's eyes. "You'll never know," he said, "how close you came."

The boy was crying now.

Mitch left him there. He gathered up the contents of the lady's purse and refilled it. Then, returning to the unconscious Oriental's form, he bent over and picked up the silver hand and attached half-triceps. Sliding behind the wheel of his Chev, he tossed his own weapon and utility pouch, along with everything else, into the back seat.

Touching his right hand to the searing pain of his left shoulder, he tore the shirt away, baring the wound, twisting his neck for a glimpse. There was only blood to see.

Starting the engine, he stared through his own tears at the crying blond boy.

X

Mitch closed the door of his third floor apartment behind him and leaned against the wall. His shoulder, bleeding freely, needed to be treated. Having lived here for only one week, there wasn't much in the place that he could think of using to stem its flow. His medicine cabinet didn't even have a bottle of aspirin in it yet.

He began unbuttoning his shirt, pulling it from his belt. The pain was intense, and accelerated sharply whenever he made any movement that affected the shoulder. Moving into the kitchen area, he finally shrugged out of the shirt, winced anew, then tossed the blood-soaked garment into the sink. He leaned forward on the edge of the counter, breathing deeply through his mouth, trying to control both his thoughts and the constant throb and sting of the wound.

He gritted his teeth as a new wave of pain stabbed at the open cut. "Shit." The word echoed in the empty apartment.

He threw back his head and bit on his lower lip. Tilting his eyes sideways, he glanced into the living area to his right. The single item of furniture in his range of vision was a wicker chair that he had borrowed from the woman on the second floor.

He had left his previous life behind.

He was alone.

And he wasn't sure that he liked that very much at all.

XI

With his one and only dish towel tied as tightly as he could manage with one hand around his shoulder, Mitch began to take stock more rationally. What came next?

He wasn't sure.

He'd live. He knew that. The quality of that life was what he didn't know.

He looked around the place that was now his home. In a previous generation, this had been the attic of the house. He had his own entry up the house's side stairs—a circular wooden stairway—that ended in the small landing outside the unit's door. It had been advertised in *The Globe and Mail* as a studio apartment with one bedroom, a den, a galley kitchen and living room combo. It measured all of about fifty square meters, Mitch guessed. Big enough for what he was bringing with him: nothing.

In the centre of the apartment where he was standing, it was fine. But as you moved toward the walls, the ceiling sloped and the headroom disappeared. He'd hit his head a number of times, and doing the dishes without stooping was impossible, so the landlady had left him a stool to sit on for that purpose. The bathroom door didn't open all the way because it hit the sink in there. But his options had been limited, as had his finances. And it had been a bargain at only a thousand a month.

His glance strayed into the bedroom. He had been sleeping on a ten-centimetre-thick piece of foam that he had purchased from Sear's in Gerrard Square. On it was the sleeping bag that had been his since he was a kid. Not much was going to be able to be transported up that winding stairway.

Except Barbie. She was the only thing from the past that he wanted. And needed.

XII

Standing on the porch of the semi-detached house on Broadview Avenue, Mitch studied the peeling paint above him as he rang the bell.

"Mrs. Wen?" He recognized her as soon as she opened the door.

The woman nodded. Then she saw her purse—its strap severed—in his hand. When she looked up to meet his face, he smiled gently and offered it to her. Reflexively, she reached for it, snapping it open, scanning its interior.

"It's all there," he said.

Her hand checking the contents of the wallet, she met his gaze again. Her eyes softened. "Thank you. Thank you very much."

"My pleasure."

"How did you get it?"

"I'm a policeman. It's a long story."

She stepped aside. "Would you like to come in? Can I get you a cup of tea?" Her smile was broad now.

Over her shoulder Mitch saw the plain kitchen at the end of the hall. Wind chimes tinkled delicately in a window. "No, thank you. I have to go."

She seemed at a loss about what came next. Then she saw his shoulder. "You're hurt."

"I'm going to get it taken care of now." He turned and started down the steps.

It was happening too quickly for her. "Officer?" she called.

He stopped at the bottom of the stairs and turned around.

"I'd like to know your name." She bowed her head slightly. His appearance had restored something in her far beyond money.

Eighty-five years in a glacier, he thought, *moving down the Italian Alps. I have no name.*

He shook his head. "No," he said. "You wouldn't."

She met his eyes with compassion.

My life, he thought, staring at her. Then: *her life*.

Oh Lord. Raise us from the dead. Please.

The wind chimes tinkled.

Bowing his head slightly in return, he got into his car and left.

The Letter

Andrew Weiner

I was on my knees in front of the filing cabinet, squinting in the light of my flashlight to read the title on the microfiche and still not quite believing my eyes. And then the lights went on.

"It was inevitable, I suppose," he said. "It was only a matter of time."

He was standing in the doorway: a tall, rather nondescript individual in a sweater and baggy pants, with close-cropped graying hair. He didn't look much like a genius, but then I knew now that he wasn't. He didn't look like much of anything, except a shabby middle-aged man with a .38 in his right hand.

I stood up, very slowly, hands stretched away from my body.

"A matter of time," he said again, and laughed, a dry croaking kind of laugh.

I didn't see much humor in the situation. But then, he was the one holding the gun.

"Your wallet," he said. "Slowly."

Slowly I pulled my wallet out of my jacket and tossed it across the floor. He stooped to pick it up, keeping the gun pointed at me all the time.

He flipped it open.

"Private investigator," he said. "Licensed in New York state. You're a little out of your territory, aren't you?"

"A little."

"And not licensed for break-ins, I imagine?"

"Why don't you just call the police and get this over with?"

"Oh no," he said. "I don't think I would want to do that."

And somehow I got the feeling that more than my license was at stake.

***

I had never been in the office of the Chief Executive Officer of a major corporation before. For that matter, I had never been in the office of the CEO of a minor corporation either, unless you count my bookie.

The office wasn't that impressive. It was smaller than a football field, and the carpet didn't come up much above my ankles. As a dining table, the desk would have seated no more than twelve. And the collection of modern art on the walls was somewhat less comprehensive than the Guggenheim's.

The Chief Executive Officer hiked around his desk to greet me. "Good to meet you, Mr. Hendricks," he said. "I'm Lou Staefler."

As if there could be any doubt in the matter. Ignorant as I was in the ways of business, even I was thoroughly familiar with that craggy face. Staefler had probably been profiled more often in the newsmagazines, been interviewed more often on TV, and had testified at more government hearings, than any other corporate executive alive. Every line of that face had become public property.

He motioned me to sit on the couch, and sat facing me.

"You've probably wondered," he said, "why I asked you to come here."

That was something of an understatement. Even if one could conceive of Staefler requiring the services of a private investigator, it was hard to imagine him dealing with anyone lower than the president of Pinkerton's.

"You come highly recommended by my friend Bud Haskell."

Haskell was one of the city's classiest divorce lawyers. I had worked for him on occasion. Not exciting work, or particularly elevating, but it paid the rent. Could Staefler be in the market for a divorce? I had always dealt directly with Haskell, not his clients.

"But you're still wondering," he said, "why I need a private investigator?"

I nodded.

"It's a little unusual," he said. "Unusual circumstances, requiring complete discretion."

"I am nothing if not discreet."

"So Bud tells me." He paused, as though unsure how to continue. "Tell me," he said. "What do you know about market letters?"

I shrugged. "They're like tip sheets, right? For investors."

"That's a fair description, I suppose, to the extent that these letters do typically claim knowledge of things to come – of movements in the markets as a whole, or in the prices of individual shares and commodities."

"Like the Wilks Letter," I said. "The guy who forecast the market crash a few years back."

"Forecast it or caused it," Staefler said. "When a letter has enough influence with investors, the two begin to blur. Wilks wiped fifty points off the Dow in half an hour. He took twenty million dollars off the value of our own shares. With one little letter."

"You don't hear much about him these days."

"Oh, he's still operating, he's still got his followers. But he called it wrong once too often. He lost the power to stampede investors, and thank God for that. But there's plenty more where he came from. It's a big business in itself. People will pay hundreds of dollars, even thousands, for what they believe to be inside information."

He crossed to his desk and picked up a bulging file folder. He started to pass its contents to me, item by item. "This one is from Fairfax, Alaska. The guy is a platinum bug. And this one is from Portland, Oregon. Specializing in gold and the activities of the Trilateral Commission. This one is into soy bean futures and laetrile. And this one -- a lot of these guys are just nuts."

He passed over the rest of the pile and I leafed through them. The letters came in all shapes and sizes. Some were professionally printed and attractively laid-out, while others were crudely duplicated. Some were brisk and business-like, but others were full of long-winded editorials about Big Government and the coming fiscal apocalypse, or else dotted with arcane references to sunspot cycles and sixty-year economic waves.

The price tags made me blink a little. People were paying two, three, four hundred dollars a year for a monthly letter. I didn't ask Staefler why, but he told me anyway.

"In good times," he said, "people don't give the economy much thought. But when things get shaky, they get scared and confused. They see their savings melting away. They have visions of pushing wheelbarrows of money down to the A&P. So they start to grope around for the right button, the one that will make it work for them.

"And who can blame them? It's a financial Disneyland out there. It's out of control, or it seems to be. The government and the banks and the leaders of the business community keep on making predictions about what's going to happen, but somehow they're always wrong. Nobody knows what's going on anymore. So they don't believe us anymore. They look elsewhere for the real lowdown. And they think they find it here.

"And of course," he said, "some of these letters are *right*. Not all of them, and not all of the time. But they're right often enough to make people keep coming back for more. Like a man playing a one-armed bandit."

"Variable reinforcement," I said.

He raised an eyebrow.

"It's a basic Skinnerian paradigm," I said. "Performance is greatest when rewards are intermittent and variable."

"Oh yeah," he said. "You used to be a psychologist."

Obviously he had checked me out carefully.

"Alright," I said. "You know all about me and I know all about market letters. What's next?"

He crossed to his desk again, and returned with a much thinner file folder. "This is the most recent issue of a fairly new letter, the *Reeve One Thousand*."

I opened the file. Inside was a skimpy document, four typed pages stapled together. Like most of the letters it was marked NOT TO BE DUPLICATED. There were a couple of unusual features. One was the price, a very steep $5000 for twelve monthly issues. Another was the number "112" in red ink in the upper right hand corner.

"What does this mean?" I asked.

"It means that I am subscriber number 112. And the letter itself is called the *Reeve One Thousand* because it accepted only the first one thousand applicants. No one else can sign up until someone drops out. I doubt that many people do."

"It's a lot of money."

"And worth every penny. Let me tell you how I came to subscribe. About six months ago I received a mailing with the first issue. A covering note invited me to check out six specific predictions made in the letter. I did. Every one of them would prove to be correct. Of course I signed up. Since then, I have approximately doubled my personal wealth."

"So what's the problem?"

"Personally, I have no problem at all. But professionally, I have many problems. Two months ago, for example, the letter recommended buying the shares of an obscure regional oil producer. A few weeks later, my own company announced an offer for outstanding shares of that company. Anyone who followed the advice in the letter made a killing. The point is, *he could not have known that.* Even my wife didn't know that."

"He's always right."

"No," Staefler said. "But he's right about 90% of the time. I had an analysis made of a number of leading market letters, testing out the accuracy of their predictions. Most are no better than chance. Some are worse. The really good ones run between 60 and 70%. And then there's Reeve."

"He's on a hot streak," I said.

"He's on an *impossible* streak. No one could predict the behavior of so many different stocks and commodities in so many markets with such precision. And even the errors—there's something very strange about them. They're not random. My analysts could explain it better, but it's almost as if they were deliberate, as if he was throwing in a few mistakes to make himself look fallible."

I looked at the letter in front of me. *Expect an upswing in the Dow by mid-February led by oil and gas shares ...Expect silver to test its 1980 high by early spring ...Prime rate will remain in the 14-15% range ...High tech shares are heading for a fall ...Sincerely yours, Reeve.*

"How are high tech shares doing?"

"On the skids," Staefler said. "Off another twenty points this morning."

"Did he call it, or cause it?"

Staefler shook his head. "Reeve wouldn't have that kind of influence. Not yet, anyway. He's still pretty low-profile, compared to someone like Wilks. He called it, alright."

"Who is this guy?" I asked. "And how does he do it?"

"Nobody knows who he is. No one has even seen him. All we know about him is his post office box number, in Burlington, Vermont."

"It's a small town."

"We don't know that he lives there. We don't know anything about him. As far as we can tell, he's got no organization, no outside advisors, no research staff. Zip. As for how he does it, that's for you to find out."

"Maybe he's a genius," I said. "The Albert Einstein of the market. Maybe he's psychic. Or maybe he just has good inside information."

"Yes, but inside information on such a massive scale? You'd need your own CIA to gather it."

"Unless you're a hacker."

Staefler nodded. "I've thought of that, of course. If you could tap into commercial data traffic, you could get advance information on stock splits, mergers, oil discoveries, government fiscal policy. Except that it wouldn't do you any good, because all sensitive data traffic is encrypted these days."

"Maybe he's broken the code."

"We're talking about heavy code," Staefler said. "Mostly using the Data Encryption Standard. That's a 56-bit key. 72 quadrillion possibilities. I don't care how good a hacker you are, you couldn't break that. Unless you had the biggest and fastest computer in the world. And if you could build a computer like that, why piddle around with a market letter? You could take over the whole economy.

"No," he said. "Any way you look at it, this thing is impossible. Absolutely impossible."

***

Tracking Reeve through his post office box was not particularly difficult, merely tiresome. I flew into Burlington and made arrangements with a local investigator for surveillance of the post office. Then I checked into a hotel and waited.

I waited four days. I watched a lot of soaps, and caught up on my back issues of the *Journal of Social and Personal Psychology*. Interesting things were happening in the cognitive-behavioral area, but I was no longer a part of them. Five years and four non-tenure track appointments, grinding out introductory psychology classes, had been enough of the academic life for me. These days I investigated other phenomena.

Finally the call came.

"It's a couple of kids," my local operative told me. "Emptied the box and then crossed the street to the diner. They're in there right now."

"I'll be right there."

My operative was sitting a table near the door. I sat opposite him. He waved his hand toward a booth by the window. They were indeed kids, eighteen or nineteen, college student casual, one male and one female. There was a large mail bag underneath their table.

"I can recommend the clam roll," my operative said. He was middle-aged and comfortably plump. He didn't have the slightest idea what this assignment was about, and probably didn't care.

"Locals?" I asked.

He shook his head. "Canadians, ten to one. After awhile, you get to recognize them. There's a Honda with Montreal plates parked at a meter down the street. Could be theirs, although Montreal plates are a dime a dozen round here."

The waitress took my order. I had the clam roll. It was good advice.

I watched the kids stroll out and get into the Honda. I followed, and got into my own rented Dodge, which was parked across the street. They led me out to the highway.

It was an easy tracking job. Obviously they weren't looking for a tail. I stayed behind them all the way to the border, where I was delayed by over-zealous customs inspector. I picked them up again ten kilometers down the road, and stayed with them all the way into Montreal.

We reached journey's end at a small brick house in the north end of the city. One kid stayed in the car, and the other carried the bag up to the porch and rang the bell. The door opened, but it was too dark for me to see inside. A few minutes later the kid came out again, holding an empty bag in one hand and an envelope in the other. The kid got back in the car and the car drove off.

I sat in my car and watched the house. Lights went on, lights went off. No one went in or came out.

It got darker, and colder. Montreal in February was colder than Burlington, which was colder than New York City. I wanted to run the engine, but didn't. I'd always hated stakeouts.

I wrote a brief report for Staefler giving the suspect's address and put it in an envelope. I realized that I didn't have any Canadian stamps. I didn't have any American stamps for that matter. I left the envelope on top of the dashboard.

It was very late now, and very cold. My feet were numb. I tried to remember the symptoms of frostbite. All the lights in the house were out now. So were most of the lights up and down the street.

I sighed to myself. It was clear to me what I had to do. I didn't much like the idea, but I couldn't think of a better one. I got out of the car and stamped my feet until the circulation started to come back. Then I walked around the side of the house and found a convenient basement window. The interior frame was so rotten, the inside catch came away with just a little pressure from a screwdriver. No alarm sounded.

The basement was low and damp. An old oil furnace rumbled away at one end. At the other was a flight of stairs.

The stairs led up to a hallway on the main floor. Kitchen, living room, dining room, office. The office was sparsely furnished: desk, metal chair, filing cabinets, microfiche viewer, Toshiba laptop. Nice enough, but not exactly a supercomputer.

I played my flashlight over the papers on the desk. I was looking at proofs of next month's issue of the *Reeve One Thousand*. Gold prices were about to go through the roof. I wondered if I should leave and call my broker. I remembered that I didn't have a broker.

I opened the top drawer of one of the filing cabinets. Files: names of subscribers, statements, payables, receivables.

I wasn't exactly sure what I was looking for, or whether I would know what it was when I found it. Bottom drawer, more files. Second cabinet, top drawer …no files. Boxes. Little cardboard boxes. I opened one up. It was crammed with microfiche transparencies.

I looked at the title on the box. I blinked. I looked at it again. I shook my head. I looked at it a third time.

And then the lights went on, and a man came through the door holding a gun.

***

"Why wouldn't you call the police?" I asked him.

He sighed.

"This is all very messy, you know," he said. "I expected to arouse interest eventually. I expected someone would track me down. But I didn't expect anything this crude. I thought I would be able to explain matters in a civilized manner."

"Explain away. I'm reasonably civilized."

"I had it all worked out, you know. I was going to say it was all a matter of computers."

"That sounds reasonable," I said. "I could buy that. Using a computer to hack your way into the data nets. We suspected something of the sort."

"Oh no," he said. He looked shocked. "That would be illegal. I was going to say that I was using a computer to generate my predictions, based on a highly sophisticated economic modelling software package of my own design.

"And if they didn't buy that," he continued, "I was going to claim that I was psychic. That I could read the future like an open book."

"I prefer the computer," I said. "You can do wonderful things with computers these days. But I suppose I could buy that, too. Actually, you must be psychic. What other explanation could there be?"

"Mr. Hendricks, you are still holding the other explanation in your hand. As we both very well know."

I looked again at the impossible title on the microfiche box.

NEW YORK TIMES, March 1995

"And that," he said, "is why I cannot call the police."

"I see it. But I'm still not quite sure I believe it. Where did you get this?"

"From the library. You can take my word for it that no one will miss it."

"What library? Where?"

"I think you mean *when*, don't you. The where of it doesn't make a lot of difference. But it was the UCLA library, circa 2003."

"You're telling me that you travelled to the future?"

"It's the other way around, Mr. Hendricks. I travelled *from* the future. Bringing with me a microfiche run of the *New York Times*,

1991 to 2001. The paper ceased publication in 2001, but of course you wouldn't know that."

"Ceased publication?"

"No power supply, no newsprint, no staff. No New York City, to all intents and purposes. Let me tell you about the future, Mr. Hendricks. You wouldn't like it."

"War?" I asked.

"Oh, certainly a few small wars, here and there. But nothing really dramatic. Not in my time, at least. I've no idea what happened afterward. But basically just a .... *falling apart.* The same process that is going on around us right now, accelerated a hundredfold. A collapse of over-strained socioeconomic structures. I could try and explain it to you, but it's not really my field. I'm a physicist, not a social scientist. Or at least I was. Now I just write my little letters."

"How did you get here?"

"Experimental process," he said. "Tachyons and so forth. We had never tried it on a human being, but the animal tests were promising. And then they closed down the university, so I figured, what the hell? How could I be any worse off?"

"But why here?" I asked. "Out of all the places and times you could have picked?"

"In fact the process only extended back twelve years. But I figured that twelve years was better than none."

"And Montreal?"

"A number of reasons. Anonymity, for one thing. Less danger here of encountering people who knew me, or my own self of this period. Keeping a distance from curious subscribers. And then, Canada will survive the collapse a little better, up to 2003 at least. Fewer people to begin with, a more centralized banking system, a smaller underclass, greater social discipline. Of course, there will be trouble here, too. Quebec will attempt unilateral independence in 1996, if I remember correctly, and there will be some bloodshed. But by then I plan to be further west, possibly in Vancouver."

"And the letters?" I asked. "Why the letters?"

"Money. By the time things get really tough around here, I plan to be long gone. I'm going to buy myself a nice little Greek island to retire on."

"But why sell the information? Why not just play the market?"

"Good question," he said. "I was only going to do this for a year, to get seed money for my own investments. But there's something a little compulsive about it. Being all-knowing, that could be very hard to give up. And apparently I *don't* give it up. Not for awhile, at least. You see, two years from now there will be an international currency collapse. It will be the first critical moment in the sequence of disasters to come. It will be triggered by a run on the yen in the New York markets. It will be followed by what, for want of a better word, people will call a Depression. According to news reports of the time, massive selling of the yen will be blamed upon a mysterious market letter, the *Reeve One Thousand*."

"You remember that?"

"No," he said. "The fate of the yen was not high on my list of interests at the time. But it's all in the *Times*."

"It will be your fault, in other words. You're going to make it happen."

"No," he said. "It's inevitable. It's inevitable because it's already happened. I may be the instrument of fate, but I'm only an instrument. I'm simply following the script."

"And what does your script say about me?"

"Nothing. Of course, I don't have copies of the Montreal *Gazette*. If I did, perhaps it would carry the sad story of the New York investigator found dead in his car. But I don't recall any mention of your name in the *Times*. Then again, I may have passed right over it. I don't really follow crime news."

"You don't have to kill me. You know that you keep on publishing your letter. I don't stop you."

He considered. "That may be true. But I think it's more parsimonious to assume that I *do* kill you, because that seems by far the simplest way of ensuring your silence. And therefore I *must* kill you. I hope you understand that?"

"What if we break the script?" I asked. "What if you don't kill me, and you stop publishing, and the yen doesn't collapse, and there isn't another Depression?"

"You think I haven't wondered about that? You think I *want* things to fall apart? I've tried to stop, you know. I've tried very hard. There are days when I've said to myself, I'm not going to work on the letter. I've even left my house, gone downtown. And then it was if this giant hand grabbed hold of me and *forced* me to come back here and write the goddam thing. I have no choice, you see, because it *has* to happen this way."

"You feel compelled," I said. "Alright. But can't you see that it's a delusion? You've been under tremendous stress. You've escaped from a terrible situation. You find yourself holding unbearable knowledge, awful power. Nobody could blame you for going a little crazy. For trying to give up responsibility for your actions. But you *do* have choices all the same."

The gun seemed to waver in his hand.

"You *can* stop, Reeve," I said. "If that's your name. You can step right off this crazy conveyor belt that's going to deliver you right back where you started from."

"Paradox," he said. "It would be a paradox. Like killing my own grandfather. I have to follow the script. The economy has to collapse. Otherwise I don't come back here at all."

"Maybe the economy will collapse without your help. Who the hell knows? It'll work out one way or another. But you don't have to be any part of it."

"I have to publish the letter. I have to invest. I need money to escape the collapse. I can't just sit around and wait for it to happen. I have to be prepared. Prepared."

"You don't have to do any of those things."

"No." He shook his head vigorously. "No. Advances in strategic metals. Disastrous coffee crop. Changes in world climate. Pollution of fisheries. Opportunities in orange juice futures. Middle eastern war. Assassination ...No."

He was decompensating before my eyes. I wasn't sure that the result was going to be any improvement. It wasn't a great moment to make my move, but I was unlikely to have a better one.

I hurled the microfiche box at his face, and he raised an arm to ward it off. I dived at his legs, and brought him down to the ground.

We struggled on the floor. He tried to point his gun at me, and I tried to force his hand down. The gun went off, and brought down a shower of plaster from the ceiling. I got a better grip on his hand, forcing it downwards. The gun went off again and shot him in the chest.

***

I thought about calling the police. I didn't think about it very long. Even if I could swing a plea of self-defense, there was a little matter of breaking-and-entering to consider. I could well serve time. I would certainly lose my license.

But that was all nearly beside the point. There was dynamite in Reeve's filing cabinets, and I had to get rid of it before it blew up the world.

There was a fireplace in the living room. I started carrying in the microfiche boxes and piling them on the grate. It took me half an hour to transfer them all. The last to go was the transparency in the microfiche viewer. It was all set up with next month's news.

I knelt down to light a match. It wouldn't light. Neither would any of the others in the matchbook.

I went into the kitchen and searched for matches, finding none. I turned on the electric burner on the stove and lit a rolled up piece of newspaper. I carried my torch into the living room and knelt again in front of the fireplace. And froze.

When the paper began to burn my fingers, I dropped it on the tiles and stamped it out.

I picked the top transparency off the pile and walked back into the office. Reeve's body was still lying on the floor. I ignored him. There would be time to dispose of him later. Plenty of time before I left for Vancouver. Or rather, I told myself, New York.

I put the transparency in the viewer and turned the machine on. I scanned to the business section and began to take notes.

Dawn was breaking when I sat down at the desk and began to write.

Interesting opportunities are developing in the long-term bond market, I wrote. *Expect the Federal Reserve to further loosen controls on the money supply, sparking upward movement in ...*

And later, *Sincerely Yours, Reeve.*

Snow flurries were developing outside my window. It would be a lot warmer in Greece.

The Newest Profession

Phyllis Gotlieb

Melba took her walks Upstreet in the bluing part of the evening during the few moments before the lights came on, and turned back downward before they had reached their peak. In her mind her hair was a long ripple, and her neck, wrists, fingers waited for jewels to add facets to the rising brilliance.

The streets were nearly bare now, shops idle. She got the occasional mildly curious, mildly contemptuous glance; she was hardly visible in the dark uniform cape, empty hands hidden behind its slits; she was a big girl in good proportion, but her face, without makeup, faded in the dimness, and her fair hair was cut mercilessly straight around at earlobe length. The long, strong legs in flat-heeled shoes paced evenly: Their only ornament was a small pedometer on a fine chain about one ankle.

When she crossed the road and turned downward there was a shadowland to pass before safety: The keepers of the shops and the servants of the rich who bought from them lived in narrow streets; they did not trouble her, but their children absorbed and vented the attitudes they did not express. When the wind howled up the street from the west and folded back her cape on the expanse of her belly, children young enough for tag and hopscotch yelled names they had likely not thought of by themselves. "Bitch," "cow," "brood mare" were mild enough; tripping and stone-throwing were not.

The stone that hit this evening landed on her temple and made her lose balance. She did not fall this time but turned her ankle and knocked her shoulder against a lamppost. The policeman who came from shadow - they always turned up afterward, never before -

reached an unnecessary hand to steady her and said, "You all right, miss?"

"Yeah."

"There's a cut on your forehead and I— "

"I'm late already and I can walk. You want to give me a ticket or somethin'?"

The hand pulled away, and she went on, limping slightly. Maybe the damn pedometer had gone bust.

Children, back of her, being called to supper, yelled:

Monster, monster, suck my tit!
Dunno if you're him, her, it!

Himmerit! Himmerit! The words slurred. She knew. It was *her* and it would never suck.

She looked outward at the bloody Sun splayed on the horizon, gross as her belly. Way out beyond Downstreet the spaceport blasts sparked, then warehouses, repair shops, hostels climbed.

Out of shadowland into near darkness. Retired Astronauts' homes and Hospice—safe enough, window lit here and there, harmonica whispering of cramped quarters in rusty scows that crossed the voids, words no cruder than the children's song. Safe enough for her to give in to the pressure pains and bend over, straighten up.

Next door, NeoGenics Labs, Inc. Home.

* * *

"Three minutes late," said the Ox in the Box, not looking up.

"Yeah. Tripped over my feet." Stiffly she bent to unhook the pedometer, not broken, and showed it at the wicket. "Two km."

The Ox looked up. Her name was Dorothy, and she and Melba were not at odds, merely untalkative. A stout woman in her forties, graying black hair chopped short and brushed flat back. Sterile or sterilized, sometimes she flushed in heats that no chemical seemed to cure. "You didn't get that thing on your head from tripping over your feet." She rang for a doctor.

* * *

When Melba reached the dining room with a patch on her head and a tensor round her ankle everyone else was half through. She picked up her numbered tray and the whitecapped jock dished out a rewarmed supper from under the infrareds. "Bump into a door?"

"What else?"

She took her seat beside Vivian. There were no rivals for it. She was Number 33, Table 5, and there were never more than fifty eaters. Alice, Pam, and Del glanced up and went on shoveling in. Vivian said, "Upstreet again."

"I like the lights, Viv."

"Second time this month. What was it this time?"

"Kids."

"Whoever made up that shit about sticks and stones will break my bones knew at least half of what he was talking about. What did the Ox say?"

"Nothing. Just got the doctor. She's okay." Melba pulled herself as close to the table as her belly would allow and stared at the little card on the tray: Meat 200 grams, starchy vegetable 150 grams, green vegetable....

Pam said, "She knows you could knock her here to hell and gone with your belly."

Melba shrugged. That was what passed for wit here, and she had little of it herself.

Vivian laughed, but she was a nervous laugher and Melba not easily offended. Viv was the smallest and liveliest of the lot, and Melba liked her for making up what she herself lacked. Her hair was black and curly, with the barest hint of premature gray at the temples; her eyes were Wedgwood blue and her lips a natural red envied by a company of women forbidden cosmetics for the risk of dangerous components.

Melba always ate quickly and finished first, in contrast - as they were contrasting friends in every way - to Viv, who was picky. Her tray was empty by the time the jock came to replace it with the pill cup.

Viv's nostrils flared: she was not among the few who were allowed three cigarettes a day and flaunted their smoke after supper. There was more harmless dried herb in it than tobacco, but it smelled like something she loved. However, she was one of the favored allowed a cup of tea to wash down her pills.

Melba drank a lot of milk fortified with yet another drug or vitamin. She turned the medicine cup into her hand and stared at the palmful of colored pills. "Ruby, pearl, emerald - and what's the yellow one again?"

"Topaz - or vitamin D. Only a semi-precious stone. Still think you'll get to wear them?"

Melba smiled her long slow smile. "I hope."

Viv shook her head. A room with fifty women in cone-shaped denim dresses. Metal chairs; metal tables with artificial-wood tops; institutional-cream walls. "Maybe you will. Maybe."

Because the money after all was tremendous. What did not get put into surroundings went to equipment, technical expertise, and the bodies of the women.

It was Melba who waited for Viv, after all, while she lingered over her tea. Pam and Del left to play euchre; Alice, yawning, deflated her cushion ring and went to bed: she was only two weeks postpartum. One or two of the jocks hung around, mildly resentful of the still cluttered table. They were men chosen for low sex drive and lack of aggressiveness. There was no sexual activity allowed the gravid women, except in their dreams, and none on the premises among inbetweeners. Whatever there was had been made difficult enough by propaganda harping on dozens of forms of VD, major and minor.

"Goddamn nunnery," said Viv.

Melba didn't mind. She liked the money. She was big, healthy, slow-thinking, and did not have much trouble pushing back her feelings. Others put up and shut up with resentment. They all knew none was considered very intelligent. No one within their hearing had ever called them cows or sows, but the essence of the words hung like a cloud, drifted like fog. The women turned their backs on the jocks, the Psychs, the Ox, and told each other the stories of their lives.

Melba said softly, "You didn't take your water pill again."

Viv gave her a look of mingled guilt and reproach. "How'd you know?"

"Saw you palming it."

"They make me feel sick."

"I don't like that rotten milk either. You get high blood pressure and you're out."

Viv had a tight water balance. Her belly specialized in dry-worlders; Melba, who bred underwater life, drank all the time, thirsty or not.

"I don't care. This one's my last."

"Not if you don't watch out. I'll be in emeralds and you'll be lying sick somewhere."

Viv, cyclonic, turned bright red and stood up quickly. Melba grabbed her by the arm. "I'm sorry, Viv, I'm sorry! Please! Take the pill."

Vivian sat down slowly. Melba's eyes were full of tears. "I'm sorry, Viv. I don't mean to be so dumb."

"Oh, for Chrissake, don't call yourself dumb. You've got a mind like one of those mills you read about that grinds slow but fine."

"Yeah, and they rot to pieces and everybody says what beautiful scenery. Don't forget the pill, Viv."

"And you never give up, do you?" Viv sighed, fished the pill from her pocket, and swallowed it with the dregs of her tea. "Four male, three female." Her belly was a small polite bulge with the third. "In a thousand years they might fill a planet. In the meantime I'm tired."

Melba had never asked if Vivian went down to the crèche, nor often what she did with her spare time, besides visiting library and bookstore. Most women here were of a class to whom steady high unemployment and the debilitation of the nuclear family gave little choice. Men in this stratum had even fewer opportunities. The Y chromosome could be found in any healthy man.

But few women went down to the crèche though none failed to promise herself to do it. Not many boasted of affairs, either with men or other women, or discussed what they did with their time, even when they visited their families, so that they were in the peculiar situation where few knew what others were doing, but all knew what everyone had done before she came to NeoGenics. Loose talk was discouraged by the Company, to preserve they said, anonymity. Nevertheless, Melba, though she did not know if Viv had seen those children, down in the huge rooms of tanks and enclosures, knew that the age limit was thirty, Viv was twenty-eight, and that both she and NeoGenics agreed that seven would fulfill her contract.

"You're lucky you've only got a couple of weeks." Viv slowed her walk to match Melba's, careless of the grateful clatter of table-clearing back of them.

"Yeah, but I still need the two males, and they're not the kind of little mousy thing you grow."

"Hey, don't insult my kids!"

"I'm not, Viv. I hope they look something like you."

"Then go down and see!"

Melba shuddered. "I'm scared. I'm scared to think what mine look like."

"Being scared is like calling yourself dumb. Working at being a cow."

Difference. They got on each other's nerves, but they got on. Viv wanted to go to a good school and learn everything she could absorb and then go out and teach anyone who would listen.

"Well, I kind of want to be a cow," Melba said mildly. "I want a nice place with a lot of good stuff in it, and I don't care if I don't spend the money usefully."

"And be a fine lady? Oh, Melba, I'm so tired of hearing that!" She leaned against the dirty cream-colored wall of the corridor and looked up at tall Melba. Her eyes were not quite like the Wedgwood in the store windows: that did not have the fine glaze. "I bet you think men will come along and load you with diamonds - if you can get a plastic job on your belly that makes you look like a virgin!"

"But I can't learn things in a school like you."

"Will I really be able to sit in a school after seven births, when my metabolism's shot and my patience is gone - and I'm hyper enough already, not just from blood pressure? It's a dream, Mel, like everybody else has. Did anybody who's been here ever come back or call or write to tell how she's done?"

"They want to forget the place. You can't blame them for that."

"It's also because they go out and find there's no other place. They're dead at thirty, with the guts eaten out of them; they run through the money; the plastic job bags out on them; they're ruined for having kids of their own." She looked away. "I have met one or two...not too keen on remembering or recognizing. They're cheap whores, or if they're lucky they get a job selling secondhand in a basement. What the hell. You aren't listening."

"But I am, Viv. I won't let it happen to me." She added, "And don't be scared I'll end up some junked-up whore either."

Vivian laughed. "I admit I can't see any pimp beating up on you."

Melba thwacked her watermelon-belly with thumb and finger and laughed with her.

* * *

Melba lay in bed and reread the letter.

Now the plant got retooled your father went back to work so we hired on Karl Olesson to get in the vegetables. With what we use and what we pay him theres not much left from what gets sold. Wesley has run off with that Sherri in the drug store that I always said was cheap. He left in the middle of the night or your father would of slammed him. He left a note which I wont repeat what he said about your father. He didn't even say Love. Half the radishes got cracked on account of the wet. Noreen is pregnant again and won't say who but I wouldn't let your father touch her on account of the one that died. Even though it was a blessing God forgive me. They dont dare give us a cross eyed look in town because I know all about THEM. She could have an abortion but she says she wants something to love. I don't know where she got that idea at seventeen. Her having something to love means I get to take care of it while she runs with dirty bikers. I just cant stand it. Its a good thing your father is working again he just sat and moped and all I got from Wesley and Noreen was a lot of mouth. You dont say much in your letters but I guess you can't help it if it's Govt work. It's hard enough writing to a P.O. number you dont even know what city it's in and I don't know what you're doing. I wish you would just get married. I dont see why not. Everybody used to say Noreen was beautiful and look where it got her so beauty isn't everything. I hope what your doing is respectable. It's enough to drive you crazy around here. I guess that is all for now. Write soon. Your loving Mother. Your father says him too.

ps I'm glad you could spare the money because we needed it.

She folded the letter away with all the others and reached to turn off the light. The intercom buzzer sounded and she switched on.

"Mel -" the voice was Vivian's but so slurred it sounded dead drunk. Viv did not even like whiskey.

"Viv? What's the matter, Viv?"

"Mel...? Come, Mel..."

She pulled her awkward terrible shape out of bed and knotted the rough terry robe. Viv's room was three away. In the few seconds it took to reach it a terror seized her, and she slid the door with shaking hands.

The lights were on. Vivian, still dressed, was lying diagonally on the bed. Her eyes were open and glazed. The left one turned out slightly, and from its corner tears were running in a thin stream; the side of her mouth dragged down so far her face was distorted almost beyond recognition.

Melba knew a stroke when she saw one. She did not ask whether Vivian had called the doctor but slammed the buzzer and yelled.

Viv raised her working hand a little. "Be all ri..."

"Oh God Viv, why didn't you take those goddamn ..."

But the one comprehending eye Vivian turned on her was terrible. "Never meant -"

Melba grabbed at the hand. "Oh, Viv -"

"So sorry..."

"Don't talk. Please don't talk."

"Stay, Mel..."

"I'm here. You'll have help soon."

The hand was moist and twitching. It wanted to say something the mouth could not speak.

"Now...who...will love..."

"Everyone loves you, Viv. I and everyone."

"Don't mean...mean, the children, Mel...the chil..."

Stretcher wheels squealed around the doorway and attendants lifted Vivian in her blanket. Her hand pulled away from Melba's and her eyes closed.

"Stroke," one of the men muttered.

"I know." She had seen her grandmother taking pills by the handful, and dying too. But her grandmother had been seventy-five.

"Good thing you found her when you did."

"Yeah."

The room was empty. Very empty. The pot of russet chrysanthemums sat on the windowsill like setting suns between the muddy blue drapes. The colored spines on the orderly bookshelves blurred into meaninglessness. Melba pulled herself up and shuffled back to her room.

Two or three heads popped out of doorways. "Viv took sick," she muttered. "I dunno if it's serious."

She lay on her bed and turned the light dim. The sea beast swam in her belly. She had become so used to its movement, the fact that she noticed it now surprised her.

Big, slow thing, like me.

Vivian, all tight wires and springs, had broken.

She'll be through here. Maybe crippled—and oh, I said—

Floors below there was a white room where doctors worked on that frail pulse. Deep below that there were tanks where monstrous children turned in sleep so that terrible worlds could be reaped and mined. For *them.* They would not care. They had the four females and two males they would breed to build their stone gardens. She beat her fists once on the unresounding drum of her belly.

Buzz

Her hand, still clenched, punched the button.

"Melba?" The Ox's rasp voice, expressionless.

"Yeah."

"Wake you?"

"No. What-" Her throat went dry.

"She's dead, Mel. Thought I'd tell you first."

"I - thanks, Dorothy."

"For goddamn bloody what!" the Ox snarled and slammed off.

She sat like stone. She had expected it. What else with her luck could happen that she could find a friend, one friend worthy of respect, and have that good fortune taken away? She was ashamed of her selfishness, and yet the fact of *death* was too painful to go near.

She lost track of time, mind blanked out, until her diaphragm buckled sharply, and she fell back on the bed, choking. Then, as if a dam had burst the waters rushed out of her, and her throat opened in an uncontrollable and unending howl.

* * *

First there was the tube in her nose. Then the cone over her mouth, oxygen tasting like dead air already breathed by everyone in the world. Tubes in the wrist and belly. Shots in the buttocks.

Tubes...and pain...in the belly?

She opened her eyes. Nurse pulling off EKG cups pop-pop. Scraggy-beard face of A.J. Yates. Her doctor. Old Ayjay.

"We had to do a Caesarean," he said. "She was a damn big walloper."

She closed her eyes and dreamed of walking Upstreet with her long hair blowing in the wind. Jewels on neck and wrist, wings on her heels, bells on her toes.

You know that's silly, Mel, said Vivian.

"What?"

Ayjay: "I said you know we can't let you go through more than one other now you've had the cut. It'll have to be the male, and it'll have to be good."

Yes. They guaranteed their product: they had tried a male once before, and aborted because it was malformed.

"But the males are a lot smaller, so it shouldn't be too much strain. Maybe we can try for twins. Um-hum. It's an idea. Hum-hum. We'll think about it later. In the meantime, you're in pretty good shape. When you graduate after the plastic job you'll be in fine shape." He stood.

"Viv. Isn't."

"Um, well...oh, I'm glad you reminded me. The inquiry's in four days, and we'll have to get you up a bit for that, as a witness, but we'll take care not to tire you."

Bye-bye, Ayjay. Her eyes closed.

That's a damn dumb idea, said Viv.

"What?"

"Drink this," said the nurse.

She drank and ran her hand over the bandaged hump, the still huge and swollen womb that slid and shifted as if another fetus were waiting there to be born.

Wings on heels, bell on toes. Twins! *Dumb*. Her eyes closed.

* * *

Four days of hell. The walls were sickly green.

"Why do I have to go to the inquiry?" she asked the nurse.

"You were her closest friend, weren't you? They'll want to know anything you can tell them about her behaviour. If she ate or drank anything out of the way, like that. After all, she's only the second death we've had here, and the way we take care of them nobody should die."

In hell it is life everlasting. *You didn't take your water pill again.*

"Will I have to go under the scanner?"

"Of course. You aborted just after I came, didn't you? And you went under when you were questioned at the tissue conference. It's in your contract. Didn't you ever read it?"

Melba said, "I only asked a polite question, Nurse."

The nurse gave her a look. She gave the nurse a look.

"I'm sorry. I have other patients to care for." Whirl away of white skirt.

* * *

On the third day, a reprieve. The Ox tippy-toed in, bearing a painted china mug filled with delicate flowers. The Ox, a friend. The friend.

"Oh, that's lovely, it smells so good. Dottie, did you think of watering Viv's flowers?"

The Ox looked down. "I took the pot to my room. You can have it when you get out, if you like."

"Oh no, you keep it, please. She'd have been happy..."

"Melba, don't cry now. Wait till after tomorrow."

"Dottie, I'm scared shitless. I'll have to go under the scanner, and I don't know what to say!"

"Tell the truth, whatever it is," the Ox said grimly.

"I'm afraid they'll twist everything around."

"They won't twist you," said the Ox.

* * *

But she did not believe that when the jock came for her with the wheelchair. At the tissue conference they had had her almost believing she was some kind of criminal. Viv had pulled her out of that, but there was no...

"It's only one o'clock. I thought the conference was at two."

"Yeah, but I'm available and so's the chair. What's it to you?"

"I've got a damned sore belly and I feel like a gutted fish. I'm not sitting around in a wheelchair doing nothing for an hour." She needed the hour to think in, but she had been thinking for four days.

"Okay, okay, I'll come back when your ladyship is ready."

A thought ripened. "No. Wait."

"What now?"

"As long as we've got this time I want you to take me down into the crèche."

"Aw, come on! First you're too sick and weak to sit in a wheelchair, an' now I'll end up bringing you up in no condition to testify at all an' I'll have *my* ass in a sling for it. I haven't even any authorization for that."

"You don't need authorization. I *have* read my contract and it says I have the right to see the whatsits."

"Conceptees."

"Yeah. So let's get going."

It was shamefully easy to bully a jock. "Listen, if there's any trouble I'll swear under the scanner that I insisted and I'm to blame."

But it was he who insisted on phoning the crèche first and was not happy to be invited to come down.

Nor was she, in truth. It was hard sitting in the wheelchair, even though her body did not look the way it had done after previous births, as if a volcano had erupted from it. The pain, in a different place, hurt as much. But she was doing something, besides having babies, that pushed at her from inside.

* * *

The white-coated woman, surprisingly, had a kind face.

"You are feeling better now, my dear?" She had sharp foreign features and some kind of accent; her hair was tightly curled blond, dark at the roots.

"Not much. I just thought ... I'd like to see..."

"Your friend came here often, and looked at many of the children. Yours too. Down this way."

A cold knot in the chest.

Her youngest, twice the size of a normal newborn, slept in a small tank of its own, but the others, chasing through the cool and weed-grown water, seemed far too big even to have been born of woman.

These were not freaks. Freaks were warped and ugly caricatures, and these were a different species. Very dark red, hairless, their lidless eyes had no discernible expression, and no glance rested on her. The noses and chins were flattened back; the creatures had no fins, webs, or scales, but long, firm rudder-tails like those of tadpoles, and their limbs fitted close to their bodies for streamlining. She felt no pity or horror. They were purely alien. She wondered if they could see beyond the glass and water.

"Can they live outside the tanks?"

"Only for a moment or two."

Upstreet. Downstreet. Undersea. Another direction. Another dimension.

"They don't look much like me."

"Only about the forehead and cheekbones. A good model."

"Oh yeah. What will happen to them?"

"They will mature in a few years, and if they breed well they will make up a little colony and be sent to supervise underwater installations on a world where the seas are suitable for them."

Servants or slaves?

"When you get a male."

"A viable one. Those are more difficult, but by the time these mature we will probably have developed modified sperms to fertilize them with, so they can breed their own males."

"Oh," said Melba. So much for twins. "Are you allowed to tell me your name?"

"Of course. Natalya Skobelev. So you will know whom to ask for when you come down again."

Again.

"You got twenty-five minutes," said the jock.

"I want to see - to see Vivian's..."

There were hours to crying time.

"Oh my God! Monkeys!"

"No, no! Arboreal hominids, with one more step to reach humanity!"

That would be some step. But she looked closer. They peered back at her, taut wiry bodies dancing on the branches of the desert tree in the enclosure. *Vivian*!

These were tailless; they had tiny capable hands and prehensile big toes. Their bodies were covered with light down but there was dark curly hair on their heads, and they had small sharp noses and neat red mouths. Vivian looked from their blue eyes.

They blinked. Melba scratched at the glass and they giggled as if they had been tickled and sucked their little thumbs.

"They look much more like her," she whispered.

"We used more of her genetic material."

"And what kind of work will they do?" she asked dully.

"Feed on and harvest medicinal herbs, at first. Then like yours, they will find other things to do as they choose, I hope. Build civilizations in seas and deserts."

Was this woman here to tell fairy tales? A publicity hack? But her sincerity seemed not only genuine but passionate. NeoGenics was a business that grew servants and slaves. Yet ...slaves had become free.

"Maybe they will. Maybe."

"Time's up," said the jock.

"I know. Thank you for showing me around, miss."

"Remember: Natalya Skobelev, my dear. It is not an easy name."

"I won't forget it."

* * *

She felt shrunk and distorted, but the scanner did not register that.

There was no broadcasting of any sort in the auditorium, and no public audience except for the carefully picked jury of six unbiased civilians. Plus the coroner, a group of company officials, and two lawyers.

She let the preliminaries run over her head. A great deal of explication. What NeoGenics had wrought, for the benefit of the jury. Circumstances leading up to, unknown. What medical staff had done for the stricken patient. Useless. All evidence given under the scanner. No one else looked frightened or sickly.

Finally she was helped to the stand and fastened to the scanner.

"Note pseudonym: Ms. Burns."

"Melba Burns. Toast."

"Ms. Burns, do you swear to answer truthfully according to your knowledge?"'

"Yeah. Excuse me, yes."

"You have been employed by NeoGenics for four years and three months, during which time you blahblahblah?"

"Yes."

"Control set," said the woman at the scanner console. The Ox slipped in and sat in the back row, a patient block of stone in her good dress, flowered navy, incongruous out of the grey uniform. No reassurance there.

Melba could not see the console screen, nor the one that was projected in back of her; the framework about her head prevented that. There was no chance of conscious attempt to control the lines of blips. She did not believe she could do it, and would not try. She was here to betray, and that was the end of it.

The lawyers were a Mutt-and-Jeff pair: the big one to protect the Company's interests, the little one acting for Vivian's relatives, to make sure the Company could not prove she had reneged on her contract, and refuse to pay out the money owing her.

Lawyer Number 1 said, "Ms. Burns, to our knowledge the deceased, Vivian Marsden, considered you her closest friend here."

"I hope so. She was mine."

"I know the company does not encourage confidences among their employees in order to protect their anonymity in the community, but - " syrupmouth, "I am sure there must have been some confidence exchanged -"

Number 2: "That is an improper question."

Mutt raised an ingratiating hand. "I am not asking the witness for gossip about personal details confided by deceased or gathered from others. I also wish to keep this questioning period brief because of the personal suffering of the witness."

Number 2: "Very sound and thoughtful."

Melba did not care. The *arboreal hominids* leaped from branch to branch, giggling.

"But the basic question rests on the physical condition of the deceased, Vivian Marsden. Not what has been reported on by medical staff, but what may have been observed by the witness, or told her by Ms. Marsden. Whether she looked ill or complained of feeling ill. Whether...she might have been harming herself, unknowingly or not, by taking unprescribed drugs, alcohol, tobacco, or ignoring dietary regulations?"

Number 2: "Mr. Coroner, my friend is asking the witness to condemn the deceased out of hand!"

"But that does seem to be the point that must be addressed," said the coroner. "Ms. Burns, will you try to answer the question as simply as possible, even though it is a complicated one?"

"Again, was Vivian Marsden taking unprescribed drugs, or alcohol, or tobacco, or not eating properly?"

Melba wet her lips. "She didn't when I was with her, and she never talked about it. She hated alcohol. I know she missed cigarettes, but she didn't smoke." Her heart was in her gut. She glanced at the Ox. The woman's face was flushed, and her eyes full of pity.

The little lawyer said dryly, "I think it has been established by general inquiry that no one has more exact information."

"There is another direction to travel," said the Company man, just as dry. "Ms. Burns, is there anything necessary to the state of her health that Ms. Marsden *neglected* to do?"

Melba stared ahead and breathed hard.

"You must answer, you know," the coroner said gently. "It concerns the health of all the other employees of the Company."

Melba did not need the screen to know that her heartline blipped like mad. "Sometimes she put her water pill in her pocket after meals. She said she didn't like taking it because it made her feel sick." *Forgive, forgive!*

"Ah. You mean the diuretic."

"Whatever took away the extra water she wasn't supposed to have."

Number 2 said quickly, "That is no proof of the cause of an aneurysm. She may have taken the pill later."

"Or not at all. It is suggestive. How often did this happen, Ms. Burns?"

Melba found herself grinding her teeth. "No more than twice a week that I knew. I kept an eye on her to see what she did with it, and when I noticed her hiding it I made her get it out and take it while I was watching her."

"She could have found ways to avoid ingesting it if she were determined. Hidden it under her tongue, vomited it up—"

Melba snarled, "Oh, for God's sake!"

"Please restrain yourself, Ms. Burns, and strike those last two remarks. What deceased did *not* do cannot be accurately inferred from what she was observed to have *done* by an untrained witness."

But the lawyers, ignoring witness and coroner, were engrossed in each other, doing some kind of mating dance.

"I suggest that we ask permission to recall the pathologist to enlarge on his report."

"I agree. Absolutely. Mr. Coroner, may we call the pathologist to witness?"

"You may," said the coroner. "Is Dr. Twelvetrees present? Ms. Burns, would you please stand down now?"

The millstones ground. "No!" Melba cried. "It's not right!"

"Ms. Burns, I know you are distraught."

"If that means I'm upset, I'm damned upset. And maybe everybody thinks I'm stupid. But I'm not crazy. Sir, please let me speak for one minute!"

The coroner sighed. "If you have a contribution to evidence, Ms. Burns, go ahead. But please keep your remarks brief and to the point, as the lawyers are supposed to do."

There was a mild snicker. Melba despised and ignored it. "Maybe I can help bring out evidence." She took breath. "I thought we were here to find out just why Vivian died but this fella here acts like she fell in a ditch when she wasn't looking, and this other one is trying to put her on trial for murdering herself. I've answered all the long questions as well as I could, and now I'd like to ask two short questions." She pointed. "This guy."

"You wish to address the Company lawyer?" He scratched his head. "This *is* an enquiry and not a trial. Go ahead, but -"

"I *will* keep it short. I want to ask, Mr. Lawyer: did Vivian Marsden have high blood pressure before she came to work for you when she was nineteen? And would she have been cured of it after she left?"

Silence fell with a dark gray thud. A man slipped out of the room, and no one blinked. The lawyer opened his mouth and shut it again. Then, "After all, Ms. Burns, everyone knows there is some risk."

"Yeah. I guess that's all. Only ...the last words she ever said to me were: *Now who will love the children, Melba?* and I didn't even know what she was talking about. I'm sorry I took up your time and

I'll stand down now. Please ask that lady in the corner if she'll take me back to my room. I don't feel well."

"You did good," said the Ox.

"Yeah. And a lot of good it'll do. Everybody will be mad at me for telling about the pills."

"Between you and me, I think a lot of people knew she was trying to hide them, but nobody else made sure she took them, the way you did, so they can be as mad as they like."

* * *

She dreamed, a layered and complex dream of creatures in tanks, and children screaming dirty words in the streets, and worlds where the children of NeoGenics stared with empty eyes and died sterile. And her sister Noreen giving birth to a ....

The door chimed.

"Come in," she said in her dream. Noreen's child was ....

"It's over," said the Ox. "Death by misadventure. Nobody to blame, officially. Vivian's heirs will get their money."

She rubbed her eyes. "I hope they don't throw it around."

"No use being so bitter."

"I have no friend."

"You can count me as kind of half of a friend. I wouldn't mind."

"I'm sorry, Dottie. I'm behaving like a crud. You are a friend." And Skobelev. She would be useful if old Ayjay got twins on the brain again.

"There were some jury recommendations. You interested?"

She said drowsily, "I guess so."

"About giving the public greater access to information about our beloved Company. Knock off some of the name-calling and stone-throwing. Not fast and not much, but some. And letting government health organizations have a hand in the choice of breeders. The shit hit the fan when they found Twelvetrees. He'd run out to dig up Viv's county health records - which he should of done in the first place and found cases of blood pressure in the family history."

"Huh. I was trying to say they'd given her the high blood pressure."

"They brought it out by accepting her without investigating enough. And there were one or two things you said that they needed to hear. Well, I guess I better get back to work, but like you, I have one more question. Now you got your brains working , the way Viv always said you ought, what are you going to do with them?"

Melba smiled. And she had not even cried yet. "Gimme a chance, Dottie. They're still awful creaky."

* * *

I did pretty clumsy, Viv, but it was the best I could. You never belonged here. You should have had a man who could give you proper kids, and I'll never know why not. I don't know why I didn't either, except the home I came from isn't the kind I'd want to have. Maybe I never thought I was good enough to make a better one, but I dunno. The old man's a bastard, but he's proud of working, and Ma won't let herself be shamed. There's nothing wrong with that, is there? But kids can't find enough work to be proud of now, and we're not ashamed of the same things. Poor Noreen. She really is stupid, God forgive me. One thing I can do with the money is get her out of there. Maybe in some kind of shelter, Dorothy'd know, but not around this place. So her baby could at least have a chance to be a person.

Viv? We had all those, and what will they do? They should have had worlds that could grow them by themselves to make their own dumb mistakes, not the ones we make for them... but I can do something for Noreen....

And if I'm very good and very lucky there'll still be some money to throw around. Aw, Viv, you know there's nothing much wrong with that either. Better than wait until....

...Emerald, ruby, diamond... and the yellowish one. Topaz. Long hair for fingers to tangle in and kind of go shivering down my back...ah....

Where'd I find a fella like that, Ma? Well, I'm not preg all the time, and I've seen other eyes on me besides yours. Looking for different things. And maybe....

* * *

She slept without a dream.

Letters Home

G.M. Cunningham

Crécy
August, 1346

To my Beloved Mother,

A visiting Prieste is generously writing down my words for you. Uncle Henry, the Village Notary, can reade them to you after I have found some way of delivering this message to your hands.

Although we are tolde our Cause is just and glorious, I have now seene the face of war with mine own eyes and it is grotesque and pitiless. Even worse than the constant torrents of missiles from those perfidious new longbowes, against which even armour is no guarantee, is the cold, the damp, the hunger and pestilence which daily claim stalwart souls from our ranks. One wonders if terryble weapons like these will soon make war impossible.

Be of good cheere, though, Mother: we are tolde that our armour is more than a match for even the Devil's own missiles, our national pride proof against pestilence. We will be home Victorious by Christmas.

Your brave soldier and loving son.

The Somme
July, 1914

Dearest Mother,

I will probably not be allowed to send you this letter, as it reveals too much, but I shall give it the old college try, anyway.

You see my letters up until now have been quite lighthearted and cheery—off to save the world and give the enemy a well-deserved beating and all that. Since my last letter, however, I have seen the true face of war.

It was bad enough to see friends disappear into the muck, develop dysentery and malnutrition, shivering in the wet and cold without sleep or proper shelter for days on end. But over the past two nightmare days, I have seen whole battalions mowed down in rows by those infernal new machine guns.

Canada has lost the flower of its young men. I am simply astonished to be alive, and actually feel a little guilty about it.

I am not surprised to hear talk of this being "the war to end all wars." At this rate, there won't be any men left to fight it!

I also find it ironic when they say we'll be home for Christmas. I don't doubt it at all, one way or another!

Sorry if this gets you down, mother, but believe me, you're in my thoughts and prayers daily, and just telling this to you—even if you never get to read it—has been a great help.

Besides, they never tell you the truth, so now you know.

Love,

Your son.

Hiroshima
September, 1945

Dear Mom:

Guess what! We're shipping out next month, so it looks like this time I really *will* be home for Christmas. Well, it's none too soon for me.

I thought serving with the occupation troops in Japan would be kinda fun, but today I saw the face of war as it looks in the "atomic age," as they're calling it.

Believe me, Mom, you may have seen newsreel scenes and newspaper photos of what happened here when the Bomb went off, but nothing can put across the sights, sounds, and smells like it really is.

The sights? They're straight from hell. An entire city levelled, people with eyes melted, skin falling off, sick from radiation. The sounds—mostly an eerie silence. Gives me the creeps. And the smells! Death and destruction, fear and hopelessness...things you think you can't smell.

Pretty depressing stuff, but like the top brass tell us, it was probably for their own good in the end. Who knows how many might have bought it if we'd had to invade and the war went on for who knows how long?

At least, as long as we have the Bomb, it means there can never be another war like this.

Have to run—being kept pretty busy. Odd, all our efforts seem to be geared towards getting this country running again...oh, well—'bye for now!

All my love,
Your son.

20 Mile Crossroad
11th lunar month, Post-Holocaust

Surprise, mom! I found this piece of cardboard under some old wreckage, and so am able to scribble a few words with this pencil stub I've been hoarding. Doing a lot of reflecting, lately. Can't help thinking that if Canada had been better prepared for war, we might have had a better chance of preserving peace. Everyone very cold, very hungry. We attacked the hydroponics facility twice so far, but they have all the advantages. Inside, they are warm and, of course, the hydroponic gardens keep them well fed. The structure itself is built into the side of a hill in such a way as to make it very difficult to use our advantage of numbers. We have excellent archers, but the enemy have a working firearm that is very troublesome. Our nerve gas canisters are kind of useless under these conditions. We'll keep trying, though. The combined effects of atmospheric degradation and radiation mean we are all dead if we don't get in there. Not to mention artificial anthrax. Funny how war has a way of reducing things to the basics. Us or them. Life or death. Funny, too, how—even after devastation and death on a global scale—the face of war still turns out to be human. I'm still confident we can take this place in time to bring you something home for Christmas. Strange...I can't shake the strongest feeling that there's something I should remember today. Oh, well, see you soon.

Your daughter.

The Price of Land

Monica Hughes

He tore open the buff envelope. "God damn! This can't be right."

"What is it, Jim? What's the matter?"

"Taxes, Lucy, that's what. How the hell can they tell us we owe this much for our land when there's no land out there any more, when it's all blowed away." He stared out of the kitchen window, bright with fresh red and white gingham curtains. Beyond the shining glass the sun bored down into the dry earth and a funnel of dust wavered across the pasture. "You'd think they *wanted* us to give up, wouldn't you? And who'd feed the country then?" He tossed the envelope onto the arborite table.

A narrow pamphlet slid from it to the floor. Lucy bent to pick it up. It was printed on shiny paper, government style. She read aloud: "'Old Age Security: The Alternative Choice.' What's this then?" She began to read, her lips moving, her breath sucking in suddenly. "It's disgusting. Honestly, Jim, I don't know what the country's coming to. It's like Hitler."

"What's it about then?" He took it from her and read it slowly.

She watched his face. "How come you're not surprised?"

"I've heard about it, down at the beer parlour. But I've never seen it explained like this before. Well, you've got to admit it's logical, the way things are now."

"Jim White! That you...well, all I can say is that life is sometimes mean and hard, and I guess there's not much to do but to bear it. But then there's downright *bad*. Evil. That's what this is...it's *evil*." She turned to the sink and filled the kettle.

Jim reread the pamphlet and put it carefully back in the envelope with the tax bill. He tucked the envelope behind the clock on the shelf.

"School bus'll be by in a minute." Lucy spoke over her shoulder. "Thought we'd have eggs for our tea. You want to lay the table while I make toast?"

He put out placemats, and laid out the knives, forks and spoons. Him and Lucy. Cheryl and Cindy. And Lucy's Gran, part of the family now since Grandpa died, all of ten years ago. Just before Cindy's birth.

"Gran still resting?"

"I guess so. Call her, will you, Jim? She likes a bit of time to recollect herself after a nap."

Jim's lips tightened. His eyes strayed to the shelf and snapped away again. He stomped down the hallway and tapped on the end door. "Gran? You awake? Teatime."

Voices outside and then the kitchen suddenly full. "Jeesh, it's hot out there today, Mom. You could fry eggs on the path."

"Mom, guess what. Liz and Jojo are leaving at the end of the year. They're going to Calgary to get jobs. Please, Mom, can I go too?"

"You're far too young to leave home yet, Cheryl."

"I'm fifteen. Gran was practically my age when she got married, Mom."

"She was sixteen. And getting married meant she'd got a man to look out for her. You...you'd be on your own. I wouldn't have an easy moment, knowing you were on your own. And Liz and Jojo—they're too flighty."

"I could board. I'd be fine. Oh, Mom, if I've got to stay here for the rest of my life, working in the Bijou cafe, 'cause there's nothing else, I think I'll go crazy. Everyone's leaving, Mom. There's nothing *here* to stay for."

"Things'll get better, Cheryl. It'll rain."

"Tuesday come doomsday it will, Mom! Hi, Gran. Gran, you're on my side, aren't you, about leaving home?"

"Taking sides isn't nice, Cheryl. It's a big decision. Give your Mom and Dad time to think it over."

"*Time!* I'm getting older by the minute. Before you know I'll be too old."

"For what, for heaven's sake?"

"To be a model. A girl doesn't last for ever, you know. If I could just get into modelling school in Toronto—that's where the jobs are. But even in Calgary I could get a start."

"Let her go, Mom. She's so pretty she's just bound to be a success. She's the prettiest girl in school bar none."

"Oh, Cindy! And you'll be wanting to go next, I suppose."

"Me? Oh no, Gran. I just want to stay here for ever and ever with all of you."

"You're nutso. Just you wait. In another three years you'll change your tune, I bet."

"That's enough, Cheryl. Come, sit, both of you. Dad, will you ask the blessing?"

"For what we are about to receive..." *Thank you, Lord, for the hens still laying, for the fact the well hasn't run dry yet. But, Lord, what am I to do with that tax bill?* "...may the Lord make us truly thankful."

"Amen."

The dishes were done and the hens fed. The slow prairie twilight crept across the farm and with it a little breeze, scented with sage. It was cooler on the porch than indoors. Lucy and Jim sat on the old couch, and the girls on the glider, Gran in her rocker close by, a basket of mending at her side.

"How's the hay coming, Jim?"

"Not that great. I guess I'll have to cut before it burns up. But next year...seed 'n' fertilizer." His voice trailed away. *And those damn taxes*, he thought.

The glider whispered to and fro. Cheryl and Cindy giggled over their homework. The rocker creaked. Gran reached for another sock and rethreaded her needle.

"You'll ruin your eyes, Gran."

"There's a little light left. I'm fine." She looked sharply at Lucy, sitting with her hands in her lap, staring at the reddening sky.

"You all right, Lucy? Don't often see you just setting."

"I'm fine. Things on my mind, I guess." She caught Jim's eye and turned away to stare at the sky again.

He cleared his throat. "Think I'll go into town tomorrow. See if they'll forgive us part of the tax, or maybe carry it over to next year."

"At least talk to them. That's a good idea, Jim."

"Seems that taxes go up every year nowadays. Why, when I was a girl..."

"There wasn't all the welfare programs then, Gran. And there were more young people working and less old people just setting."

"Jim!"

"That's all right, Lucy. It's a fact. Not that we didn't do our share. But we were the baby boomers. I guess the government just didn't think that far ahead, to when we'd all be old." She sighed. "Sometimes I feel downright *useless*."

"Gran! How can you possibly think that? You sew and knit and mend and help us with our homework. I don't know where we'd be without you."

"Thank you, Cindy, for the kind words. But still...."

"It *is* getting dark now." Lucy set a lamp out on the wicker table. A moth appeared and flew round and round. Whisper. Whisper. Closer and closer. Thump.

Cindy shivered. "I just hate it when they do that. Do we have to have the light?"

"You'll strain your eyes on your schoolwork without. It's only a moth, silly."

And what's to happen to you both? Lucy's thoughts went round and round like the moth. *What's to become of you?* Her fingers tightened around each other.

The thoughts were still there, battering round and round, after the girls and Gran had settled down for the night, after she'd got out of her housedress and washed, slipped on her cotton nightie and lain down beside Jim. "So you *will* talk to the tax people tomorrow?"

"Yep," he'd answered into the silence that hung over their bed. She didn't hear him go to sleep. Usually she did, his steady breathing a kind of signal to her brain to let go of another day. But it seemed impossible to get rid of *this* day. It was like there was something special about it. Something she'd remember in after times, though she couldn't say why. She felt jumpy with it. Jim didn't say anything, but she felt that he was awake too, silently thinking. Wrestling with something inside.

The next day was like any other, with a hurried breakfast before the school bus came by and then a little peace after it had left. Lucy did the dishes and went out to feed the chickens. Gran dusted and straightened up.

"What's this, Jim?"

He looked up from his cup of coffee. She was holding the bright pamphlet in her hand, the one from the tax department. He moved quickly and steadied his cup. "You don't want to read that rubbish, Gran. It's just government nonsense."

Gran stood by the shelf, her back as straight as a poker. She was amazing, he thought. Her hair still thick, though white as milkweed now. Her ears could hear a coyote's call over the hill and her eyes spot a hawk when it was only a dot in the sky. Good for another twenty years, he reckoned.

The shiny paper fluttered in her hands.

"It's nothing," he said again. "Forget it."

"*You* kept it. You didn't throw it in the trash. You've been thinking, haven't you, Jim?"

"I never..."

"You *should* think about it." She tucked the pamphlet back in the envelope with steady fingers. "It's a good offer." She nodded.

Her eyes were sharp as skewers and he felt his slide guiltily away.

"Lucy'd never stand for it." It was a stupid thing to say. He wished he could've taken it back. It was mean-spirited of him to hide behind Lucy's loving nature. But Gran was right. It *was* a good offer. They'd never get a better. The only chance, when you came right down to it, to get off the never-ending rat race of diminishing crops and higher taxes. And it had been said. "No, she'd never go for it. Not in a million years."

"If I signed the form and you took it in to the tax office, there wouldn't be much she could do about it, would there?"

"You'd do *that*? Of your own free will? Why? Why would you?"

"For Lucy and the girls. For your futures."

He ran a hand through his hair, harsh, sun-dried, thinning a bit on top, and looked at her tentatively. "Yes, there's the girls, too," he said slowly, feeling his way. "I don't suppose it'd be too hard to persuade Cheryl that it was okay. She's hard as nails, our Cheryl. If she can just get into modelling school, she'd go along with anything."

"She's not hard, Jim. She just knows what she wants. And that's all right."

"Cindy's something else. She just about worships you, Gran. She'd never consider...."

"It'd be hard on her, harder than on the rest of you, I know that. Just don't tell her. Don't tell none of them yet, not till it's done." She glanced out of the window, put a finger to her lips and went on dusting.

The door swung open and Lucy came in, mopping her face. "Lord, it's hot. Jim, there were coyote tracks around the chicken run. Will you just make sure there's no place they can get through?" She put a basket of eggs on the table. "Just a half dozen. Not worth taking in to town."

"It's the heat."

"Only June. Thirty-two degrees in June! And not a cloud in the sky."

"Give it a couple of weeks. There's always a soaker in July. You've got to have faith, dear."

"Oh, Gran." She hugged her mother. "What'd we do without you? Jim, what are you doing today?"

"I'll start cutting the hay this evening when it's cooler. Right now I guess I'll drive into town and talk with the tax man. Get it over with."

Gran shook out the duster. "I'll come with you, Jim. Wait till I change my dress."

"You, Gran? Whatever d'you want to go into town for?"

"I fancy a chinwag with some of my old friends. There's not as many around as there used to be. Maybe we could make a day of it, eh, Jim? You can treat me to an ice cream."

It was very quiet once they'd left. The clock ticked and the hens murmured softly outside, a sleepy sound. *I can't stay sitting here*, Lucy told herself. *I'll set bread to raise now. It'll be ready for the oven when it's cooler*. She stirred yeast into warm water. She measured out the flour. Two hours for the first raising, maybe less in this heat. She glanced at the clock on the shelf. The buff envelope had gone. Of course Jim had to take it, to argue his case. Then she remembered the other paper, the government pamphlet.

"Oh, my Lord." She ran for the door, wiping her floury hands on her apron. "Jim, you come back here! Gran!" But the truck was just a dot, a plume of white dust hanging over the road behind it. She walked slowly back to the house.

She was getting edgy, imagining things. Gran was just going for a gossip with her old friends and a dish of ice cream in the Bijou Cafe. She stirred in the flour. Dug her fingers into the soft dough, kneading, turning, slapping it smooth and silky. Refusing to think, concentrating on the creamy colour of the dough, the grain of the wooden board, the feel against her fingers. She covered the bowl with a wet cloth and left it on the table to raise. Methodically she cleaned the dough from her fingers, washed her hands, pushed the rings back over her knuckle. They were getting a mite snug. Was it high blood pressure? She ought to get a checkup. But she was probably fine. She took after Gran, didn't she? And Gran was as healthy as a horse.

She shivered suddenly. *Stop it*, she told herself. *Don't think about it.* She filled the kettle and put it on the stove. A cup of tea'd help pass the time alone. After lunch she hoed the vegetable garden. In spite of shade screens the bean bushes were drooping. The carrots were coming on, though. She went slowly down the rows, dribbling water carefully around the green fronds.

The school bus came first, with the truck at its heels. Almost as if Jim had planned it, so she wouldn't have a chance to tackle him privately and find out exactly what he and Gran'd been up to. Well, it'd have to wait till bedtime.

Frustrated, she punched down the dough and cut and shaped it into the pans. In half an hour it'd be ready to pop in the oven. Since it was on anyway she'd do baked spare ribs and potatoes.

As soon as supper was over Jim went out to start on the hay. He'd get in the best part of four hours before it got too dark to work. Lucy sent Cheryl and Cindy out to do their homework on the porch before tackling Gran. "So what were you really up to?" She hung up the damp dishcloths and glared at her grandmother.

Her face as smooth as a dish of custard, Gran proceeded to list every soul she had met, the ensuing conversations, their health and that of every relative in town and away. "And we had a real tasty ice cream to finish off," she added. "Banana surprise, they call it. I ate every speck." She chuckled. "Though Jim couldn't manage his."

"Oh, you're impossible." Lucy went out on the porch to goad Cheryl about her homework.

Jim came in late, dusty and sweaty, needing a shower before bed. She waited for him to tell her, the silence spinning a web around the room. "Well?" she asked at last.

"There's no tax relief. No way." He towelled his hair dry. It stood up like a baby's. Innocent.

She wanted to ask him right out if he'd done anything about the pamphlet, but she found she couldn't put it into words. Words were solid. Lasting. They made things more real, more possible.

He climbed into bed and lay beside her. He put a warm hand on her thigh and she could feel her muscles go hard, unyielding, like a fencepost. She didn't move. He rubbed her shoulder then, comforting. "Go to sleep, Mom." He turned on his side away from her. She continued to lie rigid, staring at the ceiling.

Jim took to being at the gate when the mail truck came by. Six days later the cheque arrived, more money than he'd seen in years, enough to cover the taxes and the cost of next year's seed and fertilizer, with enough left over for the girls. He showed it to Gran, secretly, when Lucy was out in the yard.

"You're going to have to tell them now."

"Don't worry, Gran. I'll get to it."

"There isn't much time." The cheque was postdated, cashable the day after her seventieth birthday.

"A week. Time for you to back out if you want to, Gran. I'll understand. I can just tear it up."

She looked at him steadily, seeing in his face the fear that she might take him at his word. "I've set my hand to the plough, Jim, and I won't turn aside now." She could hear his slow sigh of relief. "But you've *got* to tell Lucy and the girls."

Jim worked like a demon. He finished the haying and fixed all the fences. He was out all day, grabbing a bite and then off again. The girls whispered together on the glider, planning surprises for Gran's birthday. Lucy checked her baking supplies, making sure she had everything for the birthday cake. Jim hadn't said a word. It must be all right. That frightening pamphlet had just set her to imagining things.

She began to sing as she baked, and when they lay in the quiet dark and he put his large hand on her thigh she turned to him joyfully. This time it was he who stopped. "Sorry, love. Must be tireder than I thought."

"That's all right. You've been working too hard, that's all."

He was going to tell her then, but panic stopped his throat. He swallowed and the moment was gone.

Lucy got up early to bake Gran's birthday cake before the kitchen got too unbearably hot. It cooled on a rack all morning and the girls iced and decorated it before midday dinner.

Gran dressed in her best grey silk. She exclaimed at the decorations and opened the gifts the girls had got for her: dusting powder and a tiny bottle of toilet water. Lucy had ordered a blouse from the catalogue, pale blue with a tie neck.

It was too hot for a big meal. They had cold ham and lettuce and potato salad. And the cake. The girls chattered, while in the background the radio softly played westerns. Gran ate with relish. Jim pushed the food around on his plate and broke his slice of cake into crumbs. Lucy watched silently, a heaviness like a stone beginning to form in her chest. When the white van turned off the road and bumped up the lane towards the house it was she who heard it, looked past the gingham curtains at the plume of dust it left behind it. Like ashes.

She was on her feet. "*Jim.*" That was all. One word. Hurled at him like a stone.

"Now just a darn minute." He was on his feet too. Like combatants, one on either side of the arborite table. "I was going to tell you, Lucy. It's just...I couldn't seem to find the right moment."

"Land's sake, Jim. You mean you haven't told Lucy and the girls *yet*?"

"What's going on?" Cheryl asked, her hand to her hair.

"Mom, what's Dad done? Gran, what's the matter?" Cindy looked from one to the other.

The knock on the door was heavy, official sounding. Lucy's hand went to her mouth. "Don't open it," she whispered. "Pretend we're not here."

"Don't be foolish, Lucy." Gran's voice was crisp. "Cindy, will you get the door, please?"

The man outside was tall, big-shouldered, dressed in fresh white coveralls. His face was wide, creased in a smile. Cindy held the door wider. "Will you come in?"

"Thank you kindly. Hot day, folks." He mopped his forehead with a spotless handkerchief, shaking out its crisp creases and then tucking it into his pocket. His twinkling eyes took in the remains of the birthday feast. "A goodbye party. My, that's real nice."

"What d'you mean—goodbye? It's our Gran's birthday. She's seventy today."

"Is that a fact? That'll be Mrs. McDougal, I guess." He bowed to Gran, sitting straightbacked in her best grey silk. "Congratulations, ma'am."

"Thank you, young man. Would you care for a slice of cake?"

He hesitated. "Thanks. But no thanks." He smacked his stomach. "Got to watch those calories."

"Then I suppose we'd better get on with it." Gran began to stand.

He waved her back. "Just a few formalities first. If you'd just read this carefully."

It was a document on crisp paper, folded into three. Gran put on her reading glasses and read it through carefully. She looked up and nodded.

"If you'd just sign *here*. And *here*. That's the way."

Lucy stood, clutching the back of her chair. Her mouth twisted out of shape and the tears ran down her cheeks.

"*Mom*?" Cindy made to get up, but Cheryl gripped her arm, her polished fingernails digging in.

Gran folded the paper carefully, handed it back to the man in white and tucked her reading glasses into their needlepoint case. She got to her feet and hesitated. "Is there anything I should bring?"

"Just the way you are is fine, ma'am. I'll get you settled comfortably in the van and then I'll come back and talk to your folks."

"Thank you. I'm afraid you'll find them a little bewildered. My grandson-in-law wasn't quite able..."

"That's all right, ma'am. Nothing unusual in that. All part of the job. This way." He gave his arm to Gran.

She paused at the door and looked back at them, Cindy and Cheryl sitting at the table, Lucy and Jim standing opposite each other, clutching their chair backs. "Thank you for my birthday. Thank you for...for everything. God bless you."

The sound of the door closing seemed to waken Lucy from her daze. She leapt across the room, but Jim caught her before she reached the door.

"Let go of me, Jim White. There's still time. I won't let you."

"She signed the paper, Lucy. I didn't even have to *ask* her. It was *her* choice. Honest."

"And you tried to talk her out of such foolishness? Like hell you did! Let go of me." She turned her head and bit his hand. He swore, but held on.

"What's happening to Gran?" Cindy wailed. "Mom, what is it?"

"Hush up," Cheryl hissed. Her face was dead white, her eyes big with excitement.

Outside the truck engine rumbled. The chickens clucked sleepily in the shimmering afternoon heat. The clock on the shelf ticked. Lucy had stopped struggling and was sobbing quietly against Jim's chest, his arms holding her tight....

The clock ticked on. The engine rumbled. The radio softly played country rock.

There was another knock and the door opened.

"That's it then, folks," the man in white said gently. "It's all over. Try not to grieve. You've made the right choice. She went very quiet, very peaceful. No pain or discomfort, I assure you. Here are her rings." He laid them on the table, among the cake crumbs and wilting lettuce leaves: the thick wedding band, its gold the colour of butter, the thin engagement ring with its single small chip of diamond. "And here's the death certificate, Mr. White. You can cash the cheque tomorrow. It'll make a big difference, I reckon." He looked through the window. "There's a patch of cloud over in the northwest. Could be your luck's changing. I shouldn't be surprised if we had rain in a couple of days."

Jim let go of Lucy and held out the cheque. "Take it. Go on. I don't want it."

"It's too late for second thoughts *now*, friend. Come on, pull yourself together. You've got to think of it this way; you won't make it without this cash, that's the truth, eh? And the Government's grateful. We *need* farmers like you, hanging in there when the going gets tough, producing food for the rest of us. What the country *don't* need is old folks, right? Old Age Security. Pension. Medical benefits. There's no end to the money going out with nothing productive coming back. The country's just about bankrupt. This is an incentive payment, that's all, and a thank-you to the old lady for doing the right thing. So pay off your debts and good luck to you."

Hand on the door knob, he turned back. "Sorry, folks. I nearly forgot. Her ashes...they'll be at your door, special delivery, early next week. In a handsome urn. No charge. All part of the service. Goodbye. Have a good day."

The door slammed. The truck bumped down the lane to the road. Slowly the plume of dust settled. The kitchen clock ticked. In the background the announcer began to read the news.

"Lucy, don't look at me that way."

"How d'you want me to look at you? You're a murderer, Jim White. And I'll never forgive you. Never."

"*She* signed the paper. It was *her* choice all the way. For you, Lucy. For the girls. For all of us."

She shook her head. "No good'll come of it. It's blood money."

"Money for taxes. For seed. To get Cheryl to modelling school. Something in the bank for Cindy, when she's old enough."

When Lucy shook her head again he grasped her forearms and pulled her towards him. "*You* read the pamphlet. You knew what I was thinking. You didn't try and stop me, did you? Did you?" He shook her and suddenly released her so that she fell back against the refrigerator.

"I...." Her hand went to her mouth.

At the table Cheryl watched them with calculating eyes, while Cindy sobbed, her head down among the wreckage of Gran's birthday feast.

"Another hot day," the announcer said cheerfully. "But the weatherman is promising us that a break in the dry spell is just around the corner...."

The Art of Escape

The Falafel Is Better in Ottawa

Jean-Louis Trudel

The hunt had been long.

It that looked like a man was crouching in front of a public terminal, intent on the instructions printed in twelve languages and five alphabets. A tram whispered by on a magnetic cushion, and the lights inside washed over the form facing the grimy screen. Then returned the darkness.

The hunter climbed warily the stairs leading out of the subway station, eyes on the unmoving figure. What served it as a face was lost in night-shadows and the hunter could not see where its CCD eyes were looking. His muscles tensed, ready to react to the first sign of motion. He would allow no more escapes.

Close by, he saw that the flesh-mask was absorbed by accessing the automatic teller function of the terminal. He laid a hand on the shoulder's alien angularity.

"What if I asked you to give me that money?"

A human might have recoiled, felt for a can of mug-repellent. His prey did not even shiver.

He had waited for an answer. With his other hand, he jabbed the two prongs of his weapon into his prey's backside. There was a smell of ozone and of burnt wool, the stench of melting plastic and red-hot metal. The arm extended to pull the card out of the terminal slot stiffened.

One more joyride was over.

The hunter stared at the card half-out of the slot and a thought struck him. He pulled the card out: it was a new model, with molecular circuitry embedded under the shiny surface.

The hunter cursed. Then he shrugged. No, it was not possible.

How long is a second? Long enough for a photon to speed almost from the Earth to the Moon. Long enough for an electron to drift several hundred meters. Long enough for electronic senses to extend through specially designed fingers, make a few connections, and start an information transfer through the newly-made channels.

One function of the terminal had been data transmission. It that was dying had been aware of the potential bolthole—though it was locked—as it always was sensitive to a world half-invisible for humans, who could not perceive the shadow doors and the unseen flows of energy.

Capacity was limited, time was short, and it was forced to write itself into unused storage space of the company which owned the local network of terminals. Compress! Compress! Compress more! It savored its own dying, though the killing jolt had been too brief. The core of born flesh encased in the prosthetics died last, relaying a few desperate messages to the almost-vacated brain.

Pain. Anger. Denial. **Pain Again.** Pain. Pain. Pain.

It struggled to hold on to those last scraps of sensation. They were its own, very private sensory input that it would never share.

The lights dimmed. Could lines of code, however inextricably bound to each other, retain an identity? Could the memories sustain... resurrect? Could the questions answer themselves?

The hunter had obtained half of an ancient kitchen in the small Toronto sleepden he'd chosen. He opened the apartment's door by drawing the requisite hieroglyph on the sensitive glass. A glance down the main corridor discovered no lights filtering under the doors.

The half-kitchen had room for a washstand and even for a chemical bucket neatly tucked under the all-purpose monitor. A message light was flashing, throwing a red glare over the yellowed sheets of the bed.

He stretched out on the bunk and drew to him the strips of contact-heads hanging from their wires. Despite his deep tiredness, his hands were steady as they plugged in his crown of thorns. A soft voice instantly spoke, murmured rather, flat and genderless:

"Do you remember that day in the Museum of the Offices when you first caught sight of it? It was so new to humanity that it attempted to look at the other side of a Botticelli canvas, for it was as curious about the backside of an oil painting as it was intrigued by the curiously distorted representations of humans on the front. It was surely then that you checked in with the Firenze bureau of Stahlstadt Gesellschaft and learned of another rogue on the loose. Do you not remember?"

"Who are you?"

"A ghost?"

"What do you want?"

"Be generous to those you know and even those you don't know yet. It is not what is wanted, but what you must do."

The voice stopped and the hunter noticed there had been no background to the transmission. A click marked the end of the connection.

The hunter unplugged. His eyes focused on the minuscule stalactites of dust dripping from the ceiling. He plugged in again, drew on his dwindling credit, and confirmed that the Toronto recycling squad had indeed picked up one dysfunctioned hulk bearing the markings of a Firenze manufacture.

A sigh disturbed the dust kittens playing in the folds of his blanket. By all rights, he should send in immediately his claim for the Stahlstadt Gesellschaft bounty. Yet, he did not get up to do so.

For the first time, he felt doubt.

The message light was flashing when he woke up. It was the same voice.

"Do you not remember racing across the Piazza San Marco amid the angry flapping of the pigeons and gawkers? It crossed the Gran Canale by jumping from gondola to vaporetto to outboard, flying high in the air like an angel freed from Tintoretto's *Paradiso*, launching itself at the sun, leaving you standing at the edge of the water, a foolish little human. Wasn't the sun brilliant? Wasn't the sky pure blue, with only a few clouds coming in from the east over the Arsenal? Do you not remember?"

"You are dead." A statement of fact.

"Do you deny it was alive?"

"It was a dangerous, unsupervised, and unrestrained machine."

"Was it only that even before highjacking that new waiter model?"

"Stop asking questions!"

"Command not appropriate."

The voice clicked off and the hunter breathed out. The reaction to his last words was a revelation. What had been calling him was nothing more than a residual program hidden somewhere in the network, with hardly a vestige of self-awareness. If he wanted, next time it called, he could probably latch onto it a top of the line killer program. And that would dispose of that. Still, curiosity stirred within him. The two calls had brought back the memories of his month-long pursuit across Europe. Though he yearned to deny it, he'd enjoyed it more than any recent hunt. His prey had adapted quickly to human quirks. Few others had so prolonged his hunting. Were they making them more intelligent?

He plugged in again, reached around the world by satellite, and made a light flash in Varna.

"Marinescu here," was the answer.

"Call me Spadina."

"I believe I recognize that tone. I think we dined at the *Halàszbàstya*, when last we met."

He was only mouthing the words, to transmit them over the link, but their characteristic rhythm and syncopation were preserved. He smiled drily at the quick identification.

"What is the minimum level of consciousness?"

Marinescu did not answer instantly. She was reputed to have fallen in love with machine minds, though it was the pitiless love of the collector who pins asphyxiated butterflies to cork squares.

"Ah, Spadina, at last you question! That itself may be the first step to true self-awareness."

He glowered at nothing in Toronto and, in Varna, asked carefully:

"Can a partially programmed set of responses be conscious?"

"Dear Spadina! How many of your actions result from the running of learned programs? When you lift a cup of tea? When you flush your teeth? When you drive your car?"

He was reminded of a Taiwan hunter who'd said that a conversation with Eva Marinescu was like talking with a mirror.

"Could you be a bit more enlightening? Perhaps?"

"One question has often been asked before: is consciousness an illusion born of thoughts referring constantly to the same actor? Do you exist because you believe you exist?"

Then again, maybe she also loved the sound of her own thoughts. He tried one more time:

"Eva, could a machine mind conceived to oversee a car assembly line highjack a synthetic waiter and then transfer itself into some kind of semi-public memory, all the while retaining a hint of identity?"

There was a pause.

"Spadina, we have been creating consciousnesses in our electronic matrices and pretending that they owed us their services because we had created them. Very prudently, we keep them down to animal-level intellects. Just enough intelligence to do the job. Except that sometimes, minds that know both software and hardware, but are confined, manage to connect with a mobile unit that can be augmented and taken over. You hunt these. Others more rarely succeed in slipping fragments of themselves into the network. I hunt those. Intelligence varies, according to capacity, program, and input, but consciousness, will, survival drive—call it what you wish—remains throughout."

"Very well." He decided. "Could you send me one of your search-and-destroy programs?"

"More than mere programs, dear Spadina! Stay where you are for another thirty minutes and I'll get my latest model to you."

The hunter disconnected himself. He looked for a flashing message light, but nobody had called and he realized how much he'd looked forward to a call. And how much he'd been afraid.

He searched for something to do while Marinescu got her package to him. He never carried hard books on a hunt and didn't care to draw again on his credit to get a book from the public lending banks.

No books. No hobbies. And he didn't care for the newschatterers.

The air was becoming stale inside the small cubicle. He suddenly struggled to remember his original name. Boboli in Firenze, Montjuic in Barcelona, Vivienne in Paris... what had it been in Budapest? But those were aliases. His bank account was protected by a number string, his licenses were identified with DNA codings. He could not even remember which of his eleven languages he'd learned first. His mind threw up a word in Italiano and his memories supplied him with the equivalent in six other tongues with equal ease. Deutsch... Français... Magyar... English... no difference.

But friends, he'd certainly had friends! Marinescu, for one, even if they could hardly understand each other anymore. Varshni, but no, he'd been killed in Dar Es-Salaam by a rogue. Without-A-Cause, then... before that mental wipe ordered by... there was surely Ciorek, of course, who sent him a card every year—or two.

Too many hotels, too many sleepdens, too many trains. His life had no anchors left, apart from the regular thrill of a kill and credit withdrawals. He tried to reassure himself that to forget something, one must have known it well. Yet, such forgetfulness was the first symptom of aphasia of the ego, as the psychs called it; he knew enough to recognize it.

When the light flashed to announce an incoming data packet, he stood up, thumbed the record switch, and slammed the door open to escape. He needed more room to breathe.

Patrice Deller was the denkeeper. His two room suite even had a window, with slivers of beige sky showing between the ranks of housing towers. He got up from his desk.

"Leaving, *Monsieur*?" The soft English did not bear a trace of the man's childhood in Port-au-Prince and the hunter thought rather coquettish the use of the French honorific.

"No. I'll keep the room for another thirty hours."

"*Très bien*. I'll charge you half the nighttime hourly rate, then, since that's all of today."

The transfer between accounts was completed and the hunter started to leave when the phone shrilled.

Spadina knew before he turned to listen that he would hear the same voice as before, but it still unsettled him to have it resonate in the incense-laden air of Patrice Deller's antechamber, more forceful than when it engraved the words directly onto the aural centers of his brain.

"It knows you are there. Do you not remember Wien, where you ate in the Café Trzésniewski, standing in a corner? It spied on you then. It ate there later and the pepper sandwiches overloaded its palate input. Do you remember missing the train at the Westbahnhof and its looking at you run from a window?"

"What do you want?"

"Do you remember how it was to live, not as a tourist but as a traveller? Do you remember when tastes bit sharply, when colours shone new, when the wind blew fresh, when every feeling sliced with an edge?"

"What do you want of me?"

"What do you owe?" shouted back the voice, no anger distorting the words but with the volume suddenly raised to a deafening level.

The hunter stood, shaking, shaken. There was nothing more: the communication had ended. He gasped, but what he was trying to inhale had never been a component of earthly air. He shifted his weight, as if his body were clothes that no longer fit, and he hurried back to his room.

Tepid water trickled from the tap, but he gulped down a glass of it. The edge...

There was another edge, the edge between the human sensorium and the electron wasteland where the human soul died of thirst. It happened to those who turned too far inward, who listened too long to their machine interfaces till they could no longer decipher the buzzes and hisses of a human voice, only the binary song of dataflow. His prey was trying to maneuver him towards that edge.

He refused to fall off. Not without a fight.

He plugged in the metal points protruding around his head and wore again his crown of thorns. The killer program was summoned to his side and he waited. Would his prey take the bait?

Plugged in as he was, his ordinary senses fought with the overlay from the unused inputs. Though he was seeing, smelling, hearing, and absorbing everything that was associated with the narrow room, the built-in senses only registered a blank and reacted to the deprivation by erecting ghostly schematics of absurd circuits that superimposed purplish filigrees over the grey walls.

Images flickered in his memory. In München, he'd beaten his prey to the train station by chartering a monstrously expensive jet. Still, he'd only been on the quay in time to see the rogue debark from the train. He'd followed it to Dachau, waiting for the chance to make a quiet kill. Then he'd entered the gates of the old concentration camp. Rarely had he been so overwhelmed by the shame of being human and the rogue had regained the suburbs of München, still functional. There, in the long tree-lined streets, synthetic muscles had outlasted normal human endurance. He'd only caught up again with his prey in the train to Lausanne, where it had mingled with a band of students whose minds were dulled by looping pleasure programs. In Lausanne itself, the rogue had again outdistanced him in the steep streets, leaving him out of breath and prostrate in a corner café, cursing his lack of a weapon with a larger range of deadliness.

The message light flashed.

The hunter tensed and he suddenly knew how his prey had felt—or maybe had hoped to feel. Mouth dry, pulse rattling, stomach unquiet. Indeed, the voice was back.

"Do you remember your murders?"

He recalled his pursuit of a rogue in the maze of Barcelona's old town, before decapitating it with a laser swipe at the foot of the Roman walls. He started to unleash the killer program. To get it over with. For his peace of mind. Yet at what cost?

He did not answer.

"You are fully hooked up. Will you accept a memory transfer?"

He reflected that the abruptness of the voice's switch in subjects was the mark of the programmed mind. He let it speak.

"Will you share your sensorium? You have ample spare capacity if you dump redundant data. Do you not desire memories of compressed-to-the-collapsing-point living, fleeing, and tasting?"

The hunter paused. The suggestion did not entirely surprise him. Indeed, the hardware incrusted beneath the scalp, through the skull, and even into selected brain centers had considerable space. He could purge some unnecessary files or back them up on a separate machine. Blocks to impede the free flow between the organic brain and the inorganic appendages could be set up to allow the co-existence of two identities.

The memory of his first hunt triggered without warning. The sweat running down his spine, the nervous stalking along the canals of København, the fumbling with his weapons. The shock was dizzying.

Yes. Yes, he would.

He was heard. His gates recorded the first probings and exchanges of protocols. Meanwhile, he hastened to make space, sending useless files into public storage, and he chased away the killer program with a word of command.

Data poured in. He could not monitor the content of the flow, only register its size and the power draw as structure crystallized out of the raw accumulation. He was unable even to track the diversion of his sensory inputs or the accessing of common files.

Finally, it was complete.

I am.

What do you call yourself?

I shall call myself Ushebti.

He who called himself Spadina broke the connection to the network and stood up, leaning against the counter.

Yes. The same dry atonal voice. *Yes, do it again. It feels. It feels good.*

He was not a toy.

Again. It makes me remember.

It was then that he attacked.

Yes, remember standing at the top of the Duomo in Firenze, leaning like now against the stone parapet, drunk with sunshine, bluesky and redroofs, legs trembling slightly from the quick hard climb.

No, that is wrong, I was not...

Implacable, that was his first impression of Athina, quaint Japanese cars buzzing on both sides of a dried streambed, never stopping. Further on, a choking haze, and always the teeth-chipping roar of a city too much like an overloaded generator.

I don't remember...

But how could he forget the smell of fresh moist earth in the central square of Amboise, where he had supped outside, enjoying the late summer's gentle warmth and the African cadences of three buskers' drums?

I...

He travelled to collect memories like a miser and to compare them like a connoisseur. Stockholm and Amsterdam. Bari and Barcelona. Budapest and Paris. You could eat cheap falafel in the Spadina eateries of Toronto, but the falafel was definitely better in Ottawa. He'd been there. He knew that. He knew.

He imagined himself flying in the damp September air over the choppy waters of Venezia's lagoon, sighting the next boat that would serve as stepping stone.

He saw himself in his mind's eye, munching one of the Café Trzésniewski's open-faced sandwiches.

He dreamed of the flaming jab of a lethal weapon, the fire coursing along metal nerves, the little dyings inside the body, the twisting pain of spasming muscles before the final darkening of CCD eyes.

And then, released, he shrugged it off. The blocks dissolved. He was inside, he was outside, and he was alone.

His prey had gambled that identity could be preserved by saving selected memories, a persistent habit of interrogation, and one ingrained purpose. Yet, it was not enough. A human, a hunter especially, had too wide a gamut of experiences not to submerge the handful of memories collected by a rogue. The few tattered memories of the rogue were not nearly enough to compete with a lifetime of sampling all the diversity of a planet.

Human empathy allowed humans to assume other roles, other shapes, other bodies, as in dreams that were sometimes memories as real as any. Did rogues have nightmares? Maybe they should.

Yet, it still felt as if a friend had died in his arms.

The hunter activated the communication function of the room's terminal and typed in the Stahlstadt Gesellschaft address. The ease of the blending did bother him, even as he tried to forget it. He *had* laughed at Marinescu's fancy that consciousness might be illusory, that identity might be a trick, had he not?

The link with Firenze was established and he spoke, choosing a new name:

"Ushebti here. I want to claim a kill…"

As he described the original kill at the public terminal, he briefly wondered why he'd chosen *that* name, but he shied away from the introspection. Some illusions were better left unshattered.

Scenes From Successive Futures

Tom Marshall

"It is precisely what is invisible in the land...that makes what is merely empty space to one person a place to another. The feeling that a particular place is suffused with memories, the specific focus of sacred and profane stories, and that the whole landscape is a congerie of such places, is what is meant by a local sense of the land."

—American geographer Yi-Fu Tuan,
as paraphrased by Barry Lopez in *Arctic Dreams*

i

I had been travelling underground about half the length of the City when it first happened. I was in the longest subway tunnel in the world. I was probably under that part of the City which used to be (and, unofficially, often still was) known as "Kingston" when the thought occurred to me. I was remembering bits and pieces of a childhood excursion there. I was falling in and out of a light doze. The monotonous hollow noise of the train in its seemingly endless tunnel was combining with the dim, intermittently fading lights to undermine my waking consciousness. I could see my own shadowy reflection fade in, fade out of the darkish train-windows.

My grandmother, long dead, said clearly: "But didn't there used to be a lake? Here?" Her voice old, childish, querulous....

I jerked awake again.

ii

I was already in my forties when the Control decided to take me into its confidence. I worked for the City's largest advertising firm. My name is Jeremy Rutherford.

At the precise moment I was dreaming about my grandmother my son Monty was sitting with a girl at the very top of the large ferris-wheel in the Canadian National Exhibition grounds. It was, not untypically, stalled.

"Do you ever wonder," he asked suddenly, looking up, "what's out there?"

The girl appeared to be a little startled at this sudden change of topic. She too looked up.

"Well. There's the Dome, of course. But it's invisible. Then there's the sky. Then there's space. In the days before the Dome people from the City flew in machines through the sky." It was like a history-lesson regurgitated.

"Do you ever want to go outside the Dome?"

Her beautiful almond eyes opened very wide.

"Who would want to go there?" she said. "It's so much safer here."

"Safe," he said scornfully. "And totally confining."

Then the wheel began to move again. And they fell silent.

iii

"They were much like the medieval schoolmen," my colleague Bob insisted, "or even like the alchemists."

"I suppose," I said. He was off and running now.

"Why, as long ago as the 1980s Stephen Hawking, a British, multiply handicapped genius, had already argued that the concept of supergravity provided, for the first time, a grand unified theory of the cosmos in which all structures and processes—i.e. every damned precious thing—might be described by a single mathematical principle. Perhaps even a single equation. And there were still theories and theories yet to come. Those men were extraordinary."

"Then why," I asked, "did it all come to nothing?"

"Who knows? They were working with metaphors—as who isn't? Or zen, by which I mean the uncertainty principle, was too much for them. But Einstein's equations did check out empirically."

Outside Candace and Bob's condominium the day's last light was reflected in the windows of the nearest high-rises. Refracted, shattered there—like a splintering of planets into worlds within worlds.

"They had promising theories," Bob said. "One line of speculation was that, originally, at the Big Bang, there were ten or more dimensions of space-time, not just three or four. The extra ones are 'infolded', present but invisible to our usual senses. This is the hidden energy or mass of the universe. This means that in the very early stages of expansion, i.e. the first microseconds, there occurred the simultaneous 'compactification' of these extra dimensions while the ones we experience now were inflated. Hugely. At extraordinary speed. Three space dimensions embarked upon this inflation, like a balloon, at the expense of the others which shrank into an effectively invisible microcosmos that reveals itself only indirectly as the forces of nature. Such as gravity and electromagnetism."

"Wow!" said Monty.

"So there could be," I said, "in effect a world within the world."

"In literal, physical reality," said Bob Roberts, "there could. And who knows but that compactification in one time-direction might not be expansion in another? Even further super-dimensions might exist."

"Perhaps," I said, "the hidden universe contains the past—if time too is elastic and reversible."

"Or alternate lives," he said.

Now it was growing dark. Outside the large picture-window were other dark towers with their random patterns of bright window-squares or rectangles, and above them the faint stars int he sky. Pricks of fine white light penetrating the transparent Dome.

"Alternate lives and parallel existences—like those we glimpse only in recurring dreams. In one theory every possible happening not fixed by our perception of what is presently happening still happens anyhow at some other level of reality. This is the 'many worlds' hypothesis."

"Wow!" Monty said again.

This was the way we talked, the way we went on, in those distant days.

iv

Monty dreamed he was looking in a mirror. He was wondering what he looked like to the girl, Julia. He was thinking that the image he saw was backwards.

As he thought this his flat image began to dissolve in the mirror before him. To dissolve and darken there. The image seemed to be collapsing inward. As if another being, a shadow-self, was being etched there indelibly in acid. The shape of a man, a young man, was dissolving, collapsing before his eyes, yet the surrounding mirror-image—the blue shower-curtain, the dark blue towel hung over it to dry, the flowered pastel wallpaper behind him—remained perfectly unchanged. Only the man darkened, disappeared into the shape of a silhouette.

He could not move his feet from the tile floor. Unmoving, he felt that he was looking not forward but down, into some black, airy depth. He was being drawn into it, as if by some great undertow. A great rushing of particles.

Till he was floating in vast darkness—some vast dark womb. He had thought for a moment that he was moving at high speed but now there seemed no difference between motion and stillness. Everything was floating in this empty dark. Except—it was not dark, really, it was nothing. Not dark, not light, not colours, not anything.

Vacancy. Absolute zero. For a second perhaps. Or an eternity. Absolute desolation.

But then... It was not after all so empty. He began, slowly, to perceive, here and there, faint points of light. Starpricks. A streaming of light from all directions. Converging. He was moving at high speed again into streams of light. Or else he was perfectly stationary as light streamed past, poured through him. He was made of light. He was made of galaxies circling, spiralling...

v

"I felt as if I was being born. Out of the stars. A great wind. A kind of fluid stuff in which I floated. But before that, nothing. Nothing at all. But a nothing that seemed to have everything in it, or out of which everything comes. Oh, I don't know how to say it. It comes out contradictory.

"Everything was fading in and out. The mirror, the sink, my own reflection. Everything seemed at all times to be flowing in and out of this nothing..."

"I think," said Julia, "that you may now be ready to join us."

vi

Many of us had had intimations that all was not as it seemed. Candace and Bob noticed this in me—Candace was, after all, a therapist—but not, oddly—and this was one of their great mistakes—in Monty. They set about recruiting me. They began to speak to me of things with which Bob and my other colleague in advertising, Jones, had long been preoccupied.

"There are things," Bob said to me, "that Jones and I have wanted to speak with you about. We've been waiting until the time seemed right. And occasionally we've nudged you along. But you seem remarkably impervious to such hints as we've attempted. I'm speaking, you understand, of things that need not concern anyone else in the firm. We can use your help."

"You mentioned the Dome contract. But I don't understand."

"Jones and I have activities beyond the firm, though they naturally involve the firm.

"You could say," he continued, "that we belong to a kind of secret society, a benevolent social conspiracy, so to speak. Our aim is the regulation of an intelligently ordered, harmonious community. For obvious reasons it is helpful if some of us are in advertising, and some in the media, to do this effectively."

I was mildly flabbergasted. It sounded a little like an adolescent fantasy of power and influence. Or a businessman's lodge with its secret and childish rituals. Jones, ever ebullient and not—as far as I could tell—much given to introspection, might well belong to such an overgrown boy's club, I thought. But Bob Roberts? And Candace? Surely they were much too sophisticated.

"You too?" I said to her.

"Certainly," she said. "But I can see that you're getting the wrong idea. This isn't a game. It's how the City is run."

I had to smile.

"I've thought of you both, sometimes, I must admit, as social engineers."

"As usual," said Bob, "Candace has put it more directly, more bluntly than I. She is impatient. We constitute what the historian Toynbee called a creative minority—working its benign will upon society in general."

"The Dome contract."

"That's one of the code phrases."

"The secret password to the tree-house. Look Bob, you know, quite frankly, it all sounds rather silly."

Candace sighed deeply. Bob only smiled.

"Perhaps," he said smoothly, "we may exaggerate the extent of our influence. But if you think about it a little, you'll admit, I hope, that every society that has ever been has had its unacknowledged legislators. Often they are more important in the long run than those elected or appointed to rule."

"The City," I observed, "has a duly constituted and elected government—probably the best in the world, given our advantages here. It operates remarkably smoothly, I think."

"*We*...," began Candace. But was silenced by a swift glance from Bob.

"We influence in profound ways those who elect the government," he said. "And a few of the councillors themselves are, of course, initiates."

"Initiates," I repeated, bemused. "The mayor?"

"No. Not her. That isn't necessary. She serves our purpose anyhow."

"You make her sound like a puppet," I said. It seemed more and more absurd. The mayor was an outspoken and very feisty lady with a reputation for ruthlessness. Nobody crossed her lightly, especially when her popularity with the voters seemed to be quite undimmed by the years or even by her own occasional public outbursts of temper.

"She is," said Candace bluntly.

I wanted to laugh.

"And the Prime Minister? Is he your creature too?"

They looked at one another.

"One thing at a time," said Bob smoothly. "Let's deal with the City first."

"Oh why don't we just tell him?" said Candace, openly exasperated at last.

"Everything in time," said Bob, who now sounded mildly annoyed himself. "'One thing at a time' is always a good rule. It's too much to take in, otherwise."

"Well," I said.

"We want you to learn how we operate. Some of the older people have been dying off lately. There must always be a fresh supply of those who are qualified to continue the work. Will you trust us?"

"I always have trusted you," I said.

"Good. Now what I have in mind is that Jones is very near the top of the operation. In fact, he pretty much controls everything that happens in the east of the City."

"It sounds like the old Mafia," I said, "in pre-City times."

He ignored this flippancy.

"Jones will show you his operation. Then we'll talk again. But first I think you'd better visit his studio."

vii

The subway car is crowded today, mainly with those commuters who cross the City regularly. Their faces have largely blanked out, they all seem to have succumbed somewhat to the hypnotic, gently humming and vibrating rhythms of the high-speed automatic vehicle. It is like being lulled to sleep in some great mechanical womb. Perhaps that's just what the Dome itself, I thought sleepily, that overarching and prophylactic superglass-bubble, *is*, after all—our great technological womb.

The first huge domed-City. It was one of the genuine marvels of the age. A controlled, completely germ- and virus-free atmosphere. Utopia of a sort. But perhaps we had paid a certain price for being the sanitized wonder of the turbulent modern world. Not that most people ever thought about this. Life elsewhere, as glimpsed on the news, was basically inconceivable.

viii

"Did you happen," Jones asked me, "to watch the news last night?"

"Yes. Bob said I shouldn't miss it."

(The news. There is famine again in Africa, truly pitiable and even horrible footage of starving black children with distended bellies, and then some more heartening footage of punk rock stars in Britain performing benefit concerts. A new war has broken out in the Islamic middle east, this time between Iran and Iraq. It is feared that our already heavily rationed oil supply will be further disturbed. There is new violence in the black townships of South Africa. There is a hijacking in Karachi. So the less fortunate outside world continues on its usual depressing way. We have long grown accustomed to its violence and horror. Two more English soldiers have been killed by a bomb in Belfast.

In Newfoundland the government workers are on strike. Again. Meanwhile our porcine Prime Minister is seen romping pinkly with his children in the surf of Bermuda. At this point Fred Hancock, our blandly handsome, permanently thirty-fiveish news-anchor, favours us with an indulgent, small smile.)

"This studio is where we invented it."

"Invented it?"

"Well, not entirely—only some items. Those we can manufacture here. To these we add some distant daily news from the last century. We've been re-running the 1980s recently."

I spent a most instructive, not to mention frightening afternoon in that studio. They showed me their huge archive of twentieth-century news, encoded in tiny microchips. They had a vast repertory of items going right back to the beginnings of television. These they could "doctor" as necessary.

"We don't need," said Jones, "to repeat any one item until a whole generation or two has passed away. Jacques is our archivist—like his father and grandfather before him. An enormously important function. He passes as a janitor."

Jacques bowed ironically in acknowledgement.

"But it's preposterous," I objected. "Some of the things you've shown me—the nuclear accident at Chernobyl in the Ukraine that was on the news last week—would have made the history books. They'd have been taught in school."

"No," chuckled Jones. "*We* have 'made' the history books—for several generations now."

"I don't believe it. It's not possible to brainwash a whole people—in a democratic system."

"It was regrettably necessary," said Jones. "I mean, it became necessary in our great-grandparents' time."

"But *why*?"

He paused, as if considering what he might say next, and in what order. This was uncharacteristic. Jones was usually a fast talker.

"I gather," he said, "that you asked Bob about the Prime Minister."

"Yes, but so what?"

"He is an actor," said Jones flatly.

"*What*?"

"He is one of us. In make-up and costume he is rarely allowed to leave the studio. One or two appearances within the City per year. Most people aren't allowed very close to him. Without his prime ministerial disguise he has another identity in a remote part of the City."

"But he was vacationing in Bermuda recently. I saw him."

"You saw what we made in the studio. *Jacques*."

Jacques flicked a switch. On one of the large video screens appeared an image. Another studio in which the "Prime Minister" appeared to be rehearsing his movements. His four children also performed their parts repeatedly. Another man was directing them. All five actors wore, incongruously, bikini-brief bathing suits in the stark, mostly white, hi-tech studio.

"We combined this with ancient footage of beach and water and palm trees and all that jazz," Jacques volunteered now in his heavily accented English.

"Now you've seen behind the facade," Jones said.

"It's mad," I said.

"There is in reality *no* prime minister. There hasn't been for a long time. The national political process is theatre, or television rather. Though people still vote for the now-imaginary federal parties, of course, within the City, in all innocence. But there is no Ottawa, and no federal government."

"You mean... Outside the City there is..."

"What is outside the City doesn't bear much thinking about."

He paused, then continued: "'Human kind cannot bear very much reality.' Our manufactured news, however bad, is easier to contemplate."

"If," I said, "there is no longer any Canada"—I looked at him directly, and he nodded—"if the nation, even the world as we have known it, is a fiction maintained by television and video, then *what*, for God's sake, *is* outside the Dome?"

"That," said Jones quietly, "is what we must, I am afraid, now show you."

ix

Afterwards, travelling home again, I thought I understood. Appalling as much of the news re-run from the forgotten past was, the present "outside" reality was more than most people could be expected to bear. Better to reinforce with "ordinary" disasters their instinctive desire to stay safe within the invisible but reassuring Dome.

There seemed no alternative. Rule by a secret élite, maintained by a benevolent species of thought-control, hidden from most of the citizens, was simply a stark necessity.

It was, we all thought, the wonder of the world: this safe, clean Dome-City. No violence to speak of, few accidents, a minimum of crime, a remarkable tolerance for more or less harmless human frailty, and superb health-control. (All deadly viruses, including the AIDS of another century, had been expelled or defeated.) This was indeed a noble social experiment that had largely succeeded: the creation of a virtually germ-free environment. Not only pollution-free but biologically immaculate. That was why there were only a strictly limited number of plants and trees (outside the greenhouses) and no animals whatever larger than benevolent micro-organisms in the whole of the City.

The controlled atmosphere of the Dome allowed for a rhythmically reassuring seasonal variation which was gentle and unthreatening. The energy-plants ensured warmth but not extreme heat in summer, a cooler fall, a winter slightly cooler still, and a balmy spring. Once, apparently, these four seasons had gone to far greater extremes of heat and cold, wet and dry, and these had been somewhat erratic and unpredictable.

The water supply was strictly controlled. Plantlife outside the greenhouses was allotted moisture at regular times. But there was no rain. Rain. A word largely forgotten, though this phenomenon was described (under "precipitation") in the largely fictional official histories and dictionaries of life before the Dome. More fantastic still was the phenomenon of frozen, flaked precipitation. But it had disappeared from southern Canada even before the Dome because of a worldwide change of climate called the "greenhouse effect". The Dome had been a logical extension of this change, a creative response to it.

x

But this was only part of the truth. The Dome had also been meant to ensure survival. The planners of the Dome were visionaries as well as great scientists and engineers. They had developed with the rapidly accelerating laser-technology of the time a radiation-proof glass-substitute. This effectively insulated the great City from whatever disaster might happen outside.

Tragic events, Bob Roberts told me, had proved the wisdom of the founders. When the crunch came the Dome-City was already well on the way to self-sufficiency and independent continuance.

This is the strangest part of the story which Roberts told me. Strange because not only the great war of my great-grandparents' day but even the names and the very existence of the major participants have been utterly erased from the official maps and histories of the globe. "They didn't deserve to be remembered," Bob said.

The two "superpowers" were once known as the U.S. and the U.S.S.R. Later the U.S.S.R., a crumbling federation, split up into a number of turbulent states, some of which had nuclear weapons: gradually the military establishments in these well-armed republics came together to constitute the real supranational power, and thus presented a renewed military threat to the socially and economically declining U.S. Like mirror-images, each disintegrating empire was in its heyday possessed of a mindless and cancerously self-generating biological mania for dominance (only superficially rationalized by specious or misused ideology), and each had an advanced military science. In each case an ever-expanding military budget was gradually ruining the domestic economy and infrastructure. For a time they fought nasty little surrogate wars over the torn bodies of marginal client states whose civil divisions they were exploiting as convenient expressions of their world rivalry. Our original controllers foresaw a larger conflict and thought it desirable that something of Canada, the more peaceful and civilized but only semi-independent neighbour of the U.S.—whose own cities were then in disintegration in waves of racism, crime, poverty, unemployment, and war-fever—should survive what looked increasingly like inevitable catastrophe.

xi

At the secret CBC studio in Montreal Jones, Jacques and I had watched the postwar footage, taken with long-distance telephoto lenses from inside the Dome. We did not speak.

At first there is only rubble. Wind and dust. Emptiness. Broken buildings seen through dust-storms. Here and there rotting corpses. Sudden swirling storms, saharas of red dust. This is, of course, some distance away. Even the Dome could not have withstood a direct hit. But it was built to repel radiation.

Outside there has been nuclear winter. An overhanging dark. Cold. This lasted for two years. That quickly took care of those relatively near Canadian survivors who could not, in any case, have been admitted to the Dome. For they were contaminated beyond hope, and a quick death by cold or starvation was kindest. Outside there was only pain, hopelessness.

(A woman, half-naked, staggering, in close-up. Her hair fallen out in places. Blinded. Her flesh in strips, fluid peeling…)

Apocalypse and holocaust are followed by rusty desert. A desert punctuated with ruins. Jagged walls, the occasional corpse of an automobile. And formerly-human bodies that disintegrate slowly, surely into bones and dust. Extinction. What seems like centuries of desolation.

Then. After some years—creatures again. They seem to erupt spontaneously out of earth. Here and there. Out of the atomic desert. Sand-rats perhaps, or former fieldmice the size of large dogs or ponies, mutated beyond exact recognition. And octopus-large crablike things. Huge things that look like purple cockroaches. Things that rend and tear each other, even within species. A hawk-sized, delicately-winged insectoid thing with a lance-like proboscis that seems to inject poison. It swoops down upon the huge rats or crabs, paralyzing its victim with a single swift jab—like a lethal mosquito. But the only easily recognizable creature here is a large cat-sized spider, unchanged except in bulk. It roams the sands continually to find a sleeping victim, then swiftly entangles him in its amazingly strong rope-like nets.

It is, Jones tells me, of great interest to the biologists among the early controllers (and since) that each of these mutated creatures mates with what looks like great ferocity, after which the female seizes upon the enfeebled male, kills, and then devours him completely. She needs the protein for the species to survive. Females are also known to eat their own young, if unable to secure other nourishment, though this is obviously a malfunction of survival instinct, but more usually they protect them with fierce devotion from the attacks of other species or sometimes other creatures of the same species. If the attacker is killed, he or she is fed to the young. The mother may even sacrifice herself to the young if, as they grow, they turn on her. If the mother is killed by an invader, however, the still-helpless young are devoured as well. In whatever way, protein is exchanged, and so far each of these few observed species has survived. It is a simple and elegant new ecology, observes Jones, who likes (in his spare time) to keep up with the necessarily secret science of extra-Dome biology. You win some, and you lose some, he says in his customary cheerful way.

Within the Control Jones is known as "Tao-Jones"—an affectionate inside joke as well as a code-name. He is very close to the top.

xii

The Control decided what it was best for people to know, to remember, to want. They were not to be alarmed with truth.

It was the girl Julia who led Monty to the "Underground." Her Chinese beauty had captivated him. She took him to her grandmother Ms. Wu-Li, a seemingly ancient but still strangely handsome woman who told him he was spontaneously breaking free from his social conditioning.

"There are those of us," she continued, "who work towards a life other than that prescribed by the City."

"Can you," he asked, "take me outside the Dome?"

She smiled serenely.

"There will be a time," she said, "to show you what is outside the Dome."

xiii

"Aren't you frightened?" he asked Julia. This was at their fourth meeting.

"Sometimes," she said. "When I think of how things could go badly for us. They have most of the advantages. But I was born to this double existence. And we—the present group—have survived so far. Perhaps even undetected. But we can never be too careful. They've caused many of us to disappear over the years. My grandmother is a veteran."

"Do *you* know the true history of the City?"

"Some of it. But we're instructed gradually. As we prove reliable. You will be too."

And she spoke to him about imposed mental constructs of the world.

"Mental construct," repeated Monty, bemused.

"It's a phrase we use. I was brought up on it. Everyone has one. We live mostly in a manufactured world, I was taught, because we are instructed almost from birth how to see the world. We agree about what's what. It's *made up*. By people like your friends Candace and Bob."

"The Dome," he said.

"The Dome is there. But its purpose is different from what you have been told."

"Tell me."

Monty and Julia sat alone side by side on a low, somewhat lumpy couch. They had finished their small cups of hot delicious Chinese tea. Ms. Wu-Li had once again left them alone. He turned to her now urgently. She smiled, a bit nervously. She took his right hand in both of hers. He felt the warmth of her hands. With his awkward left hand he was gently removing the sunglasses she had been wearing all day. He needed to see her eyes. Then he was drowning again in those deep almond eyes. She lifted one of her hands, then brushed his cheek slowly with the back of it. Caressed his cheek. Her hand poised a moment there before he took her in his arms.

xiv

Something about what Jones and Roberts had told me didn't altogether ring true. I decided to go to "Kingston" once again to look at what had always intrigued me there. I would return to Bagot and Gore Streets.

Bagot Street is a street of very old mid-nineteenth-century houses, some of them row-houses. Because it embodies the imposing presence of an earlier age the street has always about it a dreamlike feeling—like a stage-set.

The Gore View Apartments, where my late grandmother once lived, looks straight down Gore Street, a street of several short blocks that begins here and slopes down to—what? An opaque, foglike, strangely amorphous space down there. This is hardly a "view" to advertise.

Intrigued anew, I walk slowly down the street to inspect once again the mystery. This greyish fogpatch.

I knew what it was, of course. But it still seemed very strange. For I had never before come so close to the wall of the Dome.

I came to a field at the end of the street, at the other side of which was the foglike opaque wall. There were some children playing in the field. They were chattering and tumbling about. But they ignored completely the Dome-wall that sealed them into their small, apparently innocent world. I suppose they had seen it a thousand times. This seemed to me inexpressibly sad. Though there was still thin sunlight from the blue sky above no light penetrated the lower wall of the great Dome. Human kind cannot bear very much reality.

I went all the way over and touched it. I half expected it to dissolve at my touch. But it did not. It felt cold, hard. The playing children paid me no heed. Or rather, they had looked momentarily as I passed by but saw nothing of interest to them. I tried, when I reached it, to look on their behalf into the great grey wall at this end of their world, the wall that seemed to stretch endlessly away on either hand, stretching round Montreal to the east and round Windsor to the west, but it was truly like a solidified fog. So finally I turned my back on it.

I looked then up Gore Street and saw the Gore View Apartments there waiting for me. At this distance the solid brick building with its numerous windows and white balcony looked quite small. When I was a child, of course, it had seemed huge.

Yes. This was where my grandmother had lived as a child. That was why we took her to visit it. There she had become unhappy and confused.

As I walked up the street I remembered bits and pieces of that visit. We were in a large apartment at the top of the house, and Grannie wanted to look out the high front window. She wanted to see that view again—in her second childhood. But it wasn't there.

"Didn't there used to be a lake?" she said. Old, querulous...

XV

"There's more to it, isn't there? That you haven't told me."

"Yes," said Candace tonelessly. "I've always thought you should know everything." She looked a little grim. Jones seemed oddly satisfied. Bob, uncharacteristically, said nothing.

"We'll go to the Control room then," said Jones.

We were seated, as we had been so many times before, in the living room of the Roberts' high-rise apartment. Bob was fiddling with the remote-control for his television. Jones was saying: "It's more precarious than you realize, we can't have revolution or civil war destabilizing everything we've built." And now, unbelievably, the room's ceiling was opening over our heads. I craned my neck upwards, half startled out of my wits. Then a stair was descending into our little space.

We went up it into a huge circular room filled with men and machines on various tiers or levels. We seemed to be directly under the Dome though this was perhaps many miles above. It was difficult to judge distances here. Numerous men and women were seated in large tiered circles and various levels at desks with complicated-looking controls and television screens or computer terminals. What were they all doing? I noticed then that there was artificial lighting from large lamps that looked like television lights—though it was day outside—and that the Dome itself was here quite dark.

"Where are we?" I gasped.

"Among the stars," said Candace.

"Open up," said Jones to a man who had approached us. He signalled to another man on the lowest level.

The dark Dome above was, instantaneous, alive with stars and galaxies. In the twinkling of an eye. We were out among them—in our floating observatory. The "television lights" had gone out like fireflies.

"And the earth?" I asked.

"Gone," said Candace.

"There is no earth," said Bob.

And Jones said: "Welcome to the giant spaceship Dome."

xvi

Now, after all this time, and anti-time, I know all or most of the compartments of the spaceship Dome fairly well. Its re-creation of the old Canadian megacity was, of course, never meant to be exact; it is a somewhat smaller selective replica. But the great spaceship had also to be large enough to accommodate the super particle-ring or accelerator that was built by the physicists and engineers of the founding generation to collide matter and antimatter in order to provide a virtually limitless supply of fuel. So that the spaceship Dome could travel across the vast galaxies, billions and billions of them, forever, if that should be necessary. If, that is, we never found a planet that had the approximate atmosphere of Earth. Meanwhile we made our own oxygen, our own gravity, our own totally controlled environment. The late-twentieth century invention of superconductors had enhanced our energy-efficiency to an enormous degree.

There are at least two versions of the history of Dome: Ms. Wu-Li's chronicle, which was kept by several generations of her family, and the videotape record assembled by Jones and his predecessors. They agree, of course, about many particulars.

Jones was able to show me much footage, hours and hours, that documented the manufacture of Dome: the greatest engineering feat in human history. Yet it had been constructed in the British Columbia interior in near-total secrecy. The opportunity arose, Jones said, after the so-called satellite-caper, that is, the sabotage of all American observation satellites by renegade elements of the Russian military who had developed a new laser-computer technology. The Americans replied to this preemptive strike immediately by blowing every Russian satellite out of the sky with their newest long-range rockets.

This engagement alarmed the more sensible leaders on each side so much that they hastily concocted a truce (even though no war had been declared). For ten years this truce held while the rival empires continued, however, to scheme at new means of definitive military superiority, since this illusion was all their power-élites cared about any more. But it came about that before any new satellites could be launched into the sky Canada had accomplished its secret project.

This was largely made possible by another phenomenon of the time. The prime minister of the day and her most powerful colleagues were, in private life, practising Holominders. This was not exactly a religion. It was a movement of people who believed that the universe was a great Mind whose parts manifested, but with distortions, the Whole—as do the images from any piece of a hologram. The object of the Holominders' study and discipline was more perfect alignment of the individual human organism with the Whole.

The scientists within Holomind conceived of the Dome. The pause in minor hostilities between the two empires seemed to them only that—a pause. Resumption of hostilities was inevitable and so, as the obvious consequence, was total atomic war and the destruction of the earth as a viable human environment.

Most ordinarily intelligent people could not, of course, bring themselves to believe this. They hoped that the "truce" would bring sanity and salvation. They refused to see its essential falsity, hypocrisy and meretriciousness. But the dynamics of imperial rivalry could not be altered so easily by a few pious lies, and the few thousand Holominders who had settled and concentrated themselves in Canada, who had felt drawn there almost by instinct from all over the planet, knew this. And the leading Holominders included several of the world's greatest engineering scientists.

So the Dome was built. In theory the builders were making only the new particle accelerator, and even this was a secret project known only to the top people of a few foreign governments. But the United States was too far gone in its preoccupation with military superiority and so with its plans for the coming war to pay very much attention. Let the Canadians find a new energy source with antimatter, that was their attitude. They had no doubt that they could effectively take over any Canadian resource.

The Dome was modelled on the central Canadian megacity. This was for the children. It was thought they should have an environment that gave them some degree of continuity with the earth that had been, or should have been, their birthright.

It was a near-thing. When the war did come all the major American and Russian cities were effectively destroyed in the first half-hour. Then there was a pause before new strikes occurred. As occur they must. For the military on each side had its own secret underground command posts, children's forts or hideouts from which the exhilarating game of destruction could continue for some time. It was the ultimate video-game.

But into the first pause in hostilities the Dome was launched like an airborne ark with its own powerful rockets. Thousands of men, women and children (but, alas, no animals) had already been living there for about two years at that point. The small children, including my grandmother, had been taken aboard in their sleep and so did not know they had exchanged their old homes for detailed replicas. Or if they did feel an inexplicable disorientation they soon forgot it, as children adapting to new circumstances will.

Long-range cameras left behind in various parts of Canada recorded Dome's ascent into space. Then they recorded the local devastation all around them after the war. The long nuclear winter and the atomic desert and the mutant animals that I had already seen. These images were received by the departing spaceship for some years. They showed that there could be no going back.

The founders planned their society in ways they thought conducive to the general happiness. Of necessity there must be an élite who charted the voyage for the benefit of the rest. Anything else was thought to be too chaotic and psychologically stressful. So there was a secret Control behind the municipal system of government by the second generation. By the third generation many who were in nominal authority believed, and certainly in my time still believed (e.g. our doughty lady mayor), that Dome was part of their ancient planet Earth. A few of these were told, as I was, about the war and the atomic desolation outside the City. This kept them compliant. But most believed they were still on the earth. And this is, we know, an illusion kept in place by the Control, which was dominated by a secret council of nine archons led by the Aristarch. No ordinary member of the Control knew who the current nine archons were unless he himself became one. They rotated in twos every four years, except for the Aristarch, who could serve longer if he or she was re-confirmed by the new council of archons each time.

xvii

Roberts and Jones explained much of this to me with great patience. Candace, for her part, exuded a kind of radiant, kindly understanding of the confusion it must be causing me. I had had to entertain repeated revelations in a relatively brief space of time. Though, now I thought of it, what did "time"—I mean, days, weeks, months, years—what could any of these phases of the earth's relationship with the sun and moon *mean*—out here?

"I'm sorry I had to deceive you," said Jones, "about our still being on the earth, and sealed inside the Dome. I thought that if I told you the whole truth right away it might prove too much for you. I mean, to lose all at once, in one fell swoop, *all* the poetry and magic that were gathered over the millennia about the earth. The memory of which, some of it, we have tried to maintain."

"I would rather know," I said. I was surprised at the relative refinement of Jones's last remarks.

"Of course you would," said Roberts soothingly. "We can all see that now."

xviii

The revolution took us all by surprise—though it had been in preparation for years. First the Epistemological Underground (as they called themselves) seized Jones's Montreal studio, and then the energy-centre where the particle-ring was managed. The Control held onto the main control-centre though it was cut off from its source and could not operate for long. But they soon put the energy-centre under heavy siege.

The rebels at Montreal proceeded to broadcast their own prepared video. And there, to my amazement, was a sober-looking Fred Hancock, familiar to every citizen of Dome as the man who read the evening news—a vastly reassuring presence. If *he* was with the Underground, then the otherwise difficult propaganda war could perhaps actually be won.

"Good evening," said Fred. "This evening all regular broadcasting is preempted by a news special. Though, really, it is more than a mere 'special'. It is without doubt the most important program you will ever see. Its subject is the true history of this city we have called Dome..."

Like thousands of others I watched, fascinated. The hours passed swiftly as the rebel telecast unfolded into the night. At the same time a battle seemed to be going on in a nearby part of the City. Explosions and gunfire could be heard. In the middle of the night.

Would there be a dawn? Might not the rebels impose continual night? Did the Control retain enough resources of energy to put down the rebels *and* keep up the usual lighting-cycle that simulated the old Earth's day and night?

Apparently not, for there was no daybreak. In later times this brief period of civil war became known as "the long night." The rebels who controlled the power supply could not allow Dome's artificial "sun" to shine: they wanted to shake the entrenched belief of the populace to its false foundations. It was a confused, disorienting time.

Dark prevailed. Outside my small house explosions could still be heard in the distance. The flares of rockets occasionally lightened the sky.

We—Monty, Julia and I—had a supply of sealed food that they (my unsuspected rebel children) had laid in. They were being kept in reserve, and also keeping an eye on me—I was to be kept from going out into the fray.

Then the world exploded.

I was lying on the kitchen floor. One window on the everlasting night had shattered near me. Smoke was coming from somewhere else in the house. It was assaulting my nostrils. I seemed at first unable to move.

Then Julia and Monty were busy clearing away the remnants of what impeded me. It was not that it was so heavy but that I was so weak.

I slept for many hours. We were still holed-up in the damaged house. But now the guns and rockets were silent.

It could be a trap, Julia said. Perhaps the Control had crushed the rebels and repossessed their strongholds. Perhaps now they waited for stray bodies like these two to emerge from hiding.

Then.

Outside. Seeping at first imperceptibly. Up from the rim of this artificial world. Greylight. *Light.* Dawnlight. Day. Day slowly but palpably returning…

The television revived. The rebels announced their victory, and advised calm.

Troops arrived shortly thereafter to escort us into the presence of the revolutionary council. It was revealed that they had long had designs on me. I must, I was bluntly informed, oversee all communications and direct the re-education of the populace. Julia and Monty would assist me. I acquiesced numbly, scarcely believing what had so swiftly happened. It all seemed like a particularly disorienting dream.

And so it proved. Emotional dislocation was rampant. In the months and years that followed there was a remarkable incidence of nervous collapse among the City's ordinary folk, despite our best efforts at rehabilitation. Individuals would—often without warning—revert to the previous "reality" and isolate themselves. Some became autistic. We had to establish clinics and mental hospitals.

Candace correctly predicted this. My old friend was now revealed, to my great surprise, as the Aristarch, the ultimate control masquerading as a therapist for children. She was now to be held personally responsible for crimes against truth and freedom. My protests at the unfairness of this went unheeded. There had to be a scapegoat for the television trial, they said. They claimed also that she had tried to kill me with a rocket aimed at my house.

Candace insisted vehemently, on television, that everything she had done, even the most ruthless measures of the Control—including the "disappearance" and "accidental death" of considerable numbers of people—was for the good of Dome, for the survival of the spacecraft. She said any ruler would have done the same.

"You think you can judge me," she said. "But as a therapist I know that people demand security, stability, certainty. We gave them that. They were content. To know that you are alone and lost in space is too much for the ordinary individual to bear. He much prefers lies. You will see. You will see mental breakdowns on a vast scale."

Her speeches in this vein were indignantly repudiated by the prosecutors. They said truth was always best. They wanted to focus the discussion on the specific high crimes and misdemeanours of the Control.

Chief of these was the failure seriously to search for a new planet; they had preferred to perpetuate their own power on Dome.

xix

But now the spaceship Dome trained its strongest telescopes on the nearest solar systems. In several generations it had travelled a small way across the Milky Way Galaxy. The new council truly believed that in recent times the Control had not seriously been charting any particular course at all, but was only concerned to hold onto power. But now several years after the revolution, a promising planet had been sighted.

By this time Monty was training to be a pilot. Julia also received some training—even through most of her first pregnancy.

Dome was to orbit the new planet while a small colony descended and attempted to establish itself—if necessary, within a completely interior controlled environment until the necessary atmosphere could be encouraged outside by the seeding of the planet with oxygen-making plants or bacteria.

I was privy to these plans which were, of course, to be revealed only very gradually to the general populace. I liked to pore over them with Monty—even knowing that he and Julia and their children would be part of the necessarily small colonizing party while I would be left behind on Dome.

After some further years we found ourselves approaching the planet we called "Hope." Our rockets, fuelled by antimatter that was collided with matter, had taken us farther and faster than any previous space-travellers from Earth had been. Now we must seed a new earth—already, according to our instruments, not altogether unlike the old and, probably, the host to some simpler forms of carbon-based life—with our own store of bacteria, algae and lichens that could eventually help to create enough oxygen to support a modest number of humans. I would not live to see this task successfully completed, but Monty and his descendants were going to overcome at last their earthlessness.

This solar system was comparable in a number of ways to the one we had left behind several generations before. The earthlike planet Hope had, it appeared, a similar distance and relationship to the moderate-sized star it orbited. Its gravity must be at least comparable. It even had a large satellite "moon" to stabilize its polar tilt. This was good luck, we felt, and indeed reason for quickening hope of a rooted future for a once-again expanding human race.

When the day of departure came we said our tight-lipped farewells, and Monty's party entered the smaller but still commodious space-vessel which had always been housed far below the main control room. This chamber reached deep beneath the City. At one end of the immense hangar were great airlocked doors to an antechamber whose doors opened in their turn on black space. The space-vessel could here be launched (as in the past corpses had been) without any alteration to the Dome that enclosed the City above. Here it had waited, tended by generations of technicians, for this day.

It was a long craft with its own control room at the front and a number of living-compartments on either side of a corridor that led back to a set of communal rooms and a storage area. Julia, Monty and their two children, Julie and Jerry, had one of the three-room living-compartments.

Monty was one of several pilots, male and female, who manned the controls in shifts. The party also included scientists and engineers of both sexes, and a medical doctor who was also a poet and official diarist of the expedition.

And so they went. My mind's eye increasingly observed them as they neared their destination. By concentrating my expanding inner resources I could see them.

Together Monty and Julia looked out a porthole at the approaching planet. It was brownish-red with what looked like white snow-peaks scattered here and there about its visible surface. It had mountains and valleys but, apparently, only rather small and feeble forms of plantlife. It looked a dry, rocky place but with those snow-peaks that could perhaps be melted to make water and oxygen. Julia and Monty watched it grow clearer and larger day by day.

"What will they do with the rest of their lives?" he wondered.

Julia looked at him. She knew he was referring to those of us left behind now by history.

"They will live on Dome," she said after a moment. "It's quite habitable, and they're used to it. It will orbit around our new world forever."

"I know. But that's not what I meant. What will they have to live for? Strive for?"

She had known what he meant. But what her grandmother had intimated to her about the future life she foresaw for Dome was difficult for her to take in.

She said, a little hesitantly, "I believe my grandmother has plans of her own involving Jeremy. And others."

"Plans?"

"Plans for a kind of mental expansion. To make up for being trapped in the Dome for the rest of their lives. But she wouldn't elaborate. She said she didn't want to distract me, or you for that matter, from our special task of colonization."

After each sleeping-period that Monty's shift-work allowed them to spend together Monty and Julia awoke, refreshed. They made love before the children began to stir in their smaller chamber. Then they lay locked in each other's arms for a while longer.

All of their homes had been temporary. But in some way they were all the same place. Always they came home to one another, to this joined body; always they floated somewhere out in deep space. Together.

Until at last...

The sandy valley between low mountains presented itself with a new clarity to their video-screens. The descent began.

Into a thin, palish atmosphere the gleaming ship gently injected itself. It hung in this planet's "air" like a vessel of insemination. A needle entering this body's delicate skin.

Everyone who could was now watching out of portholes and observation windows. The rust-coloured valley grew gradually larger and larger as the hours passed. It seemed to be constantly rising, like the bottom of an hourglass, to envelop the hovering ship.

Brooding with warm breast... Bright wings.

Julia knelt beside Monty in the control room. They did not speak. Her hand grasped his ankle.

The ground rose and rose before their eyes. The anti-gravitational engines were on full. Still the descent seemed ever more rapid. Out in space they had not felt their own super-speed. They felt now in their very bones the rocking of the ship, vibrations, a great shaking as if it might loosen any moment into parts, fragments...

The mountains had risen above them to some distance on either side. Julia gazed up at them fixedly as if perhaps they held the key, the secret meaning to this place. Beyond them was an oddly rose-tinted vault or dome of sky that now enclosed and held them. The sun had set redly behind a row of mountains.

Monty kept his eyes on the instrument panel, as did all his colleagues intent on their final tasks. Many dials and numbers were moving inexorably to their charted conclusion.

"Ahh," he sighed involuntarily as, with a great heaving and shifting vibration but without more than a quite manageable, momentary *joltshock*, the huge ship touched down...

XX

The day after the colonists were launched from Dome Ms. Wu-Li asked me to put aside an hour in late afternoon to confer with her discreetly. I was not to mention it to anyone; or if anyone took note of it, I was to say it was a purely social call on an old friend. Thinking this a little odd, I nevertheless agreed. I wondered what urgent or special problem required that we should meet in private, presumably without the immediate knowledge of the council.

When I arrived I was surprised to discover that others were already there.

"As you know," said Ms. Wu-Li, with that admirable despatch she sometimes assumed, "the builders of Dome included the greatest Terran scientists of their day. They were also Holominders. This, of course, includes your ancestors and mine.

"I want to speak with you about Holomind."

She told us many things over many sessions. She gave us meditative exercises to do. These were aimed at a transcendence of the local, delimited body that would allow us to travel mentally.

"Your mind can go anywhere at will," she said, "when you have mastered these techniques. It is subtler matter than the body. The body is bound by the laws of physics. But the subtler matter of mind infuses everything in all the universes, infinite though they be, and your minds—part of the Holomind—can go anywhere.

"Your mind contains, potentially, all that is, has been, and will be. It also contains all that might be. Beyond each black hole that opens up to another universe is Mind.

"Physically, we will never be able to leave Dome. Mentally, we already are everywhere. It is awareness of this that I want you to cultivate.

"We can, outside our ordinary bodies, travel anywhere—to all the futures there are as well as all the pasts."

I won't bore you with my initially strong resistance to these words, or how gradually this resistance was eroded by the altered perspective brought on by Ms. Wu-Li's techniques. It may even be that I reach you at a location in space-time where what I speak of is common knowledge. For those who still find it strange, I offer up this story only as my necessarily subjective experience.

There are many pasts and many futures, Ms. Wu-Li told us. In a different train of events, for instance, the earth was not made uninhabitable in a century of extraordinary folly but survived as a home. The great evil empires collapsed of their own dead weight and gave way to a new age of peace and enlightenment. In that case, however, Monty, Julia, Ms. Wu-Li and I never lived. And in another case the spaceship Dome was destroyed in the last human war, and thus never launched.

In all worlds, it seems, the continuum of space-time expands like a balloon for many more billions of light-years. But depending upon its hidden mass it may ultimately collapse again. Or one or more versions of it may collapse. Those universes will be closed, heating up again to the initial temperature of the "Big Bang."

Open universes, however, expand forever, growing colder as energy spreads out. In these life transforms itself into ethereal forms. Consciousness becomes spread out through nuclear particles linked over vast distances. It is this last and basic consciousness that constitutes Holomind itself. It is this ethereal life-state to which we join ourselves in our travels in space-time.

"In our mental travels we are anticipating the future evolution of life itself," said Ms. Wu-Li. "That is, Mind spread throughout all space and time. As it already is, of course."

And so I commenced my own journeys in space-time. While others contented themselves with the managing of Dome and the receiving of heartening reports of the progress of the colonists, those of us who felt more acutely than they seemed to do the great pathos of our confinement unto death in this enclosed bubble, this autumnal and elegiac floating leaf of a world, sought out transcendence.

Now I am old. I have seen and continue to see bizarre, hitherto unimaginable worlds—in other galaxies with other life-histories, and sometimes beyond black holes. I have felt my being spread out over vast intergalactic distances. This is immensely exhilarating.

Sometimes it is more comforting, though, to visit the otherwise lost past of my own small bit of one tiny planetary culture. I have spent highly diverting hours listening to Plato and Socrates, to Thomas More, Jonathan Swift, Aldous Huxley, George Orwell and

H.G. Wells. I say "hours" though all such travels are instantaneous in the time of Dome. You return even as you are setting forth, since Mind in its purest form is faster than the speed of light.

Meanwhile Dome is running down somewhat as the population ages and decreases. We don't need the same level of services and facilities that we did. And now our videoscreens are largely automated. I rarely look at video, but what there is to be seen is, except for public announcements of some immediate significance or the infrequent bulletins from the busy colony, largely entertainment programming from the archives, automatically recycled every so many years. I have long retired from the supervision of this, and when my successor retires in his turn the automation will continue without the need for a further supervisor.

This endless light entertainment serves to occupy the majority of the aging population not trained in the ways of Holomind. This is their unwitting substitute. These are the shadows flickering away on the impenetrable walls for those who must necessarily live out the remainder of their lives in this huge video-Cave. And even when all the humans under the Dome have finally died—perhaps in a voluntary mass-overdose when the moment seems to have come—these images will flicker on unwatched, as the power-source renews itself endlessly, until this particular version of a universe has cooled itself out countless eons from now.

So the aging population forgets at last the revolution, forgets the time of the Control before. They forget once again that they do not live on the planet Earth, or Terra—that is, until before their eyes come once again bulletins from the colonists building a new life on the planet they have recently decided to call Terra II. Now the aging perpetual voyeurs sigh, remembering for a while the Dome and its voyage. But soon they are lost again in the flickerings of twentieth-century Terran crime-shows, domestic comedies, movies of the week, mini-series, game-shows, or interviews with the once rich and famous ones, flickering shadows who have not existed in the flesh for centuries.

Is this not a particularly cruel fate, to be consigned once again to a realm of illusion—even after the re-education undertaken by the triumphant Underground in the early and more idealistic days of the revolution, and after the startling revelations offered by the new order?

Perhaps. But even after the blinding light of revelation, perhaps especially then, people need their comforts. In the long run many choose the comfort of renewed illusion. "Human kind cannot bear very much reality."

"If there were time," Ms. Wu-Li said more than once to me and to others of her initiates, "we would want to bring everyone under the Dome to Holomind. But I'm afraid it's not possible in the time that is left me. Here, that is, where a certain kind of time still prevails."

And so I and certain others continue to travel forth in Mind from the spatiotemporally-bound cave of Dome to explore both former and latter states of universe. Some of these are quite indescribable, I fear. And always, till we die, we must return to this finite place.

Nor can we well interpret what we experience. It is all too new, and we are just beginning. There are too few useful previous terms of reference. So that it all seems like a dream, an endlessly elastic dream that only opens up into further, ever more fabulous scenes of creation.

The more we see and know, the more we see there is to know. Endless. Thus the poet Rilke, one of those early twentieth-century sages who had glimmerings of Holomind, wrote: "Now, you would hardly ever hear me name him"—meaning God—"there is an indescribable discretion between us, and where nearness and penetration once were, new distances stretch forth, as in the atom..."

You are thinking, perhaps, at this very moment that everything I say, all I have told you, is itself a dream and nothing but a dream. Very well. It is all a dream. And I am still dreaming it. For this is all I can do.

And you, reading or perhaps listening to these hesitant, stumbling words of mine, listening in from some version of the past or it may be from the far future, can you be absolutely certain what kind of reality it is, which of the many many possible worlds or dreams Mind has dreamed or will dream, you yourself inhabit?

In His Moccasins

H.A. Hargreaves

If you would know a man, you must walk
a mile in his moccasins.

February 14th. It should have been a good morning; instead it was like a thousand others for Danny Mullin. He rolled out of his bunk with a muttered curse, pressed the button, and listened while a gear someplace caught, slipped, caught, slipped, and the bunk moved a couple of centimeters in small, sick jerks. With another curse he kicked the bunk, pounded a fist on the button, and gave up. Stinking bunk! Stinking ELS! It did stink. He figured there'd been water down here in the sub-levels sometime, because there was always a smell of mold or something rotten hanging in the air. A Living Space it might be, but Efficiency? No way. He palmed open the door of his washcube, slapped Depil on, and looked in the chipped mirror at his bloodshot eyes. When he pressed for hot, all that came was a trickle of lukewarm water, and he cursed yet again as he rinsed the Depil off. Running fingers through his tangled hair he wondered for the umpteenth time why he got all the lousy deals. He slotted his AP Card and the utility dispenser chattered once or twice before it reluctantly produced a cup of coffee. As he stepped back to sit on his bunk there came a sudden clank and buzz from the wall and the thing finally lurched back into its recess, leaving him squatting over thin air. He nearly threw his coffee at the wall, where there was evidence that he hadn't always stopped himself. Instead, he reached over and flipped down one of his two chairs, then sat and sipped.

To anyone who knew Danny, and precious few did, this would have seemed like unusual restraint, and he realized it. A bitter smile crossed his face as he thought of what Glasson would have said.

Yesterday Glasson had handed him his parole chit and told him sadly: "Danny, I've worked with you for a full six months, and as far as I can tell you haven't done a thing to change. You're still so blasted turned in on yourself you don't recognize that anyone else is real." He'd tried to put a hand on Danny's shoulder, and Danny had slapped it away. He couldn't stand people touching him. Glasson had started back to his desk, then turned and said: "If you don't change, you'll go back in again. Guaranteed! Keep stealing other people's property, keep beating them up, and the Stab will have your butt cooling for a lot longer next time. Remember, the Establishment have a line on you twenty-four hours a day now. That plate in your arm will tell them any time you slip up. Any way. Any place. Remember that plate, Danny!"

Sitting in his stinking hole, Danny rolled back his sleeve, looked at the oval plate, and for the first time in a long while he laughed. Glasson was so smart, him and his degrees and his plush office. Well, the plate wasn't going to stop Danny Mullin. He'd already arranged that, and he wasn't going to waste any time about it either. Glasson, like a roboclerk, mouthed his programmed crud every week, while Danny had sneaked back into Pickin', little things but worth multi-credits, stuff that couldn't be traced. He'd been building an account with the Syndies for over a month. Those Marks in the upper levels–most of them wouldn't miss the stuff for years, they were so pig-fat and loaded with high-tech gadgets. Level over level, row on row, overstuffed dolls coked out on overstuffed furniture. So stupid they left the doors of their Stretched-ELS's open half the time, thinking the security at the building entrances was all they needed. Hell, they didn't even know a level as deep as his existed: wouldn't believe the Syndie complex four corridors away, under the next building, or how easy it was to move through most of Edmonton like a mole. Well they were paying his way out of this cruddy place, out of Edmonton, out of this life! He laughed again. Today was going to be good after all. Today Danny Mullin would disappear.

It was 0630 by his beat-up chrono. He looked around his hole for the last time, pulled a little pile of jewelry from the crack behind the disposall, palmed his door and left. Ten minutes later, after doubling back and changing levels several times, he was in front of the service panel that led into the Syndie complex, eager now for the move that would give him a new life: a chance to work the Marks for everything he wanted, to do anything he wanted. After all, how could the Stab find a guy who didn't exist?

The complex was exactly that. He'd never seen more than the front office, but he knew the Syndies had as much space here under Edmonton as Western Safety Electronics had on the edge of the city. Security was even tighter than there, where he went through five checks just to get to the bay where he serviced cruddy robojans. As usual the fem at the desk made him wait, then took his bag for a tote. She took her time getting back, and shoved a slip at him with a snarly "Try a different route. We seen you come too direct." He looked at the slip and felt the usual rage, then remembered that today was the big payoff. "I got an appointment," he snapped. "Check it." Her robo-like face didn't change. She just turned to her keyboard, called up his record, and muttered: "Wait over there."

After a few minutes Danny began to pace, then went back to the desk and said: "Look, I gotta show for work, and I can't afford to be late." He almost added: "Today of all days," but even in here he wouldn't let anything slip. She might have made another smart remark, like all these desk-faces, but a door behind her slid open and a little bald-headed guy in a flashy execsuit came out. "Mullin," he called, "come with me." They went back into the complex until they came to a small white room like the ones at Emergency. A tall, skinny, rat-nosed type and another fem, in sterilsuits, hustled him into a chair. The fem rolled up his right sleeve while ratnose adjusted a hypo. "This is just to deaden the jolt," he said, as he sprayed all around the plate, careful not to hit the metal itself. Then he took out what looked like a plain chrono and carefully lowered it over the oval plate in Danny's arm. There was a paralyzing tingle when it touched, then nothing. Ratnose finished strapping it on and pressed in a tiny nib. "That's all?" Danny asked. Baldy answered. "That's all. Out!" They were into another corridor before it really sank in.

Baldy motioned him into a flipchair. "You got what you want," he told Danny, "but there are things you need to know." He flipped a switch and Danny heard a humming over his head. Looking up he saw a big machine like a vidcam aimed at him. "Just a precaution," Baldy sneered. He pushed another switch and Danny felt his brain go muddy for a second. "You'll go out a new way, and you'll never be able to find this location again." He smiled, and Danny realized suddenly that he looked vicious. Baldy continued. "Remember this. Don't ever try to take that jammer off. Ever! We couldn't care less if the Stab nab you, now. But if you try to take it off it'll blow itself and you all to hell. If you stay in Edtown we may be in touch. If you leave, someone else may be. We're everywhere." Danny started to say that he knew but Baldy kept talking. "Everywhere means every city, every country, where we can dump stuff and pick up what'll trade elsewhere." He shrugged. "If you had the right attitude we might've found a place for you. But you're trouble." He took Danny's arm and led him through another maze of corridors to an exit in a cleaning closet. With a last, steely look, he shoved Danny out. It was 0700.

His head was clearing fast, and Danny took his time, moving at random, until he arrived at the transway entrance where he always started for work. Slotting his AP Card smugly, he passed through the stile and waited on the platform, right on time. One more detail finished. The Marks said there was no way to beat the system, but he'd beat it when he was younger, and he was a hell of a lot smarter now, after four years in the Resort, listening to the pros. And if he hadn't lingered for the sheer pleasure of beating on that flabby Mark, the robocops would never have caught him back then either. But this was today, and he savored what was coming, testing and tasting it all the way out to work, watching as frost built up on the windows when they came to the surface, laughing inwardly at the stupid-cow Marks, in flashy coldsuits, huddled on the open platforms. During his lunch break he chewed a sandwich and didn't taste it, while he ran over the next moves, trying to find a flaw. There wasn't one.

At 1830, when he was just putting his equipment away after tidying up for the weekend, Berkley arrived, exactly as he always did on Friday, exactly as he had to if the plan was to work. *Mister* Berkley had been trying for months to get Danny to call him Jason, slipping in the invitations in various ways. Danny couldn't figure out why, unless this big cog, head of Design no less, had been stuck onto him by the Stab. But he came down twice a week to put test programs in a few of the robojans, replace chips, stick around, even walk out with Danny to the transway at this late hour, when everybody else was gone. Well, Berkley was going to be a help, all right.

They caught the transway, and just as always Berkley started to get off at the stop before Danny's, only this time Danny was right behind him. With a big smile pasted on, Danny said: "I need to do some shopping, Mister Berkley. Want to come along and give me some advice?" He'd said it to himself so many times it was nearly too automatic, so he added: "I mean, you been married four, five months now, right?" Berkley had looked faintly puzzled, but now he smiled back. "Don't tell me you've finally found a girl?" he asked. "Is that it? A little present?" Danny chuckled. "Almost right," he answered, "but more than a little present is what I was thinkin' of." It was perfect. The crud was grinning like an cokehead. Then the whole thing nearly blew up when Berkley put a hand on his shoulder. Danny tensed, about to swing, but then he was under control again. They were just coming to the Rent-Us Dial-up, and casually Danny slid slightly behind Berkley and whipped out a blade.

"What you're feelin' right over your kidney," he hissed, "is sharp, long, and hooked. Keep walkin' up to the booth and rent a dial-up for the weekend, with your AP Card. Try anything and your new bride will need a drawer for your ashes." Berkley had stiffened and stopped, but a prod started him off again. This, the toughest part of Danny's plan, had to work. If Berkley tried anything or went to pieces Danny'd be hiding deep in the sub-levels for a long time before he could get out of Edmonton. But Berkley, no more than a little pale at this point, did what he'd been told, and with the keys handed over by the roboclerk headed for the proper dial-up. Once there, however, he looked Danny in the eye. "I can't operate one of these things," he said. "I had ... a bad experience in one when I was a kid." Danny was stunned, disbelieving. "Quit stalling," he snarled. "All you Marks know how to drive." Berkley sagged against the side of the dial-up, sweating in the cool air. "I'm telling you true," he half-whispered. "I hate the bloody, killing things." Danny fought down panic and accepted that he must be telling the truth. It changed things, but only slightly. Carefully, he steered Berkley to the other side of the vehicle, slammed the door, and ran around to the driver's side. He'd been happy-hopping these things on back roads and even on the Ed-Cal Motorway since he was eleven or twelve, back in Rimbey. He flipped the doorlock and belt switches before Berkley even had a chance to move. So much for keeping him quiet while they drove, though he looked as if he was going to pass out anyway. Good thing it was a roboattendant at the entrance, he figured, pulling the yoke out the the dashboard. A Mark would notice that something was wrong, for sure.

He was careful to punch a standard route going east out of the city, though it was a long way round, and it was only when they moved onto the open motorway that he punched a new route for the outer ring road going south. As they hit the approach to the Ed-Cal Motorway he waited till the last split second, then punched again. On the Motorway and headed for Calgary he dialled up, moving lane by lane to the next fastest before switching to cruise. Only then did he think to check the charge meter, noting with a sigh of relief that the needle was up against the peg. At 180 kph the landscape went by fast, but Danny could see that not much had changed from five years ago, and he was certain now that the plan would work.

Berkley didn't seem to be seeing much of anything He was sitting rigid, eyes closed, teeth clenched, sickly white. The stupid Mark had really meant it then. It was even better than Danny had expected, and a wave of happiness swept over him that was almost like too much Alkade on Saturday night. Disappearing was the big goal—but what a bonus, stiffing a cruddy Mark too.

Outside the vehicle slanting bars of snow began cutting down visibility, and the blinking caution ops slowed his speed automatically to 150 kph. He'd wanted to make it as quick as possible, but this still wasn't bad, only he had to be very careful to watch for landmarks. South of Ponoka he flipped off automatic and moved back down to the slow lane. The snow was really belting down now, but he still found the little exit he wanted, north of Lacombe. The dial-up slewed slightly as he swung onto the back road he knew so well, and traction was lousy. Two kilometers in he figured he was at the best place he could get. There had never been any buildings around here before, but the snow was too heavy for him to check. Not that it mattered.

He flipped the lock and belt switches, and Berkley slumped down. Danny pushed the yoke back in, swivelled, and gave him a shove. "All right, Berkley, out." Berkley's eyes snapped open and he looked around dazedly. "Out!" Danny repeated, and shoved him harder. Berkley suddenly realized what he meant and blurted out: "You can't." "You bet your credits I can ... and will," Danny growled at him. "Listen," Berkley said earnestly, "You'll be picked up by the Stab in no time. Your implant ... ," but Danny swung a full left backhand that caught Berkley across the mouth. "Shut up and get out," he yelled. It felt so good that he did it again, and Berkley's head bounced off the frame. Blood trickled out of both corners of his mouth. Danny reached across him and opened the door. "So long crud," he shouted, and raising his foot he kicked Berkley savagely with every ounce of strength. Berkley grabbed at the door as he was catapulted out, but his legs flipped up after his body and he landed on the ground, rolling away as Danny pulled the yoke out and dialled up. Snow and gravel whipped back into Berkley's face, and the last Danny saw of him in the rearview he was kneeling in the road in the driving snow. Then Danny was punching to make the entrance into the slow lane, aware that in this weather the Ed-Cal Motorway was always dangerous. As the chill left the vehicle he felt so happy that he hummed a tuneless song. Yes, the weather. There'd be no witness, would there?

Berkley had looked like one of those advertising simuls outside a wraparound show, Danny gloated. They were usually bloodied up too. He might even take in a wraparound once in a while once he got settled in Calgary, though he hadn't much liked them before. They made you feel creepy, takin' you into the middle of other bodies, like. Maybe he would, maybe he wouldn't, but at least it would be his choice. He'd find the Syndies or they'd find him. There was a rumor that not even they could make you a new All Purpose Card, but you could get by on stolen ones if you only used them once or twice, and trading with the Syndies was "all purpose" enough for most needs. He'd been so deep in his thoughts that he was almost on the edge of Calgary before he could dial down and punch a local route. He knew where he was going--to drop in on his cellmate at the Resort. Not a friend, yet bound by the code to help him. But suddenly, there was a robocruiser alongside him and his vehicle was under remote control. It was his turn to be completely stunned as the robocop dragged him out and he heard his rights read.

It was 2210 exactly. Danny had been escorted into the Trial Chamber by another robocop and was facing a bank of TriVid cubes identical to those he'd faced when he was tried and sentenced the first time. He still couldn't understand how they'd known so quickly, how they'd tracked him down when the jammer was snug over his plate. The damned thing must have been working, because the Stab had gone through a very cautious and elaborate procedure to get it off him. They respected it, all right. The impossibility of the whole situation made his head spin. But now one of the cubes was lighting up, and a judge faced him from his office someplace else.

The robocop spoke. "Daniel Richard Mullin, RIM3597ALT20478. Apprehended 2140. Charges: 291, driving a stolen vehicle; 324, unprovoked assault; 121, attempted manslaughter; Federal–726, interference with a PenSyst implant. Accused was read his rights. No response to questioning." The Chamber was quiet for a moment as a pair of discs dropped from a slot onto the Judge's desk. Then he spoke. "Daniel Mullin, before we begin this trial, do you wish an attorney?" Danny stared ahead. The Judge intoned: "Let the record show that the defendant did not request counsel." Then he continued. "How do you plead?" Still Danny made no answer and the Judge intoned flatly again: "Let the record show that the defendant entered no plea." He inserted one of the discs into his viewer and read with total concentration, then said: "For the record, no misconduct while serving previous sentence. However, no cooperation in rehabilitation except minimal skill retraining." He inserted the other disc and read with the same concentration. "For the record, Parole Officer Glasson's final report. No perceptible improvement in societal interaction. Extremely high ego-set intensified by non-acceptance of other egos." The Judge sat back and pushed one of a row of buttons in his desk. The second TriVid cube sprang to life and Danny was shocked to see Berkley lying in a hospital bed, feet and hands swathed in bandages, face swollen into a grotesque mask by bruises and frostbite. But the ultimate shock was to see, just below where a tube entered his bare right arm, an oval plate glistening in the dim light. He only half-listened while Berkley gave his testimony in a weak, uneven voice. In a crescendo of revelations Danny understood a number of things. Why Berkley had been bound to take the extra interest in him. Why he'd been found and rescued so quickly by the Stab. Why he … why he'd said something about Danny's implant just as Danny hit him. Stupid! Stupid! He'd been so busy licking his chops over getting rid of the only witness to his escape that he'd missed it altogether. Slowly he became aware that the Judge was talking straight at him, that the sentence was due. He'd probably go in for a long, long stretch this time. But it was only his second offence; he had that to fall back on.

"Daniel Richard Mullin," the Judge said in a voice completely empty of emotion, "you have heard the evidence against you. Do you now wish to say anything in your own defense?" Danny stubbornly remained silent, figuring there was nothing he could say that would help, and silence couldn't hurt. The Judge sat even higher in his straight-backed chair and continued. "I have considered all the facts known to me in this case, and in the absence of any defense I must pass sentence now. You will be placed in confinement for a minimum of eight years on the charge of attempted manslaughter, sentence on all other charges left pending." He stopped and polished his old-fashioned glasses.

"However," he leaned forward slightly, "I must take into consideration one more factor: your psychiatric record. So long as you regard other individuals as no more than objects, to be brutalized or, at best, used for your own gratification, you will never become a productive member of society–the goal to which all must aspire. You would be sentenced again and again, a menace to the community while free, and a drain on the economy while confined. Before removal to an institution for retraining, you would normally receive a memory erasure for this offence, with possible loss of productivity. For you particularly, however, we have a new form of remedial treatment, which will be administered immediately, and repeated as often as necessary. Stand down!"

Danny listened with growing bewilderment and anger, less and less certain that he understood what was happening. As he was led by a robocop to a far wing of the building, he compared this to his last sentencing. They were so totally unlike that he began to feel a gnawing fear. He became even more frightened when the robocop drew him into a room complete with table and massive machine from which wires and plates hung loosely. A muscular fem seized his arm securely and whipped a hypo shot into him. Almost immediately he lost control of his body. From far away he heard her say to the sterilsuited man who entered, "Here's the Berkley recording, just transmitted from Lacombe General Hospital." They led him to the table, strapped his body down, pasted the many plates to wrists, ankles, temples. Then, abruptly, he was back in the dial-up, out on the back road. Something was different, though, and as the belt dropped away and the doorlock next to him clicked he turned, the wrong way, to receive a smashing backhand. Through blinding pain he heard … himself, but not himself … shout "Shut up and get out," and the hand caught him again, so that his head bounced off the frame and he could taste warm blood welling from his mouth. The door was opened and a foot caved in his left ribs as he cartwheeled from the dial-up to a shouted "So long, crud." As he knelt in the road the dial-up's wheels spun snow and mud unto his eyes and mouth, choking and blinding him, leaving him in terrible pain to feel the first, incredibly-intense sweep of frigid air through his light jumpsuit.

The Immaculate Conception Photography Gallery

Katherine Govier

Sandro named the little photography shop on St. Clair Avenue West, between Lord's Shoes and Bargain Jimmie's, after the parish church in the village where he was born. He had hankered after wider horizons, the rippled brown prairies, the hard-edged mountains. But when he got to Toronto he met necessity in the form of a wife and babies and, never having seen a western sunset, he settled down in Little Italy. He photographed brides in their fat lacquered curls and imported lace, and their quick babies in christening gowns brought over from home. Blown up to near life-size on cardboard cutouts, their pictures filled the windows of his little shop.

Sandro had been there ten years already when he first really saw his sign and the window. He stood still in front of it and looked. A particularly buxom bride with a lace bodice and cap sleeves cut in little scallops shimmered in a haze of concupiscence under the sign reading Immaculate Conception Photography Gallery. Sandro was not like his neighbours any more, he was modern, a Canadian. He no longer went to church. As he stared, one of the street drunks shuffled into place beside him. Sandro knew them all, they came in the shop in winter. (No on eought to have to stay outside in that cold, Sandro believed.) But he especially knew Becker. Becker was a smart man; he used to be a philosopher at a university.

"Immaculate Conception," said Sandro to Becker. "What do you think?"

Becker lifted his eyes to the window. He made a squeezing gesture at the breasts. "I never could buy that story," he said.

Sandro laughed, but he didn't change the sign that year or the next and he got to be forty-five and then fifty and it didn't seem worth it. The Immaculate Conception Photography Gallery had a reputation. Business came in from as far away as Rosedale and North Toronto, because Sandro was a magician with a camera. He also had skills with brushes and lights and paint; he reshot his negatives, he lined them with silver, he had tricks even new graduates of photography school couldn't (or wouldn't) copy.

Sandro was not proud of his tricks. They began in a gradual way, fixing stray hairs and taking wrinkles out of dresses. Then he met with a situation that would have started a feud in the old country. During a very large and very expensive wedding party, Tony the bridegroom seduced Alicia the bridesmaid in the basketball storage room under the floor of the parish hall. Six months later Tony confessed, hoping perhaps to be released from his vows. But the parents judged it was too late to dissolve the union: Diora was used, she was no longer a virgin, there was the child coming. Tony was reprimanded, Diora consoled, the mothers became enemies, the newlyweds made up. Only Alicia remained to be dealt with. The offence became hers.

In Italy, community ostracism would have been the punishment of choice. But this was Canada, and if no-one visited her mother, who was heavy on her feet and could not get out and sat on the sofa protesting her daughter's innocence, if no-one invited her father out behind to drink home-made wine, Alicia didn't care. She went off to her job behind the till in a drugstore with her chin thrust out much as before. The in-laws perceived that the young woman could not be subdued by the old methods and, this being the case, it was better she not exist at all.

That was why Diora's mother turned up at Sandro's counter with the wedding photos. The pain Alicia had caused! she began. It was Diora's mother's very own miserable wages saved these eighteen years that had paid for these photographs! she wept. The money was spent, but the joy was spoiled. When she and Diora's father looked at the row of faces flanking bride and groom there she was - Alicia, the whore! She wiped her tears and made her pitch.

"You can solve our problem, Sandro. I will get you a new cake, we will all come to the parish hall. You will take the photographs again. Of course," she added, "we can't pay you again."

Sandro smiled, it was so preposterous. "Even if I could afford to do all that work for nothing, I hate to say it, but Diora's out to here."

"Don't argue with me."

"I wouldn't be so bold," said Sandro. "But I will not take the photographs over."

The woman slapped the photographs where they lay on the counter. "You will! I don't care how you do it!"

Sandro went to the back and put his negatives on the light box. He brought out his magic solution and his razor blades and his brushes. He circled Alicia's head and shoulders in the first row and went to work. He felt a little badly, watching the bright circle of her face fade and swim, darken down to nothing. But how easily she vanished! He filled in the white spot with a bit of velvet curtain trimmed from the side.

"I'm like a plastic surgeon," he told his wife. "Take that patch of skin from the inner thigh and put it over the scar on the face. Then sand the edges. Isn't that what they do? Only it isn't a face I'm fixing, it's a memory."

His wife stood on two flat feet beside the sink. She shook the carrot she was peeling. "I don't care about Alicia," she said, "but Diora's mother is making a mistake. She is starting them off with a lie in their marriage. And why is she doing it? For her pride! I don't like this, Sandro."

"You're missing the point," said Sandro. The next day he had another look at his work. Alicia's shoulders and the bodice of her dress were still there, in front of the chest of the uncle of the bride. Removing them would leave a hole in Uncle. Sandro had nothing to fill the hole, no spare male torsos in black tie. He considered putting a head on top, but whose head? There was no such thing as a free face. A stranger would be questioned, a friend would have an alibi. Perhaps Diora's mother would not notice the black velvet space as where a tooth had been knocked out, between the smiling faces.

Indeed she didn't, but kissed his hand fervently and thanked him with tears in her eyes. "Twenty-five thousand that wedding cost. Twenty-five thousand to get this photograph, and you have rescued it."

"Surely you got dinner and a dance too?" said Sandro.

"The wedding was one day. This is forever," said Diora's mother.

"I won't do that again," said Sandro, putting the cloth over his head and looking into his camera lens to do a passport photo. In the community the doctored photograph had been examined and re-examined. Alicia's detractors enjoyed the headless shoulders as evidence of a violent punishment.

"No, I won't do that again at all," said Sandro to himself, turning aside compliments with a shake of his head. But there was another wedding. After the *provolone e melone* ,the veal piccata, the many-tiered cake topped with swans, the father of the bride drew Sandro aside and asked for a set of prints with the groom's parents removed.

"My God, why?" said Sandro.

"He's a bastard. A bad man."

"Shouldn't have let her marry his son, then," said Sandro, pulling a cigarette out of the pack in his pocket. These conversations made him nervous.

The father's weathered face was dark, his dinner jacket did not button around his chest. He moaned and ground his lower teeth against his uppers. "You know how they are, these girls in Canada. I am ashamed to say it, but I couldn't stop her."

Sandro said nothing.

"Look ,I sat here all night long, said nothing, did nothing. I don't wanna look at him for the next twenty years."

Sandro drew in a long tube of smoke.

"I paid a nice bundle for this night. I wanna remember it nice-like."

The smoke made Sandro nauseated. He dropped his cigarette and ground it into the floor with his toe damning his own weakness. "What am I going to do with the table?"

The father put out a hand like a tool, narrowed his eyes, and began to saw, where the other man sat.

"And leave it dangling, no legs?"

"So make new legs?"

"I'm a photographer, not a carpenter," and Sandro. "I don't make table legs."

"Where you get legs is your problem," said the father. "I'm doing well here. I've got ten guys working for me. You look like you could use some new equipment."

And what harm was it after all, it was only a photograph, said Sandro to himself. Then too there was the technical challenge. Waiting till they all got up to get their *bonboniere*, he took a shot of the head table empty. Working neatly with his scalpel, he cut the table from this second negative, removed the inlaws and their chairs from the first one, stuck the empty table-end onto the table in the first picture, blended over the join neatly, and printed it. Presto! Only one set of in-laws.

"I don't mind telling you, it gives me a sick feeling," said Sandro to his wife. "I was there. I saw them. We had a conversation. They smiled at me. Now ..." he shrugged. "An empty table. Lucky I don't go to church any more."

"Let the man who paid good money to have you do it confess, not you," she said. "A photograph is a photograph."

"That's what I thought, too," said Sandro.

The next morning Sandro went to the Donut House, got himself a takeout coffee and stood on the street beside the window.

"Why do people care about photographs so much?" he said to Becker. Becker had newspaper stuffed in the soles of his shoes. He had on a pair of strained brown pants tied up at the waist with a paisley necktie. His bottle was clutched in a paper bag gathered around the neck.

"You can put them on your mantel," said Becker. "They don't talk back."

"Don't people prefer life?" said Sandro.

"People prefer things," said Becker.

"Don't they want their memories to be true?"

"No," said Becker.

"Another thing. Are we here just to get our photograph taken? Do we have a higher purpose?"

Becker pulled one of the newspapers out of his shoe. There were Brian and Mila Mulroney having a gloaty kiss. They were smeared by muddy water and depressed by the joint in the ball of Becker's foot.

"I mean real people," said Sandro. "Have we no loyalty to the natural?"

"These are existential questions, Sandro," said Becker. "Too many more of them and you'll be out here on the street with the rest of us."

Sandro drained the coffee from his cup, pitched it in the bin painted Keep Toronto Clean, and went back into his gallery. The existential questions nagged. But he did go out and get the motor drive for the camera. In the next few months he eradicated a pregnancy from a wedding photo, added a daughter-in-law who complained of being left out of the Christmas shots, and made a groom taller. Working in the darkroom, he was hit by vertigo. He was on a slide beginning a descent. He wanted to know what the bottom felt like.

It was after a year of such operations that a man from the Beaches came in with a tiny black-and-white photo of a long-lost brother. He wanted it coloured and fitted into a family shot around a picnic table on Centre Island.

"Is this some kind of joke?" said Sandro. It was the only discretion he practiced now; he wanted to talk about it before he did it.

"No, I'm going to send it to my mother. She thinks Christopher wrote us all off."

"Did he?" said Sandro.

"Better she should not know."

Sandro neglected to ask if Christopher was fat or thin. He ended up taking a medium-sized pair of shoulders from his own cousin and propping them up behind a bush, with Christopher on top. Afterwards, Sandro lay sleepless in his bed. Suppose that in the next few months Christopher should turn up dead, say murdered. Then Mother would produce the photograph stamped Immaculate Conception Photography Gallery, 1816 St Clair Avenue West. Sandro would be implicated. The police might come.

"Adding is worse than taking away," he said to his wife.

"You say yes to do it, then you do it. You think it's wrong, you say no."

"Let me try this on you, Becker," said Sandro the next morning. "To take a person out is only half a lie. It proves nothing except that he was not in that shot. To add a person is a whole lie: it proves that he was there, when he was not."

"You haven't proven a thing. You're just fooling around with celluloid. Have you got a buck?" said Becker.

"It is better to be a murderer than a creator. I am playing God outplaying God at his own game." He was smarter than Becker now.

He knew it was the photographs that lasted, not people. In the end the proof was in the proof. Though he hadn't prayed in thirty years, Sandro began to pray. It was like riding a bicycle: he got the hang of it again instantly. "Make me strong," he prayed, "strong enough to resist the new equipment that I might buy, strong enough to resist the temptation to expand the gallery, to buy a house in the suburbs. Make me say no to people who want alterations."

But Sandro's prayers were not answered. When people offered him money to dissolve an errant relative, he said yes. He said yes out of curiosity. He said yes out of desire to test his skills. He said yes out of greed. He said yes out of compassion. "What is the cost of a little happiness?" he said. "Perhaps God doesn't count photographs. After all, they're not one of a kind."

Sandro began to be haunted, in slow moments behind the counter in the Immaculate Conception, by the faces of those whose presence he had tampered with. He kept a file—Alicia the lusty bridesmaid, Antonia and Marco, the undesired in-laws. Their heads, their shoes, and their hands removed from the scene with surgical precision, he saved for the moment when, God willing, a forgiving relative would ask him to replace them. But the day did not come. Sandro was not happy.

"Becker," he said, for he had a habit now of buying Becker a coffee first thing in the morning and standing out if it was warm, or in if it was cold, for a chat. "Becker, let's say it's a good service I'm doing. It makes people happy, even if it tells lies."

"Sandro," said Becker, who enjoyed his coffee, "these photographs, doctored by request of the subjects, reflect back the life they wish to have. The unpleasant bits are removed, the wishes are added. If you didn't do it, someone else would. Memory would. It's a service."

"It's also money," said Sandro. He found Becker too eager to make excuses now. He liked him better before.

"You're Tintoretto, painting in his patron, softening his greedy profile, lifting the chin of his fat wife. It pays for the part that's true art."

"Which part is that?" said Sandro, but Becker didn't answer. He was still standing there when Diora came in. She'd matured, she'd gained weight, and her twins, now six years old, were handsome and strong. Sandro's heart flew up in his breast. Perhaps she had made friends with Alicia, perhaps Diora had come to have her bridesmaid reinstated.

"The long nightmare is over," said Diora. "I've left him."

The boys were running from shelf to shelf lifting up the photographs with their glass frames and putting them down again. Sandro watched them with one eye. He knew what she was going to say.

"I want you to take him out of those pictures," she said.

"You'd look very foolish as a bride with no groom," he said severely.

"No, no, not those," she said. "I mean the kids' birthday shots."

They had been particularly fine, those shots, taken only two weeks ago, Tony tall and dark, Diora and the children radiant and blond.

"Be reasonable, Diora," he said. "I never liked him myself. But he balances the portrait. Besides, he was there."

"He was not there!" cried Diora. Her sons went on turning all the pictures to face the walls. "He was never there. He was running around, in his heart he was not with me. I was alone with my children."

"I'll take another one," said Sandro. "Of you and the boys. Whenever you like. This one stays like it is."

"We won't pay."

"But Diora," said Sandro, "everyone knows he's their father."

"They have no father," said Diora flatly.

"It's Immaculate Conception," said Becker gleefully.

But Diora did not hear. "It's our photograph, and we want him out. You do your job. The rest of it's none of your business." She put one hand on the back of the head of each of her twins and marched them out the door.

Sandro leaned on his counter idly flipping the pages of a wedding album. He had a vision of a great decorated room, with a cake on the table. Everyone had had his way, the husband had removed the wife, the wife the husband, the bridesmaid her parents, and so forth. There was no-one there.

"We make up our lives out of the people around us," he said to Becker. "When they don't live up to standard we can't just wipe them out."

"Don't ask me," said Becker. "I just lit out for the streets. Couldn't live up to a damn thing." Then he too went out the door.

"Lucky bugger," said Sandro.

Alone, he went to his darkroom. He opened his drawer of bits and pieces. His disappeared ones, the inconvenient people. His body parts, his halves of torsos, tips of shiny black shoes. Each face, each item of clothing punctured him a little. He looked at his negatives stored in drawers. They were scarred, pathetic things. I haven't the stomach for it, not any more, thought Sandro. As he walked home, St Clair Avenue seemed very fine. The best part was, he thought, there were no relationships. Neither this leaning drunk nor that window-shopper was so connected to any other as to endanger his, or her, existence. The tolerance of indifference, said Sandro to himself, and tried to remember it to tell Becker.

But Sandro felt ill at ease in his own home, by its very definition a dangerous and unreliable setting. His wife was stirring something, with her lips tight together. His children, almost grown up now, bred secrets as they looked at television. He himself only posed in the doorway, looking for hidden seams and the faint hairlines of an airbrush.

That night he stood exhausted by his bed. His wife lay on her side with one round shoulder above the sheet. Behind her on the wall was the photo he'd taken of their village before he left Italy. He ought to reshoot it, take out the gas station and clean up the square a little. His pillow had an indentation, as if a head had been erased. He slept in a chair.

In the morning he went down to the shop. He got his best camera and set up a tripod on the sidewalk directly across the street. He took several shots in the solid bright morning light. He locked the door and placed the CLOSED sign in the window. In the darkroom he developed the film, floating the negatives in the pungent fluid until the row of shop fronts came through clearly, the flat brick faces, the curving concrete trim, the two balls on the crowns. Deftly he dissolved each brick of his store, the window, and the sign. Deftly he reattached each brick of the store to the west side to the bricks of the store to the east.

I have been many things in my life, thought Sandro, a presser of shutters, a confessor, a false prophet. Now I am a bricklayer, and a good one. He taped the negatives together and developed them. He touched up the join and then photographed it again. He developed this second negative and it was perfect. Number 1812, Lord's Shoes, joined directly to 1820, Bargain Jimmie's: The Immaculate Conception Photography Gallery at 1816 no longer existed. Working quickly, because he wanted to finish before the day was over, he blew it up two feet by three feet. He cleared out his window display of brides and babies and stood up this new photograph - one of the finest he'd ever taken, he thought. Then he took a couple of cameras and a bag with a tripod and some lenses. He turned out the light, pulling the door shut behind him, and began to walk west.

Living in Cities

Candas Jane Dorsey

In the city, time becomes visible.
-Lewis Mumford

I have lived in cities until my heart is lost to them: beautiful random human constructions with their geometry chaotic and their rhythms arbitrary. I dive deep into their oblivious centres, and their darkness and danger does not deter me from loving them. To me, it is no surprise that cities are dangerous. Any lover so deep in the heart is dangerous. Any group of that many intentions, that many dreams and cynicisms, is bound to conflict and occasionally to terrify.

But set against that are the moments when the sun reflects from the mirrored glass of the old buildings and down into the shadowed streets, and walking through an alley I see a corner of even older brickwork alight with that golden reflexion. Restless energy, surprising times and places of tranquility, dreamlike scenarios glimpsed from car windows: everything placed in conjunction, or maybe unplaced completely but still emerging arranged.

I live in an old apartment, with wood floors and doors which like other luxuries I can afford because of my previous profession, and big windows which strangers say look out on nothing. But it is not nothing: it is city and cloud. Buildings brick and glass, short and tall; displayed against ever-changing, clean, beautifully-decorated sky: both are essential.

I work across the alley, in a building with an imposing, comparatively-new façade, but an archaic back where iron fire escapes funnel down to a concrete parking lot. There I have my tiny suite of offices, where I keep my computers, my collection of old laser discs, and, even more eccentric, my books. All of them insured to the hilt — I may be crazy but I'm not stupid — inside doubled walls I installed myself, and protected by better security systems than the building deserves, all carefully invisible.

In front of the building, where the façade was modern over fifty years ago, the streets are immaculate; in the alley the material detritus of prostitution and drug use drifts eventually up against walls or into the cracks and rough spots in the pavement. Less obvious are the people who leave these traces, for they are transitory; the police patrols are the most visible, making my walk to work or home in midnight, through streets said to be mean, safer than most I take through more genteel districts.

No one builds there any more: no one can. The zoning regulations are strict, and protect the trees and parks equally with the brick and glass. Only those who will do no harm can work here, or those who cannot be regulated: I claim I am both, but only to myself. It is so easy to slip over the edge and become precious in these late-night monologues.

I retired to this city many years ago, having outlived my past but being still young enough in body to begin a new career. I live by a curious mixture of the ascetic and the profligate, and I do what interests me or—sometimes the same thing—what I think is indicated.

I tell you this to preface my story, to say cities are where I centre; in fact, in this one preserve of the genre I have been settled now for some years, and intend to stay for the one lifetime left to me.

This city where I live now, I know deeply; knowing it this way is not easy nor does it lend itself to analysis. So when Aaron asked me if I could show my city to a stranger, one particular stranger, I wasn't sure I wanted to do it. I could have refused, but as I thought about it, I realised what an interesting challenge it was: a tourist tour of my own skin? Finally I thought I'd try.

The stranger was different than I had expected. Small, a woman, with a heavy braid of black thick hair almost to her waist. Instantly, unexpectedly, I wanted to undo that braid, comb that wild hair with my hands; her pale face was serene and I wanted to take that serenity apart with passion.

I hoped my face showed nothing. "All right," I said to Aaron. "I'll do what I can. Tomorrow."

"Do you know what you're dealing with?" he asked me, pulling me aside for a moment. "She's..."

"I don't want to know." My city is the same for everyone, if they look at it from the right direction, but even I, governed now only by my enthusiasms, do not say such things aloud. "I'll do my best."

The next morning, we drove away from the hotel in my old Vivair with the cracked windscreen. I'd cleaned out the cab for this but there was no way to hide the crazing in the old plastic, the faded lettering on the readouts, the dents and scratches in the body. The seats are worn beyond repair, held together with silver gaffer's tape (a stolen roll I keep under the edge of the passenger seat, wedged in with work gloves, the chamois and the squeegee).

She made no comment. Good manners, I thought. After she was seated, though, she leaned forward and reached out one small forefinger to the long crack in the windscreen, running her fingertip along it for as much of its length as she could reach. She actually touched it: her finger made a tiny streak in the dust. Then she sat back again and tightened her seatbelt.

"So this is Earth," she said, and I laughed.

"Yes, indeed," I said. "How do you like us so far?"

"I was born on Earth. Were you?"

When I shoulder-checked a glance at her controlled face, she was smiling a little, but looking away out the window. All right. That one to her.

Imagine a hollow in the land, a deep wide trough scooped out by a river, ready to take a sandcasting of air, of sky. Imagine that between this molding and the air it shapes, crystals begin to grow, complicating and recomplicating into jagged fantastical accretions which seem to have order and purpose but which obey only internal rules. Imagine that these crystals spread, and push the sky away, creating a thin, wide interstitium which at certain nodes thickens—or, more accurately, deepens—and complexifies. Compared to the earth and the atmosphere, this layer is the thinnest of rimes and hardly worth study, yet in the chinks in and between those crystalline constructions lives an admixture of human, animal and vegetable: in cities.

I took her to the edge of the bowl of sky, where on the opposite bank the tall buildings rise precipitously, while below and across the autumn trees appeared, from that distance, like contours of variegated moss filling the valley below. An old bridge, its span painted blue, conducts traffic across the river there; soon we would be crossing it and I wanted her to see where we were going.

It was day: I could not show her where either of us had been.

"This city is under three hundred years old," I said, "young for an Earth city. There was a time when everything that the people here called old was younger than the buildings I consider to be new: at that time, the earlier architectural artifacts were destroyed so that those—" (I indicated the towers) "—could be built. They were modern. Now, the city is frozen in time; no more will be done thoughtlessly. But you know all about that."

"Pretend I don't. Pretend I am new."

"We grow our habitats on the planet like algae on a pond, a scum across its clarity. But ah, they are pretty, don't you think?"

"I am sure algae is pretty too. I wouldn't know."

"Hydroponics is not your specialty?"

"I have no specialty. Shall we move on?"

I took her first to streets where poor people still live.

We parked the Viv behind a broken-down movie theatre which still sold adventucons and pornoflicks to addictives and pros and streetsleepers. I paid the credits to take us inside. The smell of popcorn and burned oil from the antique machine was classic; so were the seats with their cracked plastic coverings, creaky hinges and mysterious stains. Obviously unafraid of contamination, she touched everything.

"You have a lot of these plastic artifacts?" she said.

"Shhh!" said a stubble-faced derelict a row ahead. On the screen, jasmine flowers surrounded a naked couple whose exercise seemed almost academic, their faces were so disinterested.

The scent of jasmine was heavy in the theatre, almost drowning the smell of vomit and old come.

"This is ancient," she said, wrinkling her nose. "We have..."

"You have advanced the science of pornography to greater heights than these?"

"Unmind, it doesn't matter. Do you think we can call a truce for today?"

"No, we can't. If we could, do you think they would have sent you here?"

You know what I mean. But she didn't say it. Because "Shhh!" came from behind us, and a whisper in elided urban dialect, which I could translate as: "You there! Shut it up!"

A burly usher was starting down the aisle. She stopped when she recognised me, but crooked her finger. I went with her back to the lobby.

"What's the story?" said the usher.

"She's a visitor…"

"What's this, a new sideline for you?"

"Sure. There's a big future in tourism,'' I said. "See home first, eh?"

She laughed. "Who is she?"

The visitor still stood halfway down a row of seats, watching the screen. The sea was washing a jungle beach. Salty air slowly swept the jasmine scent away. She lifted her face as if into a wind off the ocean, but the air came in from the side vents with smells prepackaged, and shattered her illusion.

"Just a stranger," I said.

"Well, get her out of here before the others smell her out. You know how it is."

I knew how it was, more than she thought. I went back down, took the visitor's sleeve, and brought her back out of the darkness.

We walked down the sunlit sidewalk in the real breeze. On a day like that, with autumn counting down but summer holding strong sway, the doorways are full.

"I have read about Earth addicts," she said. "What are they addicted to?"

"Whatever they can afford," I said, "just like us."

"What can you afford, all of this?"

But I didn't want to answer. Ahead of us, a beautiful native woman laughed up into the face of a scarred but compelling-featured man whose skin was deeply dark. The contrast of their disparate skin colours with the scarlet and saffron clothing they wore shocked the day. I did not realise I was smiling until I saw the visitor looking at me.

She said nothing more, however, and we walked on.

She turned into the import shop herself, though if I had thought, I would have taken her there. This was not one of the shiny consumer-wise shops for rich tourists and visiting politicians and officers. No, here the people of this inner city bought cheerful eerie unfamiliar trinkets, cloths and baubles to take home and use: hang in windows, use for cooking, cover tables, give to babies, wear for jewellery. How to control xenophobia with consumer principles. She turned over the cheapwares as gently as she would touch something valuable, I imagine: as gently as she would touch me? The thought was insupportable. I turned back out into the sunlight. Behind me I heard her soft-voiced transaction with the merchant. She had a credit card: I heard the machine chitter. When she came out, though her hands were free.

We walked on to a tiny triangular park at the end of the block. There used to be a café there where I liked to sit and read, in the front of a three-storey, ramshackle brick rooming house. Two years ago it had burned half-down and an artist with the city had stripped the brick of leftover plaster, ash and soot. The result was that half the lot was filled with a hollow, airy skeleton of a building; the other half had been turfed-over with hardy grass, and a few benches surrounded a central semicircle of flowers.

She stopped within the semicircle, like a natural actor unconsciously choosing the centre of the spotlight, and, reaching into her pocket, brought out a string of tiny wooden fishes. Concentrating, she separated half the string and handed it to me, careful that her hand did not touch mine, compelling me with her gaze until my hand reached out to receive the gift.

Or, not a gift, an obligation. As if she thought she had to bind me with such an exchange. I was already bound by her black hair, by her anger and my own.

I took the smooth string of tiny carvings, meaning to put them into my pocket without looking. But their texture was so seductive that I glanced down, and the fine-grained wood, bright paint thin enough to let the grain show through, caught my imagination. I brought the ends of the string together and hooked them, completing the circle. Metaphors occurred to me and I twisted my lips into what I think I managed to make into a smile at the last moment.

She watched what I did, and for a moment I though she would do to her own half-necklace the same thing I had done. Instead, she coiled the brightly-painted fishes around her small fingers, put them into her pocket without looking at them, as if putting away a duty.

I had the lack of grace to feel satisfaction.

The health clinic on our left; the Christian mission on our right, gaudy advertising and all. Cheap cafés, shops selling secondhand appliances, and a secondhand car lot. Finally, around the block and back to the Viv.

Not three blocks away from the porno theatre, the young rich still hold their colonised river bank, crowding themselves between the poor people and the view, as if poverty and lack of vision were related. The cars here are not secondhand, the cafés not cheap, the storefronts not filthy with city grime. The awnings are bright, the architecture is deliberately retro, and the colours are refreshed each year.

We walked there too, and I withheld the editorial comment. I could see by her smile that she knew it. I toyed with the fish worry stones in my pocket, and the day seemed very long.

We drove to the far north end of the city, came around the ring-road freeway to the west. I don't like getting out of the car in the burbs, but I took her into one of the sprawling malls, with their apartments and hotels and stores linked in towers and corridors. Myriad and wondrous, I suppose, are the sights we saw. I always find them a depressing part of the time capsule, if necessary for now.

We left the periphery of the mall and came out into patchy sunlight again, blocks away from the corner where I had parked the Vivair. We walked through unlinked housing complexes, old apartment developments, and even past some ancient row housing, half-restored and uninhabited. But everywhere else there were people: parents and nannies walking babies in strollers, young kids on trikes and older ones riding bicycles, and teenagers walking with dataflats and schoolbags.

I don't know why I hate this part of it. It's as if those old builders didn't know when to stop, when they were ahead. They could have taken up satellite cities decades earlier, but they didn't, and we are left living in the impossible sprawl they made. I have tried to fix it, but to fix some things it is necessary to start again. And what would happen to the people who live there, even if they agreed to the change? So my best-loved places have cancer, or so it sometimes seems, and waiting for the lesions to heal from within, putting pressure but losing every direct battle, I am a beleaguered immune system making such slow progress that I show it off only because I have to be fair.

As a consequence of which, as we drove east and then south around the ring route, then cut straight north into the historic preservation zone, to return to the river, I subjected her to as didactic a lecture on urban growth and development over the last four centuries as any I have ever given. Coming back, we were snarled in midday traffic. I swore at an idiotic move another aircar driver made; she looked out the window the other way.

"This is permitted for reasons of nostalgia," I said. I felt far from my city, inside a social studies textbook for backward adolescents. I had managed to suppress some memories, some feelings in order to produce that diatribe—which eventually contained enough truisms to have pleased the censors of both our respective governments. I hadn't said anything I considered completely false, luckily; still, I was starting to dislike myself, the day, and even, thank all the gods and goddesses, her.

She, however, broke into one of my brilliantly vapid sentences unconcernedly.

"There are too many people in this world," she said, her quiet voice sounding almost vicious. Surprised out of my protective cloud, I looked again at the way she was watching the cars, and was even more surprised to see that her face, instead of looking angry, looked sad. Was she really almost crying?

"They don't think so," I said.

"And you?"

"It's not up to me." The traffic cleared away from in front of the Viv suddenly, and I turned down the sweeping hill into the valley, speeding up across the chunky old silver bridge that is the first upstream from the blue span: that's where we were now. Circles and crossings: all very symbolic, I'm sure.

"How noble. Certainly it is. Didn't you ever think of it?"

"Every day I think of it." Turn right, and up again on the other side. Out her side window, the expanse of river valley again in subtly different array, but she had her back to it.

"For goodness' sake, don't fence like that," she said. "You were asked to guide me for a reason; you must know that. Certainly not for your wit."

"I don't care about reasons," I said sharply. "I live here now. I no longer believe in reasons." Sand on the pavement under the Viv grated as I braked. "This is where we are eating."

Once, fiction-writing romantics posited that sushi would become the food of tomorrow, but in reality, when tomorrow arrived there was not enough fish to feed it. The food of today, now, was rice, indeed, but the rest for most people was spices and salt and protein-high meat-substitutes. I remembered my grandmother's story about Soviet citizens, visiting her mother in this same city which was then Canadian, admiring those who could afford meat. I could afford fish.

Taking her to this sushi restaurant was showing off.

As we got out of the Viv and prepared to cross the street, I automatically put my arm behind her, my hand on the small of her back. She stopped instantly and turned to face me, spreading her arms in a warding-off gesture.

"Untouch me!" she said sharply.

I spread my arms in denial, an unconscious echo of her gesture. When I noticed that, I put my hands angrily in my pockets, the left knuckles bruising against those damned fish, and turned to walk on.

"Excuse me," she said. "I had forgotten." A sparrow hopped and picked in the gutter, bronze in the early-evening glow.

"Yes," I said, "you certainly have. I don't see why you would put yourself in the way of it again. You could have stayed safe." In the golden light of the low sun, our shadows went on ahead of us.

"These days there is no safety," she said. We came to the door of the restaurant. Inside the entry there was a 'phone booth. "One moment, please," she said. "I must do a little business."

I let her go in ahead of me, and leaned against the wall of the entry. What business on this world? She could not, as in the old film, call home. Neither could I, but for my own reasons.

She stepped into the booth and I watched her talking to thin air, heard none of it of course, thought I'm sure Aaron would have wanted me to try, and, still angry and reminded of him, I thought that I would tell him tomorrow to forget this experiment. The light glinted on strands of her hair which had over the day escaped their binding. It was not the first time that afternoon that I had thought of combing her hair, restoring its order—or encouraging its disorder. Chaos and information have also been used as metaphors too many times in the last hundred years. The only metaphor I can stomach any more is the city itself: perhaps because it is so blatant, it soothes me instead of causing more pain.

She came out of the booth and we went in to eat. Through dinner she was charming. She knew all the names of the nigiri sushi, and the difference between Tokyo and Osaka styles of eating. Old knowledge. My anger had left my nerve endings very receptive, and watching her lick her fingers, I was back at the beginning (those protective hours in traffic reduced to nothing): taken with her beauty, at a loss as to her character, and deeply suspicious of her purpose here. But I was not going to fight any longer.

When we had finished there was no cheque. She had somehow charmed the owner too, had put her credit card down. Credit indeed. That was twice today. She was showing off too. "How long has it been since you were on Earth?" I asked.

"I don't remember," she said, and turned in through the doorway of a souvenir shop beside the restaurant.

"Come away from here," I said impatiently.

"I may as well see some of the tawdry," she said. "You've overwhelmed me with quality."

And holding up a nasty little statuette, she made a face like its clumsy little face. I had to laugh.

"They have a nice line in spies," I said.

"Spies?" She laughed too, and clowned some more among the shoddy trinkets. The fish chain grew warm from my fingers clenched around it.

In old books the solution would have been to kill her, but that was no solution any more. Another solution would have been to talk until we understood each other. But I have already said that I think I have only one lifetime.

The sun was almost ready to set, a good time to go down to the river, so we walked through the trees, raising dust from the piles of already-fallen leaves as the sunlight came in lower and lower through the varicoloured screen of branches. As the sun began to sink below the horizon, glaring around the superannuated university buildings on the south bank and reflecting from the old glassine towers of downtown, we plunged down the bank on a precipitous path which brought us right to the shore of the river at a gravelly sandbar.

There was still enough light for me to show her how to pick among the chunks of rock there until she found petrified wood, washed into layered definition by the current. The first piece she saw was fine enough to please me with the performance of my home place; the second piece she found, so accidentally that it almost seemed to jump into her hand, was etched with millions-years-old leaf tracery, and layered with the edges of scores of fossil leaves. Except for its grey colour, it was not that different from a section of the muddy leaf litter around our feet.

"Do you take credit for this too?" but her tone was gentle.

"We have been having autumn here for a long time," I said, and she smiled.

We climbed back up to a small plateau to sit, to watch the protracted post-sunset sky-show that is native to this northern land until the last technicolour cloud wisps had faded to grey, the river reflected only grey; and then waited some more until the sky was a vivid dark blue and the first stars showed bright among the dispersing clouds. The moon was rising against the intricate towers of the industrial tangle to the east: no smoke there any more, but worth leaving the structures for the patterns they make in the air.

She took the fastener out of her hair, and combed it until it was in order again, and refastened it, all unconscious, all businesslike, and I held my hands very still, and hoped that maybe she knew nothing about me.

Then we climbed the rest of the way back to the parking area, and for revenge against my tumultuous heart I took her to a play at a small, experimental, uncomfortable theatre whose seats were clones of those in the porno theatre of the morning. The usher here knew me too, but was not burly; rather, he was young and thoroughly insubstantial-looking—though I knew he had written the night's entertainment.

"Who is she?" he whispered when the visitor had found her seat.

"Never mind," I said, but I knew that there would be talk backstage. Usually I am alone.

The play was about Travellers and Visitors. Of course. Because the playwright knew me, it was (possibly) less xenophobic, more subversive than it could have been—but neither Travellers nor Visitors are well-loved these days, no matter what dramatic techniques are considered.

She was silent throughout, at intermission and afterward when the first-night celebration overflowed the lobby, out into the raked garden under the now-clear blue-black sky. Clouds would have made the sky orange-red with reflected light. I wondered if she knew that, or would be here long enough to find out.

I said goodnight to my friends, hugged the playwright again, and saw the woman back into the Vivair, which was beginning to seem like a spaceship, shabby and claustrophobic and fuggy. This time, though, we were only going a few blocks. We had stopped and were out of the car, standing on the leafstrewn grass of a residential boulevard, before she spoke.

"They know you were a Traveller," she said.

"They are not likely to know."

These days everyone knows where the only Travellers worth noting go. And depending on where the notes are made, any admission can be dangerous. That's what the play had been about: it was all wrong of course. Reality was here amidst the orange darkness streetlights bring.

"But you came back for good," she continued.

I looked at her. It was too late to worry about danger as the Travellers in the play had constantly done. Besides, everything happens quietly, even this. We were among quiet houses, except that on one side there was a deep bank of trees. She did not know yet what I had brought her here to show her.

"And I know why," she said.

"Then you are wiser than I am," I said, and behind her, above her, the streetlight went out. It was thirty-four minutes after eleven.

In the dark her moon-dim face moved slowly to look up, and as she did so the lamp began to glow again, dimly.

"Well done," she said.

"It does that every night just at this time," I said. By now the light was glowing with its former lustre. I walked back toward the Vivair. She walked the other way. The street curves there, and I watched her around the corner, then put my feet up on the dash and waited.

"We can go now," she said, sliding into the other seat a few minutes later.

"Find anything?" I asked offhandedly.

"Solitude, that's all. Just what you might expect." The emphasis on the "you" might have been in my attenuated imagination. In the orange bylight, her hair gleamed darkly. Her face she turned away, looked out at the night city as we passed through many streets drifted with falling leaves.

Down another long hill I steered, and above us the skyscraper row of apartments glittered against the sky. The valley at night is dark with parkland and the dark river seems oily and restored to its primitive danger. The bridge we crossed this time has low parapets over which I glanced downstream at the river, while she gazed upstream, still turned, deliberately or not, fully away from me.

We climbed the mirror-similar hill on the south side, and glided onto the long sweeping drive which bounds the university campus on the north.

"Yes, I have been away from the earth," I said.

"Yes?"

"Yes, I came back."

"Yes." As if I had told her something.

Read anything I want into her compliant reticence. If I had taken her home, suggested sex, would she have said as calmly, yes?

"What is it?" she said unexpectedly, and I found her looking at me.

"Nothing," I said. "Never mind. Here is the university."

I was beginning myself to speak in her laconic style. I turned the Viv into one of the small laneways of the campus with a flourish of centrifugal force, and stopped with, shall I say, directness.

"People who are being eaten alive are always attractive," she said, looking not at the graceful Edwardian library but at me. I turned off the Viv, and we got out on opposite sides, like yet another metaphor.

"You had better say what you mean," I said. "Otherwise I'll just think I know, and that's not data."

"I will die of this," she said. "Ambition, fire, return to Earth, gravity and defying gravity, defying everything. So of course you see it in me, and you want me."

"I wanted you before I knew anything," I said, "except that I wanted to take down your hair. Take your calmness away. You say I see fire, I say just beauty."

"You have seen beauty before."

"Not yours. Not there, not so quickly. It's none of my business what's eating you. Ambition? I gave it up. Politics? I gave those up too."

"You say so. Everyone says so."

"I left here. Now I'm back. That's my only proof. Turned into a tour guide for spoiled space travellers."

"Spoiled," she said. "Yes. Hmmm. This must be the Fine Arts Building, they always have these self-conscious murals."

"Everywhere?"

"Everywhere I have been. Artists are the same all over, you know."

"How would I know?"

"You have travelled—been off Earth, you say."

"I was not among artists. I worked."

"So do we."

By that was I to know that she was, or saw herself as, or wanted me to see her as an artist? I didn't ask, deliberately, so she would know I didn't want to know.

"Come on," I said. "I'll show you this tomorrow, when the studios are open."

"If I'm here."

"If, as you say, you are here."

There was one more bridge I wanted to cross with her.

A high black old trestle took us back to the glittering mound of the city core, from lip to lip of the valley without having to dive yet again into, or emerge shaken from, the depths. The crisscross iron webbing gave us glimpses of the moon, the river and the valley if we looked to the side, but ahead, the bridge seemed a long, brightly-lit and vaguely-walled tunnel, leading to a dead end.

Through it toward that imagined imminent collision but emerging unscathed as the road veered to the side to exit, then back into the core on streets near-empty for the midnight, past my office building where her unprompted glance up at my office window only added to the turmoil I felt. Down the long central avenue, east and then northeast until abruptly we were among houses again: old, single-family dwellings which had been converted back and forth from apartments and businesses to dwellings for rich professionals so many times in the last two hundred years that their architecture was rambling and laden with strange tumorous addenda.

I stopped the Viv at the cap of the street, a true dead-end this one, and took her to a view that was the mirror twin of our beginning vista. Where in sunlight the trees with their green, orange and yellow of autumn had been substantial and reassuring, under full moonlight they were dark, dangerous and ephemeral. The river was silvered by the moon and flecked with the reflexions of city lights until its bijou gaiety seemed masklike.

The sky was starry and moon-struck; suddenly a curtain of aurora borealis shot across the south, its lucence coloured green and red like a celestial nocturne of the autumn day, clothing the rising Orion with cold fire.

From the dark residential mass across the river came, suddenly, a gunshot, single and flat and anachronistic. By my watch, its echo marked midnight.

The wind rolled down the valley from the west, edged with the cold of the winter to come. I shivered, put my hands into my pockets. The chain of fishes lay there; they were cold until my fingers' warmth passed through to them. Their mixture of smoothness and angularity was compelling. It seemed that my thoughts and my body were not one, then one as the moon wind shook me and the northern lights performed miracles above. I sighed without wanting to, without meaning. Her voice startled me, real into the mystery.

"It is a beautiful thing you have done, making this whole again," she said, "but it will not work."

"I think it will."

"For that, they must love you."

"They do not know it is me. I do not want them to have to love me to be able to live here."

"You want to be loved simply for being, not for being their salvation. I understand, though I think it is foolish."

"I think it has to be foolish, or it is wrong."

There was more silence, more night. Behind us, a cat called sharply. "I would love you, if I could," she said finally. "But I seem to have no heart left in me."

She looked out at the city. The cold wind had parched my lips, so I had to lick them to speak.

"Let me give you mine," I said.

"Oh, no," she said. "Untalk that nonsense. I know what that is all about. Making yourself feel better, but it does nothing." I did nothing.

"Look," she said, gesturing out at the buildings, their lights patterning the night; "it looks all right, from here."

I couldn't help laughing. "Thank you!" I said, and I took her into my arms. To warm her, and indeed, after a few moments, she stopped shivering.

"I'll take you back to your hotel," I said, but instead we stood silent and quiet then, looking out at the lights both moving and still. We stood still then looking, and the glimmering night went on.

Eco/Logical

Memoirs of the Renaissance

Douglas Fetherling

It was not like it is here because then was different from now. Those of us born in the first generation grew up in areas that had become relatively safe by then but were still full of debris, literally full. Shells of buildings that had long ago been looted of anything that was useful were now full of what wasn't, sometimes 10 or 15 feet deep. Finalists could remember when everything worked and nothing was broken and every place was safe (I don't know which I found hardest to believe). They spent their time trying to make order in one little patch of ruin. That's how they honoured the order they remembered. It was hard for them because suddenly there was only a fraction as many people as there had been before and this made them sad. Everybody they saw reminded them of someone else who was gone. For people my age it meant, I suppose, that though there was plenty of most things about us, the whole accumulated residue of everyone who had lived there before, it was all either broken or unsafe to touch. To answer your question, that's how I became an artist.

I remember well the very day, or think I can. We ate our food from bowls, and one day the last bowl but one got broken somehow. My mother was distraught and lapsed into one of the sad unbearable silences that were, to our young eyes, a characteristic of finalists. In my childish mind, I thought I knew how to cheer her up by replacing what we needed. The sectors where I usually searched turned up nothing, though I spent what seemed like hours climbing over busted furniture, mouldy cloth, all the foul-smelling muck of the old world. Then I began making bowls out of mud and setting them in the sun to harden. When I tried eating from them they returned to mud which I got in my mouth. A finalist saw me and told me that I needed clay and a kiln to bake my pieces of clay in. I don't remember whether he pointed the clay out to me or whether I already knew where it was, but I laboriously dug some red earth from the side of a cliff I knew where the chemo-rains had caused a wall to topple over. It was like fudge when it was wet, but I managed to fashion some crude bowls, a little lopsided I'm sure. Baking them was more difficult. I used a rusty steel drum to make a crude furnace with two openings, one of which I sealed up after placing my precious bowls inside. My garbage fire wasn't hot enough and eventually I had to unseal the hole partway to blow air inside. Then I experimented with other fuels that would burn longer and hotter. In the end I did have something resembling bowls but I had done nothing about a glaze. My mother didn't think I was as brilliant as I thought I was, for she remembered more than I could ever learn. But I had managed to figure out a problem for myself. I suppose it wasn't more than six months later that I used the first kiln to fire clay bricks from which I made a better one.

Sometimes I got sidetracked. I began wondering how I could gather up all the broken pottery that everyone had and melt it down and make new. But the answer eluded me. And though I was able to keep improving my kiln, my clay remained poor despite constant experiments to haul it from other places where it was redder or less red than what I'd begun with. My mother had lost much of her caring by then and used what I made not because it was made by her daughter but because it was there to be used. Most days she ate from my bowls and drank from my cups in silence.

Someone had told me about throwing clay on a wheel. I made a good one right off the bat by drilling a circle of holes in a suitable piece of wood and punching it out, then attaching it to the wheel from a baby carriage I found at the end of a ruined street. With practice this improved the work I was turning out. It was only a question of time until I used the rotating wheel to decorate my bowls and pots, first applying other kinds of clay with my fingers or making designs by dragging pointed objects against the pot, finally by learning glazes too.

I am often asked: Why make something new in a world full of old, some of which can be mended? I say: When the world became small again and the calendar grew thick, we started over at the beginning and had to make discoveries to live.

Anyway, this is how I began. Eventually I made improvements to my tools and acquired more skills. Some of the tricks were painfully simple. Using wire to cut off gobs of clay didn't occur to me for a long time—I'm embarrassed to say just how long. Glazes became an obsession until they threatened to replace the obsession for the pottery itself. What I did steadily became more distinctive, quite unlike what anyone in the standing had seen before. Varying the speed of the wheel was the secret, of course, that let me evolve my own shapes in the dishes and flasks and ash-shrines that became so popular. The making satisfied me only for a short time; the decorating continued to reward me long after I had forgotten a particular piece.

I began taking what I produced to the browse, at first attracting little notice. In the aftermath everything else was broken junk; people weren't used to anything that wasn't broken junk; it was the same situation—the same junk in fact everywhere, in all the standings. In time, however, I began to draw some attention when people recognized the newness, and I got offers of food and clothes and other useful items. It was the decorative motifs people responded to. They would talk about them with me, and I found myself having to put my ideas into words that I found true and that they could understand. An incomer from some ways away offered to take some of my pieces to the browse in a distant standing he was headed for and to swap them there in return for half what he received, and I agreed for by now I was making far more than I could swap among people I knew, and incomers were still rare enough that he might return with objects not known in our standing. And so it went.

I decided that I could do other work just as easily and began painting scenes on our walls with colours and stains I made from different varieties of earth and later from roots and foods. I liked the results at first but soon began to see errors. I was discovering so many mistakes and failed opportunities, in fact, that in looking back much later I could date a picture almost to the day by the primitive condition of my skill that allowed such and such to remain. This was in addition to basic problems I was years in overcoming. At first I had trouble working on a big scale on people's walls (for soon they all wanted theirs decorated too). The junk neighbourhoods were full of pictures, millions of old images that were so familiar to us that our eyes hardly noticed them, and these, I realize now, held me back for a long time, because most of what I had to look at came from the other time and had been made with cameras. In the aftermath no one took camera pictures because they had no film and probably no chemos to develop film. The whole process gradually lapsed. Finalists cherished the photographs they had of the old world until they became creased and faded. The process was lost, the object revered. I had no knowledge but only a respect I didn't, couldn't, fully understand. When I was growing up the custom of using photographs as grave goodies was just beginning, and they very soon became the holiest kind of grave goodies, better than coins or plastic. Which is by way of saying that here again my great discoveries were all so simple that their greatness was in their simplicity and my renown was merely that I was able to rediscover the obvious by thinking back to what the old world had actually been—not the old world as the finalists taught it.

I slowly came to understand how through patches of colour I could create depth. However, it was years before I tried to paint shadow directly. Finalists reacted badly to attempts at shadow, being reminded, I suppose, of the long darkness (there were still traces of it when I was very young). But then that was the dilemma, wasn't it? That what they had lived through made them believe everything was hopeless because the past was gone, but that what my generation hadn't yet endured made us hopeful or at least curious. I covered our walls and other people's walls but comparatively few people saw the results. I sought new surfaces to paint that I could swap at the browse and send by others to be swapped at browses two or three standings distant. This search led me, much to my frustration, to be more a scientist than an artist many days, and with at times the usual abuse scientists are subjected to.

When people ask me about those early days, of how I made my own materials and vanguarded certain techniques, I say, yes, we had to scrounge and improvise and hoard precious supplies. But the rarest commodity, I tell them, the rarest commodity was accurate information. To the degree that people could see beyond their own sorrow or thanksgiving they were eager, almost fanatically driven I'd say, to compare their own lot with that of other people beyond the next standing—and no one really knew how many standings there were or how much bigger the biggest ones might be. "How is it where you are?" became the salutation people gave at the beginning of communications, as when a safe incomer turned up, as a small but growing number did, or when a written message went out, which was rather less often. I wanted to make small things that would say how we were here and other things in which I could imagine how it might be elsewhere, even how it had been beforetimes. I hoped that others would send theirs to me somehow, that images would be exchanged freely. So I knew I would need some means of printing.

Ink was never any problem, oddly enough. I started with some tar diluted and thinned and later I mixed this with berries and juices. The basic idea always worked well enough. I still found it necessary to conduct experiments but these were enjoyable and profitable, though I never knew how long any ink would last and could never get one batch to look exactly like the last. The problem wasn't ink but paper. Old paper, scattered books mostly, was rich. I tried everything I could think of to bleach the pages clean but nothing worked; the paper was so fragile and acidic that I often ended up destroying it instead of repurifying it as I intended. In frustration one day I even tried covering old paper in black ink and drawing over that in white ink I had made from tar and bird droppings. Finally I had to make paper of my own. I knew it could be made from cloth but didn't know how and couldn't find anyone who might once have known. I wasted much effort until I discovered that I needed cotton rags, which weren't easy to come by. The cloth was bound to be very old, but so old, I found, that I could easily enough break it down into pulp by boiling and pounding. Two pieces of screen cut from blind windows of a collapsed house proved the right size when laid one over the other to reduce the size of the pattern by half. I made moulds from splintered crates. Soon I had several people helping me make paper but could never keep up with my own needs and of course could never make two sheets that looked the same even though I was able to regulate the way my paper generally would grip the various inks.

I had almost unlimited amounts of wood and so I began making woodcuts but found it very rough going, for I didn't have the tools (only knives) or the ancient skills. For a while I tried incising the lines of the drawing and leaving the rest of the block in its natural state, to create the opposite of a woodcut, a sort of etching, but the results were thin and strained. Then I discovered linoleum. The fact that there were twenty-five, maybe fifty times more buildings than people to use them was my salvation once more, for old buildings were full of linoleum flooring, filthy, broken and with hardened black glue stuck to the bottom side and perfectly usable once I had ripped up the size I needed and trimmed the edges. It was so plentiful that for once I could afford to ruin many pieces before getting the one I thought suitable. Full of optimism I started making better tools. The most friendly was the simplest: a gouge I created by cutting a length of small diameter copper tubing in half lengthwise, sharpening one end, putting a bone on the other for a handle. How stupid I felt when one summer day I retrieved some linos that I had been drying in the sun after cleaning off the gook with soap and water and discovered how much easier they are to cut when they are warm. Even now I sometimes stumble on the obvious in this manner. It still makes me feel what I remember thinking back then, that pre-finalists must have known everything, even though others call them primitive because of the way they preferred technology to learning.

In any event, I began sending linocuts and paintings and pots out into the world and established some contacts with the small number of others interested in these things. I had the feeling that we had to make great concessions in liking one another and one another's work simply because we were so few. I was always sad when precisely the opposite happened—when because there was so little attention to be divided up we all grew greedy for it and fell to arguing over great distances and hating each other except when word filtered back that one of us had died. I say we because I was just as guilty as the others. Maybe sometimes I was worse. I find it odd that I always got along better with other kinds of artists different from myself.

I was most successful in the case of producing decorations for the votive dancers who came each autumn to all the survival meets and performed many pre-event dances they had heard about but had never really seen. What they did was to make up new dances and call them by the ancient names, just as the religioners did with their own ceremonies. It was queer that despite this common ground the religioners always hated the dancers and in fact hated all the artists, except their favourite little makers of grave goodies who they rewarded with praise. The great spring-up made the religioners more powerful than at any time in the past and they wanted to see art made in their own image. This caused the rest of us years of worry and anger, though today I think all civilised people feel it's natural that we should make most of what we need and make it our own.

This is the message I try to tell students when we gather to pass on our information and show our works. However hard it was for people like me, it was good that it was so hard, for there was little danger that we would ever acquire our information too easily and fall into the habit of satisfying powerful people and not work very hard for ourselves alone. When I was your age, I tell them, I gradually became dissatisfied with the terror of the finalists but I was never bored amid the despair.

The Weighmaster of Flood

Eileen Kernaghan

At exactly quarter to nine Jack Buchan's milk-wagon rattled around the bend. The Weighmaster glanced up at the sun, then pulled his watch from his overall pocket. Every morning for the past twenty-five years Jack Buchan's wagon had reached this weigh-station at a quarter to the hour; and the Weighmaster's watch, which was made before the wars and ran on the sun's energy, had lost not so much as a second since the day he had inherited it from his father, along with his title and his duties. Nonetheless, each morning when the milk-wagon arrived, the Weighmaster consulted first the sun, and then the watch, to be certain everything was in accord; and only then did he wave the wagon towards the scale.

Jack Buchan's gaunt bullock raised its head and shuffled forward. The wagon creaked onto the platform. Deftly, unhurriedly, the Weighmaster slid the counter-weight along the beam.

Jack Buchan waited, tight-mouthed and dour, the reins drooping from his hands. Once, on a blazing August morning, in the days when the Weighmaster was still new at his job, Jack Buchan had asked him to waive the ritual of weighing-in. He was in a hurry, he said; the milk was spoiling; and if the Weighmaster had any doubt, he need only look into the wagon and count the number of cans.

The Weighmaster had not argued. It was not his practice to argue. He was a man of no more than average height, and slightly built, but like his father before him, when he put on his badge he seemed to gain stature and girth. His voice deepened, his spine straightened, and he drew the dignity of his office around him like a greatcoat.

"The Weighmaster's title is to be worn with pride," his father had said. "But never forget it carries obligations with it. To remain at your post in all weathers, to preserve your scale in good order, and to preserve the law. To treat all men alike, whoever they may be...and above all, to let no man question your authority."

On that August morning (it must be ten summers ago, now), the Weighmaster had stood his ground, as once his father had stood his. Jack Buchan had cursed and spat, had sworn that farms would fail and babes would starve on account of the Weighmaster's obstinacy; but in the end he had shrugged his shoulders, and had driven sullenly onto the scales.

Buchan handed the Weighmaster his toll—not milk, which in this heat would sour before supper—but a small hard wedge of cheese. The Weighmaster pocketed the cheese; then he took out his punch and clipped yet another hole in Jack Buchan's stained and battered card.

"See you tonight," he said amiably. Jack Buchan grunted and gathered up the reins. The milk-wagon jolted off towards the bridge.

At noon a donkey-cart approached with half a load of turnips. When the Weighmaster had checked the load and punched it through, the driver tossed him down three or four turnips tied up in a bunch. The Weighmaster examined them glumly. They were the size of crabapples, twisted and gnarled and full of worm-holes. He knew they would be tough as wood inside, and bitter-tasting, like all the turnips he had had this season. Still, Sylvie would be glad of them. Maybe they would do for soup.

There was no traffic to speak of in the afternoon. The Weighmaster used the time to sweep the platform and wipe the morning's accumulation of grey dust from the top of the balance beam. Then he polished all the weights with a soft clean rag. As he worked, he whistled softly. The tunes were ones his father had taught him: The Maid of the Mountain, The Miller and his Lad, John Plowman's Lament.

When he could find nothing else that needed doing, he retired to the shade of an overhanging rock and gazed down into the valley, watching the shadows of the girders lengthen along the river-shore. They reminded him of the spider's web of ditches and canals that had once covered the bottomlands, farther west where the valley widened. In those days the valley was filled with houses and dyked fields and lush green garden plots. The Great Flood had washed them all away, in one huge wave of black, boiling water. Afterwards, no one had had heart or strength to rebuild. The survivors had gathered up their children and had gone away into the hills. There was nothing left, now, but sour swampland, insect-ridden, and clogged with reeds and sallows. Only the Weighmaster's family remained, in their house at the top of the bluff. Soon after the flood the Weighmaster's mother, seeing so much good land going to waste, had tried to make a garden on a patch of ground by the river; but she said the floodwaters must have poisoned the soil, for nothing ever came up.

The bridge was part of the high road, suspended between two bluffs and spanning the narrowest end of the valley. Ever since the Great Flood, it had been in need of repair; but it was a wooden bridge, and there was no longer any timber to be found. The best they could do was to enforce the load limit, and hope that when the girders finally gave way, nobody was caught halfway across. It would be a long slow journey from the hills to the market towns, once the bridge was gone. There was a low road winding down the cliffs into the valley, but the first part of it was steep and dangerous; and where it followed the river-bank much of it was eaten away by marsh. Moreover—as the Weighmaster was fond of reminding people—the next river-crossing was forty miles to the west.

Just before dusk Joe Morgan's two sons arrived with a load of granite boulders, bound for the village of Westmead two valleys away. Their three steep acres grew nothing but thorn-scrub. Stones were the only crop they had to sell.

"You'll never make Westmead tonight," said the Weighmaster, as the stone-boat groaned to a halt.

"Then we'll sleep by the side of the road," said the older son. He was a pleasant youth, cheerful and sweet-tempered, though like so many of the hill-folk simple-minded.

"Not too wise," said the Weighmaster. "These days, they say the Heights are full of bandits."

Both of them grinned. "They're welcome to steal this load," the younger one said, "if they can haul it away. There's plenty more rocks where these came from."

"Good," said the Weighmaster, making a note on his pad. "Because half of them are staying here."

By the time they had unloaded the surplus weight it was almost dark. They paid their toll with a handful of biscuits, so dry and hard they too might have been granite. Though the sight of food made his stomach rumble, the Weighmaster stuffed the biscuits into his pocket beside the cheese, to share with Sylvie later.

He stood in the warm dusk, listening to the creak of timbers as the stone-boat ground its way across the bridge. There would be no more traffic tonight. It was time to go home.

He laid a rug over the balance-beam to keep off the worst of the damp. Then he put his polishing cloth and his broom away in the shed. He had just snapped the lock when he heard the clatter of wheels coming over the hill.

He turned to look, saw a big horse-drawn wagon advancing out of the gloom. He wondered how long it had been on the road; the last draught-horses in these mountains had been dead for fifteen years. The load was covered by a tarp lashed down with cord. It rose in a smooth mound above the siderails.

The driver reined in beside the weighing-platform. He wore a hat of grey leather pulled down over his eyes, and a grey homespun jacket. A lad of about twelve --his son, presumably--sat beside him.

"You're too late," said the Weighmaster. He tried not to let his voice show the irritation he felt. "I've locked up, I'm going home to my supper."

"It's not our fault we were held up," the driver said. "There was a rockslide across the road."

"You'll have to wait till morning," said the Weighmaster. "Even if I were of a mind to open up, it's too dark to read the scales."

"I'll lend you a lamp," the driver said. "And I don't mind making it worth your while."

The Weighmaster waited. "Eggs," said the driver. "Fresh eggs, from my own hens." The words hung seductively between them.

To his shame, the Weighmaster felt his mouth watering. How Sylvie would squeal with delight, if he brought her eggs—real eggs, from proper chickens.

"Show me," the Weighmaster said.

There were half a dozen of them, small thin-shelled pullet's eggs, each one nested in its own bed of tree-cotton to protect it from the shocks of the road.

"Four for you," said the driver. "That's twice the usual, seeing as I'm keeping you overtime."

"That's fair," agreed the Weighmaster, imagining those eggs lying white and gold and ever-so-slightly crisp at the edges in Sylvie's big cast-iron pan; and he went to uncover the scales.

"You're pushing the limit," he told the driver. "Another kilo and I'd have to turn you back." He did not inquire what the load was, that made the wagon rest so heavily on its wheels. That was not his business, so long as the limit was observed.

"This is not a road I'd want to travel in the dark," the Weighmaster remarked as he punched the card.

"I've seen worse," the man said. He rattled the reins. "Anyway, I'll take it slow, and the lad will walk out in front with the lamp."

The Weighmaster watched as the darkness swallowed them; when the timbers had stopped squeaking and everything was quiet again, he covered the scale and went home.

***

"Oil to waste for lamp-fuel," said Sylvie, marvelling. "And trees..." She stroked a wad of the cotton, snatched from their predatory she-goat, Alice, in the nick of time. "Well, there's no way he could have come from anywhere around here."

"No," said the Weighmaster. He watched her eat her egg in small careful bites, making it last as long as she could. She had been thin in a limber, willowy kind of way when he married her; now her flesh was pared down to the bone, and she looked starved, haggard, too old for her thirty years. If only he could bring her eggs every day of the week, instead of turnips, hard biscuits, handfuls of millet.

"Maybe in distant parts, things are getting better. Did he look like a man who came from a long way off?"

"Very like," said the Weighmaster, thinking of the horses; and remembering that the man's clothes had been cut in a different fashion from any he had seen before.

"You must ask him, when he comes back over the bridge. You must ask him where he comes from."

"Why should I ask him that?"

"Because it sounds like a good place, with trees and chickens and horses, and oil for lamps. Surely they would have plenty of cows as well, in such a place."

He should have guessed at once where this conversation was leading. She hungered for a child, his poor Sylvie, as other folk hungered for meat. Sometimes children rode with the wagons to the weigh-station, and she would come out of the house to stare at them, with such terrible greed in her eyes that he felt sad and ashamed.

"You know we must stay at Flood," he said. He spoke gently, reasonably. "A Weighmaster cannot leave his post."

She stared at him across the table, twisting the cotton in her fingers. He knew what was in her mind, that he was not married to his office, that another man could be Weighmaster in his place. He knew also that she would not speak these thoughts aloud.

"Then we can raise the child here," she told him.

He stared at her.

She smiled, and put her hands on her concave belly.

Sorrow welled up in him. "Sylvie, how long?"

Proudly she held up four fingers. "Nearly a month," she said.

"This is a great foolishness, Sylvie. How can we feed a child? Look at you, your breasts are no bigger than a child's, and Alice is old, she gives us scarcely enough milk for our porridge..."

She was not listening. How often had she heard these arguments before?

"I am strong," she said. "The milk will come. Other women in these valleys have had children, and they have managed to suckle them."

"And have you seen those children, Sylvie? Undersized and sickly; simple-minded, most of them, with twisted limbs, and tumours, and all manner of deformities. It's true what they say, the blight on the grain has blighted our seed as well."

Stubbornly, she shook her head. "It's the river water," she said. "We must not drink any more water from the river. I will go up into the hills and find a spring."

He had to smile at that. "And where do you think the river comes from?" But she paid no heed.

***

Next day the man in grey returned. In daylight, the Weighmaster could see that though the horses were swaybacked and underfed, the boy who rode beside the driver was straight-limbed, firm-fleshed, with healthy colour in his face. Maybe Sylvie was right, the Weighmaster told himself. Maybe there was a far-off place where the curse on the grain was lifted. Maybe where this man and his son came from, the ears of the corn and the udders of the cows were full, and children thrived.

"A safe trip?" he asked the man in the grey hat.

"Safe enough."

"And a good market?"

The man's eyes were grey as well—a cold dark grey, like river-stones. They studied the Weighmaster carefully from under the pulled-down brim.

"Good enough."

The Weighmaster decided to press his luck. "Things are looking up, then, in your part of the country?"

"I have no complaints, friend," said the man. "No complaints." And he rattled the reins and moved off.

***

At the end of July the man in grey returned. The load was heavier this time—the Weighmaster could see the horses straining as they came up the rise just in front of the weigh-station.

He doublechecked the scale, then showed the man the numbers he had written on the pad. "Barely under the wire," he said.

"But under it, all the same."

"This time," said the Weighmaster. He punched the card.

"I'll be on my way, then," the man said. He dropped a small grain-sack at the Weighmaster's feet.

When the wagon had gone, the Weighmaster opened the bag. It was buckwheat—a change from their everlasting diet of millet. Sylvie should be pleased.

He could no longer deny the fact of Sylvie's pregnancy. Though she was thinner than ever, her stomach made a small round bulge under her skirt. For two months she had been violently ill each morning; now, suddenly, she was ravenous.

Sylvie shooed Alice away from the sack of buckwheat and locked it in the cupboard. She did not look as pleased as the Weighmaster had hoped.

"That's all?"

"It's all I was due. You can't expect eggs every time, my girl."

"Those who have more, should be made to pay more," she said.

"And let the Murphy boys go free?"

"Why not?" She sounded angry—his mild-tempered, patient Sylvie, who never raised her voice, except sometimes to Alice. "Anyway, next time this man comes back, you must ask for something better than buckwheat. I need eggs, and lentils, and fruit, too, if the baby is to grow strong."

"When have any of us seen fruit?" he asked, trying hard to keep his patience.

"This grey man of yours will have fruit. Maybe that is what he has in his wagon."

"More likely a great many sacks of buckwheat," said the Weighmaster. "But if he comes again, I will ask."

***

It was early autumn when the grey man returned—a hot, clear September morning. Perfect harvest weather, in this country where crops no longer grew.

The Weighmaster choked down his pride. "My wife's expecting," he explained to the grey man. "I'd be much obliged if you had any eggs, or fruit, or something nourishing of that sort."

"Sorry, nothing of that sort," said the man. "But seeing as how you're expecting a young one, I could let you have an extra sack of wheat."

"I'd be obliged," said the Weighmaster, with a sinking heart.

"Safe journey," he said, as the horses moved off. But just this side of the bridge he saw the wagon draw off to the side of the road. In a few minutes the driver was back at the weigh-station, on foot, and scowling.

"One of the traces broke," said the grey man. "Is there a harness-mender hereabouts?"

"There's old Higgins, over in the next valley. But it's a ten-mile ride."

"Will you keep an eye on my load?" asked the grey man.

The Weighmaster nodded.

"I'll be back as quick as I can," said the man. He unharnessed the horses, and watered them in the trough beside the weigh-station shed. Then he and the boy and the horses plodded off into the hills.

By suppertime they had not returned.

"Old Higgins won't mend that trace in an afternoon," said the Weighmaster. "They'll be lucky to be on their way by tomorrow midday."

Sylvie wet her finger and picked up a last crumb of wheat-cake. Then she pushed herself back from the table and stood splayfooted, belly thrust out, tying a scarf around her head.

"Where are you going?" asked the Weighmaster.

"Out to look at this wagon I've heard so much about. What better chance?"

"I'll come with you," said the Weighmaster anxiously. She was full of strange notions these days; there was no guessing what foolishness she might take into her head.

"What do you really think is in there?" asked Sylvie. She prodded the tarp where it bulged above the siderails. The Weighmaster seized her hand and pulled it back.

"I told you. Buckwheat. Or millet."

"We'll never know till we look. What if he's carrying apples, or cheeses, or cabbages?"

"It's none of my business what he's carrying," said the Weighmaster. "So long as it's not overweight."

"But suppose he's carrying apples, and pays you in buckwheat?"

"Food's food," said the Weighmaster. "Now come into the house, there's a good lass. You've seen all you're going to."

He heard the sudden sharp intake of her breath, and thought the babe had kicked her. But then she whispered, "Look, there under the wheels."

He crouched and peered under the wagon, seeing first the dark patch of damp spreading across the ground, and then the slow drip of water from the floorboards. Sylvie was on her knees beside him, catching the drip in her outstretched palm.

"It's cold," she said softly. "It's ice-water. Tom, there's ice in the wagon."

He understood, all at once, why the load was so heavy. Sylvie was on her feet now, staring down at him.

"Meat," she said. "He is carrying meat, and he has not paid his proper toll. Tom, it is not fair, you must tell him to pay us in meat. You must think of the child."

"Next time," he said. "Next time, Sylvie. Remember, this time he has already paid."

"Promise?" she said. "For the child's sake?"

He nodded. "For the child," he agreed.

***

On a bleak November morning the man in grey returned. The horses, breath smoking, plodded patiently over the rimed stones; the man and the boy huddled together on the seat, sharing a single ragged blanket.

"Cold journey?" said the Weighmaster.

"Cold and hard," said the grey man. "I'll be thankful to see my own hearth."

The Weighmaster slid the weights along the beam. The metal was searing cold on his gloveless hands. He shook his head. "Twenty kilos too heavy," he said apologetically.

The man jumped down from his seat and came to look for himself.

"Twenty kilos? You would turn me back for that?"

"Yes," said the Weighmaster. "The law is the law."

"Whose law? Not mine."

The Weighmaster was sorely tempted to reply, "The Law of Gravity," but he thought better of it. He must maintain his dignity at all costs.

"If I let you go on, and the bridge collapses, everyone will suffer," he pointed out.

"I have treated you fair," said the grey man. "You can't argue that."

Sylvie would have argued, and loudly, thought the Weighmaster; but it was not his place to do so. "Yes," he said. "You've treated me fair. And I'm treating you fair. Over the limit, and you must dump the extra weight, or turn around and go back."

"I can't afford to dump twenty kilos," said the grey man. "And in this weather, on these roads, you tell me to turn back?"

"One or the other," said the Weighmaster. "I can't check you through."

"Can you stop me, little man? Supposing I just pick up the reins and drive right over you?"

"You wouldn't want to do that," said the Weighmaster quietly. As he spoke he reached under his winter coat and drew out his pistol. There had been no bullets in it since his father's time, but the grey man was not likely to know that.

The man looked at him with his cold grey eyes, weighing the situation. Finally he said, "I'll tell you what's fair. Let me pass, and I'll split the difference with you. Ten kilos for me, and ten for you."

Under the shrill keening of the winter wind, the Weighmaster thought he heard his father's voice. "Remember your obligations," the voice said. "Treat all men alike, let no man question your authority. And above all, preserve the law." And at the same moment he heard Sylvie speak, clear and loud as though she were standing beside him. "Think of the child," she said. Her voice was not soft and compliant as it had once been, but harsh and urgent-sounding. He thought of her gaunt, exhausted face, drained of the last vestiges of color by the fierce imperatives of the womb.

"Yes," said the Weighmaster. "Ten kilos for you, and ten for me. That's fair."

***

The Weighmaster threw the sack over his shoulder and headed back to the house. The contents were frozen hard, and seemed heavier than ten kilos. He pushed open the door, and in the close, dark kitchen, smelling of boiled grain and dung-smoke, he dropped the sack at Sylvie's feet.

Hands trembling with excitement, she untied the cord and reached inside. Then he heard her scream, again and again, as though a knife had been thrust into her heart.

And he ran to pry from her rigid fingers the small cold perfectly fashioned limb, with its five perfect tiny nails.

What Mrs Felton Knew

Timothy Findley

On October the sixteenth a car pulled onto the shoulder of the road at about 10:45 a.m.

The driver was a man called Green, and beside him sat his wife and two-year-old daughter. In the back seat of the car, his mother, his father, and his aunt lay asleep and his four-year-old son was stretched out across their knees.

The car could be described as beige, the colour of dust. The license plates were black, and the chrome of the fenders had worn away. It was the sort of motorcar you would call "serviceable"—but little else.

Neither of the children stirred or showed any sign of life, but Mrs Green was partially awake and she said, without opening her eyes, "Where are we now?"

Mr Green said, "This road is called the eleventh concession road of Horace Township but I can't tell you what county we're in."

And she said, "Oh. But I had a dream and I thought we were climbing." It was at this point that she opened her eyes. "We're not alone," she said. "There's a house right there."

"Yes," said Mr Green. "I've been looking at it. Wondering."

"Wondering what, Harry? What?"

"It looks lived in."

"Yes, it does," said his wife, "and there are flowers in the garden too."

"Those are Scarlet Runners," said Mr Green. "Not flowers. Beans."

"Do you think ...?" said Mrs Green.

"I am thinking," he said. "I am. Be quiet."

Mrs Green watched him as he thought. Her eyes were a dusty colour and for some reason she had no eyelashes and no eyebrows. She was thirty. There was a sore on her hand. She was afraid to comb her hair. Her nostrils and the roof of her mouth were in constant pain. And she touched her daughter but her daughter did not wake.

"The children are hungry." She whispered automatically.

"Be quiet, Verna," said Mr Green. "Just be quiet."

"But Harry. A house. Red Runners. A rocking chair, for Christ's sake!"

"I know it. I know. I'm thinking."

They both sat quiet and listened.

A dog barked and Verna Green caught her breath.

"A dog, Harry. Oh, God—a dog ..."

Mrs Green gave a frantic look through the windows. They did not want a dog to find them. A dog could be very dangerous. Two weeks ago they had found a car by the side of a road with its doors standing open and three dogs...

"Get that out of your head," said Mr Green. "Right now. This instant. Quit it."

"I'm sorry."

"Roll up the windows. Forget it. That isn't going to happen. To us."

"Yes, Harry. I know it. All right. I'm fine."

She watched him carefully. His eyes, like her own, looked terrible. His hands shook involuntarily. She wanted to touch him, to calm him, to calm herself—to let him know, irrevocably, that she was right there with him, but she knew that they mustn't touch. That much she remembered. That much she knew.

Outside, the weather was calm and warm and brilliant. The sunshine hurt them, but it was beautiful if you squinted to see it. The road they had pulled onto rose and fell before them in a straight line, passing over hills and valleys with farms down either side.

"It's a little like our own road was," said Verna. "And our own farm. Eh?"

He didn't answer.

Instead he tried to glance at his parents, aunt, and son in the back of the car. He had to use the rear-view mirror to see them because he could not turn around. They were gray-coloured and he was not certain this was because of fatigue. He thought of trying to force his way into some town.

And then there was an old man all of a sudden standing with a dog on the lawn across the road.

"We'll have to move on now," said Harry.

"No," said Verna. "He has the dog on a rope. Wait and see what he does."

The old man, whose name was Turvey, stared at the Greens and the Greens stared back.

"Shouldn't we speak to him?" Verna asked. "Please? He looks so nice and quiet over there."

"Don't open the window," said Harry. "The dog might smell us."

"But I'm not afraid any more," she said. "The dog is on a rope."

"That man might let go of the rope. Do as you're told and leave the window alone."

"But Harry—the *children*. Move on? Jesus! Move? There are *beans* over there..."

"Look at the children," said Harry. "Look at them."

She did. "But Harry—please—moving on is crazy anyway."

"Look out the window. At that man."

"He's a nice old man is all ..."

"Look at him. He knows what we are."

Verna stared and knew that her husband was right. The old man had bitten off the look of compassion in his eyes and his lips were set with that awful resignation everyone knew about now. It was second nature to read this look and never to have to hear the words "get out—I can't help you—I want to but I can't." You just considered all that said and moved on.

"Should we wave at him to say we understand?" said Verna.

"No. He knows we understand. See? He's trying to find the right things to say ... so—we'll just go. Are you with me? *Shall* we leave?"

"Yes, Harry. All right. Yes. we'll leave. I love you." She looked down at the pale head in her lap. "If I was still a mother—but I'm not. So we can go..."

Harry Green looked at his wife. He broke the rule and touched her. "You mustn't cry," he said. "You'll hurt yourself so bad."

"I can't help it," said Verna. "After all, my god, I'm still human—whatever they say."

She held their child and Harry started the car and they began to leave.

The old man across the road raised his hand and Harry nodded.

"The old man saluted us," he said to Verna.

"Yes," said Verna, "I saw him. He was a nice man. He understood."

"Yes," said Harry and they were driving now, back on the highway, with their eyes out for the tanker trucks or any other signs of danger.

"Did you notice," said Verna, "the church at that corner? Across from where the old man lived?"

"No," said Harry. "I didn't."

"Well, yes. There was a church. There really was. Isn't that just crazy?"

Driving faster, Harry said yes, that it was crazy, and Verna held on tighter to the body in her lap.

"I wonder," she said, "if it's going to happen to them. There, on that road."

"Of course it will," said Harry. "It only takes time."

Better they should kill themselves now, she thought. But I mustn't say that. And I won't.

They just drove.

And the next day was Sunday.

The first sign that it was happening to them, that it was their turn, came late on that Sunday evening.

An airplane flew over.

But not everyone was quick enough to leave.

Only Arthur King arose before first light on that Monday morning to set his remaining animals free in the valley. By four-thirty, rigid with silence, he had completed loading their truck with supplies and necessities and his wife had roused the children from the last ignorance of sleep.

At sunrise there was the putt of a motor. No one had spoken yet. Not even a child. Arthur and his wife gazed with stoic regret upon all that they left behind them—house and happiness, land and animals, and then, with their children beside them, they clambered into the cab of the truck and went away.

They did not say good-bye to their neighbors, knowing that whoever was left behind would understand their leaving and, hopefully, do likewise. At once.

The eleventh concession was exactly two-and-a-half miles long, corner to corner, and the Kings' farm was located more or less centrally. All told, there were six farms and up west, near the highway, the abandoned church. Right by the highway you could not really say there was a *farm*, but there was a small house and two acres and old man Turvey.

Perhaps Turvey was a Mennonite, because his house was unpainted shingle and on a day of winter sunshine it shone silver with age like a grey mirror in the snow. Turvey had only the dog—no wife, no children, and very little identity. No one ever saw him except on summer mornings when he would sit on his small green lawn, scratching the head of his dog. By late autumn, man and dog had retired into the house and did not emerge till spring. Like everyone else, Turvey had been dispossessed of radio, television, and telephone, but unlike everyone else, he did not fall back on gossip for news. People said that of all those allowed to live along the road, only Turvey had found the Secret of Life—which was silence. For all speech had become synonymous with Fear.

Moving east, then, from the old man and the church, you came to the Jewell place, Kings', and Feltons'. Past Feltons' there was a breach of wilderness which was cut by the river. On the west bank of the river were the Cormans, and beyond them on the other side of the road, was Barney Lambert. By Lambert's the road turned and was gone. It disappeared townward into the trees.

Monday at noon, the childless Jewells got into their station wagons and went away, leaving their farm to the whisper of mice—and there remained then only the Feltons, Cormans (by the river), and Barney Lambert—plus old Turvey.

At 2:00 p.m., Monday, the second airplane flew over. It cut a few high white lines into the sky and departed without making its presence more than obliquely obvious. It was there; it was gone. Its meaning remained a question.

Harvey Felton phoned Joe Corman and said, "Well, are you staying?" and Joe Corman said, "Yes, until we're absolutely certain."

But Felton was feeling more than mere apprehension now because his neighbors, the Kings, had already left. Through binoculars there was something very unnerving about their barn door standing wide open like that, and the horses gone and the cows gone and only the cat wandering lost and sitting silently magnified at the back door of the King house, which did not and would never again open for it.

So, at four o'clock, Harvey Felton, his wife and two sons got into their truck and drove down the road to the Cormans'. One boy sat between them and Mrs Felton held the other on her lap. As they went along, Kate Felton stared quietly at the annual tragedy of the falling leaves and thought: this is so natural. It's natural. Why can't they just leave us alone with what's natural like this?

Joe Corman's house was particularly small, so the two families, replete with babies and dogs, held their meeting on the bridge, while the children threw stones into the water.

Felton had long, rustic bones and gray skin—except on his face, where the bones were feminine small and the skin remarkably pink. He had great thick fingers whose dried, cracked skin had not been flesh-coloured since he'd ceased, at twelve, to be a schoolchild—and standing on the bridge he kept trying to jam these fingers down the closed collar of his denim shirt, or into the belt loops of his pants, or, fisted together, into his armpits. To no avail.

It couldn't ever be right to leave, Felton's erratic posture seemed to say. It was wrong. No matter what the Government said, or how many licences they issued or denied, these people had always been here—always—all of them—for generations impossible to tell—and it didn't matter that they *should* leave or that they *must*, according to law—it was just wrong, and he simply could not get over that. He could not reason any more and his wife became afraid.

Mrs Corman, so large that she was semi-invalid, was not afraid but she was curious. She stacked her bulk against the stone abutment of the bridge and watched the laconic animation of the men and the stilled, waiting face of the only other woman—Kate Felton. Mrs Corman cleaned her fingernails with an old guitar pick of her son's, but Mrs Felton was pale and catatonic with a blanket thrown over her emotions.

Mrs Corman felt so sorry for Kate Felton that it was difficult to watch her and to stand so close to her. Stay or go. She herself was relatively relaxed in the knowledge that her own husband could make up his mind to act on a set decision. But poor Kate was caught in a terrific panic of wanting to go *now*—of having to get out clean without the delay of debate—even without the delay of thought—but her husband, Harvey, just stared with a reminiscent eye into the sliding water, not knowing what to do. Afraid to stay, fearful of going, Harvey Felton was beyond being able to save his wife and children—and Mrs Corman knew it. She wanted to say so, but it was not her place to speak. A family was a family; you simply didn't interfere.

She could not quite hear the voices of the men and she could no longer bear to look at Kate, so she turned away and looked back at her own beloved house—semi-lost among the trees by the river. We've lived here all our lives, she thought. Joe laid that shingle only last May, and I planted the bulbs on Thursday. Why, they renewed our licence in July! So why won't they let us stay here now? And what'll we do with the dog?

At five, the E.R.A. Forestry Siren began to wail on the outskirts of town and the meeting on the bridge broke up. If another plane came that night, it was decided, or if there was even a hint of tanker trucks on the highway, then the Cormans would leave. But if there were no plane and no activity on the road, then they would be satisfied that it was not happening yet and they would stay. For a while. Until it did.

Still, Harvey Felton went home from their meeting not knowing.

And it happened.

At 3:10 a.m. a helicopter stuttered through the night and was above the road for at least fifteen minutes before it finally departed. The Cormans had lain awake and now they began to rise and dress, knowing exactly what to do. They started in to fill the back of their truck and both the men, father and son, went down to set the livestock loose.

Up at the Feltons', Harvey heard the helicopter and sighed and got out of bed and went into the bathroom and locked the door. He was thinking that if he could be alone, with just the lightbulb and the mirrors and the mesmeric glitter of being bathed and warmed and steamed in memory—if he could just sink into this roomful of pleasures, womb-like, with the comfort of water—if he could only stay there a moment—an hour—he would be safe. Perhaps he could even gain admission to his courage, if he could be alone with the sanity of the past.

But Kate got up and hadn't slept either and went down the hall to the door and stood there scratching at it lightly so as not to wake the children. And she wanted to get in, through to him, but he would not let her and so she stood there (leaning, really), whispering through the door but thinking that she was shouting, until at last she lost her voice. And when all she got was a stammered protraction of Harvey's indecision of the afternoon (in fact, she thought, of all his life), she wandered from the door so quietly that he was not aware she'd left.

The Arthur Kings being gone, there were no immediate neighbours to hear her when she fired a gun, point-blank, into the temples of each of her sleeping sons. Or when she prayed and turned the thing into her own mouth without amen because she didn't want time to think about conclusions or how you came to them. She simply pulled the trigger and the whole thing was over.

For her.

So, at about five-o'clock, when Harvey Felton rode away on the back of Joe Corman's pick-up truck, his feet dangled bare from his long-boned legs, and one hand was over his face. He hadn't even dressed, and as if to fortify his reason, he'd gone over to Kings' in just his pajamas, and had brought along the abandoned cat when he'd walked down the road to the bridge.

Neither Joe nor Joe junior spoke of the blood that covered him, and because of it, no one asked after his wife and his sons. In her mind, little Nella Corman was certain that Harvey had committed murder, but Mrs Corman, having taken her private look at Kate on the bridge the previous afternoon, merely sighed and tried to remember whether they had brought with them their own guns. And saw that yes, they had.

Barney Lambert's wife was many years dead and his daughter had some time ago been accepted for Government-approved marriage in the City. So he lived alone.

Barney had set the expression on his face the day his wife died and no one had seen it alter since. It was not a dour expression, or even sad. It was just set and there was never animation.

But he was liked. His eyes showed you his whole life and sometimes yours, too, as you stood talking to him. Through his silence he could make the wisdom or the foolishness of what you said apparent. For a man who did so much listening, he had remarkably small ears, and when he was in his twenties and thirties, people had regarded him as the best-looking, the most athletic, and the kindest young man in the district. He had married Ethel Felton, a cousin of Harvey's. But that was all a long time ago, before you had to have a licence to live, and Barney was fifty-two years old now, living on remembrance.

When his daughter met and married her man and was given her clearance to live in the City and was gone, Barney closed the gates down by the road and without ill will of any kind, just removed himself from the people around him and became inaccessible. But he remained all that he had been—kindly, intelligent, friendly if met—and silent. He took to cultivating cabbages (a difficult crop) and to raising a menagerie of animals culled from their world without any apparent thought for their usefulness to him. Only of his usefulness to them. He had three burros, a mule, two goats, a cow, three Canada geese, and a dog. In the house he kept a cat and another dog who was too old to get around.

He lived a plain life within a certain discipline that was neither rigid nor lax. He was aware of time but never ran to do anything. He was not a paragon of tidiness, but he never threw a paper or a pillow on the floor.

Barney had heard all that was going on—the aircraft, the various leave-takings, and the E.R.A. Forestry Siren. When the Cormans drove by from the river on the Tuesday morning, Barney was watching from the upstairs windows of his house, moving from room to room to see them out of sight. He noted the posture of Harvey Felton as he slumped there, holding the cat and his own face, and he remembered his own grief and he knew, more or less, what had happened to Kate Felton, and maybe to the boys, too. Barney had ceased at about the same time as everyone else to be aware that there was a God, and so he did not pray, even mentally, for these would-be survivors. A few women could tolerate prayers, but men could not, and children were alarmed by the ridiculous posture of prayer and by the closed eyes and the silent, moving lips. Still, Barney had respect and awe for something and that something was Nature and so, when he saw his neighbors depart and one of them was in grief, he slapped his thighs with the palms of his hands and gave the Universal sigh.

Then he went down to the kitchen where the old dog was asleep under the stove, and he lit the fire to make coffee.

Five-thirty, and a pale, high light beyond the windows.

Barney went outside and remembered where the wheelbarrow was and brought it round to the back door. It was a sizeable barrow of the kind used for carrying manure—not one of those small, neat, garden types, but large and serviceable. He piled blankets and two pillows into it and then went back.

He got out a cardboard carton and a can opener and filled the carton with tinned and bottled food and put the can opener in his pocket. He filled two five-gallon tins with water. Then he stuck toilet paper and a First Aid Kit under his elbows and lifted the carton and carried it outside. He came back for the water and out again, and then back again.

At last, about 6:00 a.m., he sat down to smoke a cigarette and to drink coffee and he tried most of all not to look around the room he was in, and not to want to get up and go through the house, memory by memory. He wanted everything to be as it was now in his mind, even if he remembered it wrong, without the pain of refreshment. So he sat still and squinted at the cup and at his hands and at the cigarette. He did not even look at the table top. He just thought about right now and he saw only what was right there.

There was, however, one very bad moment when the sun made it absolutely all the way over the horizon and had ceased being red or orange or any other colour and was just light—and Barney felt a terrific urge to put his head down and hide. He did then, for one faltered second, give his glance to the rifle in the corner and his mind to the box of bullets in the drawer. But he got out of it by standing up. His pride reminded him that his child had been accepted into Civic Society, that one of them at least had made it and that he could make it, too, if he tried.

He took a spoonful of honey and ate it and another spoonful which he carried over carefully to the old dog.

"Come on," he said, "it's time to wake up now. And go."

And he got to his knees and the old dog, still lying down, licked the spoon clean, and then Barney put the spoon down on the floor and left it there forever—and pulled the dog's box out from under the stove and soothed the old dog with a litany of hums and haws and lifted him up so that the old dog's head could rest against his neck and he walked out of the house and laid the old dog very carefully in the barrow on the blankets and pillows and surrounded him with the tinned water and the boxed food and the toilet paper and the First Aid Kit and, at the very last, the cat—and they set off toward the barn.

And all the while the E.R.A. Siren screamed at the edge of the town: This is the End. This is the End. This is the End.

In some instances there were spectators, but this depended on the season and on the direction of the wind. It also depended upon the availability of masks and on whether the event took place on a weekday or on a weekend.

Civic people, rich in safety, could afford to watch from the privacy of the air, and there were usually a few groups of trainees who went up, too, in University helicopters, but as with all such things, Time creates tolerance and even boredom and on this particular day the only people who were by were there to work.

You may wonder what the townspeople made of all this, and probably question the morality of their silence, because they were so close to these events and even neighbours of the victims. But they were neighbours only in the tactical sense. In fact, they formed a bulwark—a wall of protective innocence—between the City-dwellers and the Rural Expendable. The townspeople smiled among themselves and nodded at the sounding of the E.R.A. Forestry Siren and said things like "Goodness, another fire" or "When will it ever end?" and they went inside on these days and closed and locked their doors and pretended through the following weeks that they did not smell or see or hear what patently they did—what certainly they had to. They were particularly adept at going blind.

Barney went down the lane unnoticed and got to the barn and opened the doors.

He had known all along that when the time came he would not leave his animals, as most people had, so there was an air of well-rehearsed ritual to all that he did. His plan was to get as deep into the swamp in the valley as possible, and thereby to try for temporary survival, at least. If he could save himself or even one of his animals, then his protest would register with Nature, which was all that mattered to him.

Barney hitched the mule to the wagon and transferred the contents of the barrow onto the wide, long planks, together with several bales of hay, three bags of feed, and the cage with the three geese. The old dog lay trustful and quiet on the nest of blankets and the stable dog got up on the seat beside where Barney would sit. The cat dug a hole in the barnyard and relieved itself and afterwards leapt up beside the old dog and lay down to stare at the geese.

It was at this point that Barney remembered his sheepskin coat and knowing that without it he might perish in the cold of the swamp he went all the way back to the house to get it.

When he got into the house the echo of the opening door leaked into distant emptiness upstairs like a prowling animal and Barney closed his eyes and waited for the silence to return.

But it didn't.

A new sound shied in behind him and beyond him and it came from so far away that he could at first only imagine that he heard it.

Trucks.

Tankers.

The highway.

Barney gained his composure by remembering anger.

They were coming now and he was to be the next victim of the new E.R.A.

And so he went very calmly into the back hall and got down his sheepskin coat from its peg and put it on—for all that it seemed to be a summer's day—and he took his binoculars and went onto the road to see what he could see.

In his mind he practised the moment when he must leave the road and run to the barn in order to save the animals and then he sat down on a large rock near the gate and watched, through the binoculars, the distant end of the road where there was a hill beyond which you could not see the deadly highway.

He wondered if Turvey and his *old* dog had got away. And he thought not. He wondered if he could get the beautiful old church into his mind, but, along with God, he couldn't. He thought of Myrna Jewell's chickens and what might have become of them and of Arthur King as a boy when they were both boys and he tried to get by the Feltons' house in his mind, without going inside, but he kept thinking that he knew Harvey too well and too long not to guess at what had happened and for the first time since she'd died, he blessed his own wife's death as a prize of good fortune that she should not have had to face this moment now because she might have had to do what he instinctively sensed poor Kate had done.

And then he was able to take a real look through the glasses at the Cormans' new roof and to go along by the lenses into their barnyard and to see there some stupid cow who'd come back from the swamp in the valley and he wavered on the brink of going over with the gun to drive her off or to kill her but there wasn't time.

The E.R.A. Forestry Siren gave another earnest wail at the moment, rising into a steady blast—a wail that would continue into the night and perhaps even into the next day depending on whether it rained or not and on whether a wind rose or not and on whether anyone was seen along the road.

It was not until rehearsing that sequence in his mind, as he sat there waiting and listening to the siren that Barney knew he was going to let himself be seen.

He was going to do what perhaps no one else had done till now. He was going to force a pair of eyes to look into his own. Someone had to *see* someone.

The incongruous sun blazed down and Barney loosened the sheepskin coat around him, lit another cigarette, and gave a look through the glasses at his own barnyard.

All was quiet. The dogs and the cat and even the geese seemed to sleep and the other animals just waited as if they must know, and had trusted that he would do this. He smiled. He would do it. He would start a conscience. Somehow. In someone. Right here. On this road.

There was no wind at all—not even a breeze—and it was so clear that when the first sign that the tankers were in operation came to him, it was in the thought that the sky was filling with beautiful great clouds and that he might be saved by rain.

But the sweeping hiss of the distant hoses cut that hope short before it was real.

They were spraying.

Barney tried not to, but could not avoid rising to his feet. Instinctively he threw down his cigarette, stood up, and began to breathe great gulps of the last pure air. He felt dizzy, both from fear and from too much sudden oxygen. He fought back the temptation of paralysis which wanted to conquer him. The end of the road was alive.

Great swaying flowers of spray arched into the blue, topped with a rolling flood of cloud.

This was what they called E.R.A.—or, to give the solvent its soothing Administration name: "Environmental Redevelopment Agent." Sprayed from hoses, its crystal drops burned the oxygen from the air, killing every single living thing within the circumference of their fall. It wasn't rain it formed—it was beautiful snowy mist. And when a thing died, it died in a flameless acid fire so intense that only ashes remained.

The E.R.A. tanker trucks were yellow and they were manned by suited E.R.A. Foresters in orange and green who wore oxygen tanks on their backs and asbestos gloves and shoes, and who could only be faced through the treated plastic visors of their helmets and who had no voices except amongst themselves, inside the safety of their suits.

They came along the road in mechanical procession, stepping out in unison to the spurting rhythm of their hoses.

The siren had mounted to its ultimate wail now—continuous.

All Barney wanted was one face—just one pair of eyes before he ran. He knew that he could only hope to see them through his binoculars, that he could let them get no closer than the Cormans' by the river, but he knew, too, that from that distance he could see the moment of recognition and that was all he wanted: a look to mark his own existence in another man's eyes, before he fled.

They were approaching the river now—three tankers, each leashed by hoses to six men, and behind the tankers a travesty of hope so insidious that Barney could not believe his eyes—an ambulance, marked by huge red crosses. How could it ever stop to take in survivors when of course, by the very nature of the solvent, there could be no survivors? It was there only to satisfy the grotesque conscience of the Government and of all the World Bodies that were dedicated to Cities and that supported this scheme for the control of rural populations.

He had risen now and was standing, poised on his toes, so completely flooded inside with adrenalin that he was virtually ill and retching. But he jammed the binoculars against the bones of his face and waited.

It was unfortunate that he did not run instead. But it was too late. The meeting of eyes was adhesive when it happened and once he found them and was staring and being stared at, everything but panic stopped.

He heard himself saying, "Child—child—child—they're only children" and he felt his stomach heave over and the sickly sweet taste of curdled honey rise into his mouth. For he had seen the eyes of a boy no more than sixteen years old. And they had not been what he'd thought he'd see. For there was no fear in them and not an ounce of human recognition and he had not known that that could be—that such eyes existed as he saw there beyond the glass and the plastic—blind, but cognizant. Signalling sight, but reflecting nothing more than the reaction of a meter when it registers the presence of electrical force. The boy's eyes looked and let him go, without a flicker of human response.

Barney threw down the glasses and ran.

And all this while, old Turvey and his dog had been ashes for almost half an hour.

When he got to the barn, Barney threw open all the remaining doors, letting free the cow, the goats, and the burros, and he began to shout at the mule in such a peculiar way that he himself did not recognize the language. Perhaps there were no words any more. Perhaps there never had been and certainly there never would be again. He could not even gather the sentence of a thought. He was noise and movement and something that seemed furious, but was only afraid.

The wagon slugged off toward the top of the hill and as it went it rolled so slowly, drawn by the mule and pushed by Barney, that all the animals, Barney included, had the time and misfortune to catch the smell of E.R.A., which is to say, the time and misfortune to begin to burn.

There came screams, utterly unlinked to any pain that can be described—because as they pushed and pulled and dragged themselves forward, parts of them were already turning to ash.

The clouds of E.R.A. mounted back along the road in the terrible beauty of their purity and they were rolling up like walls around them hissing with the massive immolation of trees and grass and flowers and insects—birds, mice, and anything that lived that comes to mind.

Barney only knew to push and the rest was all pain.

Until he got to the top of the hill.

And was saved. With his three geese, the old dog, the cow, three burros, two goats, and the mule.

By the dying thought of green.

But he had tried.

There is no ending to this story. There is only what is and was and will be. How can I possibly say that any one of the survivors survived? For how am I to know? But you must have seen as many abandoned cars and trucks and trailers as I have. And heard as many packs of wild dogs. And come to as many "Detour: Road Closed" signs as I have.

I, too, live in a house by a road.

So, perhaps, do you.

But I'm not fooled, as I fear many are, by the current propaganda.

For instance, they recently moved the yellow tankers up to a station near us. Now they're telling us (and certainly many have believed it) that these trucks are only oil tankers. Some new delivery system for a factory that hasn't been built yet. How gullible we are. The other day I saw two men in green and orange suits and I actually heard some fool describe these costumes as a new snowsuit to wear skiing. And they've blown the Forestry signal constantly this last week and there hasn't been a single fire—so why is that, I ask you? And last night there was a helicopter ...

But my neighbours are believing. They trust. Why, a government man was around here just last week selling bug killer. D.D.T. they call it.

And my neighbour bought it.

Now *why*, do you think, in the present scheme of things, would he do that?

Outport

Garfield Reeves-Stevens

You can smell the ice and you can smell the fear and sometimes the fear's so strong you can't tell one from the other. And sometimes, it's just the excitement of the passengers who don't know enough to be afraid yet. Going into the outports. What's left of them. Looking for the survivors.

"Never did know why they called them *survivors*." Burl Finn asks the question. He's an American. They all are, seven of them this time, the passengers. Only ones who can afford the trip. Only ones desperate enough to want to take it. This one, Burl, made his money building the dykes around Florida. A lot of them did. Getting rich not by making something new but by saving what was old. There's too much that's old left in this world.

Burl's drinking beer from a small can in his huge gloved hand. He's a big man. They all are. Food's easy to get down south. Not like St. John's where we sailed from. Not like the outports where we're going. Things still grow outside down south, under the UV nets at least. Burl drinks some more and then he belches. The sound's swallowed by the mist and the pulse of the ship's engines churning. But the stink of the ice and the fear is overcome for the moment.

"'Cause they're still here," I say, close enough to the truth. I don't like Burl. I don't like any of them. But I'm leaning on the railing with him just the same, watching the sea out here grey and thick, carved by the ship's bow like molten glass, almost solid. I can believe that someone might walk across this water. I wish someone would. It would be an easier path to salvation than what I'm doing now.

"Not for long," Burl says, sort of snorting. He horks down what's left of the beer like he's cleaning out his nose through the back of his throat, like the beer's part of him, some liquid made by his body that he's reclaiming, recycling. The plastic can splinters easily in his glove and he tosses the shards over the side, and they spin like ice crystals all the way down. If there were fish left out here, those shards probably would've killed a few, when they'd tried to swallow them. But that's nothing to worry about anymore. The Banks aren't what they used to be and most of the fish are long since sucked up into the factory ships that used to sweep these waters worse than the ice does now.

There're fish inshore of course. Lot's more than there used to be, too, back when the outports were real fishing villages, not any ever big enough to be towns, not without roads, no way in and out in the winter. It's just that those inshore fish can't be caught. Not by the survivors anyway. They've got too much else to think about. Too much else to do. Getting ready for a summer when the ice won't melt at all. Supposed to be soon now. Winter all the time.

Burl doesn't care about any of that, though. Not that I've tried telling him what it used to be like, the way my father and mother told me it was. I've tried telling them before, other passengers, other trips, but they never were much interested. Used to bother me then, when I was younger and I thought it was important that they understand what was going to happen to them, when it happened to them. But it doesn't anymore. Makes it easier, really. Part of the process.

We stand there for a long while till Linda gives me a call from the cabin. Shore's coming up, she says. Can't hear the breakers in the fog, not over the engines, but the cliffs of Newfoundland like black clouds are suddenly there, a storm front roiling up, solid, twisted, puckered like something that's grown in place, like some of the plants down south that still hold out on their own, without protection, no matter what the UV does to their DNA. They know about DNA in the outports. The survivors know what's important. If they didn't, they wouldn't be survivors, would they?

Linda cuts back on the engines and we almost coast. She's looking for markers, something familiar. Can't use the radar or fix on the NavStars with the Maritime Command in the same waters. The big red ships, all metal and composites, with brilliant white lines across their hulls blinding like ice when the sun breaks through the fog, they don't really care about us, as long as we don't rub their noses in it. They know what we say we're doing, and they know what it is we really do, and either way you look at it, it's illegal. But if you look at it just one particular way, you can't say it's wrong. And after the summer comes when the ice won't melt at all, who's going to care?

"Should we get the stuff ready?" Burl asks. The black wall of rock has changed his mood, made the beer courage go away.

"Leave it be for a while, yet," I tell him. "Maritime Command's got better things to do than search us if they find us out here, but if we've got the guns on deck, they won't have any choice but to board us and take us in."

Burl nods at that. I know he's relieved. Jerry Bright, his partner, is still belowdecks, sleeping off last night. Jerry's not nervous, not like Burl. Jerry fought in the Mex-American. When he gets drunk enough, he tells us he was first across the Rio Grande, first to march into Mexico City. Wish I had a dollar for every American I've met said he was the first to do those things. I could buy another boat or ten. A couple of others are belowdecks with him. I saw them using their knives to cut crosses into the soft ends of bullets to make them break apart when they hit. The others are in the galley complaining about the cold. And this the summer.

"I hear sometimes it's easy," Burl says after a while.

I pretend to not know what he's talking about.

"You know," he says, "that they know how bad things are getting so they, they just like, leave the children there, on the shore, and you just have to leave something in exchange. You know, guns, food, even whiskey."

"Yeah, I've heard that, too," I tell him. It calms him down a bit. Burl wasn't in the Army, but he knows there's a hell of a difference between a Mexican regular and what he's going to find out on those rocks. The Mexicans were fighting for a wasteland, stripped bare by the exodus from Central America, fried by the sun, scourged by disease. It was a country already lost and no matter what the American politicians said, it wasn't a police action to restore order to their neighbour to the south, it was a war to keep the starving millions on their own side of the border until nature had run her course. The Mexicans didn't have a whole lot of reason to fight. They'd already lost.

Of course, nature doesn't stand a chance out on those rocks and Burl knows it. The survivors aren't fighting for a wasteland. They've been a colony, a Dominion, a colony again. Even been another country's province for awhile. But the land never changed through all of that. And the people never changed. They're fighting for a future, same as always. And as long as the ice keeps ploughing down from the north, keeps the mist and the fog in the air to shield this place from the UV, there will be a future here. Something new, like the name says.

And by being new, that makes it something that Burl and Jerry and none of their countrymen can understand. I've seen it happen to them. Their thoughts are like their country now, constrained by dykes that will never withstand the thousand-year patience of the sea. Their dreams are walled in by armed borders that might, for now, be keeping disease out, but just as certainly choke off what little life remains within, a tourniquet applied too tight and too late. At some level the Americans know that.

At some level their government lets enough of them out beyond their iron borders to search for the life they know they need. Searching here, in Australia, through what's left of the EC. Just like the Maritime Command lets my boat cross the Banks, the US Coast Guard blinks when men like Burl and Jerry slip out to sea. Looking for survivors, they say. But in Australia, and through what's left of the EC, all they ever find are those who *have* survived and now are only waiting without purpose. Out here, they find those who *are* survivors, and still survive. None of my passengers has ever understood that difference until it was too late.

Linda angles the boat closer toward the shore and now the breakers sound over the barely idling engines. Burl grabs the railing hard as we rise and fall with the growing grey swells.

"Are we getting close?" he asks.

"Seems so," I say, though the bright patch of fog that's the sun is still high enough over the cliffs that I know we won't be setting off for an hour or two. I tell Burl so.

"It's better at night?" he asks.

"That's right," I say. "Especially for the children."

That always works on these passengers. After all, they say, that's what they're doing it for. Never for themselves. Never for the adoption bounties. Not even any mention of their country's gene pool slowly evaporating in the heat of a century's worth of toxic, mutagenic pollution. This is *all* for the children, they say, the poor, poor children, thinking that the children of the outports need rescuing from their bleak dismal life among the rocks and the ice, as if for some reason they'd enjoy the new and better bleak and dismal life of a country that already has begun to live by night, afraid of the sun, choking on its own waste, its own past, inflicting genetic instability to the point of sterility to all that were trapped within the delimiting borders first forged by geography, now set even more immutably within a fixed inertial intellect.

Burl stumbles away from the railing toward the cooler and pulls another can of beer from the coldpacks. As if keeping the beer exposed to the air wouldn't keep it cold enough, as if just the fact that it is summer is enough to require beer to be chilled. They do that a lot, I've found, ignoring reality for what they *know* is real.

"Watcha see, Linda?" I call out.

Through the window of the cabin I see Linda wave one hand ahead and down, flashing three fingers. I track the cliffs according to her instructions and spot the grey smudge of what we call Old Mike's cabin, the first of the landmarks we need to find our way. The cabin is in ruins, really, little more than a bleached jumble of timber atop the rocks. But it lets us know we're close to Dunder's Cove.

"That where we're going?" Burl asks, beer in hand. I can tell the difference between the stink of ice and fear now. He's truly scared. As if he knows what's going to happen.

"Just an old shack," I tell him and he believes me. It's easier. "Lots of old things on the cliffs out here."

"But you know where we are, don't you?"

I nod. There's not much left to hide from him anymore.

"So there's an outport near?" He likes that word. Uses it a lot. Maybe it sounds alien to him, as if the trip has taken him to another planet, as if he won't be facing humans, as if that makes it easier, too.

I nod again.

Burl stares at the cliffs and the fog. I wonder if they remind him of the walls he's built against the sea down south, and how useless those walls will be. "How do you find them?" he asks me.

That's one of the things still to hide, until we get close to shore and the sun gives way to night. My passport doesn't say so, and I've learned a mainland accent, but I know how to find the outports because I was born here. Because my mother and father were born here, as were their own. Because the folds of these cliffs are the folds of my skin and the crash of the breakers is the pounding of my heart and because the ice that's ploughing down from the north in unending sheets that soon will defeat the summer for the next ten thousand years is my soul. Cold, perhaps, with features hidden, but more enduring than the sea it engulfs.

Burl waits for my answer, knowing I have one, but Jerry's down below with the guns and the others are cutting their bullets into dum-dums and we're not yet in position so I can't tell Burl what he wants to know.

So I tell him, "Sometimes you see a boat, a dory, going into the outports. Old and creaky, tied up some places, dragged up in others, usually hidden, not very well. Sometimes you see just splinters from where the ice took hold. Sometimes you see a building, too, like that one. Most of them are wood, like the boats, dragged over from the west, the valleys, back when what roads there were, were clear, when there were still forests."

Burl nods in time to the rise and the fall of the deck. I like to think he senses the life of the land and the sea here. Something he's not familiar with. Something new.

I tell him that the real outports are long since flooded. That the buildings we see are the ones that were built high enough. Scattered like barnacles across black rocks all craggy and sculpted and ragged. As if the ice took hold of the land once and splintered it, too. Eventually, the ice will reach to Florida. I see Burl understands that, that he knows the true worth of his useless dykes, though he says nothing.

"Sometimes you see lots of buildings," I tell him, and this is true. You see them underwater. When there's not much ice. Whole villages caught like paintings melting in rain. Rippling a bit where the water's clear. Disappearing softly, with no lines, no borders or boundaries, where the water's murky. Those buildings, trapped like that, quiet and still, make me think of waiting. The feeling of waiting, looking down off the side of the boat with the passengers. There have been a great many Burls over the years. I haven't liked any of them. Though sometimes, I have felt sorry for a few. I don't know yet if I will feel sorry for this Burl.

Burl looks over the railing, beer held forgotten in his hand, as if trying to peer beneath the waves and the years, trying to see the past. Typical, I think.

They used to walk those ghost streets, narrow, twisting, the first survivors did. Their parents, anyway, before the ocean rose up, swallowing the outports like the factories swallowed the fish. Lobsters live in those streets now, scuttling, and crabs. And the fish. Lots of fish inshore where the factories can't get them, lazy schools of them weaving through the streets like flocks of slow birds, silvery white reflections of the gulls that used to follow the factories, back when there were gulls.

"Why do they do it?" Burl asks.

"Do what?" But I know what he means.

"Just give them up."

"Give what up?"

"The children," he says.

I stare at the cliffs. We're getting closer to where we need to be. "They don't give them up, Mr. Finn. You've got guns," I remind him.

"But you said, sometimes, they just, they just leave the children there, for the ships to take."

"I said, I've heard the stories."

"Then they don't?" he asks. "Leave the children?"

Sometimes, I find it painful to be around these people. "Under current conditions, what would you do?"

"I'd do what was best for the children."

"I assure you that that is what they do, too."

The poor man smiles in relief. That's another common trait among them, the stubborn insistence that there's only one way of looking at things. Their way. I don't try and set him straight.

By the time the patch of sun has passed behind the cliffs, all the passengers are gathered on the foredeck, sidelit by running lights. Four have blackened their faces with camouflage paint. They're the ones used to be in the Army. All of them wear laden equipment belts, local transponders, and carry their rifles. All of them pose like commandos prepared to take on a vicious enemy. But they're only doing this for the children.

Linda and I keep them occupied with a transponder and weapons drill while John and Eleanor wrestle with the launching gear aft, dropping the dinghy into the dark water with enough splashing and grinding of winch gears to drown out the other sounds from the ocean.

We check the transponders twice so that no one will lose his way, we tell them. Linda starts talking about using the handheld infrareds to see where the fires have been burning. The passengers listen attentively, in love with their technology.

"Above all, be safe," Linda tells them. "Don't fire unless you have to." But by the intensity of their eyes, we see that the four with the painted faces have no intention of restraining themselves. To them, this is not an adoption run, this is not an attempt to rescue the poor children of the decaying world to bring them to safety within Fortress America. This is a hunt, pure and simple, a make-good for the killing fields lost now that Mexico is uninhabitable. They're right, of course, but they have the wrong idea of who is to be the hunted.

Linda looks to me but John still hasn't given the signal from the winch. "Let's check those safeties one more time," I tell them. "We want this to go as smoothly and as quickly as possible."

Burl gurgles with a beer laugh. "So you can get back home and spend all the money we paid you!"

I laugh with them, though the money's already spent and what it bought is sitting in the hold.

I hear the winch grind for a moment when I know it shouldn't. Eleanor stands by the aft railing, lit by a floodlight fastened to the top of the cabin. She flashes two fingers.

"The dinghy's almost ready," I say. Then I tell them that the sea is choppy and I'd feel a whole lot safer if they'd just unload until we hit shore. Stop any chance of an accidental discharge.

One of the men with a painted face is unhappy at the suggestion but I point out that everyone on shore will be hiding away from the cliffs. No one's going to attack while we're in the dinghy, heading for land. He hears the truth in my voice and reluctantly disarms his weapons.

By now, of course, the Dunder's men have worked their way up the netting from their dory. I sense them moving in the shadows of the unlit half of the ship as Linda and I wave our disarmed passengers aft, keeping them distracted.

The Dunder's men are silent but they make no other attempt to hide now. Their dingy white jackets and pants, padded thickly for insulation and protection, almost glow in the darkness of the deepening night. Even their faces are encased in white sacks. An old tradition brought back to life to forestall any identification, in case any passengers escape.

But no passengers ever escape.

Burl goes down easily with one blow. The rest except for two ex-soldiers follow in seconds. Those two men whirl at the first sign of the silent attack, assuming positions of martial arts combat.

But they are not facing other soldiers. They're facing pale apparitions who scream at them with wailing indrawn breaths, even as they swing their bladed pikes.

One ex-soldier goes over the railing and hits the sea. I mourn the loss of his equipment, but the cold will claim anyone in that water within minutes and I have long ago learned to respect the cold and give it its due.

The other ex-soldier goes cleanly, his final breath leaving his severed trachea like a mummer's wail, bubbling just a bit at the end like Burl finishing a beer.

The attack takes less than thirty seconds. The passengers hadn't been expecting it, so of course it is easy.

We work the rest of the night offloading the supplies we bought with the passengers' payments. Book disks. Tools. Seeds for the greenhouses. The transactions were all in cash so there are no records and no trail. Burl and Jerry and the five others will be just another group of Americans who have slipped illegally from their country to disappear in the dying world. Perhaps, as sometimes happened, a brother or friend will come looking for them. And when and if that happens they will have no difficulty in hiring a ship to take them up through the ice, searching the outports. This land, this sea, this ice, my home, is admirably efficient in dealing with those who don't respect it.

I explain this to Burl as he sits tied on the deck, just as the sun rises, a pale glow in the mist. Without his beer, Burl looks more frightened than ever. He cringes when Linda says everything's been offloaded.

"What happens to us now?" he asks. His lips are tinged with blue. It's the summer and it's getting that cold.

"You get offloaded, too," I tell him. I help him to his feet. He is unsteady. "You'll finally get to see an outport."

"What happens then?" His teeth are chattering. This is not his climate, not his world. He really might as well be on another planet, or from one.

"That's up to the doctors," I explain. The other passengers are being led to the railing. If they have cooperated, then the Dunder's men untie their hands to let them climb down the rope ladder to the dory more easily.

"Why doctors?" he asks. I don't know yet if I should untie Burl's hands. The ship rocks up and down with the swells, the pulse of life.

"To see what you can add to the community, Mr. Finn. It's very small, very self-contained, and sometime soon is liable to be cut off by a winter that will last for centuries."

He tells me he doesn't understand what I'm saying.

"Contributions to the gene pool," I tell him. "We've found that not all of you are as badly affected as you think. In time, given a proper diet, a rest from contaminants, there's a chance that you'll produce healthy sperm again."

"You're going to *breed* us?" He seems shocked by the suggestion.

"You've taken so much from this world, Mr. Finn. Isn't it time you put something back?"

His cheeks go splotchy, angry red against the stark white of his skin. "And if I can't? If I *can't*?"

I'm always surprised when they don't figure it out for themselves. "One way or another, you will," I tell him. "Food's hard to get up here. But we do get it."

He trembles badly, tied hands resting on the rail. I watch his eyes as they go to the sea, as if they look beneath its grey surface, struggling to find ghost cities of the past, as if he knows that the past is his only future. And in that moment, I sense something more about Burl Finn, something hidden. Perhaps he's had an operation, perhaps an accident or exposure to something so toxic that his gametes will never run clean and error free. Whatever, he seems to know that there will only be one way he will give something back to the world. I think of him sucking on his beer, as if he were recycling his own fluids.

"Why?" he asks.

I know that he knows the answer, but I tell him anyway. "For the children. For the future."

"But like this?"

"Like what?" I ask him gently.

His wide, panicked eyes are so easy to read. Kidnapping, they say, theft, murder, cannibalism. A dozen other terms of one world's horror. Another world's necessity.

"*This*!" he says by way of briefer explanation. "How can you?"

I didn't like him throughout the trip, and standing with him by the railing, with no more reason to hide anything at all from him, my mission done, I find that I still don't like him. But I do, at last, feel sorry for him. I look at the slow pulse of the sea long enough that his eyes are drawn to it as well, and at that moment, I cut through the rope that binds his hands, giving him his final freedom. The dory creaks below us, beneath the waiting rope ladder. The fog is rose and yellow with the dawn.

"We're not jetsam, not dredges, not the forgotten waiting for our time to be over," I tell him. "We're not like you are." I step back from him, knowing what he must do even before he does. "We are survivors. Always have been. And will be."

Tears freeze to his cheeks in the cold wind of this summer morning. There's ice nearby, beyond the fog, closing in, inexorable, enduring. "What about me?" He forms the words but doesn't say them.

I shake my head. "You might have been able to ask that once, perhaps. But no longer."

A Dunder's man, impatient, wails up from the dory, white arm waving Burl down and down.

Burl doesn't look at me again. I smell the ice waiting offshore. And his fear. This time, they are the same again, brought into balance.

Burl Finn goes over the railing, spinning like a large shard of something old and fragile. And when he hits the thick grey surface of the water, it parts for him, drawing him down to the ghost streets of the outports that so fascinate him. I wonder if in his last moment he thinks that there still might be an escape for him, that the water might hold and that he might walk upon it. Sometimes, I get that impression from my passengers. That that's the type of people they think they are.

But not this time.

He leaves only a ripple, and only for an instant. And then there is only the splash of the sea against the boat's hull as the Dunder's men push off with the last of my passengers, heading for shore.

I wave a final time to them, then signal Linda to swing us out.

The sun almost breaks through the fog then, and on the wind that comes to me, I scent the continent of ice that grows out there, coming from the north, invincible.

I stand at the railing, eager to meet it.

It smells like home.

Greenhouse

Geoffrey Ursell

His senses flicker awake. Become aware of the trickle of water, of green light. Warm air full of strange, sweet scents.

He opens his eyes. Masses of leaves fill them up with a myriad of green shapes. His eyes swim in a sea of leaves. He turns his head from side to side. Leaves, everywhere leaves.

And silence. Except for the slow trickling of water.

His limp hands close slowly, clutch crumbling soil, spongy with leaf mould. His body floats on the soil.

Silence.

Where? He turns his head, looking about. The leaves are a thick, multi-layered barrier to sight.

He leaps to his feet, pushing through the leaves, trying to find an open space, someplace he can *see*. The leaves rustle and sigh as he pushes them aside, flailing them away from his skin, from his eyes. They caress his skin, licking at it with their green tongues. He twists and turns. In his ears is the sound of leaves, of water.

He tries to run. Forcing his way through the leaves, the parted leaves swishing together behind him. The leaves slowing him, pulling at his flesh.

Where am I?

He runs free of the leaves and has a brief vision of open space before he hits full-tilt an invisible wall. He bounces back, staggers, falls to his knees in earth soaked with moisture. His head is a black void spinning with sharp blades of stabbing light. He holds his hand over his face, gasping. He rubs his eyes. Stands up. Steps forward into a space of wet earth free from plants.

In front of him is something flat, cool, and smooth. Curving slightly inward as he moves his hands up. Through the frame of arms raised, palms outstretched above his head, he looks out across a flat plain towards a low line of hills. A layer of cloud presses down, promising no rain, leaving only a narrow band of sky in which the sun bleakly hangs.

The hill is thronged with a multitude of figures, hardly more substantial than their long, wavering shadows. The restless figures form and unform serpentine columns that move up into and down from the hills, drifting across the plain. The masses of figures move slowly, heads bent, as if searching the earth. A thick powder of grey dust puffs up around their shuffling tread.

Around small fires closer to him, he sees clumps of gaunt figures. They have strips of grey cloth wound around them. Their skin, grey and wrinkled, hangs limp on fleshless bones.

Into his sight are lifted the fingers and palms of a hand. The parched skin has shrivelled, changing the fingers into claws; has split open at the tips, peeled back from bone. At the centre of the palm an open wound festers, oozing thick grey juice. The hand reaches for his face, stops in front of it. Cannot reach through the invisible barrier to touch.

He steps back from the glassy wall. He looks down at the creature that has raised the hand into his vision. Looks down at a body withered and twisted, the limbs thin sticks jutting out from a hollow chest in which all the ribs show, from a belly puffed out as if stuffed with food. The hair sparse and straggling. Breasts shrunk flat. A woman.

He looks into the eyes of the woman. Clear eyes. Eyes that do not plead; eyes that search his own.

He hits the wall with his fist. Hits it again, again. He begins to pound upon it with both clenched fists, trying to smash it open. The wall will not break, will not move at all.

The woman turns away, lowers herself to the ground, gazes out towards the hills. The sun has vanished up into the clouds. Dark figures, casting no shadows, swarm upon the hills and the flat plain.

He sees that there are many people clustered near the wall.

Some huddle against it, trying to pull a small part of the heat it holds into their shivering bodies. Others, cupping their hands around eyes, stare longingly in, entranced by the warm, green world they cannot reach.

***

Exploring the wall for some distance in either direction, he can find no opening in its smooth, unbreakable surface. Eyes amazed at his presence cling to him as he passes. Over his head the mass of foliage arcs away from the slow, inward curve of the crystal barrier.

He does at last find the place where a stream emerges from the brush, forming a pool that oozes into earth, making it moist for a long way on either side. He tries to make his way by walking up the stream, but the water is too cold. So, pushing through the first layer of leaves, he once again enters the murky green light of that realm of plants. He immerses himself in the ocean of leaves.

He loses sight of his legs, cannot see where he is putting his feet. His hands, held in a wedge in front of his face as if he is a diver, vanish. The leaves wash over him, submerging his body, until he can see nothing of himself except by bringing it close before his eyes. He keeps the sound of the stream nearby.

As he walks cautiously on, he can feel the ground begin to slope gently upwards. Then the slope quickens, the mass of vegetation thins and gives way to a forest whose branches are filled with pliant pale-green needles. Their pungent odour revives him. He climbs more strongly, gliding between their close-growing bodies covered with rough-textured bark, brown and red. The water burbles quickly down, glistening and pure.

Now the hill slopes even more, so steeply that he bends half-forward as he climbs. Abruptly, the pine forest ends, and he steps out into sunlight. He looks up. Far above, the vast crystal dome, lifting high, pushes its top through the heavy stratum of grey cloud. The clean azure of the sky surrounds a dazzling disk of sun.

From the top of the hill, the stream leaps out from a lip of stone, plunging in a spray and smashing into foam on exposed rocks near the trees. A rainbow hangs on the rising mist.

He goes forward, his hands grasping the long grasses that cover the hill, helping to pull himself higher. The hill rounds off, the slope lessens. He reaches the top of the rise and pauses, gasping for breath.

Across a verdant meadow, the fronds of grass utterly still, rise rank after rank of trees, forming a woodland whose edges curve away on either side. The boughs of the trees shimmer thick with colour, pink and white, purple and golden, hiding the bark of twigs and branches. The boughs droop, laden heavily with brilliant clusters of red and orange and yellow fruit. He stands, listening to his own easing breath and the fall of water behind him. The hot sun falls on his body, the colourful masses of blossoms and fruit fill his eyes.

He walks across the meadow, following the straight course of the water, into an astonishing aura of fragrance from the multitude of flowering and fruit-bearing trees. The sweet smells suffuse the air entirely. He cannot remember such an intensity of scent. Moving slowly forward, he closes his eyes, breathing deeply again and again.

Leaves and blossoming twigs delicately brush his face. He stops and opens his eyes. Before him, boughs bend down, offering fruit. He plucks an orange, squeezes it in one hand until the skin splits open, and sucks the sweet juice that trickles out. He takes fruit after fruit, sucking their juice, the pale liquid sliding down his chin, dripping onto his body.

He moves farther into the orchard, takes glistening red apples in his hand, bites into the crisp and aromatic flesh. Then pale yellow pears, the lucious white core melting into his mouth. And lustrous clumps of cherries, hiding in their hearts hard pits that he spits out. And, trailing from the branches of tree, vines that dangle dense clusters of amber, rose, and blue or purplish-black grapes.

He eats and eats, pushing the fruit into his mouth, revelling in the wonderful mixture of taste and smell, eating until his face and hands run thick with juice and pulp, until his chest, his belly, his thighs, drip with nectar.

He goes deeper and deeper into the shelter of the trees, and when at last he can eat no more, he stops and looks about. He has moved away from the water and no longer knows which way he has come.

All around him the woods are still. He listens. Hears at last a faint, distant sound. He turns his head, trying to find its direction. When he thinks he has, he walks a few steps and listens again, then another few steps, then listens. He does so until he knows he has it right. Then he weaves his way through the intricate maze of trees, ducking under trailing vines, making his way back to the stream, whose sound grows more and more musical as he approaches it.

Pushing aside a veil of blossoms and leaves, he steps out into a glade. The circling woods enclose it completely. Not a blade of grass stirs. In the utter stillness, the sound of water lifting and falling in a stone fountain at the very centre of the glade is clear and melodious.

Around the fountain rests the base of narrow stairs made of silver metal. The stairs rise in two strangely interwound tight spirals around the jetting water, a shining double helix ascending into the air. He tips his head back, trying to see how high it goes, trying to follow the spirals up to where they seem to become no more than a thin, glistening needle, to where they seem to touch the apex of the crystal dome far, far above.

In the fountain, the soaring water rises and falls so smoothly that it scarcely ripples the wide surface of the pool. The melody of the water comes from four sluices that lead it away to the four quarters of the orchard. He dips a hand into the water. It is cold as ice. He bends his head down and drinks. The water stings his mouth and throat with its chill. Gasping at the cold, he splashes it on his chest, washing away the sticky sweetness of the fruit. Then on his belly, his legs. Then he ducks his entire head in the water, and, lifting it out, shakes it from side to side, drops of water spraying off his long, curling hair.

At last, refreshed and alert, he moves to the base of the stairs. He pauses, glancing about at the glade, the woods. Then he makes the first step onto the spiral, feels the metal amazingly warm beneath his foot, and begins, once more, to climb.

***

There are no clouds anymore. A descending, pale, distant sun sheds cold light over the land.

He stands on a silver platform that trembles and gently sways under his weight. He has climbed the interwoven spiral of stairs, thousands of stairs, before he has reached this lookout. Directly below, he sees the symmetry of the orchard, quartered by streams that plunge in falls of water down into the pine forest and vanish in the thick green brush, emerging once more only at the enclosing crystal wall. He can also see clearly in all directions out to the horizon, through the crystalline walls of a small bubble that pushes up from the top of the dome like a nipple on a breast.

He sees a settlement to one side, a core of tall buildings made of some grey-white material, with no windows at all, squatting rigidly in rows. Around them, a ramshackle mass of hovels clusters.

Undulating lines of people move ceaselessly in and out of this place, powdery grey dust rising in thin streams into the air from their passage.

The lines trail haphazardly off in all directions, forming the shape of a web constructed by an insane spider. Thin strands of people are strung out across a steel slab of land, vanishing beyond the hills, fading into the grey shadow of the encircling horizon.

***

By the time he has returned to earth, everything has changed.

The fountain no longer lifts and falls; the trickling rills it fed have dried. The flowing grass of the glade is now brittle chalk-yellow. It crackles and breaks at the press of his feet. The blossoms have withered upon the boughs, the leaves turned colour and let loose, fluttering russet and gold to carpet the soil. The marvellous fruit, over-ripe and pulpy, falls down to wither and rot, or shrivels upon the vines. The branches, once covered by the flesh of leaves, raise their naked bones into the quickly-cooling air.

Walking towards the edge of the orchard, he hears the groaning squeal of metal behind him and spins around to see the silver spirals sway and bend, twisting down upon themselves in a screaming crash. He flings himself to the ground. The stairs smash into the fountain, the steps leaping apart, spikes of metal flung in whistling arcs, slashing into the trees all around, the impact of the jagged fragments lopping off branches, ripping trees apart.

Unscathed, he picks his way carefully through the devastation. He reaches the encircling meadow, now sere, the ground cracking. Comes to the slope of the hill. There is no fall of water. He slides down, dust rising up, settling upon his limbs.

The pine forest has toppled in the loosening soil, the needles turning brown, brittle and piercing. He clambers over the deadfall, his flesh scratched and stinging. Where he had swum through a sea of soft leaves, now he plunges into a dry bramble that snaps, whipping his body. But he pushes on to reach the base of the dome, desperate to find a way out.

***

Eyes. Endless pairs of eyes.

Filled with sorrow for what has become of the green world. For the loss of something that cannot be borne to be lost.

The endless eyes watch him as he circles the base of the dome, through air turning parched and hot. Eyes astonished, disbelieving. Weeping eyes.

He walks, walks, walks. The unbroken clear barrier always beside him. The eyes always there. Flesh tight on sticks of limbs, all the ribs showing through. But the eyes moist and full. Unblinking.

The touch of eyes everywhere upon his body. His strong, young, healthy body. Eyes caressing the body. Eyes locked in an embrace with the body. Eyes kissing the skin, the flow of muscle under glistening skin. Eyes twining in the curling hair of head and crotch.

The world of warm green gone.

Only this to look at now.

This body.

Where The Heart Is

Robert J. Sawyer

It was not the sort of welcome I had expected. True, I'd been gone a long time—so long, in fact, that no one I knew personally could possibly still be alive to greet me. Not Mom or Dad, not my sisters…not Wendy. That was the damnable thing about relativity: it tended to separate you from your relatives.

But, dammit, I'm a hero. A starprober. I'd piloted the *Terry Fox* all the way to Zubenelgenubi. I'd—communed—with alien minds. And now I was home. To be greeted by the Prime Minister would have been nice. Or the mayor of Toronto. They could even have wheeled in a geriatric grand-nephew or grand-niece. But this, this would never do.

I cupped my hands against naked cheeks—I'd shaved for this!—and called down the flexible tunnel that had sucked onto the *Foxtrot*'s airlock. "Hello!" A dozen lonely echoes wafted back to me. "Yoohoo! I'm home!" I knew it was false bravado. And I hated it.

I ran down the corridor. It opened onto an expanse of stippled tile. A red sign along the far wall proclaimed *Welcome to Starport Toronto*. Some welcome. I placed hands on hips and took stock of the tableau before me. The journalists' lounge was much as I remembered it. I'd never seen it empty before, though. Nor so neat. No plastic Coca-Cola cups half-full of flat pop, no discarded hardcopy news sheets: nothing marred the gleaming curves of modular furniture. I began a slow circumnavigation of the room. The place had apparently been deserted for some time. But that didn't seem right, for there was no dust. No spider-webs, either, come to think of it. Someone must be maintaining things. I sighed. Maybe the janitor would show up to pin a medal on my chest.

I walked into an alcove containing a bay window and pressed my hands against the curving pane. Sunlight stung my eyes. The starport was built high on Oak Ridges moraine, north of Toronto. Highway 11, overgrown with brush, was deserted. The fake mountain over at Canada's Wonderland had caved in and the roller coasters had collapsed into heaps of intestines. The checkerboard-pattern of farmland that I remembered had disappeared under a blanket of uniform green. The view towards Lake Ontario was blocked by stands of young maples. The CN Tower, tallest free-standing structure in the world (when I left, anyway), still thrust high above everything else. But the Skypod with its revolving restaurant and night club had slipped far down the tapered spindle and was canted at an angle. "You go away for 140 years and they change everything," I muttered.

From behind me: "Most people prefer to live away from big cities these days." I wheeled. It was a strange, multitudinous voice, like a hundred people talking in unison. A machine rolled into the alcove. It was a cube, perhaps a metre on a side, translucent, like an aquarium filled with milk. The number 104 glowed on two opposing faces. Mounted on the upper surface was an assembly of lenses, which swung up to look at me. "What are you?" I asked.

The same voice as before answered: a choir talking instead of singing. "An information robot. I was designed to display data, including launch schedules, bills of lading, and fluoroscopes of packages, as required."

I looked back out at where my city had been. "There were almost three million people in Toronto when I left," I said.

"You are Carl Hunt."

I paused. "I'm glad someone remembers."

"Of course." The tank cleared and amber letters glowed within: my name, date and place of birth, education and employment records—a complete dossier.

"That's me, all right: the 167-year-old man." I looked down at the strange contraption. "Where is everybody?"

The robot started moving away from me, out of the alcove, back into the journalists' lounge. "Much has happened since you left, Mr. Hunt."

I quickly caught up with the little machine. "You can call me Carl. And—damn; when I left there were no talking robots. What do I call you?"

We reached the mouth of a door-lined corridor. The machine was leading. I took a two-metre stride to pull out in front. "I have no individuality," it said. "Call me what you will."

I scratched my chin. "Raymo. I'll call you Raymo."

"Raymo was the name of your family's pet Labrador Retriever."

My eyes widened in surprise then narrowed in suspicion. "How did you know that?"

Raymo's many voices replied quickly. "I am a limb of the TerraComp Web—"

"The what?"

"The world computer network, if you prefer. I know all that is known." We continued down the hallway, me willing to go in the general direction Raymo wanted, so long as I, not the machine, could lead. Presently the robot spoke again. "Tell me about your mission."

"I prefer to report to the Director of Spaceflight."

Raymo's normally instantaneous reply was a long time in coming. "There is no person with that title anymore, Carl."

I turned around, blocking Raymo's path, and seized the top edges of the robot's crystalline body. "What?"

The bundle of lenses pivoted up to take stock of me. "This starport has been maintained solely for your return. All the other missions came back decades ago."

I felt moisture on my forehead. "What happened to the people? Did—did one of the other starprobes bring back a plague?"

"I *will* explain," said Raymo. "First, though, you must tell us about your mission."

We exited into the lobby. "Why do you want to know?" I could hear an edge on my words.

"You are something new under the sun."

Something new—? I shrugged. "Two years ship time to get to Zubenelgenubi, two years exploring the system. I found intelligent life—"

"Yes!" An excited robot?

"On a moon of the sixth planet were creatures of liquid light." I paused, remembering: two suns dancing in the green sky, living streams of gold splashing on the rocks, cascading uphill, singing their lifesongs. There was so much to tell; where to start? I waved my arm vaguely. "The data is in the *Terry Fox*'s computer banks."

"You must help us to interface, then. Tell me—"

Enough! "Look, Raymo, I've been gone for six years my time. Even a crusty misanthrope like me misses people eventually."

"Yet almost a century and a half have passed for Earth since you left—"

Across the lobby, I spied a door labeled *Station Master's office.* I bounded to it. Locked. I threw my shoulder against it. Nothing. Again. Still nothing. A third time. It popped back on its hinges. I stood on the threshold but did not enter. Inside were squat rows of gleaming computing equipment. My jaw dropped.

Raymo the robot rolled up next to me. "Pay no attention to that man behind the curtain."

I shuddered. "Is this what's become of everybody? Replaced by computers?"

"No, Carl. That system is simply one of many in the TerraComp Web."

"But what's it for?"

"It is used for a great many things."

"Used? Used by who?"

"By whom." A pause. "By all of us. It is the new order." I pulled back. My adrenalin was flowing. To my left was the office. In front of me was Raymo, slipping slowly forward on casters. To my right, the lobby. Behind me...I shot a glance over my shoulder. Behind me was—what? Unknown territory. Maybe a way back to the *Terry Fox.*

"Do not be afraid," said Raymo.

I began to back away. The robot kept pace with me. The milky tank that made up most of Raymo's body grew clear again. A lattice of fluorescent lines formed within. Patterns of rainbow lightning flashed in time with my pounding heartbeat. Kaleidoscopic lights swirled, melded, merged. The lights seemed to go on forever and ever and ever, spiraling deeper and deeper and...

"A lot can happen in fourteen decades, Carl." The multitude that made up Raymo's voice had taken on a sing-song up-and-down quality. "The world is a better place than it has ever been before." A hundred mothers soothing a baby. "You can be a part of it." I knew that my backing was slowing, that I really should be trying to get away, but...but...but... Those lights were so pretty, so relaxing, so...A strobe began to wink in the centre of Raymo's camera cluster. I usually find flashing lights irritating, but this one was so...interesting. I could stare at it forever...

Head over heels sharp jab of pain goddammit! I tripped as I backed, falling away from the lights. Scrabbling to my feet, I shielded my eyes. My fingers curled into a fist. I hauled back and rammed my arm into the centre of Raymo's tank. As the glass shattered, the tank imploded. I ran through the lobby. Pausing at a juncture with two corridors, I looked at my carved and bleeding hand. I rubbed it, winced, and dug out a splinter of glass.

Left? Right? Which way to go? Dammit, it'd been six years since I'd last been in this building. Seemed to me the loading docks were back that way. My stride slowed as I ran, partly due to pain, partly because Raymo was already eating my dust.

"Believe in us, Carl." The same torrent of voices—but from up ahead. Out of the shadows rolled a second robot cube, identical to Raymo except that this one's sides glowed with the number 287. I looked over my shoulder. Raymo, sparks spitting from its shattered image tank, had castered into the end of the hallway. Sandwiched.

"We have your best interests at heart," said Raymo.

I shouted: "Where are all the people?" *Easy, Carl. Panic's the last thing you need.*

The voices came in stereo now, from robot 287 in front and Raymo in the rear. "The people are *here*, Carl. All around you."

"There's nobody here!" Keep calm—dammit—calm! "What the hell's going on?"

Robot 287 was edging closer. I could hear the faint hum of Raymo moving in, as well. The voices surrounded me, soft, so very soft. "Join with us." Lights began to coalesce in 287's tank, all the colours of the starbow that had accompanied my ship on its long, lonely voyage. Swirling, dancing colours. I pivoted. Raymo was a dozen metres away, its tank dark and charred. I exploded down the corridor, legs pounding, pounding, pounding. I crouched low and leapt. Up, up, and over top of Raymo, my boot crashing through the jagged glass wall of the tank's far side. I ran back into the starport's lobby.

"Listen to us, Carl Hunt." Voices, like those the robots had spoken with, but clearer, more resonant, coming from nowhere, coming from everywhere. I halted, spread my hands. "What do you want from me?"

"We want...you. Join us!"

I found myself shouting. "Who are you?"

#

The beautiful woman sitting opposite Carl tried to sink down in the crushed-velour upholstery. "Sssh, *Carl. You're making a scene."*

Carl slammed his fist onto the restaurant table. Wine sloshed out of his glass. "Dammit, Wendy, don't lie to me."

"Professor Cayman and I spent the entire weekend digging for arrowheads. I'm his research assistant—not his playmate."

"Then what were you doing sharing a tent with him?"

"You wouldn't believe me if I told you."

#

"You wouldn't believe me if I told you," said the voices. I ran through the lobby, swinging my right hand up to rub sweat from my forehead. Blood splattered across my face. My hand was more seriously hurt than I'd thought. A bloody archipelago of splotches trailed behind me across the lobby floor.

The voices again: "We're human, Hunt. A lot has happened since you left." I burst through a double doorway into the deserted press gallery. "We are the TerraComp Web. We are the sum of humanity." I ran past the tiered seating to the door at the other end. Locked. Breathing raggedly, I beat my hands against the mahogany, the injured one leaving a bloody mark each time it hit. "Think of it," said all the voices. "By joining with the global computer system, humankind has achieved everything it could ever want."

A woman's voice separated from the vocal melee. "Unlimited knowledge! Any fact instantly available. Any question instantly answered."

A man's voice followed, deep and hearty. "Immortality! Each of us lives forever as a free-floating consciousness in the memory banks."

And a child's voice: "Freedom from hunger and pain!"

Then, in unison, plus a hundred more voices on top: "Join with us!"

I slumped to the floor, my back against the door. I tried to shout but the words came out as hoarse whispers. "Leave me alone."

"We only want what's best for you."

"Go away, then! Just leave me the hell alone."

The lights in the gallery began to slowly dim. I lay back, too tired to even look to my slashed hand. Another robot, different in structure, rolled up quietly next to me. It was a long flatbed with forklift arms and lenses on a darting gooseneck. It spoke in the same whispering multitude. "Join with us."

I rallied some strength. "You're…not…human—"

"Yes, we are. In every way that counts."

"What…What about individuality?"

"There is no more loneliness. We are one."

I shook my head. "A man has to be himself; make his own mistakes."

"Individuality is childhood." The robot edged closer. "Community is adulthood."

With much effort, I managed to pull myself to my feet. "Can you love?"

"We have infinite intimacy. Each mind mingling—solute and solvent—into a collective consciousness. Join us!"

"And—sex?"

"We are immortal. There is no need."

I pushed off the wall and hobbled back the way I'd come. "Count me out!" I fell through the doors into the lobby. There had to be a way outside.

I turned into a darkened hallway. Bracing against a wall, I caught my breath. Suddenly, I became aware of a faint phosphorescent glow at the other end of the hall. It was another information robot, like Raymo, with the number 28 on its sides. I held my arm out in front of my body. "Stay back, demon."

"But you're hurt, Carl."

I looked at my mangled hand. "What's that to you?"

"Asimov's First Law of Robotics: 'A robot may not injure a human being, or, through inaction, allow a human being to come to harm.'" As the voices spoke, the words materialized in glowing amber within 28's tank. "If I do not tend to your hand, it may become infected. Indeed, if the bleeding is not stanched soon, you may suffer shock due to blood loss."

"So you respond like a classical robot?" My tone grew sharp. "I order you not to come any closer."

Twenty-eight continued to roll towards me. "Your health is my primary concern."

I peeled open a Velcro fastener on my hip and removed a metallic wedge. The thick end was peppered with the holes of a speaker grille and a numeric keypad checkerboarded one major face. I held it up in front of me, as if to ward off the approaching robot. "This is a remote tie-in to my landing module's on-board computer. If you come any closer, I will cause the landing module's fusion motors to overload. You, me, and what's left of the city of Toronto will go up in one giant ball of hellfire."

The robot stopped. I could hear the pounding of my heart. I stared fiercely at 28. The robot's crystalline eyes stared back. Stand-off. Five seconds. Ten. Fifteen.

The voices were plaintive: "I only wish to tend to your wounds." The box-like automaton eased forward slightly.

I hit keys in rapid succession. "Back off!"

#

Carl rolled off Wendy and she slipped into his arms. "You know," he said, gently stroking the small of her back, "they're going to announce who gets Starprobe 12 tomorrow. If it's me, I'm going to go."

Wendy stiffened ever so slightly. "Everybody you know will be dead when you get back."

"I know all that."

"And you still want to go?"

"More than anything."

Wendy moved to kiss him. "You're such a stubborn man."

#

The robot came to another halt. "You're such a stubborn man."

I looked quickly to my left and right. "How do I get out of here?"

Silence.

I fingered the tie-in wedge again. "Answer me, damn you."

"There are unlocked doors leading outside down the corridor on your left. But you must tend to your injury."

I looked down at my hand, caked with dried blood. Thick liquid still welled from shredded knuckles. Damn. I nodded slowly. "Where can I get a first-aid kit?"

"I brought one for you," said 28. A small slot opened in the base on which the robot's image cube rested. A hinged plastic box with a red cross flexographed on its lid clacked to the tiled floor. A dull hum, almost a white noise, issued from 28's twin speakers.

"Back away from it," I called. Twenty-eight retreated slightly. "Damn it, move right away. Fifteen metres back." Casters whirred as the robot receded perhaps a dozen metres. "More!" Twenty-eight slowly slid farther back. I stepped forward, crouched, set the interface wedge down, opened the box, and proceeded to mummify my hand in white gauze.

"You really should clean the wound first," said the multitude from 28's speakers. "And disinfect it. The plumbing isn't running anymore, but there is an old supply of bottled water in the men's room. If you should require—"

"I require nothing from you."

"As you wish, Carl. We only want to—" I whirled around, pivoting on my heel. Another robot had slipped up behind me, its approach masked by the droning noise from 28. It scooped up my remote control and wheeled across the lobby. Number 28 careened around to block my pursuit. I didn't know the damn things could move so fast. "We could not allow you to keep that device." The voices were almost apologetic. "We can allow no harm to come to you."

Football. I'd played some in high school. Deke right! The robot lurched to block. Deke left! The cube moved again, but ponderously, confused. Right! Left! Right! I barreled past the robot and ran down the corridor to my left. Golden sunlight poured in through glass doors at the end of the hall. I stretched out both arms as I ran, one to push open each of the double doors. Home free!

Another of the info cubes was waiting for me outside. This one was labeled 334. I wondered how high the bloody numbers went.

Like all the robots, this one spoke with the voice of hundreds. "Do not be alarmed, Carl."

One side was blocked by a high hedge. Number 334 stood too far in front for me to fake it out. In the distance I could see a pack of assorted robots rolling in from the loading area.

"There is really nothing to worry about." A few flashes of colour appeared within the robot's tank.

"Why don't you leave me alone?"

The voices were soothing. "We will. Soon."

The lights began to dance more rapidly within the cube. Soon the seductive strobe began its hypnotic flashing. "There, now. Just relax, Carl."

Dammit, I'm a starprober! Keep a level head. Don't let them...Don't...Don't...

The image cube exploded in a shower of sparks. A brick lay in the centre of the smoldering machine. "Over here, boy!"

From across the asphalt a ragged, filthy, old, old man beckoned wildly to me. I stared for a second in surprise, then hurried over to the bent figure. We ran on and scuttled under a concrete overhang. He and I both collapsed to catch our breaths. In the confined space I reeled at the man's smell. He reeked of sweat and wood smoke and more sweat: a rag doll made from ancient socks and rancid underwear.

He cut loose a cackling laugh showing popcorn-kernel teeth. "Bet you're surprised to see me, boy."

I regarded the old coot, crumpled and weather-hewn. "You bet. Who are you?"

"They call me String. Cap'n String."

I felt a broad grin spread across my face as I extended my hand. "I sure am glad to see you, String. My name's—"

"You're Hunt. Carl Hunt." String's knobby fingers shook my hand with surprising strength. "I've been waiting for you."

"Waiting for me?" I shook my head. Relativity is a crazy thing. "You weren't even born when I left."

String cackled again. "They talked about you in school. Last of the starprobes. Mission to Zubenelgenubi." The laugh again. "I'm a space buff, you know. You guys were my heroes."

For the first time, I noticed the filthy, tattered jacket String was wearing. It was covered with patches. Not mismatched pieces of cloth repairing rips and tears: space mission patches. *Friendship 7. Apollo 11. Apollo-Soyuz.* A host of *Vostoks.* The *Aurora* missions. *Ares. Glooscap.* And, yes, the Starprobes. A complete history of spaceflight. "String, what happened to Toronto? Where are all the people?"

String shook his grizzled head. "Ain't nobody else. Just me and the sandworms. Plenty of food around. No one to eat it."

"So it's true. The computers have taken over."

"Damned machines! Harlie! Colossus! P-1! Men got to be men, Hunt. Don't let them get you."

I smiled. "Don't worry about me."

String had a far-off, sad look. "They canceled the space program, you know. Your flight was the last." He shook his head. "Only thing kept me going all these years was knowing one of the spacers was going to return."

"Spacers?" I'd never heard that term before outside of a comic book.

String's gaze came home to roost above his bird's-nest beard. "What was it like...out there? Did you have a"—he lowered his voice—"sense of wonder?"

"It was beautiful. Desolate. Lonely. I met intelligent aliens."

He whooped and shoved his scrawny arm high. "All right!"

"But I'll tell you, String, I felt more at home with the liquid lights of Zubenelgenubi than I do here on Earth."

"Liquid lights! Dragons of Pern! Tharks of Barsoom!"

"What—?"

"The Final Frontier, boy! You were part of it! You—" String jumped to his feet. A robot had slipped up on us. "Run, boy! Run for all you're worth!"

We ran and ran through the starport grounds, past concrete bunkers and concrete towers, through concrete arches, down concrete tunnels, and along concrete sidewalks. Ahead, in the centre of a vast concrete platter sat my boomerang-shaped landing module, the *Foxtrot*.

String stopped, rubbed his arm, and winced in pain. Two info robots and a cargo flatbed rolled out from behind the *Foxtrot*. The one in the middle, a cube labeled 101, moved slightly forward. "Let me tend to the old man. He requires medical aid."

"Leave me alone, machine," String shouted. "Hunt, don't let them have me!"

So near, so near. I turned away from my waiting ship and ran with String in the opposite direction. I could feel my own chest heaving and could hear a ragged, wet sound accompanying String's pained breathing. Once we were well away, I stopped running and reached out an arm to stop the old man, as well. We leaned against a gray wall for support. "String, you've got to tell me. What happened to everybody?"

He managed a faint cackle. "Future shock, boy! They built computers bigger than they could handle. It started before I was born; just after you left. Everybody was numbered, filed. A terminal in every home. No need to go to the office. No need to go shopping. No need to go to the bank. *No need!*"

I shook the man. "What about the people?"

"If you've got machines to do everything for you, you just fade away, boy. Obsolete. You end up as just a shell. The 'New Order,' they called it."

"People don't just 'fade away.'"

"I seen it with my own eyes, boy! It happened!"

I shook my head. "There's got to be more to it."

The voices spoke from the PA horns mounted high on the walls. "There is. Much more. Hear us out, Hunt."

String ran off and I followed. Suddenly, the old man stopped and grabbed at his chest. I put a hand on his shoulder. "Are you all right, String?"

"I don't feel so good."

"Let us help him," said the voices.

"Keep them away from me, Hunt." String forced the words out around clenched teeth.

"I—"

"Keep them away! Swear it!"

I looked up. An info robot was approaching fast. "I swear it."

The old man doubled over, clawing at his chest. He reached into a tattered pocket and pulled out an ornate, gaudy pistol. "Here, take my gun."

I grabbed it, turned, and aimed at the robot, now only a few metres away. My finger squeezed the trigger. A jet of water splashed against the robot's image cube.

I looked down, dumbfounded, at the dying old man. "A spacer," said String, almost incoherently. "I'd have given anything to have been you."

I felt my eyes stinging. "String…"

The crab-apple head lolled back, dead eyes staring up at the sky. The robot rolled slowly next to me. "I'm sorry, Carl," it said softly.

I exploded. "If you hadn't chased us, he wouldn't have had the heart attack."

The robot, number Four, responded quickly. "If you'd let us treat him, we could have prevented it."

I looked away and rubbed my eyes.

"What was Earth like when you left, Carl?"

"You seem to know everything," I snapped. "You tell me."

"It was filthy. Polluted. Dying. People starving across three-quarters of the globe. Petty wars raging in a dozen countries. The final conflict perhaps only days away."

"What's your point?"

"Look around you," said robot Four, its lens assembly swinging to and fro. "Things are better now. Cities are gardens and forests. Breathe the air: it's sweet and clean. There is no violence. No hate. No misery. Computers made this possible."

"By getting rid of the people! Some bargain!"

The symphony of voices grew deep, hard. "*You* left. You knew your mission would take a century and a half of Earth-time. You took a gamble. Some might say you hit the jackpot. You've come home to Utopia."

I measured my words evenly. "If there are no people, then this is Hell."

The robot rolled slightly closer. "Individual memory patterns are still separable from the whole." The image tank became transparent. "Recording began scant years after your departure." The tank filled with a matrix of glowing cubes, each perhaps ten centimetres on a side, each slightly tinged with a different colour. "It took decades to process all six billion humans." The cubes subdivided, like cells undergoing mitosis, each splitting into four smaller cubes. Near the top of the tank the cubes were black, farther down, a rich almond. "Only a handful resisted in the end." The cubes divided again, tiny holographic pixels, making up the head and shoulders of a young woman. "The old man, String, was the last surviving holdout." The cubes split yet again, refining the grain, growing richer in colour. "Now, all that is left is you...and your past."

I felt myself grow flush with excitement. "Wendy!"

The image remained still, but I tingled at the sound of that single, lyrical voice emanating from the robot's twin speakers. "Hello, Carl."

"Wendy, darling—" I shook myself. "No. It can't be you."

"It *is* me, Carl."

"But it's been a hundred and forty years since—since I left you. You're...dead."

"I was one of the first to transcend into the computer." She paused, ever so briefly. "I didn't want to lose you again. I would've tried almost anything."

"You waited over a century for me?"

"I would have waited a millennium."

"But how do I know it's really you?"

The voice laughed. "How do *I* know it's really *you*?"

I set my jaw. "Well?"

"You always wear your pajamas inside out."

"That damn robot even knew the name of my dog. Tell me something no one else could possibly know."

She paused for a moment. "Remember that night in High Park—"

New tears dissolved the yellow crystals String's passing had left at the corners of my eyes. "It is you!"

The voice laughed again. "In spirit if not in body."

But I shook my head. "How could you do this? Give up physical existence?"

"I did it for you. I did it for love."

"You weren't this romantic when I left. We used to fight."

"Over money. Over sex. Over all the things that don't matter anymore." Her tone grew warmer. "I love you, Carl."

"We said our goodbyes a long time ago. You didn't say 'I love you' then."

"But in your heart you must have known that I did. It would have been unfair for me to tell you how deeply I felt before you left. You were like String, your head in the stars. I couldn't ask you to give up the thing you wanted most: your one chance to visit another world." She was silent for a moment, then said, "If you love something, set it free..."

She'd sent me a card with that inscription once. Somehow it had hurt at the time: it was as if she was telling me to leave. I didn't understand then. But I did now. "If he comes back, he's yours..."

"If he doesn't, he never was."

"I love you, too, Wendy." I lightly touched the robot's image cube.

"Join with *me*," said the beautiful voice from the speakers.

"I—"

"Carl…"

"I'm—afraid. And—"

"Suspicious?"

"Yes." I turned from the image. "I've been chased all over and warned against you by the only living soul I've seen."

"The robots followed you for your own protection. String's warnings were those of a worn-out mind."

"But why did you try to—absorb—me without my consent?"

"You've seen what none of us have seen," said Wendy. "Other intelligent beings. We crave your memories. In our enthusiasm to know what you know, to feel what you have felt, we erred."

"You erred?"

"'Tis human."

I looked deep into the image tank. "What if I choose not to transcend into the world computer network?"

"I'll cry."

"You'll—cry? That's it? I mean—I have the choice?"

"Of course. You can live the life of a scavenger, like String."

"What if I want to go back to Zubenelgenubi? Back to the liquid lights?"

Her voice was stiff. "That's up to you."

"Then that is what I choose." There was silence for a moment, then Wendy's image slowly began to break up into coloured cubes. The little robot started to roll away. "Wait! Where are you going?"

It was the multitude of voices that answered. "To help prepare your ship for another journey."

I followed behind. Wendy, dear, sweet Wendy…

The cube rounded out onto the landing platter. A variety of robots—flatbeds, info cubes, and some kinds I hadn't seen before—were already at work on the *Foxtrot*; others were rolling in from various places around the starport. I looked at the ship, its sleek lines, its powerful engines. I thought of the giant, lonely *Terry Fox* up in orbit. I thought and thought and thought. "Stop," I said at last.

The robots did just that. "Yes, Carl?" said the multitude.

I hesitated. The words weren't easy. But they were the truth. "I—I just had to see for myself that it was *my* choice; that I still had my free will." I cleared my throat. "Wendy?"

The tank on the nearest info robot became transparent. Interference-pattern cubes coalesced into the pretty face within. "Yes, darling?"

"I love you."

"You know I love you, too, Carl."

I steeled myself. "And I'm staying."

Her voice sang with joy. "Just relax, darling. This won't hurt a bit."

Her image was replaced by dancing and whirling prismatic lights. I was aware of a new image forming in the tanks of the other info robots, an image growing more and more refined as cubic pixels divided and subdivided: an image of the two of us, side by side, together, forever. I let myself go.

I was home at last.

Political Alienation

Centrifugal Force

John Bell

It took longer than they had expected to hunt down the three campers. In fact, the man—the father, Sally assumed—almost escaped, but Wolfe, ever alert, found him hiding behind some fallen trees. Sally heard the two men talking for an instant, and then she saw a flash of light. She flinched. Wolfe walked back to her, his eyes glowing red.

The smoke billowing around them was acrid, and Sally wanted very much to leave. As they headed for the canoe they had left just north of the campsite, she caught a glimpse of Wolfe tossing a card near the charred remains of the other family members. It fluttered like a butterfly to the ground. She knew the words on it by heart: *These executions represent one more battle in the struggle to liberate Atlantic Canada. No peace for foreign visitors until we control our own land. Free Atlantica!*

Wolfe joined her, pushing off the canoe. As she disassembled their blasters, a kingfisher darted overhead. Her eyes followed its piercing blueness into a copse of birch, and then, turning from Wolfe, she vomited.

* * *

From *The Halifax-Toronto Globe, August 21, 2010:*
ALF TERRORISTS MURDER US FAMILY
Kejimkujik, N.S.

Three members of a Connecticut family have become the latest victims of Atlantic Canada's rising tide of terrorism. Robert Blake and his wife, Janet, and son, Gregory, were brutally killed yester-

day as they were preparing breakfast at their Long Lake campsite. They are the fifth, sixth, and seventh Americans to be slain this summer in the Kejimkujik National Park area.

A communique issued shortly after the murders confirms that the slayings were the work of Atlantic Liberation Front (ALF) terrorists, who have recently embarked on a ruthless campaign to disrupt tourism, the Atlantic region's only remaining industry.

All four Atlantic premiers have denounced the murders, as has the Federal Minister of Atlantic Affairs, Samuel Lemieux. Furthermore, both provincial and federal officials have admitted that the economic impact of such incidents could be extremely deleterious. In fact, US and Canadian tourist traffic is already beginning to decline markedly.

Clearly, pressure is mounting on all levels of government to respond to separatist demands for regional independence and control of the offshore.

Meanwhile, local Canadian Guard commanders are stepping up anti-terrorist measures. Since January, four ALF members have died in blastencounters with the CG. Authorities have been unsuccessful, though, in capturing any ALF members alive.

* * *

As Sally listened to Wolfe, she turned the ID card over and over as if looking for a third side that was somehow eluding her. It identified her as Sheila Peterson of Providence, R.I., a desirable persona in a province starving for American dollars.

"William has located a Yank couple at the far end of the park, near Little Cook Lake. They've been there for several days and are very isolated. We could burn them without too much risk of attracting attention. It'll take a few portages, but I figure if we left after we eat, we could get in there tomorrow about lunchtime."

Sally stared at her hands, her fingertips touching to complete some secret circuit. She almost wished she could pray.

"I don't want to kill any more people in Nova Scotia, even if they are outsiders. We're fouling our own nest. Why don't we take the war to Canada? Export all the violence and hatred."

Wolfe stared at her, his face alternating between surprise and anger. "Jeezus, Sal. We've been over this before. Why don't you drop it? It's not just the Upper Canadians we've got to pressure but our own sell-out politicians. Take away the tourists and the friggin' economy will collapse. Then we'll be called in to pick up the pieces."

Sally wasn't convinced, but she recognized the futility of arguing. As she watched Wolfe carefully fillet the three trout she had caught at dawn, she wondered what sort of country he would make for their coming child? Did he dream of death or life? She wasn't sure anymore.

* * *

TOP SECRET

PMO/Ottawa
10.8.29
PO/Halifax

Dear Premier:

As agreed, Canadian Guard Commander Riel is commencing arrangements for secret negotiations with the ALF leadership. Provincial representatives should arrive next weekend to lay groundwork for first contact. Fed/Prov Security Council will define strategy. Majority decisions to prevail.

Sincerely,
Shirley Davis
Prime Minister of Canada

* * *

TOP SECRET

PO/HFX
10.8.30
PMO/OTT

Dear Prime Minister:

Prov. rep. to arrive Fri. She will advise re recommendations. While we recognize the necessity for negotiations, we would urge utmost caution. CG should not abandon military option.

Sincerely yours,
Willard Zwicker
Premier

* * *

Since smoking was outlawed at the turn of the century, only the very wealthy or the very powerful were able to obtain tobacco. Riel was both. Sucking on a hand-rolled cigarette, he watched Dr. Barks weave his pointer through a maze of diagrams. Riel had had just about as much of the scientist's meandering presentation as he was willing to take.

"Doctor, my diagnosis is logorrhea. Cut the crap and tell me, in English, whether your device can be of use to the CG. And, please, be succinct."

"I'm sorry, sir. In a nutshell: memory erasure can be reversed with my invention. It's like an arc lamp in which two wires do not meet, but are sufficiently close to enable a current to leap across the void. We can do the same for destroyed memory circuits."

"In other words, if I supply you with a man whose memories are selectively removed and stored, you will be able to retrieve the missing information without access to ED banks?"

"Precisely."

"Cigarette?"

"Thank you very much, sir."

* * *

Atlantic CG
Keji Office
15:00 Hrs.
Atlantic CG HQ
Halifax

VT couple murdered at Little Cook Lake. Reginald D. Parks and wife, Wendy R. Freeman. Laser destruction. Little evidence available: ALF calling card, boot prints, woman's barrette. Probably 2 terrorists arrived and departed by canoe. Man & woman? Search underway. Expect ALF communique to reach media in few hrs.

Commander Lewis.

* * *

Sally liked Rhode Island. It reminded her of the Maritimes and was probably her favourite ALF base outside the region. Wolfe was late, and she couldn't help but feel nervous. The child seemed to share her tension, because it too was restless. First one kick. Another. Another. Then a knock.

She let Wolfe in. He looked tired but not as tense as he had been during the drive down yesterday.

"Where have you been?"

"Memory erasure. I'm going to TO"

"Toronto. Why?"

"Ottawa is getting ready to deal with us before the regional economy is irreparably damaged. It's tentative, of course, because they can't gauge our strength. So they're not sure whether to call a truce or not. Incidentally, you're going with me."

"I'm not erased."

"You will be. And listen: they might be playing games, so be prepared to self-destruct with maximum force."

"Wolfe?"

"Yeah."

"If I suicide, I'm not just killing myself."

"I know."

* * *

CG Security
Classification: Top Secret

Commander Riel:

CGS has learned that all ALF terrorists are systematically implanted with very powerful Self-Destruct Units activated, it appears, by verbal commands of 2-3 words. If we opt for seizure of the ALF representative later this week, we will have to neutralize his/her voice within seconds in order to protect CG personnel as well as to ensure survival of the captive—not to mention bystanders at the meeting place.

Please advise whether you require special staff members to control the situation. If so, would recommend Mjrs. Boudreau and Bryson.

* * *

While the drive to Toronto was uneventful, once Wolfe and Sally were in the city their anxiety level increased dramatically. Wolfe relied on enormous quantities of uppers to get him through the three days of preparations that they had planned before the CG conference.

In addition to his SD unit, Wolfe was carrying a broadcast/receiver implant which would permit Sally to monitor and record all discussions. For security reasons, however, they decided to establish range so that she could be as far away as possible from the meeting. After determining the unit's power in the city's cavernous downtown, they then spent another day finding a site for the meeting. The deal was that Wolfe would tell the CG on Thursday where he wanted to meet Friday night. This would give the CG time to clear the location, however public or open it might be.

Eventually, they couldn't resist the obvious symbol of Upper Canada's pretensions: the CN tower. Wolfe phoned Riel with the news, blacking out the video.

"We'll meet you at the top of the tower."

"I should have known."

* * *

Thursday night Sally and Wolfe checked into the Holiday Inn. After making love, they went to Chinatown for a meal. Later that night, they visited Toronto Island for a stroll. To find a moment of peace deep in enemy territory was something they relished. A forest of lights, the city seemed distant and no more hostile than the Keji woods.

On Friday, Wolfe rose early, poring over ALF memoranda and research material. When Sally awoke, he ordered brunch and then spent the remainder of the day discussing strategy with her. After supper, they showered and then rested.

* * *

PO/HFX
CG HQ/TO

CMDR Riel:

The NS Govt. has decided to withdraw from ALF negotiations. We are convinced that both the CG & Ottawa are overestimating terrorist strength. We are certain that a CG counter-offensive would negate ALF.

Premier Zwicker

* * *

As Sally awaited Wolfe's broadcast she thought about the three campers they had killed at Long Lake. One of them was just a child. Somehow, the violence should end. Surely the CG could see how Atlantic Canada had been ruined by Confederation, that the provinces deserved their independence. For Upper Canada to ignore the ALF would simply mean more dead people. More dead kids.

Falling back on the bed, she reached over and touched the still-visible impression that Wolfe's body had made on the covers. On the floor he had left a half-finished cup of coffee and a book propped open like a tent. His Yeats. Wolfe and Yeats were inseparable. For the new Atlantic Canadians, it would be guns and poetry.

Rising, she went to the window, where, amidst the mountains of Toronto's wealth, Wolfe carried his life. It was a valley of shadows.

Suddenly her monitor spoke in his voice: "Broadcast commences. Elevator door is about to open. I love you."

Her heart racing, Sally listened.

"Welcome, Mr....?"

"Howe."

"Mr. Howe. How appropriate. I am Riel. Allow me to introduce my CG associates: Major Boudreau and Major Bryson."

"Hello. Hell..."

"Don't hurt him unnecessarily. Bring him here. Tape his mouth. Where's the stretcher?"

"When you've secured him bring him to the car port. We will meet you at the Medical Centre for memory reconstruction."

Sally turned off the monitor. She was weeping and couldn't hear the words. Wolfe's memory would lead the CG to every cell in the ALF. And without a verbal command, he couldn't self-destruct.

And she didn't know his code. Usually it was just a few words, but it was truly a private thing, something you just didn't share. Like a mantra. Hers was her great-grandmother's name, in full—not the sort of thing you'd blurt out accidentally.

As she wept, she cried not so much for Wolfe as for the end of the dreams they had shared, the future they had offered their child. Wolfe deserved a better death. A death to inspire. Falling back on the bed, she raised her arm, about to throw the monitor against the cold Toronto skyline that filled her hotel-room window, and then she remembered Yeats.

Grabbing the volume, she switched the monitor to broadcast and began to read the poem at which Wolfe had left the book open:

> Turning and turning in the widening gyre
> The falcon cannot hear the falconer;
> Things fall apart; the centre cannot hold;
> Mere anarchy is loosed upon the world,
> The blood-dimmed tide is loosed, and everywhere
> The ceremony of innocence is drowned;

Outside, the Toronto sky became fire. Dropping the monitor, she stretched her fingers over her belly and felt her baby swim to freedom. Wolfe's freedom.

Shopping

Margaret Atwood

Doubled I walk the street. Though we are no longer in the Commanders' compound, there are large houses here also. In front of one of them a Guardian is mowing the lawn. The lawns are tidy, the facades are gracious, in good repair; they're like the beautiful pictures they used to print in the magazines about homes and gardens and interior decoration. There is the same absence of people, the same air of being asleep. The street is almost like a museum, or a street in a model town constructed to show the way people used to live. As in those pictures, those museums, those model towns, there are no children.

This is the heart of Gilead, where the war cannot intrude except on television. Where the edges are we aren't sure, they vary, according to the attacks and counterattacks; but this is the centre, where nothing moves. The Republic of Gilead, said Aunt Lydia, knows no bounds. Gilead is within you.

Doctors lived here once, lawyers, university professors. There are no lawyers any more, and the university is closed.

Luke and I used to walk together, sometimes, along these streets. We used to talk about buying a house like one of these, an old big house, fixing it up. We would have a garden, swings for the children. We would have children. Although we knew it wasn't too likely we could ever afford it, it was something to talk about, a game for Sundays. Such freedom now seems almost weightless.

We turn the corner onto a main street, where there's more traffic. Cars go by, black most of them, some grey and brown. There are other women with baskets, some in red, some in the dull green of the Marthas, some in the striped dresses, red and blue and green and cheap and skimpy, that mark the women of the poorer men. Econowives, they're called. These women are not divided into functions. They have to do everything; if they can. Sometimes there is a woman all in black, a widow. There used to be more of them, but they seem to be diminishing.

You don't see the Commanders' Wives on the sidewalks. Only in cars.

The sidewalks here are cement. Like a child, I avoid stepping on the cracks. I'm remembering my feet on these sidewalks, in the time before, and what I used to wear on them. Sometimes it was shoes for running, with cushioned soles and breathing holes, and stars of fluorescent fabric that reflected light in the darkness. Though I never ran at night; and in the daytime, only beside well-frequented roads.

Women were not protected then.

I remember the rules, rules that were never spelled out but that every woman knew: don't open your door to a stranger, even if he says he is the police. Make him slide his ID under the door. Don't stop on the road to help a motorist pretending to be in trouble. Keep the locks on and keep going. If anyone whistles, don't turn to look. Don't go into a laundromat, by yourself, at night.

I think about laundromats. What I wore to them: shorts, jeans, jogging pants. What I put into them: my own clothes, my own soap, my own money, money I had earned myself. I think about having such control.

Now we walk along the same street, in red pairs, and no man shouts obscenities at us, speaks to us, touches us. No one whistles.

There is more than one kind of freedom, said Aunt Lydia. Freedom to and freedom from. In the days of anarchy, it was freedom to. Now you are being given freedom from. Don't underrate it.

In front of us, to the right, is the store where we order dresses. Some people call them *habits*, a good word for them. Habits are hard to break. The store has a huge wooden sign outside it, in the shape of a golden lily; Lilies of the Field, it's called. You can see the place, under the lily, where the lettering was painted out, when they decided that even the names of shops were too much temptation for us. Now places are known by their signs alone.

Lilies used to be a movie theatre, before. Students went there a lot; every spring they had a Humphrey Bogart festival, with Lauren Bacall or Katherine Hepburn, women on their own, making up their minds. They wore blouses with buttons down the front that suggested the possibilities of the word *undone*. These women could be undone; or not. They seemed to be able to choose. We seemed to be able to choose, then. We were a society dying, said Aunt Lydia, of too much choice.

I don't know when they stopped having the festival. I must have been grown up. So I didn't notice.

We don't go into Lilies, but across the road and along a side-street. Our first stop is a store with another wooden sign: three eggs, a bee, a cow. Milk and Honey. There's a line, and we wait our turn, two by two. I see they have oranges today. Ever since Central America was lost to the Libertheos, oranges have been hard to get: sometimes they are there, sometimes not. The war interferes with the oranges from California, and even Florida isn't dependable, when there are roadblocks or when the train tracks have been blown up. I look at the oranges, longing for one. But I haven't brought any tokens for oranges. I'll go back and tell Rita about them, I think. She'll be pleased. It will be something, a small achievement, to have made oranges happen.

Those who've reached the counter hand their tokens across it, to the two men in Guardian uniforms who stand on the other side. Nobody talks much, though there is a rustling and the women's heads move furtively from side to side: here, shopping, is where you might see someone you know, someone you've known in the time before, or at the Red Centre. Just to catch sight of a face like that is an encouragement. If I could see Moira, just see her, know she still exists. It's hard to imagine now, having a friend.

But Ofglen, beside me, isn't looking. Maybe she doesn't know any more. Maybe they have all vanished, the women she knew. Or maybe she doesn't want to be seen. She stands in silence, head down.

As we wait in our double line, the door opens and two more women come in, both in the red dresses and white wings of the Handmaids. One of them is vastly pregnant; her belly, under her loose garment, swells triumphantly. There is a shifting in the room, a murmur, an escape of breath; despite ourselves we turn our heads, blatantly, to see better; our fingers itch to touch her. She's a magic presence to us, an object of envy and desire, we covet her. She's a flag on a hilltop, showing us what can still be done: we too can be saved.

The women in the room are whispering, almost talking, so great is their excitement.

"Who is it?" I hear behind me.

"Ofwayne. No. Ofwarren."

"Show-off," a voice hisses, and this is true. A woman that pregnant doesn't have to go out, doesn't have to go shopping. The daily walk is no longer prescribed, to keep her abdominal muscles in working order. She needs only the floor exercises, the breathing drill. She could stay at her house. And it's dangerous for her to be out, there must be a Guardian standing outside the door, waiting for her. Now that she's the carrier of life, she is closer to death, and needs special security. Jealousy could get her, it's happened before. All children are wanted now, but not by everyone.

But the walk may be a whim of hers, and they humour whims, when something has gone this far and there's been no miscarriage. Or perhaps she's one of those *Pile it on, I can take it*, a martyr. I catch a glimpse of her face, as she raises it to look around. The voice behind me was right. She's come to display herself. She's glowing, rosy, she's enjoying every minute of this.

"Quiet," says one of the Guardians behind the counter, and we hush like schoolgirls.

Ofglen and I have reached the counter. We hand over our tokens, and one Guardian enters the numbers on them into the Compubite while the other gives us our purchases, the milk, the eggs. We put them into our baskets and go out again, past the pregnant woman and her partner, who beside her looks spindly, shrunken; as we all do. The pregnant woman's belly is like a huge fruit. *Humungous*, word of my childhood. Her hands rest on it as if to defend it, or as if they're gathering something from it, warmth and strength.

As I pass she looks full at me, into my eyes, and I know who she is. She was at the Red Centre with me, one of Aunt Lydia's pets. I never liked her. Her name, in the time before, was Janine.

Janine looks at me, then, and around the corners of her mouth there is the trace of a smirk. She glances down to where my own belly lies flat under my red robe, and the wings cover her face. I can see only a little of her forehead, and the pinkish tip of her nose.

Next we go into All Flesh, which is marked by a large wooden pork chop hanging from two chains. There isn't so much of a line here: meat is expensive, and even the Commanders don't have it every day. Ofglen gets steak, though, and that's the second time this week. I'll tell that to the Marthas: it's the kind of thing they enjoy hearing about. They are very interested in how other households are run; such bits of petty gossip give them an opportunity for pride or discontent.

I take the chicken, wrapped in butcher's paper and trussed with string. Not many things are plastic, any more. I remember those endless white plastic shopping bags, from the supermarket; I hated to waste them and would stuff them in under the sink, until the day would come when there would be too many and I would open the cupboard door and they would bulge out, sliding over the floor. Luke used to complain about it. Periodically he would take all the bags and throw them out.

She could get one of those over her head, he'd say. You know how kids like to play. She never would, I'd say. She's too old. (Or too smart, or too lucky.) But I would feel a chill of fear, and then guilt for having been so careless. It was true, I took too much for granted; I trusted fate, back then. I'll keep them in a higher cupboard, I'd say. Don't keep them at all, he'd say. We never use them for anything. Garbage bags, I'd say. He'd say…

Not here and now. Not where people are looking. I turn, see my silhouette in the plate-glass window. We have come outside then, we are on the street.

A group of people is coming towards us. They're tourists, from Japan it looks like, a trade delegation perhaps, on a tour of the historic landmarks or out for local colour. They're diminutive and neatly turned out; each has his or her camera, his or her smile. They look around bright-eyed, cocking their heads to one side like robins, their very cheerfulness aggressive, and I can't help staring. It's been a long time since I've seen skirts that short on women. The skirts reach just below the knee and the legs come out from beneath them, nearly naked in their thin stockings, blatant, the high-heeled shoes with their straps attached to the feet like delicate instruments of torture. The women teeter on their spiked feet as if on stilts, but off balance; their backs arch at the waist, thrusting the buttocks out. Their heads are uncovered and their hair too is exposed, in all its darkness and sexuality. They wear lipstick, red, outlining the damp cavities of their mouths, like scrawls on a washroom wall, of the time before.

I stop walking. Ofglen stops beside me and I know that she too cannot take her eyes off these women. We are fascinated, but also repelled. They seem undressed. It has taken so little time to change our minds, about things like this.

Then I think: I used to dress like that. That was freedom.

Westernized, they used to call it.

The Japanese tourists come towards us, twittering, and we turn our heads away too late: our faces have been seen.

There's an interpreter, in the standard blue suit and red-patterned tie, with the winged-eye tie pin. He's the one who steps forward, out of the group, in front of us, blocking our way. The tourists bunch behind him; one of them raises a camera.

"Excuse me," he says to both of us, politely enough. "They're asking if they can take your picture."

I look down at the sidewalk, shake my head for *No*. What they must see is the white wings only, a scrap of face, my chin and part of my mouth. Not the eyes. I know better than to look the interpreter in the face. Most of the interpreters are Eyes, or so it's said.

I also know better than to say Yes. Modesty is invisibility, said Aunt Lydia. Never forget it. To be seen—to be seen—is to be—her voice trembled—penetrated. What you must be, girls, is impenetrable. She called us girls.

Beside me, Ofglen is also silent. She's tucked her red-gloved hands up into her sleeves, to hide them.

The interpreter turns back to the group, chatters at them in staccato. I know what he'll be saying, I know the line. He'll be telling them that the women here have different customs, that to stare at them through the lens of a camera is, for them, an experience of violation.

I'm looking down, at the sidewalk, mesmerized by the women's feet. One of them is wearing open-toed sandals, the toenails painted pink. I remember the smell of nail polish, the way it wrinkled if you put the second coat on too soon, the satiny brushing of sheer pantyhose against the skin, the way toes felt, pushed towards the opening in the shoe by the whole weight of the body. The woman with painted toes shifts from one foot to the other. I can feel her shoes, on my own feet. The smell of nail polish has made me hungry.

"Excuse me," says the interpreter again to catch our attention. I nod, to show I've heard him.

"He asks, are you happy?" says the interpreter. I can imagine it, their curiosity: *Are they happy? How can they be happy?* I can feel their bright black eyes on us, the way they lean a little forward to catch our answers, the women especially but the men too: we are secret, forbidden, we excite them.

Ofglen says nothing. There is a silence. But sometimes it's as dangerous not to speak.

"Yes, we are very happy," I murmur. I have to say something. What else can I say?

Invasion

Sansoucy Walker

"But why should they come here?" bleated the prime minister, nervously smoothing the long strands of hair that failed to hide his bald spot. He did not question the truth of what he had been told—not after seeing the man from the other universe materialize out of thin air in his office a few minutes earlier—but he failed to understand the situation.

The man, who had given his name as Yagol, had produced a sort of photograph, which projected its 3-D picture in vivid colour and nauseating detail in the air in front of it. As the prime minister hastily turned his gaze away from it, Yagol said, "These creatures may be coming through to this universe any hour now. I head a group from a different universe which is prepared to set up defences here and destroy all of the creatures that get through. We can guarantee that none of your people will be in danger, provided they keep out of our way. There will be no cost to you and very little damage to property—"

At this point the prime minister made his query as to why the creatures should choose to attack Canada as their first target, rather than one of the powerful nations.

Yagol shrugged. "They know nothing of your political or economic power distribution here, and they don't care, anyway. Humans mean nothing to them. My group specializes in exterminating those of these creatures that get through into other universes. We're a crack unit, and we've never failed to get every gonsegule—That's what they're called in my world."

Still floundering a bit, the prime minister asked, "Should I declare an emergency?"

"What for? Unless I've misjudged your technology, there's nothing you could do about an inter-universe invasion. Still, it's up to you—If you'd rather try to handle things yourselves, we'll pull out. There are strict rules about interfering in the affairs of other universes."

"No, no, don't go," said the prime minister hastily. "I—We appreciate your help."

"That reminds me," said Yagol. "I'll have to get your authorization for our operation." He felt in a couple of pockets in an off-hand manner, and pulled out a document which unfolded without a crease. "You sign the paragraph requesting us to destroy any gonsegules that get into your land—See, there's a picture of one to make clear what we're talking about—and I sign the paragraph guaranteeing all I've said: no damage to your world or any of its inhabitants; no fee of any sort; we finish off the gonsegules within one day, and leave your universe ourselves within that same period. If we damage any property, we'll pay for it in gold, uranium, or whatever you choose—except technological stuff, of course; that's forbidden."

"But must you go so soon? I might have to prove what's been happening!"

"We leave immediately to prove that *we're* not invading. That's for our own sake—the Inter-Universe Authority would have *our* hides if we didn't leave promptly and without doing any damage."

"Then I'd better get my publicity people on this immediately."

"I'd advise you not to," Yagol said. "If you want to send observers along with us to record everything, fine; but if you're hoping to gain political advantage from this event, think again: if you publicize it immediately, you'll get panic; later, you'll get disbelief and rumours about your sanity. We've checked the contact point, and it's in uninhabited country, so there'll be nothing you have to explain. You'd do better just to put your records in archives, and leave it to posterity to appreciate your decisive handling of the matter."

"Perhaps you're right." The prime minister thought gloomily of the problem of explaining and proving everything to suspicious voters, then preened himself a little as he thought of some future day when his universe would achieve full contact with others, and his story would be released from the archives...

Yagol signed the contract under his guarantees, then gave it back to the prime minister, who picked up his pen, then hesitated once more, his dreamy look changing to a stubborn pout. "It's not bilingual," he complained, putting his pen back down.

Yagol cast his eyes heavenward, then gathered his patience with a deep breath and said, "It's in your own first language, so *you* understand it. Now make up your mind. It's your universe, not mine."

The prime minister picked up his pen again. Then both men jumped as another figure suddenly materialized beside the desk—a woman this time. She plucked Yagol's document from under the politician's hands and read it. Yagol looked annoyed, then resigned.

The woman raised her gaze to the other-universe man, dislike crossing her features. "Scram, Yagol," she said evenly.

"Here, wait a minute!" cried the prime minister. "Who are you? You can't make him go. He's offered to help us—"

"No," said the woman. "He's been very careful not to phrase it as help, or I'd have him for misrepresentation. I'm Veth Tilvaxin—Inter-Universe Fraud Squad."

"Fraud!" gasped the prime minister, staring at Yagol.

"I've never defrauded anyone in my life," said Yagol with a lofty sneer.

"Not within the legal definition," conceded Tilvaxin. "But one of these times you'll slip up. I'm looking forward to that day."

"Well," shrugged Yagol, "since you're determined to interfere here, I suppose I'd better go call off the arrangements—and start making new ones, somewhere else." He vanished.

"What's going on?" demanded the prime minister, disarranging his careful strands of hair in agitation. "Was it all lies? Are there no gonsegules after all?"

"There are," said Tilvaxin, "but they won't be coming here now. They're a harmless, non-sapient, endangered species which Yagol lures into universes that don't have laws protecting them, so that the sport-hunters who hire him can come and massacre them. He cons the local government into authorizing the slaughter; but he's very slick at staying just within the legal limits. Usually one look at the poor, ugly gonsegules is enough to convince a weak-minded politician that they're evil and dangerous; so Yagol just builds on that impression."

"Madam!" spluttered the prime minister furiously. "Do you realize to whom you are speaking?" But he found that he himself was now speaking to the empty air.

User Friendly

Spider Robinson

When he saw the small, weatherbeaten sign which read, "Welcome to Calais, Maine," Sam Waterford smiled. It hurt his mouth, so he stopped.

He was tired and wired and as stiff as IRS penalties; he had been driving for … how long? He did not really know. There had been at least one entire night; he vividly remembered a succession of headlight beams coring his eyeballs at some time in the distant past. Another night was near, the sun low in the sky. It did not matter. In a few more minutes he would have reached an important point in his journey: the longest undefended border in the world. Once past it, he would start being safe again …

He retained enough of the man he had once been to stop when he saw the Duty-Free Store. Reflex politeness: a guest, especially an unexpected one, brings a gift. But the store was closed. It occurred to him distantly that in his half-dozen trips through these parts, no matter what time he arrived, that store had always been closed. The one on the Canadian side, on the other hand, was almost always open. Too weary to wonder why, he got back into his Imperial and drove on.

He had vaguely expected to find a long line-up at the border crossing, but there was none. The guards on the American side ignored him as he drove across the short bridge, and the guards on the Canadian side waved him through. He was too weary to wonder at that, too—and distracted by the mild surge of elation that came from leaving American soil, leaving the danger zone.

It was purely subjective, of course. As he drove slowly through the streets of St. Stephen, New Brunswick, the only external reminders that he was in Canada were the speed limit signs marked in metric and the very occasional bilingual sign (French, rather than the Spanish he was used to in New York). Nonetheless, he felt as though the invisible band around his skull had been loosened a few notches. He found a Liquor Commission outlet and bought a bottle of Old Bushmill's for Greg and Alice. A Burger King next door reminded him that he had not eaten for ... however long the trip had lasted so far, so he bought something squishy and ate it and threw most of it up again a few miles later.

He drove all the rest of that evening, and long into the night, through endless miles of tree-lined highway interrupted only seldom by a village speed-trap, and once by the purely nominal border between the provinces of New Brunswick and Nova Scotia, and he reached the city of Halifax as the sun was coming up on his left. Dimly he realized that he would shortly be drinking Old Bushmill's and talking, and he expected both to be equally devastating to his system, so he took the trouble to find the only all-night restaurant in Halifax and tried eating again, and this time it worked. He'd had no chance to change his money, but of course the waitress was more than happy to accept Yankee currency: even allowing him a 130% exchange rate, she was making thirty-seven cents profit on each dollar. The food lifted his spirits just enough that he was able to idly admire Halifax as he drove through it, straining to remember his way. It had been many years since any city in America had looked this pleasant—the smog was barely noticeable, and the worst wino he noticed had bathed this year. As he drove past Citadel Hill he could see the Harbour, saw pleasure craft dancing on the water (along with a couple of toothless Canadian Forces destroyers and a sleek black American nuclear sub), saw birds riding the morning updrafts and heard their raucous calls. He was not, of course, in a good mood as he parked in front of Greg and Alice's house, but he was willing to concede, in theory, that the trick was possible.

He was still quite groggy; for some reason it seemed tremendously important to knock on the precise geometrical center of Greg's door, and maddeningly difficult to do so. When the door opened anyway it startled him. His plans stopped here; he had no idea what to do or say next.

"Sammy!" His old college buddy grinned and frowned simultaneously. "Jesus, man, it's good to see you—or it would be if you didn't look like death on a soda cracker! What the hell are you doing here, why didn't you—"

"They got her, Greg. They took *Marian.* There's nothing I —"

Suddenly Greg and the front of his house were gone, replaced by a ceiling, and Sam discovered that he was indoors and horizontal. "—can do," he finished reflexively, and then realized that he must have fainted. He reached for his head, probed for soft places.

"It's okay, Sam: I caught you as you went down. Relax."

Sam had forgotten what the last word meant; it came through as noise. He sat up, worked his arms and legs as if by remote control. The arms hurt worse than the legs. "Got a cigarette? I ran out—" He thought for a moment "—yesterday, I think."

Greg handed him a twenty-five-pack of Export A. "Fill your boots. Have you eaten more recently than that?"

"Yeah. Funny—I actually forgot I smoked. Now, that's weird." He fumbled the pack open and lit a cigarette; his first puff turned half an inch to ash and stained the filter. "Did I drop the bottle?"

"You left it in the car." Greg left the room, returned with two glasses of Irish whiskey. "You don't have to talk until you're ready."

Sam restrained the urge to gulp. If you got too drunk, you had *less* control of your thoughts sometimes. "They took her. The aliens—you must have read about them up here. They *appropriated* her, like losing your home to municipal construction. Sorry, railroad's coming through, we need your universe. No, not even that polite—I didn't even get the usual ten percent of market value and a token apology."

"Christ, Sam, I'm sorrier than I know how to say. Is she ... I mean, how is she taking it?"

"Better than I would. She's still alive."

Greg's face took on the expression of a man who is not sure he should be saying what he is saying, but feels compelled to anyway. "Knowing you, the way you feel about such things, I'm surprised you didn't kill her yourself."

"I tried. I couldn't. You know, that may just be the worst part."

"Ah, Sam, Sam—"

"She begged me to. *And I couldn't!*"

They waited together until he could speak again. "Damn," he said finally, "it's good to see you." And it would be even better to see Alice. She must be at work, designing new software to deadline.

Greg looked like he'd been missing some sleep himself. Novelists often did. "You might as well get it all out," he said. "How did it happen?"

Sam nodded slowly, reluctantly. "Get it over with. Not a lot to tell. We were laying in bed together, watching TV. We'd ... we'd just finished making love. Funny, it was better than usual. I was feeling blessed. Maybe that should have warned me or something. All of a sudden, in the middle of David Letterman's show—do you get him up here?"

"We get all the American shows; these days, it's about all we get. Go on."

"Right in the middle of Stupid Pet Tricks, she just got up and left the room. I asked her to bring me back some ice water. She didn't say anything. A few moments later I heard the front door open and close. I didn't attach any significance to it. After five or ten minutes I called to her. I assumed she was peeing or something. When she didn't answer I got up and went to make sure she was all right. I couldn't find her.

"I could *not* figure it out. You know how it is when something just does not make sense? She wasn't anywhere in the apartment. I'd heard the door, but she couldn't have gone out—she was naked, barefoot, her coat and boots were still in the hall closet. I couldn't imagine her unlocking the door for anyone we didn't know, certainly not for someone who could snatch her out the door in two seconds without the slightest sound or struggle. I actually found myself looking under chairs for her.

"So eventually I phoned the police, and got all the satisfaction you'd expect, and called everyone we knew with no success at all, and finally I fell asleep at four AM hoping to God it was some kind of monstrous joke she was playing on me.

"Two government guys in suits came that night. They told me what had happened to her. Sir, your wife has been requisitioned by aliens. Quite a few people's husbands and wives have been. And we wouldn't do anything about it if we could, which we can't. They were good; I never laid a hand on them. When I calmed down enough they took me to the hospital to see her. She was in pretty good shape, all things considered. Her feet were a mess, of course, from walking the streets barefoot. Exposure, fatigue. After the aliens turned her loose, she was raped by four or five people before the police found her. You remember New York at night. But they didn't cut her up or anything, just raped her. She told me she almost didn't mind that. She said it was a relief to be only physically raped. To be able to struggle if she wanted, even if it didn't help. To at least have the power to protest." He stubbed his cigarette out and finished his drink. "Strange. She was just as naked while she was possessed, but no human tried to touch her until afterward. Like, *occupado*, you know?"

Greg gave him his own, untouched drink. "Go on."

"Well, God, we talked. You know, tried to talk. Mostly we cried. And then in the middle of a snuffle she chopped off short and got up out of the hospital bed and left the room. I was so mixed up it took me a good five seconds to catch on. When I did I went nuts. I tried to chase after her and catch her, and the two government guys stopped me. I broke the nose of one of them, and they wrestled me into somebody's room and gave me a shot. As it was taking hold I turned and looked sideways out the window, just in time to catch a glimpse of her, three flights down, walking through the parking lot. Silly little hospital gown, open at the back, paper slippers. Nobody got in her way. A doctor was walking in the same direction; he was a zombie too. Masked and gloved, blood on his gloves; I hope he finished his operation first ...

"She came home the next day, and we had about six hours. Long enough to say everything there was to say five times, and a bunch of other things that maybe should never have been said. This time when she left, she left dressed, with an empty bladder and money to get home with when they let her go. We had accepted it, taken the first step in starting to plan around it. Only practical, right?" He shook his head, hearing his neck crack, and finished off the second drink. It had no more effect than had the first.

"What happened then?"

"I got in the car and drove here."

For the first time, Greg looked deeply shocked. "You left her there, to deal with it *alone*?"

Someone grasped Sam's heart in impersonal hands and wrung it out. Greg must have seen the pain, and some of the accusatory tone left his voice. "Jesus wept, Sam! Look, I know you. You've written three entire books on brainwashing and mind-control, 'the ultimate obscenity,' you call it: I know how uniquely horrible the whole thing must be to you, and for you. But you've been married to

Marian for *ten years*, as long as I've been married to Alice—how could you possibly have left her?"

The words came out like projectile vomit. "I *had* to, God damn it: I was *scared*!"

"Scared? Of what?"

"Of *them*, for Christ's sake, what's the matter with you? Scared that the thing would look out of her eyes and notice me—and decide that I looked ... *Useable*." He began to shudder, and found it extremely hard to stop. He lit another cigarette with shaking hands.

"Sam, it doesn't work that way"

"I know, I know, they told me. Who said fear has to be logical?"

Greg sat back and sighed deeply, a mournful sound. There was a silence, then, which lasted for ten seconds or more. The worst was said, and there was nothing else to say.

Finally Sam tried to distract himself with mundane trivia. "Listen, I saw the 'No Parking' sign where I parked, I just didn't give a damn. If I give you my keys, will you move it for me? I don't think I can."

"Can't do it," Greg said absently. "I don't dare. They could fine me four hundred bucks if I get caught behind the wheel of an American-registered car, you know that."

The subject had come up on Sam's last visit, back in 1982. Marian had been with him, then. "Sorry. I forgot."

"Sam, what made you decide to come *here*?"

He discovered that he did not know. He tried to analyze it. "Well, part of it is that I needed to tell somebody the whole thing, and you and Alice are the only people on earth that love me enough. But there wasn't even that much logic to it. I was just terrified, and I needed to get to someplace safe, and Canada was the nearest place."

Greg burst out laughing.

Sam stared at him, scandalized. "What's so funny?"

It took Greg quite a while to stop laughing, but when he did—despite the smile that remained on his face—Sam could see that he was very angry.

"Americans, no shit. You're amazing. I should be used to it by now, I guess."

"What are you talking about?"

"About you, you smug, arrogant bastard. There are nasty old aliens in the States, taking people over and using them to walk around and talk with, for mysterious purposes of their own—so what do you do? Take off for Canada, where it'll be safe. You just *assume*, totally unconsciously, that the aliens will think like you. That they'd never bother with a quaint, backward, jerkwater country like Canada, The Retarded Giant On Your Doorstep! Don't you read the papers?"

"I don't—"

"Excuse me. Stupid of me: it probably wouldn't make the Stateside papers, would it? You simple jackass, there are *three times* more Canadians hagridden than Americans! Even though you've got ten times the population. They came here *first*."

"First? No, that can't be, I'd have heard—"

"Why? We barely heard about it ourselves, with two out of the sixteen channels Canadian-originated. It ain't news unless and until it happens in the friggin' United Snakes of America!" He had more to say, but suddenly he tilted his head as if he heard something. "Hell. Stay there." He got up and left the room hastily, muttering to himself.

Sam sat there, stunned by his old friend's inexplicable anger. He finished his cigarette and lit another while he tried to understand it. He heard a murmur of voices elsewhere in the house, and recognized the one that wasn't Greg's. Alice was home from work. Perhaps she would be more sympathetic. He got up and followed the sound of the voices, and it wasn't until he actually saw her that he remembered. Alice hadn't worked night shift in over a year—and she had a home terminal now anyway ...

She was in pretty fair shape. Face drawn with fatigue, of course, and her hair in rats. She was fully dressed except for pants and panties; there was an oil or grease stain on the side of her blouse. She tried to smile when she saw Sam.

"He caught me sitting on the john," she said. "Hi, Sam." She burst into tears, still trying to smile.

He thought for a crazy second that she meant her husband. But no, of course, the "he" she referred to was not Greg, but her—

—her *rider*. Her User ...

"Oh, my dear God," he said softly, still not quite believing. He had been so sure, so unthinkingly convinced that it would be safe here.

"Naturally the Users came here first," Greg said with cold, bitter anger, handing his wife the slacks she had kicked off on her way out the door some hours before. "We were meant for each other, them and Canadians. Strong, superior parasites from the sky? Who just move right in and take over without asking or apologizing?" His voice began to rise in pitch and volume. "Arrogant puppetmasters who show up and start pulling your strings for you, dump you like a stolen car when they're done with you, too powerful to fight and indifferent to your rage and shame? And your own government breaks its neck to help 'em do whatever they want, sells out without even stopping to ask the price in case it might offend 'em?" He was shouting at the top of his lungs. "Hell, man, we almost didn't even notice the Users. *We took 'em for Americans.*"

Alice was dressed again now. Her voice was soft and hoarse; someone had been doing a lot of talking with her vocal cords recently. "Greg, shut up."

"Well, dammit all, he—"

She put a hand over his mouth. "Please, my very beloved, shut your face. I can't talk louder than you this time, my throat hurts."

He shut up at once, put his own hand over hers and held it tightly against his face, screwing his eyes shut. She leaned against him and they put their free arms around each other; the sight made Sam want to weep like a child.

"Greg," she said huskily, "I love you; part of me wants to cheer what you just said; many Canadians would. But you're wrong to say it."

"I know, baby, I know *exactly* the pain Sam's going through, don't I? That's why I got mad at him, thinking his pain was bigger 'cause it was American. I'm sorry, Sam—"

"That's only part of why you're wrong. This is more important than our friendship with Sam and Marian, my love. Pay attention: *you would never have said what you said if there'd been an Inuit in the room.* Or a Micmac, or a French Canadian, or a Pakistani. You'd never have said it if we were standing in North Preston, talking to someone who used to live in Africville 'til they moved all the darkies out to build a bridge approach. Don't you see, darling, everybody is a Canadian now. Everybody on Earth is now a Native People; a Frog; a Wog; a Paki; a Nigger—gradations of Niggerhood just don't seem all that important any more.

"Gregory, some of the Users wear a human body as though it ought to have flippers, or extra legs, or wings—I saw one try to make an arm work like a tentacle, and break it. There are a lot of different races and species and genuses of User—one of the things they seem to be using Earth for is a conference table at which to work out their own hierarchy of power and intelligence and wealth. I've heard a lot of the palaver; they don't bother to turn my ears off because they don't care if I hear or not. Most of it I don't understand even though they do use English a lot, but a few things I've noticed.

"If two neighboring races discover that one is vastly superior to the other in resources or wisdom or aggressiveness, they don't spend a lot of time whining about the inequity of it all. They figure out where it looks like the water is going to wind up when it's finished flowing downhill, and then they start looking for ways to live with that.

"I've never heard a User say the words, 'It's not fair.' Apparently, if you can form that thought, you don't reach the stars. The whole universe is a hierarchy of Users and Used, from the race that developed the long-distance telepathy that brought them all here, down to the cute little microorganisms that are ruthlessly butchered every day by a baby seal. We're part of that chain, and if we can't live with that, we'll die."

The three were silent for a time. Finally Sam cleared his throat. "If you two will excuse me," he said softly, "I have to be getting back home to my wife now."

Alice turned to him, and gave him a smile so sad and so brave that he thought his heart might break. "Sam," she said, "that's a storybook ending. I hope it works out that way for you. But don't blow your brains out if it doesn't, okay? Or hers. You write about mind-control and the institution of slavery because subversion of the human free will, loss of control, holds a special horror for you. You're the kind that dies fighting instead. Marian isn't. I'm not. Most humans aren't, even though they like to feel they would be if it came to it. Maybe that's why the Users came here.

"It may be that you and Marian can't live together any more; I don't know. I do know that you need twelve hours sleep and a couple of good meals before it's safe to let you back on the highway—and Greg and I badly need someone to talk to. My User won't be back for another ten hours or so. What would you say to some eggs and back bacon?"

Sam closed his eyes and took a deep breath. "I guess I'd say, 'Hello there—do you mind if I use you for twelve hours or so?'" *And turn you into shit in the process*, he thought, but he found that he was ashamed of the thought, and that was something, at least. "Can I use your phone?"

"Only if you reverse the charges, you cheap Yankee son of a bitch," Greg said at once, and came and hugged him hard.

Patches

Lesley Choyce

It was not until we had occupied the Academy offices in Halifax and surgically removed our patches that my memory of previous lives began to trickle back.

At first it was like the sound of a hollow echo inside my brain. I looked around at the other faces. They felt it too. Gina, the dark intellectual. Victor, the angry young man with the pointed beard. And Delisle, one of the many among us who was two-sexed. These were all my friends. And I could see in their eyes that the memories had begun to return. Now, at long last, we began to understand our rebellion. Soon we would know what had been hidden from us.

Gina was the first to speak, in hushed tones of soft confusion, and to me only. "Derek, the memory is crowding back. I see so many faces and hear so many voices but I don't understand why it was kept from us."

I nodded. "This is what we were feeling in our hearts. This is where the anger has come from. They have stolen our past from us and now we have a chance to see who we are and where we have been."

"There may not be much time," Victor cut in sharply. "They will know by now this is more than a student prank. They will know we have disconnected, that our patches are removed. What we can expect is psychic jamming to begin at any time."

Victor had a cold, rational mind. Gina could follow him. I myself was lost in a crazy entanglement of images and emotion. I had not considered *this* past. I had only accepted what had been taught to me by my teachers through the patching to the Network.

I looked around at the many other students. Some were huddled in corners sobbing. Some spoke to each other with tears in their eyes. Some looked crazed and bewildered. And what now?

Now we were only beginning to realize the knowledge that was stolen from us. And we didn't even understand why it was taken, why we had been artificially filled with other knowledge, so damn much of it, but always lacking this.

There would not be much time. Perhaps we would die quickly knowing only the first hints of true memory. The Network—our teacher, our source of all knowledge and history, the great unifier, was a great ganglia of lies.

I looked hard at Gina and saw the first of many haunting shadows to come. I saw in her others that I recognized. A child in rags with large round eyes, a beautiful brown-skinned woman with an angel's face, and then the face of a man, a confused young man. I had known her many, many times before in other lives. Why had this obvious evidence been denied? What was so delicate in our great Unimerican civilization that this realization of the past was to be hidden from us?

The first wave of numbness surged through my body. The Network had now begun to react to our rebellion. Since the patches had been removed, the Network could no longer induce direct punishment but other means would be almost as simple. I expected the terrible sharp pain I had felt as a child, as my parents first learned to use the patch for discipline. It had always been followed by reassurance, however, that there was love, parental love after the punishment. The punishment was a mere necessity, a means to learn and to grow. This would be different.

But it was not a sharp piercing pain at all. Instead, a great tide of loneliness swept over me, a monumental regret for having disconnected. Behind loneliness and regret was a terrible paralysis of the senses. This was all part of the price, the punishment. The physical numbness began to go away but a pain of the heart rose up like a volcano within. Others around me began to wail. But Gina did not. She took my hand and looked deep into my eyes. Then she took Victor's hand and Delisle's. Soon we were all gathered around the floor of the Great Hall in a circle. A new sound began with Gina but soon spread around the room—a gentle but powerful tone shaped like a vast balloon...and it filled up the space around us and the hollowness in our hearts. It was a sound we all knew and had shared in other lives. Now I was convinced. We all had lived before, many times. As we chanted, we felt it as a physical fact.

But we were on the defensive. A new, more intense pain grew within us as the psychic jamming intensified. I wanted to claw at my skin and pull my nerves from my body to avoid the terrible perforating torment. But instead, our chanting grew louder. We looked around into each other and there was recognition all around.

Then I searched deep within myself and saw that it would no longer be necessary, it could no longer be possible, to be alone. I would never need the Network again.

The big question remained: why had the Network found it imperative to shield us from our communal past?

There was a knock at the door. The chanting ceased. But the pain and loneliness did not return. The door was not locked, not barred. Why didn't the Network guardians simply storm in and kill us? Or simpler yet, why had they not filled the room with anaesthetic gas and knocked us out, then sent in a team to reconnect us? Perhaps there was more that I didn't understand.

I stood to answer the door. Gina grabbed my wrist but Victor knew that one of us must go and he removed her grip. The circle of thirty sat silent. I heard my own footsteps echo as I walked across the floor of the great domed room.

I opened the door slowly, expecting the worst.

Instead, before me was a very mild figure of a human. Five foot five, he stood. He was dressed as casually as a man was permitted, in loose pants and an old flannel shirt. He carried nothing. He smiled nervously and seemed mildly embarrassed.

"Come in," I said. As he walked before me towards the group, I saw from the back of his head that he had no patch. He had no need for one, of course; he was an android, the kind manufactured in the Censtates and brought into breathing life by the Network itself. More than any of us had ever been, he was one with the Network. He could never doubt his maker.

He sat down in the very centre of our circle, still seeming somewhat uncomfortable. This, I knew, was also part of his programming, intended to put us at greater ease. Every human nuance had been built into him. Although fully bio-engineered, he was no mere creature of sophisticated circuitry. He was flesh and blood. In so many respects there was very little difference between him and us. Yet he had never needed a patch. For him it was completely unnecessary.

"My name is Niven," he said. "Can we talk freely?" He almost stammered with a mock nervousness.

"Is the Network present?" Victor asked.

"Of course. The Network is always present. But the Network operates for the common good, for the individual good as well. It can be no other way for that is in the programming."

"Then, Niven, tell the Network we want to be left alone. We will leave the academy but we do not want to be reconnected." It was Delisle who spoke. We all nodded in agreement.

"By doing so, you will be depriving yourselves of the tremendous knowledge that is available free to you. Human memory cannot contain all that is in the Source. You are asking to return to a very primitive state."

"Yes," asserted Gina. "Primitive. Self-contained."

Niven looked perplexed. He shifted his legs into a full-lotus position. He was programmed to know that this would appeal to our group. Every micro-second, he was processing each trace of everything we did. Levels of confidence, eye movements, every rise or fall in pulse or twitch of eye movement. As an android connected to the Network, he could not help but feed each bit of information automatically to the Source. The Network had made him human; he still used his eyes, nose, and ears as much as we did. But the information processing was much more thorough, rapid and efficient than ours could ever be.

"Do you like being alone, Niven?" I asked him.

"This is a non-sequitur, my friend," he answered. "As part of the Network, I can never be alone. You, a student of the technology that made me possible, should know that."

I laughed nervously. "How much do you really know about me?"

"You know very well that I know everything."

"That's not possible," I said. "If you knew everything...if the Network knew everything...it would have predicted our action today."

Niven sat silently. After careful thought, he said, "Perhaps we did know this would happen. We did not know precisely when."

"Then there is already a plan for us?" Gina asked.

"Of course, in the Network there are a great many plans of action for any emergency."

"But why is this an emergency?" Delisle wanted to know.

"Because you have removed your patches. You are depriving yourselves of full knowledge and therefore crippling your abilities. We cannot let you continue with this handicap in a society where all are equal."

"Then what do you plan to do?" I found myself crawling across the floor on my hands and knees toward Niven. I felt an instinct, a most volatile, primitive instinct to wring his neck. I felt threatened.

Niven understood all too well. He smiled that programmed smile, reached into his flannel shirt and pulled out a handful of fresh patches, those tiny sending and receiving explants that provided so much available information from the Source, direct to the brain.

"No!" Gina said. We all looked directly at her. Suddenly, as I heard her shout that single word, something for me was different. It wasn't Gina speaking. It was me. But that's not quite right. It was not my voice. I feared at once that Niven and the Network were already playing some sort of trick on us. I looked around at the other faces and recognized them, as if for the first time.

I closed my eyes and I felt myself swept up and away. I was no longer Derek. I was in a room in an old building surrounded by the smell of...baking bread. The smell was overpowering. Then suddenly I was no longer there but swimming for my life in a warm but turbulent sea. Then again, I was a woman frightened and asleep in a cold, dark basement. I opened my eyes, looked around at the others who were now as confused and dazed as myself. As I began to lose my focus, as I became more and more diffuse in my identity,I knew I must do something, anything, if I was to maintain a focus. I reacted primitively and instinctively.

I lunged for Niven and yanked his arm behind his back, pushed his face to the floor. He was no stronger than any of us. There had never been need to build physical strength into an android. "Cut out the tricks!" I shouted. "We want our freedom and nothing less."

Gina could see that Niven was genuinely frightened. My attack was unexpected. The others in the room seemed shocked. I let go and sank to the floor. I had no idea where such anger had come from.

Niven tried to resume a dialogue. "That reaction, Derek, suggests you are acting on impulse without the aid of Freethought back-up response. You are deluded into believing that you are trying to free yourself when, in fact, you have always been free, by law, since your birth. The Network has added infinitely to your ability to be free by providing access to any and all empirical knowledge." He held out the patching devices again. "Without these, you have deprived yourself of the most vital element of freedom—knowledge."

"No, not knowledge," Gina said. "Information."

"They are both the same," Niven responded.

It was Delisle who suggested we begin to chant again because something very weird and wonderful had already begun to happen to us. Something none of us understood but that perhaps, given another chance, we would comprehend. We were all floundering in images long hidden in our brains, images suppressed perhaps by the overwhelming influx of clean, orderly ideas, of pure unlimited information. I knew there was something very valuable in the horrendous confusion that now teemed within me and within the others.

Niven composed himself and did not intrude. "Do as you wish," he said. "Perhaps I will learn something."

Thus, we began to chant a single sound that opened up our minds to visions, to smells, to sensations that came fast and furious. Utter confusion gave way at length to startling awareness. Perhaps an hour passed. Perhaps it was days. When we opened our eyes, Niven was lying face down on the cold stone floor. At first I thought he was dead.

I touched his shoulder and he was startled. He sat up.

"You were asleep," I said. "I thought maybe you were dead."

He seemed amused. "No, just sleeping. There was no information to be gathered. I watched you all. Nothing happened. I grew bored, weary, fell asleep. I suppose it was a bit unprofessional." He blushed, slightly embarrassed.

"Not at all," Victor said, smiling. For him, the experience was as clear as it had been for me. He looked at me with true recognition for the first time. We had met before, many times. The same was true for all of us in the room.

"What have you learned, Niven?" I asked.

"Nothing, as I said. You sang a one note song which eventually bored me and put me to sleep. I have learned I do not like your music. But I can certainly tolerate it. Our society is nothing if not tolerant."

If Niven did not understand, then neither did the Network. Unless the Source was lying and we now realized that was a distinct possibility.

"Then you really don't understand?" I said, tentatively trusting that Niven was only being honest.

"No," Niven said. "I don't. Perhaps you are suffering memory loss from having cut your link with the Source." He held out a patch to me again.

Gina moved beside me, touched my arm. I felt a warm tingling sensation that I had never before realized in this life. "Let me," she said. "I can explain to Niven."

Now it swept over me like a warm tropical wave. It was no longer the old respect I had felt for Gina, the intellectual. It was deeper. My recognition was complete. She had shared herself with me before in other lives. Again and again, we had found each other. We had all lived many lives before and, for some cruel reason, the Network had jammed our ability to remember.

I was so afraid of losing her now that I pulled her back but she only smiled warmly and kissed me as gentle as a summer cloud upon my cheek. And before I knew how to stop her, Niven had most quickly and efficiently applied the patch to the back of her neck. I saw Gina wince, then close her eyes. Niven too closed his eyes.

We all waited for several long minutes. Niven, eyes still shut, spoke first. His voice was more clinical now, less friendly but certainly not threatening.

"What you are going through is undoubtedly a very interesting malady of group memory. We have record of such things before. The Source is very impressed by the depth and scope of such delusions and has considered storing these fantasies for future study. However, in the end, it was decided that since there is no valuable empirical evidence here, no concrete basis for any such memories, the information should be discarded. Such ideas could yet act as a virus to the entire information system and must be eliminated."

"But why?" I shouted. "Why not tolerate these aberrations?"

Gina looked very tired. I took hold of her, cautiously moved my hand toward the patch. I was not certain now that it would be safe to remove it as I had removed the others before. Before we had the element of surprise. Now the Network had regained one of us. It would not let go so easily. Should I simply force it from her skull?

"I wouldn't do that," said Niven. "She will die if you do." The earlier persona was replaced now by a much stronger authoritative voice. "The aberrations negate the present unity of all in the Network. The very idea that a human...or an android for that matter...is anything more than his current biological and intellectual composite is absurd."

Gina opened her eyes and looked at me, then the others. "No, Niven. You're wrong," she said with absolute certainty. "The Source recognized my memory of previous lives. I could tell. Threshold dampers flashed back at me with each new memory image I filed. It does not want us to believe we have come before." Then her face contorted in a mask of pain.

Niven seemed genuinely concerned for her and reached out to hold her hand. "What you speak of as memory is merely history, historical data fed to you from the Source. You have confused its meaning, that is all." Niven was shouting now. "It was learned through the Network, file after file of history. That is what you possess. Not some foolish memory of previous lives."

Victor was walking towards the door, opening it. He looked out into the courtyard. All was quiet. The grass was green. The Nova Scotian sky was blue. There was no one there. No one waiting to punish us. Such primitive methods would not be necessary. "Perhaps you have fulfilled your mission here, Niven."

"No, I haven't. I have failed at that. I have not yet been able to make you see your mistake. Such a failure will be regarded as information debit. I have inadvertently broken the law." The door closed just then of its own accord.

"Tell us the truth, then," I requested. "Perhaps the truth will help us to see our error."

Niven looked frightened. He swallowed hard. He put his hand on Gina's neck and I jumped to grab him but Gina motioned me away. Deftly, Niven removed the patch. "I persuaded the Network that this controlled disconnection would appeal to your primitive sense of trust." He held the patch up to the light. "The truth, someone once spoke, will set you free," Niven said in a quavering voice.

I held Gina tightly to me, echoes of past lives swarming in me as I felt her warmth. We would never be students again, not here. We would never again debate, using our favourite analogies; we would never again feed together on the endless empirical information that came through the open floodgates of the Network. But we would savour these moments, live them larger than any that had come before with all the freedom of endless learning.

"I have only momentarily held onto some of what Gina filed to the Source," Niven said. "I am still on the Network and quite soon, my current file will delete. I will not be able to retrieve what the Source will now closely guard...or destroy...or simply ignore. But I have a theory I will share, for what it is worth. And that is this.

"Just suppose you can remember the past from before you were born. Perhaps it is ancestral memory; maybe you were born with it."

"It's more than that. We've all felt, remembered things today far too deeply for it to be simply something inherited like hair colour." Victor spoke defiantly, convinced of our previous communal lives.

"Well, this is very hard for me to accept, having been raised by the Network. Yet, I was able to read what Gina has provided me. The images are very strong, perhaps accurate. We know that the mind had evolved very far from its origins before the Network was developed. But the need for information was greater than the storage capacity of the brain. That was why it was necessary to create the Source. Yet in order to maximize the brain's ability to use such tremendous amounts of information available from the Source, it was necessary to erase...no not erase...sublimate these other...memories...or whatever they are. Any rational mind can see that it was a fair trade. Unlimited information in exchange for these enchanting but, you must admit, irrelevant and highly confusing memory files of the lives of your ancestors."

Niven was genuinely trying to be helpful but he didn't have the whole picture. Raised as he was by the Network and limited to only the Source, he could not fathom what was happening to us. "But this is why we rebelled!" I had to say it out loud because up until that moment I had no clear understanding as to why we had made this unaccountable takeover of the Great Hall of the Academy. There was no record in the Source of any such action before. We had instinctively known we were being deprived of our past. "The Network has been cheating us out of our immortality," I now stated flatly.

Niven smiled. "There's no need to get metaphysical, my friend. A man's immortality, as we all know, rests in his knowledge. And the memory of each man and woman who lives and dies is logged into the Source and available to all through the Network. No one dies. The body perishes, but his thoughts, his ideas, his information live on."

Of course. It was what we had been taught in the Unimer Church from childhood. But now I knew it was not enough. "You can't store a man's soul, only the bits of his memory that the Source decides are useful to others."

"Quite right. Why else save the irrelevant fragments that can not be filed and retrieved in a rational manner?" He beamed a broad smile as if his point was somehow convincing. It wasn't.

I was really just fumbling to understand it but Gina had a full grasp. "Then the Source has robbed us of our richest commodity; it has robbed us of access to our past lives, our very souls."

"Nonsense. What are you talking about? This is the sort of madness that happens when you remove the patch. Denied access to the full empirical knowledge of the Source, you begin to lose the faculty of reason and revert to this ancient mysticism, this gibberish."

"I can understand," I said, "that this is all gibberish to you. You can not be disconnected. And we pity you. But it does not mean you are right."

"But *right* is a matter of a full understanding of the maximum amount of information. And since you presently have no access to the Network, you are not reasoning properly. I suggest you allow me to make repairs on all of you immediately."

A stony silence came over us. "Please," he pleaded. "I only want what's good for you."

But I saw a terrible look in his eye. He was at this minute being punished somehow by the Network. We were getting to him.

"You know that you are missing something vital. And you envy us," Victor taunted him.

"No!"

"Before the Source," Victor continued, "each one had the opportunity to make contact with his other lives through memory. But the Network could not allow such random fragmentation. The Source was too limited to cope with the memory of so many lives, past and present, all at once. It knew that the only way to attain efficiency was to delete the 'unnecessary' elements of the past."

"No," Niven said. He was bent over in pain and confusion. "Not delete. Sublimate. It could not be erased but it could be made inaccessible. Through the patch and the Network feed. I can only see now that this is the case. I did not know this before. Now I must go. I can say no more."

Niven rose and tried to make a dignified exit to the door.

Delisle stopped him. "Now what?" he asked. "Now that the Source knows we are aware. Will it find a means to erase our memory or simply destroy us?"

"I don't know," Niven answered. "There has never been such a confrontation. Whatever will be done will be done in the name of empirical good. The Source will decide if the resurgence of these old thought tracks will be useful or not useful. If it is found again to be a virus that slows down the processing of vital information, it will continue to make that memory inaccessible. Perhaps it will decide otherwise."

Niven's hand was on the door. He pushed but it would not open. He tried again but the building had sealed itself. He looked around at the high austere walls and the shining dome above our heads. The Great Hall of the Academy had become an immense tomb.

When I closed my eyes, the images from past lives swam vividly up before me. We all gathered again in a circle to chant. As the sound rose like beautiful thunder in that dome, I saw the others before me and now began to see precisely how our lives had intermingled before, many, many times. The past stretched out like a wide, familiar lush landscape and I could see that the present, too, was a limitless expanse. Should we all fall dead in the next split second, it would still allow for many lifetimes of pleasure and dream and pain and experience. And knowledge.

Gina squeezed my hand ever so lightly.

When at last I opened my eyes, it was because I heard a painful wailing. Niven was kneeling in the centre of our circle.

"Niven, you do not need to feel sorry for us," Victor spoke softly to him. "All the Network can do is to kill us. This seems of such small consequence now that we understand the cause of our rebellion."

But Niven continued to wail. "It is not for you I am crying, my friends but for me," he said.

And at that moment our compassion was so great for this lone android that we all wished we could have assembled a thousand previous lifetimes to give Niven, and a thousand future ones for him to look forward to as well.

These Changing Times*

W.P. Kinsella

Axgard tramped through the marble corridors of the House of Nations, crimson robes billowing behind making his massive body look even larger than it really was. The echo of his footsteps thundered and crashed through the empty halls. Axgard enjoyed thunder. It reminded him of war.

He entered Phillipet's office without knocking, brushed past the Commander's small dog-faced orderly and through the open door of Phillipet's private conference room. The heavy carpets silenced his heels; he stopped, bringing himself silently to attention, saluted, and waited for the commander to speak.

"Well, Axgard, what do you find so important that you can crash into my private office without being announced? Perhaps I should remind you that you're only an assistant to the board and not until you become one of my three board members like Soloway or Banks can you enter without my permission!"

"What I want to tell you, sir—it's about Banks. I've made a very important discovery—he's a Perfidian."

Axgard smiled, a broad ugly smile, showing large crooked yellow teeth.

Phillipet let the words enter his mind slowly; he weighed them, turned and examined each one before speaking.

"That's a serious charge, Axgard. Have you any way of proving it?"

Axgard smiled again, and produced a tiny roll of film.

"It's all there, sir, a whole sight and sound recording of a Perfidian meeting in Bank's cellar. Can you think of a less likely place for a Perfidian meeting than in the home of a Director of Nations, but I found them. I've suspected Banks for a long time."

Phillipet's thin face was white now, almost as white as his Commander's silks. He pulled his skeleton-like form to its full height, and wavering in the air like a marble pillar advanced towards Axgard.

"I don't think you realize just how clever you are, Axgard. Tell me why you didn't take your ingot gun and cremate the lot of them."

The big man shifted his robes uneasily, unwilling to answer the truth yet afraid to lie. He settled for the truth.

"Well, sir, I thought if I brought the film to you and told the story you might see fit to give me Banks' place on the Board."

"You'll get along alright, Axgard. You do think once in a while, but you still haven't seen the point. What would the masses think if it was suddenly revealed that one of the chosen Board was a Perfidian? Even if he had been destroyed on the spot, think what it would have done for their cause. Now, Banks will simply resign his position because of illness. We'll keep him carefully guarded in his home for a few months and then do away with him. You've earned yourself a place on the Board, Axgard—even if you don't entirely understand why."

The big man's nervousness was gone now. He paced quietly about Phillipet's office, adjusting his robes and tunic, and smiling his crooked smile on unseen admirers. Phillipets interrupted his reveries by asking:

"Why did Banks do a ridiculous thing like that? He's always been one of our top men, and he was second only to Soloway for my job."

"It's about two years ago, I think, sir. You remember when Soloway got his Spaceman's Honor Bar for breaking up that Perfidian meeting and killing all twelve that were there. That was what ranked him ahead of Banks. The next day I remarked that I would have given anything to have been there when Soloway killed the Perfidians, and Banks hit me. I believe it was right then that he joined with them. After all ,we haven't killed more than a half dozen Perfidians in the last two years."

"Can you imagine it, though? Axgard, here it is nearly 3000 A.D. and a clear-thinking man like Banks still believes in the Perfidian way of life."

"I believe he only felt sorry for them at first, sir, but they're awfully persuasive if you start to listen to them. I guess that Banks just has a weak spot somewhere."

"Still, it's hard to think of Banks as a Perfidian," Phillipet said. "Their system has been outdated nearly a thousand years. Can you imagine any clear-thinking educated person believing in freedom for the masses and, of all things, the principles of that ancient political system—democracy?"

*This was my first published story, written in 1954 when I was nineteen and working at my first full-time job as a correspondence clerk with the Government of Alberta, Department of Lands and Forests in Edmonton. As a writer, when I look back at my finished work, I'm generally pleased with what I read, and often say, "Gee, I don't remember it being this good. Did I really write that?" As I reread *These Changing Times*, amateur as it is, I still feel it is a pretty good story from a ninteteen-year-old beginner.
Bill Kinsella, Palm Springs, California, February 1992

Afterword

by Judith Merril

Once upon a time, in the shining years of the youth movements, the time of turning on and tuning in, the days of draft dodgers and deserters and Fuller domes, first moon landings, and Whole Earth Catalogues, there was a high rise building in Toronto called Rochdale College: a "free university", student-owned and run, dedicated to a concept of education that had everything to do with learning and almost nothing to do with teaching. The elder members, like me — anyone over 35 was an elder — were not Professors, but "Resource Persons". It was a good place to be, for a while; and of course, it lasted only a short while. But for a few years, Rochdale was a moiling boiling collective centre for people — artists, social scientists, planners, politicos — trying to create (yes!) a truly new world order, to carve the future to a shape and in a substance better suited to the planet and its humans than the painful present we were experiencing, let alone what we knew of the past.

Most of the people at Rochdale read science fiction.

The Rochdale building is now a senior citizens' residence, and I, for one, am now a senior citizen. The Space Race fell off the pop charts long before the US-USSR wargames (and the Soviet Union itself) collapsed, and the liberation generation students of the 60s and 70s are now mostly struggling with middle-age middle-class mortgages and migraines. The new youth are addicted to nostalgia instead of novelty, and prefer medieval fantasy to speculative future fiction.

The future seems to be on hold.

I came to Rochdale in 1968 from a fairly cushy spot in the world of US science fiction — a world that was just then in the process of exploding out of a dirty-little-genre ghetto into both literary and commercial respectability. I came to Rochdale, and for that matter to Canada, for the same reason I have invested the largest part of my adult life in speculative fiction: I wanted to change the world.

I still want to change the world. We are supposed to get over that as we "mature". Perhaps I just got old without maturing. (No mortgages, no migraines.) The longer I live, the more urgently, the more thoroughly the world seems to need changing— in wider, deeper and more demanding dimensions. At thirteen, when this lifelong obsession was just seizing upon me, I had sure simplistic/socialist goals of reshaping the political economy, establishing social justice and eliminating war as a game for powerfreaks and hunger as a byproduct of profiteering. At thirty, I was beginning to think it might be at least as urgent to open our eyes and mouths and bodies to sensory awareness and full communication potentials. At sixty, I was no longer willing to indulge in triage politics and sociology: all logic insists that food for the belly comes first; yet people still die of hunger for love, dignity, "honor" and simple human contact; still others are killed for refusing to starve, or suppress, their minds.

Now I approach three-score-and-ten, and in the past decade many of us Earthlings have come to understand that all our hungers, honors and ailments may be irrelevant in view of the damage inflicted by humanity on Gaia, the earth, the planet from which our very lives derive, and without which we can not as yet survive.

Somewhere in this progression, I seem to have lost the personal compulsion to make my statement through science fiction. Perhaps it was just the suspicion that any medium both profitable and respectable can hardly be subversive. Perhaps the fancy-dress, the masque, of fiction now seems too frivolous: we are living in truly terrifying times, where utopias become literally inconceivable and the visibility ahead is closing down to zero.

Many — most — of my generation of science fiction writers seem to have succumbed to the same malaise. Some of the best have moved to writing (splendid, and sometimes, some ways, still speculative) mainstream mimetic fiction; others have turned clear around to write (clever, delightful) historical "what-if's." Most, sadly, have acceded to the bottom-line blandishments of mass-market publication and now write endless formularized sequels, sets, and set-in-the-world-of read-alikes.

The future is on hold?

Not quite.

This Ark of Ice has no solutions, few fine visions or vistas; but it is blessedly full of the seeds of discontent, of finely visualized delineations of problems for which we have little or no precedent and small scope for understanding. Some of these stories are simply refinements of by-now "standards" of SF, but many others are probing attempts to expose new realities at the center of life-and-death decisions we must, very soon, find the energy and acumen to deal with.

The questions that come at us here have much to do with bio-technology, the new or imminent ethics and practices that relate to birth and death and sustenance in a changed and changing set of ecological equations. But, equally, they deal with the technology — both electronic and psychological — of control and decision-making. And, finally, with the act of perception itself: how do we penetrate the multi-veils of illusion (education, media, tradition, authority, sciencism, mysticism, high-tech glitz) so as to perceive the (real?) problems?

If future fiction cannot, or does not, at this juncture show us a way forward, perhaps it can at least illuminate some barriers and byways: point us toward explorations of new paths to hope — or to as-yet undefined hazards.

Unless we can find and move through or around the obstacles we have set in the paths we already know, the future will no longer be on hold; it will be out of service.

Contributors

Margaret Atwood is one of Canada's most important writers with over thirty books of poetry, fiction and criticism in publication. She won the Governor General's Award for poetry in 1967 and for fiction in 1985 for *The Handmaid's Tale* which also won her the Arthur C. Clarke Award for Best SF in 1987. Her most recent book is *Wilderness Tips*.

John Bell was born in Montreal, grew up in Halifax, and now lives in Ottawa. Active as an editor and writer in the fields of Canadian popular culture and Atlantic-Canadian literature, he co-compiled the first bibliography of Canadian SF and fantasy, co-edited the anthology *Visions from the Edge* (1981), and co-authored the first survey of Canadian comic books, *Canuck Comics* (1986). He also edited *The Far Islands and Other Tales of Fantasy* (1984) by John Buchan and *At the Harbour Mouth* (1988) by Archibald MacMechan, as well as two urban anthologies, *Halifax: A Literary Portrait* (1990) and *Ottawa: A Literary Portrait* (1992). The author of the poetry chapbook *The Third Side* (1983), he edited a special SF issue of the poetry magazine *Arc* in 1985. A co-founder of the Canadian Science Fiction and Fantasy Award, he was also a co-chairman of the Tenth World Fantasy Convention (1984).

Lesley Choyce was born in New Jersey in 1951 but moved to Canada and became a citizen when he was a young man. He teaches part-time at Dalhousie University, runs Pottersfield Press and has over 20 books in print. Lesley surfs year round in the North Atlantic and is considered the father of transcendental wood-splitting. He's worked as a rehab counsellor, a freight hauler, a corn farmer, a janitor, a journalist, a lead guitarist, a newspaper boy and a well-digger. His volume of collected SF stories is titled *The Dream Auditor* and was published by Ragweed.

Malcolm Cunningham has spent the past 20 years toiling anonymously at his craft in the employ of radio stations, a nonprofit organization and, most recently, government. Although he had a fair amount of freelance material published in the mid-seventies, the exigencies of scratching out a living and raising a family have since absorbed all of his time and energy. The ideas wouldn't stop buzzing around in his head, however, and his family has been raised about as high as it's going to get, so he has resumed writing some of those thoughts down in the hope that such activity will lower the level of the humming and might even save some of them from joining the growing mound of dead ideas on the floor of his brain.

Candas Jane Dorsey was born in Edmonton in 1952. She writes fiction, poetry and essays. Three books of poetry were published by blewointmentpress in 1973, 1974 and 1976. In 1986, with Nora Abercrombie, Candas won the Pulp Press International Three-Day Novel Writing Contest for *Hardwired Angel*. This was followed by a book of speculative fiction short stories, *Machine Sex and other stories*, published in 1988 by Porcepic Books. The first story in the book, "Sleeping in a Box", was the winner of the Canadian Science Fiction and Fantasy Award in 1989 for Best Short-Form Work in English in 1988. With Gerry Truscott, Candas co-edited the third anthology of Canadian speculative fiction writing, *Tesseracts3*. A freelance writer specialising in arts journalism, social issues and commentary, she is also a founding member of SFCanada, SFWorkshop Canada Ink and the Institute of Future Studies, an anarchic organization of creative futurists and visionaries.

Douglas Fetherling is a poet and a painter who lives in Toronto. He is the author of *The Dreams of Ancient Peoples* (ECW Press), *Blue Notebooks* (Mosaic) and *Moving Towards the Vertical Horizon* (Subway Books). He is employed variously as a journalist and editor, including duties as editor of *Canadian Notes and Queries*.

Timothy Findley is a distinguished Canadian novelist who first came to literary prominence with *The Wars*. He is also the author of *Famous Last Words*, *Not Wanted on the Voyage*, *The Telling of Lies*, *Stones*, and his recent autobiographical work, *Inside Memory*. In 1986 he was made an officer of the Order of Canada. His home is in rural Ontario.

Phyllis Gotlieb was born in Toronto in 1926 (Phyllis Bloom). She received a BA in 1948 and an MA in 1950 from the University of Toronto. In 1949 she married Calvin Gotlieb, now professor emeritus of Computer Science at the University of Toronto. They have three grown children. Phyllis lives, and has lived lifelong, in Toronto where she is a novelist (mainly science fiction) and poet. Her books include *Sunburst* (Fawcett, 1964), *O Master Caliban* (Harper, 1976) and *Heart of Red Iron*.

Katherine Govier was born in Alberta and lives in Toronto. She is the author of two collections of short stories and four novels, the most recent of which is *Hearts of Flame* (Penguin, 1991). "The Immaculate Conception Photography Gallery" was a winner in the CBC Literary Contest in

1989 and was first published in *Saturday Night* magazine. It has also appeared in several short fiction anthologies.

Terence M. Green was born in Toronto, where he still lives, in 1947. He is the father of two sons, aged 14 and 11. He holds a BA (English) and BEd from University of Toronto, and MA (Anglo-Irish Studies) from University College, Dublin. Terry has taught secondary school English in Ontario for over 20 years. His books include *The Woman Who is the Midnight Wind* (short story collection), Pottersfield Press, 1987; *Barking Dogs (novel),* St. Martin's Press (NY), 1988; and *Children of the Rainbow* (novel), McClelland and Stewart, 1992. Stories, articles, interviews, and reviews have been published in such places as *Books in Canada*, the *Globe and Mail*, *Isaac Asimov's SF Magazine*, the *Magazine of Fantasy and Science Fiction*, *The Twilight Zone*, *Aurora: New Canadian Writing*, *Tesseracts*, *Tesseracts2*, *Conversations with Robertson Davies.*

H.A. (Hank) Hargreaves lives in Edmonton. His SF stories have appeared in such diverse publications as *On Spec*, *Calgary Magazine*, and *Alberta Motorist*. University of California Press has also published his translation of Fontenelle's *Conversations on the Plurality of Worlds.*

Monica Hughes was born in Liverpool, England, and spent her early years in Egypt before returning to be educated in England and Scotland. She was in the WRNS (Women's Royal Naval Service) during World War II, and then spent two years working in Zimbabwe in a dress factory and a bank. Monica emigrated to Canada in 1952 and worked for five years at the National Research Council in Ottawa before marrying Glen Hughes. They lived in various Ontario cities between 1957 and 1964, when they moved to Edmonton with four children. Between 1974 and 1990 she had 23 juvenile novels published, of which the great majority are science fiction.

Eileen Kernaghan is the author of three fantasy novels set in Bronze Age Europe: *Journey to Aprilioth* (1980), *Songs from the Drowned Lands* (1983), which won the Canadian Science Fiction and Fantasy Award, and *The Sarsen Witch* (1989). Her poems and short fiction have appeared in a number of magazines and anthologies, including *Prism international*, *The Magazine of Speculative Poetry*, *On Spec*, *Tesseracts*, and *Light Like a Summons* (five BC women poets). Born and raised in the North Okanagan Valley, she now lives in the Vancouver suburb of Burnaby, where she and her husband operate a used bookshop, Neville Books.

W.P. Kinsella is the author of the remarkable novel, *Shoeless Joe*, from which the movie *Field of Dreams* was created. He is the author of nearly 20 other books of fiction including the recent release, *Box Socials*. He has won the Stephen Leacock Medal for Humour, as well as the *Books in Canada* First Novel Award. In 1989, Bill and his wife, Ann Knight, co-authored *Rainbow Warehouse*, published by Pottersfield Press.

Tom Marshall was born in Niagara Falls, Ontario, in 1938. As a child he lived in and around Memphis, Tennessee and Joplin, Missouri, where his father, a chemical researcher, did war work from 1940 to 1944. He grew up at Niagara and attended Queen's University, where his parents had met in 1930, and where he is now a Professor of English. He is the author of twenty books, including *The Elements*, selected poems; the recent collection of new poems *Ghost Safari*; *Harsh and Lovely Land*, a study of Canadian poetry; *Multiple Exposures, Promised Lands*, his selected essays on Canadian poets and novelists; and the fictional works, *Rosemary Goal*, *Glass House*, *Adele at the End of the Day*, *Voices on the Brink*, *Changelings*, and *Goddess Disclosing*. He is presently working on a novel about his ancestor, John Montgomery, and the course of Canadian history.

Judith Merril was the editor of the first *Tesseracts* anthology, published by Porcepic Books in 1985. She is a leading authority on science fiction; she has edited twenty anthologies, written several novels and many short stories. She founded The Spaced-Out Library in Toronto where she is a broadcaster, consultant and peace activist .

Garfield Reeves-Stevens is the author of several novels with science fiction and horror elements, including *Bloodshift*, *Nighteyes*, and *Dark Matter*. With his wife, Judith, he has also co-written two Star Trek novels, *Memory Prime* and *Prime Directive*, as well as the near-future, ecological thriller, *Clyde*, and the ongoing fantasy adventure series, *The Chronicles of Galen Sword*. Various Reeves-Stevens novels have been translated into Dutch, French, German, Hebrew, Italian, Polish, and Japanese. Reeves-Stevens was born in Oakville, Ontario, and grew up in Toronto. He and Judith now live in Los Angeles, which has the largest Canadian population of any non-Canadian city. They are not sure what the significance of this is, though they think it has something to do with snow.

Since **Spider Robinson** began writing professionally in 1972, he has won three Hugos, a Nebula, the John W. Campbell Award for Best New Writer, an E.E. ("Doc") Smith Memorial Award (Skylark), the Pat Terry Memorial Award for Humorous Science Fiction, and Locus Awards for Best Novella and Best Critic. His book *Callahan's Crosstime Saloon* was named a Best Book for Young Adults by the American Library Association. He was born in the Bronx in 1948, on three successive days (they had to handle him in sections), and holds a Bachelor's degree in English. He has been married for eighteen years to Jeanne Robinson, a modern dance choreographer. The Robinsons collaborated on the Hugo-, Nebula- and

Locus-winning 1976 classic *Stardance* (Baen Books), which created the concept of zero-gravity dance, and on its 1991 sequel, *Starseed.* They currently live in Vancouver, British Columbia, with their teenage daughter, presently named Terri.

Robert J. Sawyer's first novel, *Golden Fleece* (Warner, New York), was named by critic Orson Scott Card as the best SF novel of 1990, and it won the CompuServe SF Forum's HOMer Award for best first novel of that year. Rob is also the author of *Far-Seer* (Berkley, New York, 1992) and *End of an Era* (Berkley, 1993). His short SF has appeared in *Amazing Stories, The Village Voice, Leisure Ways,* and the anthology *100 Great Fantasy Short Stories* edited by Isaac Asimov, Terry Carr, and Martin Harry Greenberg. Sawyer also writes and narrates documentaries on SF topics for CBC Radio's *Ideas* series and is *The Canadian Encyclopedia*'s authority on Science Fiction. He lives in Toronto with his wife Carolyn.

Jean-Louis Trudel is a creature of the night — presently pursuing a Ph.D. in astronomy at the University of Toronto. When he's not up till early morning observing variable stars, he's probably busy editing SF Canada's newsletter or writing SF. Born in Toronto, he spent most of his life in Ottawa before being irresistibly drawn back to Toronto. He has published stories in French in *imagine ..., L'Apropos* and *Solaris.* One of his earlier stories was translated and published in Tesseracts^3. He has also written in collaboration with Yves Meynard two short stories, the first published in *L'Année de la Science-Fiction et du Fantastique Québécois 1988* and the second in *Solaris. The Falafel Is Better in Ottawa* is his first publication in English.

Geoffrey Ursell is an award-winning writer of drama, poetry, fiction, and songs. His plays, *The Running of the Deer* and *Saskatoon Pie!*, have won him national playwriting awards. He has also written drama for radio and television. His first novel, *Perdue,* won the prestigious *Books in Canada* First Novel Award. His most recent books are *Way Out West!*, a collection of stories, and *The Look-Out Tower*, a collection of poems. Ursell has also edited ten short story anthologies and two anthologies of writing for children. At present, he is working on a new novel, a small-scale opera, and is the Editor of *Grain.* Ursell was born in Moose Jaw, Saskatchewan in 1943 and grew up in various Prairie cities. He studied at the University of Manitoba and the University of London, England, where he completed his Ph.D. He and his wife, Barbara Sapergia, both write full-time and live in Saskatoon.

Sansoucy Kathenor Walker has had four stories published in professional SF and F magazines and anthologies in the United States, as well as assorted work in semi-professional magazines in Canada and the United

States. She has won seven short story awards, including a Writers of the Future (1985) and a "Best of Year" from *Leading Edge* (1987), and two Epstein awards in poetry. She has also had a book of poetry, *Temple into Time*, and a songbook, *Maplecon Folksong Book*, published.

Andrew Weiner was born in London, England in 1949. He came to Canada in 1974, and is now a Canadian citizen. He lives in Toronto with his wife and son. Weiner has published more than 30 stories in magazines and anthologies including *Fantasy and Science Fiction*, *Isaac Asimov's Science Fiction Magazine*, *Interzone*, *The Twilight Zone Magazine*, *Chrysalis*, and *Proteus*. His stories have been translated into French, Italian, Japanese and Polish, and have been nominated for the British Science Fiction Award and for the Canadian Fantasy and Science Fiction Award. Two of his stories have been filmed for the U.S. TV show *Tales from the Darkside*. He has published one novel, *Station Gehenna* (Congdon and Weed, 1987 & Worldwide Library, 1988), and one collection of short fiction, *Distant Signals* (Porcepic Books, 1989).

Acknowledgements

All stories are published by permission of the authors.

Introduction © 1992 by Lesley Choyce.

"Blue Limbo" © 1992 by Terence M. Green.

"The Letter" © 1982 by Andrew Weiner; first appeared in slightly different form in *The Magazine of Fantasy and Science Fiction*, November, 1982.

"The Newest Profession" © 1992 by Phyllis Gotlieb.

"Letters Home" © 1992 by G.M. Cunningham.

"The Price of Land" © 1992 by Monica Hughes.

"The Falafel is Better in Ottawa" © 1992 by Jean-Louis Trudel.

"Scenes from Successive Futures" © 1992 by Tom Marshall.

"In His Moccasins" © 1979 by H.A. Hargreaves; first appeared in *Calgary Magazine* in August 1979.

"The Immaculate Conception Photography Gallery" © 1990 by Katherine Govier; first appeared in *Saturday Night*, April 1990.

"Living in Cities" © 1992 by Candas Jane Dorsey.

"Memoirs of the Renaissance" © 1987 by Douglas Fetherling; first appeared in *Quarry*, Fall 1987.

"The Weighmaster of Flood" © 1992 by Eileen Kernaghan.

"What Mrs. Felton Knew" © 1984 by Timothy Findley/ Pebble Productions, Inc.; appeared originally in *Dinner Along the Amazon* published in Canada in 1984 by Penguin Books Canada Limited.

"Outport" © 1992 by Garfield Reeves-Stevens.